TWO LANDS

Stories from Canada and Ukraine

NEW VISIONS

TWO LANDS

Stories from Canada and Ukraine

NEW VISIONS

EDITED BY
JANICE KULYK KEEFER & SOLOMEA PAVLYCHKO

TRANSLATIONS FROM UKRAINIAN BY
MARCO CARYNNYK & MARTA HORBAN

First U.S. edition, 1999.

Edited by Janice Kulyk Keefer and Solomea Pavlychko.
General editor, Geoffrey Ursell.

Cover painting, "Seasons," by Khrystyne Haidamaka.
Cover design by Kate Kokotailo.
Book design by Duncan Campbell.
Printed and bound in Canada.

This publication has been funded in part by the Ukrainian Canadian Foundation of Taras Shevchenko.

The publisher gratefully acknowledges the financial assistance of the Saskatchewan Arts Board, the Canada Council for the Arts, the Department of Canadian Heritage, and the City of Regina Arts Commission, for its publishing program.

Coteau Books celebrates the 50th Anniversary of the Saskatchewan Arts Board with this publication.

Canadian Cataloguing in Publication Data

Two lands, new visions: stories from Canada and Ukraine
ISBN 1-55050-134-8

1. Short stories, Canadian (English)—Ukrainian-Canadian authors.*
2. Canadian fiction (English)—20th century.*
3. Short stories, Ukrainian—Translations into English.
4. Ukrainian fiction—20th century—Translations into English.

I. Keefer, Janice Kulyk, 1953-
II. Pavlychko, Solomea, 1953-

PN6129.92.U48 T86 1998 C813'.018891791
C98-920124-4

COTEAU BOOKS
401-2206 Dewdney Ave.
Regina, Saskatchewan
Canada S4R 1H3

AVAILABLE IN THE US FROM
General Distribution Services
85 River Rock Drive, Suite 202
Buffalo, New York, USA 14207

UKRAINE

CANADA

Introduction

SOLOMEA PAVLYCHKO

The world of literature, unlike a literary textbook, is always a world of creative chaos, an absence of logic. Ukrainian literature is no exception. The biggest paradox is unfolding today: contemporary literature, that which is being written after 1991, the year independence was obtained, has lost its optimistic and romantic tone. Nobody yearned for independence as much as writers; however, literature today has lost its bearings. The writers of the older generation are stressed out, and some have even stopped producing; young writers wallow in depression and pessimism: they view the world through the eyes of the grotesque and satire. Writers have largely lost interest in social issues, which were their age-old concern, and instead delve into self-reflection, cue in narcissistically on their bodies, and explore their sexuality – frightening conservative nationalists who are still convinced that Ukrainians had their origins in Immaculate Conception.

After independence, the writer's role in Ukrainian society altered radically. The Ukrainian writer was born over a thousand years ago as a chronicler, noting the events of Kyivan Rus. Following the Byzantine style, the writer had little leeway. The important thing was accuracy, a minimum of individuality, and strict adherence to canons. In time things changed. Five hundred years passed, and monks had taken to writing philosophical tracts and comedies, and hetmans (Cossack rulers such as Ivan Mazepa) wrote poetry.

Two hundred years ago the Ukrainian writer came into a new role: that of educator, preacher, builder, prophet, servant of an idea, fighter for the freedom of Ukraine, a country which at that time had been divided between two mighty empires – the Russian and the Austro-Hungarian. And although this new beginning coincided with Romanticism and was heavily influenced by it, there was nothing idyllic about the predicament of Ukrainian literature in this period. This was not the struggle for freedom à la Byron, who in a theatrical gesture ordered a helmet of an ancient Greek warrior en route to liberating Greece. In Ukraine there were enormous losses and suffering: prison and censorship under Russian rule, which entailed the banning of the language itself, not only individual works. Then came the Soviet period with its mass executions, prison camps, and the gulag. The ten-year forced conscription, in the nineteenth century, of Taras Shevchenko into the tsarist army (which he served in the deserts of Central Asia) because of derogatory lines about the empress, and the death in Soviet camps some fifteen years ago of another poet, Vasyl Stus, defined the scale of values of Ukrainian literature in the last two centuries.

Now everything has changed. Writers have lost their role as political and spiritual leaders. This change has greatly influenced individual styles and genres, the short story in particular.

The contemporary Ukrainian short story does not resemble classic national instances of the genre, which is, by the way, the leading genre of fiction, in the sense of masterpieces created by predecessors. One can affirm without hesitation that the contemporary short story is undergoing a time of experiment that never occurred before. The main tendency of these experiments lies in the furious destruction of the old form, the old content, the old language, the sense of writing, and sometimes even the sense of the author's own "I."

The next peculiarity of the new Ukrainian short story (and of fiction as a whole) is a pessimistic minor key, an interest in the dark side of consciousness, the absurd, macabre, and "dirty" sides of life. For several years now, the most optimistic era in Ukrainian history has been spawning terrible fantasmagorical plots, a world without dawn or hope. In the official Ukrainian literature – called socialist realism – of recent Soviet times, there was so much saccharine falsity and mendacious optimism that the accentuation of the "terrible" truth is a sign that literature is convalescing. Our time in Ukrainian literature can be called a return to the truth. It is tied to a need to grasp previous experience of Ukrainian life – Chornobyl, Afghanistan, Soviet totalitarianism.

Political independence has brought into the culture the phenomenon of rereading and rethinking the past in a broad sense. Consciously or subconsciously writers have been trying to grasp both the preceding era of the Soviet regime and the legacy of the two empires to which Ukraine belonged until 1918 – the Russian and the Austro-Hungarian, and the Cossack state that flowered in the seventeenth century and declined in the eighteenth, and finally the even-earlier experience of the principalities of Kyiv Rus, Galicia, and Volhynia. The re-examination of history and its mythologemes is taking place together with a redefinition of the principles of Ukrainian "civilization": literature deconstructs its age-old complexes and fears, at the same time modernizing and liberalizing the general cultural discourse.

Another thing that is taking place today and touches all fiction writers is a rethinking of the nature of the short story itself. In the canons of Soviet literature narrativity was a political requisite along with ideological loyalty and a variety of taboos: against sexuality, against censorable language, against the language of the streets. It seems that this very "fortress" of the past – narrative – has for contemporary Ukrainian fiction writers become especially intolerable. Throughout the nineties a war against narrative has been waged. Among writers it has become fashionable to talk about writing fragments of prose that exist beyond the framework of genre. It seems that the social aggressivity that is present in contemporary Ukrainian society is also directed against the short story, which is single-mindedly destroyed, quartered, and dissected into separate phrases and sounds, depriving it of any of the logical ties that are characteristic of real life. For this reason, perhaps, the traditional short story with a plot and real life is again being received in the late nineties as a gust of fresh air.

Besides the general tendency to the breakdown of narrative, the Ukrainian short story of recent years demonstrates a number of specific features: conceptual, regional, and gender-related. The latter are perhaps the most interesting. Only in the last ten or twenty years has Ukrainian literature seen the return, after a long period of silence or some puzzling boycott of socialist realism, of women. They have brought their point of view on women's lives, an as-yet unknown confessionalism, an openness in conveying feeling, feminist aggression, and a sarcastic rejection of patriarchal Ukrainian life with its stereotypes and set roles and norms. The women's prose, and especially of the authors included in this book – Oksana Zabuzhko, Yevhenia Kononenko, Svetlana Kasianova, and Roksana Kharchuk – can probably be compassed by the one notion of "diversion." This diversion is particularly central, for it touches not the surface of life, but undermines the notions of traditional masculinity and femininity ostensibly fixed forever by the national culture.

The feminist tradition, which began to develop in the fin

de siècle, was silenced in the Soviet period. Today women for the first time in many years are speaking in their own voice. Their stories have little in common with the image of the idyllic happy peasant-mother in an embroidered blouse; rather they are brutally honest and explore hitherto forbidden themes. In the eighties Ukrainian fiction was subdivided thematically into village and city prose. Village prose, or more precisely prose about the village, was an encoded version of resistance to a hostile regime. For only in the village was Ukrainianness able to survive, evading the Russification that was integral to every aspect of urban existence. It was village prose with its naturalism, psychologism, and political allusions, hidden behind a style of authorial non-comment, that commented, criticized, and spoke the truth about Soviet life.

From village prose evolved the naturalistic tendency of the present day, not devoid of a certain moralistic quest. Writers like Vasyl Portiak or Oles Ulianenko no longer turn their gaze to the village or even the city, but to marginal types who do not belong to either village or city – the homeless, the social "bottom," to use a term from Emile Zola's time. In a society that is experiencing a global economic crisis, mass unemployment, and the marginalization of entire social strata, a huge number of such people have emerged. The writers of this tendency have tried to find in the naturalistic mire some sense of the present and a cleansing of it, and behind anti-intellectualism and simplicity hides an explosive force of truth on an almost-mythological level. Portiak and Ulianenko represent the only school that has some continuity with the literature of pre-independence times. They are writers of eastern Ukraine and Kyiv.

The western, Galician, writing phenomenon is entirely different. This is not surprising in view of the historical legacy. At a time when Russia ruled, writers from Ukraine were denied the right to publish in the Ukrainian language. Their colleagues in the more liberal Austro-Hungarian empire issued newspapers and journals, held professorships, and wrote doctoral dissertations. At the end of the last century, western Ukraine also had a bohemian, artistic milieu in tune with the cosmopolitan currents of the modern. This was inconceivable in Russian-ruled eastern Ukraine. Moreover, writers there lived in the shadow of Russian literary influence, whereas the writers from the western region were influenced by Austrian, Polish, and other Central European influences.

At the centre of contemporary Galician writing is the intellectual, the artist, the tragic actor. The carnivalesque style of his life is reflected in burlesque, lucid prose. This prose is based on the multilingual literary tradition of the Austro-Hungarian empire, of which Galicia was a part. The intellectual freedom of the eighties, reinforced by the political freedom of the nineties, resurrected the vibrant personalities of the region: Bruno Schulz from Drohobych, Leopold von Sacher-Masoch from Lviv, and Joseph Roth, born in Brody near Lviv. And even though not one of them wrote in Ukrainian (the former wrote in Polish and the latter two in German), their presence and that of such giants of Austrian literature as Kafka and Musil is palpable and substantial in the contemporary Galician phenomenon. Galician writers are also heavily influenced by Latin American fiction of the second half of the twentieth century, especially Borges, and the deconstruction of Derrida, and the postmodern theorizing of Lyotard. Once again, as before 1918, authors and their heroes travel to Vienna, Prague, or Cracow, with an obligatory return to Lviv or Stanyslaviv, as they all prefer to call present-day Ivano-Frankivsk.

Thus Ivano-Frankivsk/Stanyslaviv has reappeared recently on the map of Ukrainian literature. Possibly the most interesting and promising contemporary writers, represented here by Yurii Izdryk and Taras Prokhasko (in fact the group includes significantly more names), have emerged in this city. These authors do not record life, but model it, conceptualizing and ruining narrative at the same time as they ruin other fundamentals and truths. For them, nonetheless, the problems of the genre with which they are experimenting and of their own identity and their place in Central European culture are still unresolved. They have chosen a Central European identity. All that remains is for them to win recognition from this culture, and this is gradually happening, especially through translations of these authors into Polish or German.

As always, there are figures who stand apart and do not belong to any groups or trends. The most sarcastic humour, the most brilliant narrative, and an inexhaustible quantity of plots are being produced in the nineties by Bohdan Zholdak from Kyiv and Yurii Vynnychuk from Lviv. Both began writing in the seventies, both managed to survive the period of writing for the drawer and to come out, it seems, completely undamaged. This is a wonder in itself, for non-publication or its threat broke many writers. Zholdak and Vynnychuk were among the first of those who broke norms and canons themselves, touched on forbidden themes, and introduced a new language.

Language merits a separate comment. It has changed radically in the last decade, that is, the language of literature has come closer to the language of life than ever before. This means that it has integrated dialects, slangs, "surzhyks": the Russian-Ukrainian creole in the east, which is a sign of political and social processes and cataclysms, and the entirely different, "noble" Galician dialect, which does not have the aggressivity of a surzhyk, in the west, with its numerous and now entirely organic Polish and German elements. The expansion of the latter barbarisms is pleasant and unthreatening, while the Russian-Ukrainian creole of eastern Ukraine has the destructive power of its bearers. Surzhyk is no longer just a language, but a state of tangled, dark consciousness that interests writers of a naturalistic-realistic orientation in the first place. No wonder that stream of consciousness (of a Faulknerian sooner than a Joycean order) is one of the most widespread fictional devices today.

"As never before" – these are the words used most frequently to characterize contemporary Ukraine as well as its literature. Indeed, Ukrainian life is, as never before, dramatic, dynamic, multifaceted, and creatively and intellectually stimulating. The atmosphere of liberty and constant change that has lasted for years now is inebriating as never before. Ukrainian writers, as never before, have something to talk about. The stories they tell are, as never before, interesting and captivating, terrible and funny. I hope that they will be interesting for the English-language reader as well, as a new piece in the mosaic of contemporary literature.

– Solomea Pavlychko, Kyiv, Ukraine, 1998

INTRODUCTION

JANICE KULYK KEEFER

In 1987, an anthology edited by Jars Balan and Yuri Klynovy, *Yarmarok: Ukrainian Writing in Canada Since the Second World War,* gave us glimpses of the work of forty-nine contemporary poets, dramatists, and fiction writers, upcoming and established, immigrant and native-born, all of them members of the Ukrainian diaspora in Canada.

Two Lands, New Visions has a different scope and aim: it brings together samples of contemporary fiction from Canada and Ukraine by writers who might be described not so much as "distant" but as "distance" cousins. For the term "distant" conveys an emotional as well as spatial sense, suggesting estrangement and the loosening of bonds, whereas "distance" stresses the fact that politics and history, rather than any desire to abandon mutual ties, have dictated the fact and terms of separation. Until Ukraine gained independence from the Soviet empire in 1991, Ukrainian-Canadians could return to their originary homeland only as heavily-chaperoned tourists with no freedom of movement – temporary prisoners might be a better term to use.

This combination of an imposed separation from and an intense desire to connect with Ukraine has profoundly influenced a great many Ukrainian-Canadians: often you will hear people whose ancestors came to Canada in the 1880s speak of going "back" to Ukraine as they plan their first-ever journey to that country. For them, ethnicity means more than those superficial, festive markers of difference from a dominant norm: food and dress. I would argue that in order for the term to be meaningful at all the ethnos, or distinguishing culture of a given community, must be seen through the complexities of history, both "old-world" and "new." We must also recognize the dynamic and varied nature of what it means to be "ethnic," for the distinctive culture of Ukrainians in Canada is anything but fossilized and monolithic: differences of class, gender, politics, and religion complicate the relations within families and between the larger social groups that comprise any given Ukrainian community.

The writers whose work makes up the Canadian portion of this volume present a variety of perspectives on this complex matter of ethnicity. At times, the "Ukrainianness" of the fictive world created by the author is entirely subsumed, as in Mary Borsky's story "Myna," in which the precision of the prose and the writer's gift for telling observation make us hear one of the world's oldest stories as if for the very first time. In Barbara Scott's elegiac "Oranges," however, the Ukrainian icons and traditions both revered and rejected by the characters are powerfully present. Ray Serwylo's "The Lost Winters of Emerald and Silver" gives us a haunting vision of life in a Ukrainian community composed of those who "were not born in this place, [b]ut treat it as...home." Lida Somchynsky gives us another perspective on the experience of Displaced Persons in "The First Lady," whose setting reminds us that not all Ukrainian-Canadians come from or live on the Prairies.

Three of the Canadian stories in this collection deal, in very different ways, with the mesh of memory and identity as they figure in the experience and construction of family – Patricia Abram's "Green Sundays," Chrystia Chomiak's "The Still-Boiling Water," and Marusya Bociurkiw's "The Children of Mary." In "Ways of Coping" and "Two Triangles," Myrna Kostash and Martha Blum extend the province of memory to incorporate public history in a way that acknowledges the irony, brutality and terror of events in "the old country." And Martha Blum's story reminds us of how varied and complex the mesh of culture, geography, and history can be, and of the truly multicultural nature of the country of Ukraine.

Finally, the closing story in this volume, Kathie Kolybaba's "Lunch Hour with a Soviet Citizen," returns us to the Prairies where Canada's first Ukrainian immigrants once settled, giving us two radically different responses to place – that of a young woman recently arrived from Ukraine and rampantly on the make, and that of a descendant of those first Ukrainian pioneers, a modern working woman who still longs "to come home to this ancestry…this earth I love…my country."

WHILE THERE ARE INTRIGUING SIMILARITIES between some of the Canadian and Ukrainian stories in this volume – for example, the eroticism and concern with violence that figure so strongly in Myrna Kostash's and Martha Blum's stories, and in the work of Bohdan Zholdak and Yurii Vynnychuk – it is the differences which are most striking. Whereas many of the Ukrainians emphasize the complex historical and political contexts which have formed and deformed imaginative possibility in their country, most of the Canadians tend to interpret history within the personal and private terms of family. The speculative fantasy and often savage irony of many of the Ukrainian contributions are largely absent in the Canadian. All but one of the Canadian writers are women; the majority of the Ukrainians are men. And while frequent references are made by the Canadians to *borshch* and *pyrohy*, these near-talismanic items of cuisine are nowhere to be found in the stories of the

Ukrainians, whose cultural identity, even after centuries of foreign domination, seems assured enough to give us the the kind of literary or media-centred cosmopolitanism embraced by a Taras Prokhasko or Oksana Zabuzhko.

Indeed, the most striking difference between the writers from these "two lands" would seem to be the fact that the Ukrainians are so obviously at home in the literary and larger culture of their country, whereas their Canadian counterparts are still defining for themselves what their own place within or relation towards Canadian society and culture might be. One of the most welcome and conspicuous developments on the Canadian literary scene over the past twenty years has been the surge of what I would call "transcultural" writing – literary work that recognizes, in a dynamic and reciprocal way, the multicultural nature of Canada; that crosses the borders and boundaries that have so often divided and ghettoized different ethnic, religious, and "racial" groups. Some of our most gifted and applauded writers have emerged from communities that were previously silent or silenced: the First Nations, and Black, and Asian. Yet while there has been at least one major Canadian writer of Ukrainian background – George Ryga – it seems that Ukrainian-Canadians, in contrast to their peers from the Mennonite and Jewish communities, for example, are just beginning to make their voices heard and stories known within the changing canon of this country's literature.

The ten Canadian writers who appear in *Two Lands*, and the dozens more whom this anthology, regretfully, was not able to accommodate, are extending that act of ground-breaking which *Yarmarok* began eleven years ago. They are labouring not only to articulate the ethnos of their families and communities, but also to reinvent what it means to be Ukrainian in this country. Their task, as I see it, is one not of simple preservation but of transformation, too; it requires the courage of critique as well as the pleasures of celebration. By critique I mean occupying a position that I regard as indispensable for any artist: that of being both within and outside of a formative community, of being free to observe, analyse, and judge as you will, without the kind of censorship so often exacted by blind loyalty to "our own." For one of the writer's crucial tasks has always been to play the role of the *enfant terrible* in that fable of the Emperor's New Clothes – to point to contradictions, injustices, or absurdities that many may have noticed, but lacked the will or means to address.

To be aware of how and what our heritage has made us, to understand the dangers as well as the delights of such making, and to search for new ways of exploring and expressing our ethnicity – these are invigorating as well as daunting tasks. They would involve Ukrainian-Canadians in mining an extraordinary wealth of material, archival and otherwise, pertaining to the lived experience of Ukrainians in Canada, from the days of the first pioneers, to the internment of immigrant Ukrainians as "Austrian Nationals" during the First World War; from the arrival of Ukrainians in Canada after World War II as Displaced Persons, to the traumas of displacement and acculturation suffered by new Ukrainian immigrants today. But an equally important task involves the asking of difficult, necessary questions about problematic aspects of the culture Ukrainians have brought to and attempted to preserve in this country, questions that involve vital issues concerning gender and the construction of "Others."

CANADIANS OF WHATEVER BACKGROUND and ethnic derivation have the opportunity, with this volume, of discovering something of what it is like to live in contemporary Ukraine – the hopes and frustrations, the continuing shock of the old and the comparable shock of a runaway and often hostile "new." They will also gain a sense of what Ukrainian-Canadians have made of their inheritance from that far-off country which, in however central or vestigial a way, has made them who and how they are. What Ukrainians who have grown up in Kyiv or Lviv will make of the work of those "distance" cousins who grew up in Ottawa or Edmonton will be interesting to see. And this is perhaps the most exciting aspect of the production of a volume such as *Two Lands*: that it has the potential to begin a lively discussion between people who are in the paradoxical situation of being both strangers and intimates.

In this context, I would like to end by quoting Ukrainian-born poet Lydia Palij, who emigrated to this country in 1948. Though she has continued to write in her native tongue, winning wide recognition in Ukraine, she has become part of the writing community in Canada as well. In "Juncture without Sign Posts," from a volume entitled *Son-kraina – Dream-realm*, the poet carries on a conversation, from Canada, with a lover whom she met on a visit to Ukraine, and had to leave behind. This inevitable separation leaves her "mourning/for all the years/spent on foreign soil." Yet it also compels her to begin a new and more powerful relationship with the absent beloved. For the fact of distance has finally conferred equality, however bitter-sweet, upon the lovers, as the poem's ending shows:

> We parted at a junction
> without sign posts.
> Now only the east wind
> brings letters from you
> telling me
> that strange birds
> patter over your desk
> and gaze into your eyes.

Forgive me, but I forgot
the colour of your eyes.
I will write you too,
and send a paper boat
down the St. Lawrence River.
Look out for it on the shores
of the Sea of Azov.

This anthology is just such a paper boat – ink and paper remaining one of the strongest ways we have of connecting with each other over the farthest, deepest distances.

– *Janice Kulyk Keefer, Guelph, Canada, 1998*

UKRAINE

Father

YURII IZDRYK

My dad doesn't have any eccentricities. He doesn't collect anything, doesn't play the violin, doesn't chase women, doesn't have any phobias, and he doesn't pick his nails with a comb. For all his positive qualities – culture, decency, intellect – and in spite of his rather important position on the city council, Dad has a taste for the lifestyle of the average citizen. He goes to work regularly, consumes food regularly; in fact he likes to eat, and in the evening he has no objection to stretching out on the sofa with a newspaper or a book. He has no urge to fix anything or to solve crossword puzzles without an audience. He tries to do away with any deviation from the established order as quickly as possible, and even though he manages to get out of unusual situations, even precarious ones, with surprising dignity, any disturbance naturally takes a heavy toll on his spirits. Dad is forced to compensate for such losses with extended walks in the woods. In the absence of any other eccentricities, his urge to take solitary walks in the woods could probably be considered an eccentricity, but in that case we'd all be taken for pathological deviants. What's more, Dad has no use for hunting, picking mushrooms, or fishing. For this I respect him.

My respect for him was conceived and confirmed a long time ago, when I was still a teenager. I remember well how we were coming home late one evening from a tailor's shop where I was having my first pair of trendy pants made and I, dizzied by the starry sky and the anticipation of a fashion make-over, asked Dad about the meaning of life. I was at that happy age when people take an entirely sincere interest in things like that and have an entirely sincere belief that every question has an answer. Perhaps it was precisely my existence at that time under a particular kind of sky without a particular kind of pants that aroused a suspicion as to the meaninglessness of being, but I was still hoping for a miracle, for there being a meaning that I just wasn't grasping because of my immaturity. Dad dispelled these last doubts of mine. And, to his credit, he did so openly, without stuttering, but also without superfluous affectation.

My respect grew and strengthened when in time I observed my father at work. As has already been mentioned, he occupied a rather important position on the city council – head of the control commission for the educational process or something like that. It was a revelation for me that Dad, who was so gentle and accommodating at home, could be so firm and principled in managing all sorts of riff-raff at work.

In the course of my life in general I often had occasion to make such discoveries for myself, and this only strengthened my father's authority. For example, when everyone all around was no less than gagging with hatred and disdain towards Russians, Dad said, "But you can't just reject a great people as simply as that. In spite of everything (of anything, of nothing at all) the Russians did create a great culture." A similar loyalty and tolerance distinguished him with regard to the Polish and Jewish questions as well.

Without ever trying to do so directly, my father nevertheless had a significant influence on the formation of my personality. He had an appealing image thanks to his restrained conduct and dignified lifestyle. He seemed to live by the principle that "all is vanity." And although we rarely – actually, almost never – got into any sort of frankness, so-called heart-to-heart talks or baring our souls, I always valued our feeling of oneness, which only people who are really close can experience.

Besides the absence of eccentricities, it is also worth mentioning that Dad didn't have any of the status symbols with which people like to enhance their own value – antiques, securities, or family heirlooms, say. Thus, for example, Dad didn't even own any weapons.

That's why we were forced to use an automobile.

Actually, my father's car was also as average as you can get, maybe even too unimposing by today's standards.

Right at Christmas, after a good supper, we got in the car – Father at the steering wheel, me at his side – and drove to the town square. As usual we drove unhurriedly, almost cautiously, religiously observing the traffic rules. In the square, across from the city hall, shone a tall Christmas tree, with merry, tipsy citizens frolicking around it and singing carols. Driving into the square, we speeded up a bit and cut into the circle of carollers, splattering slush as we went. The first incursion was very successful, because no one had had a chance yet to get scared and run away. Our second try, after a U-turn in the course of which, driving in reverse, we managed to knock down a few people, wasn't too bad either. The crowd got flustered and couldn't get its bearings for about fifteen seconds. But the rest was more complicated. People started running in all directions, and although the panic was actually playing into our hands, it was hard to play an aiming game, and accidental victims were just getting in the way. What saved us was the fact that the car kept skidding on the wet pavement, and slipping and sliding like that was how we knocked down probably the most of our fellow countrymen. But it was hard to pick up speed, and slow driving was becoming dangerous – some of the citizens had come to their senses and naturally decided to fight back. Sticks and rocks found their way into the hands of these daredevils, and they used every chance they could to strike a blow at us. The corpses, of which there weren't all that many, but enough to get in the way, deprived us of our manoeuvrability, and this gave our foes more chances. We managed to knock down a few who were armed with sticks, but the people, aroused by alcohol and the sight of blood, were no longer reacting to the danger and constituted a serious threat.

Finally one of them managed to throw a rock into our windshield, and for a moment the world disappeared from view, covered with a dense screen of cracks. I hit it with my fist, the glass shattered, the cold air whipped our faces, and the car ploughed full force into the trunk of the Christmas tree. More rocks flew in our direction, and we were quickly being surrounded. Still, Dad didn't get flustered, and within a second or so we were already rushing at the rank of our attackers. Blows thudded on our roof; the rear window also shattered, and several men who had obviously lost their minds ran to intercept us, putting out their arms as if they meant to catch a pig. Dad was unerring. From what I could tell, we managed to put down three at once. One corpse got stuck on the hood, but we slammed on the brakes and knocked it off.

"Well, that's enough," Father shouted. "The radiator's cracked. We have to go before the engine stalls."

And we left the city behind.

Christmas Night was turning into a quiet morning, and Dad and I were standing on the roof of the car under a spreading tree. It was certainly the first time in a long while that Dad wasn't alone in the woods. He was looking at the sky and the ravens that had settled all over the branches of our tree. And I was looking beneath my feet at our beat-up car.

"So, *jazda?*" I said in Polish. "Ready?"

"*Jazda,*" said Dad. "On the count of three."

"One."

"Two."

"Three."

This, I must confess, was the first time I tricked my father, and even though he will never find out about it, I still have a grave sin on my conscience. I did what little boys often do when they're competing to see who can stay under water longest. Everyone dives in on the count of "three," but the cleverest one stands there laughing or dives in later. And so I didn't jump on the count of "three" and saw how Father's body swung in the noose, how the frightened ravens took to the sky, and how a convulsion ran through his body. I sinned, but before I died I had time to repent and managed to jump before the birds came back to the tree.

Orders

OLES ULIANENKO

He clearly heard the short, hollow sound. Something like "fra-uf-k-s-s" wheezed in the pristine air. The ensign ran his tongue over his parched and crusted lips, which had swelled up overnight from drink. Or, rather, he sensed it, because it was time. He stirred in the slimy, stuffy darkness. A wave of heat struck him in the nape of the neck. Pain clawed down from the crown of his head, pulsed in his temples, coursed through his softened muscles, and stabbed at his fingertips. He could tell by the thudding of boot heels on the baked, trampled earth and by the strident isolated cries of the crew beside the barbed-wire enclosure that this was a car from headquarters and not an armoured personnel carrier. Pushing aside the camouflage net, he tried to look around, but did not see anything. A swarm of gnats cut through the rectangular piece of illuminated space, and the blanched sky highlighted his strong, jutting cheek-bones and the bulging arteries in his neck. He twirled an empty bottle and then flung it into the corner. He flared his nostrils at the sour, acrid smell of his own body and sweat. He flapped his greasy shirt. The sun was scattering wisps of light from behind the flattened crests of the low mountains. The sky was turning the colour of rust.

In a minute the car spurted, sputtering and spreading exhaust fumes along the valley. Its tires crackled over the packed gravel and echoed between the barbed wire and the rows of modules as it rolled away. Even now Didenko did not see the car. It was only from the way the door slammed and from the way the shadows were lengthening that he guessed that they were coming in his direction. He sat motionless, like a paralytic. He let out a thick, drunken belch. The door squeaked and cut out a luminous square, and on it appeared a long, black hunched figure. Behind it another, smaller, figure kept trying to slip in ahead of the first. Through the lit rents Didenko saw two figures passing by the fence. The shadows quivered briefly on the peeling boards and crawled along the walls of the modules. Behind them were two more men, with sub-machine-guns, sleepy and bleary-eyed. "Motherfuckers." The thought flashed through his mind and then went out.

The man who was standing in front of him was short-sighted. Without his glasses he seemed a bit insolent, or more frightened than insolent. This wasn't the way Didenko remembered him from the year before, when they had marched on Djalalabad. For a minute the short-sighted man felt around the darkness with a colourless gaze, and his shape darted like quicksilver in the square of light.

"Who's there?"

"Who are you looking for, lieutenant?"

"Are you Didenko?"

"I guess."

Something stirred in the module. The camouflage net fell onto the threshold and spread out like a hand. Water bubbled in the gullet of the kettle, and there was a croaking sound. The lieutenant dropped his head, then raised it and heard a muffled, contented smacking of lips: "Right, there's no fucking tea. Well, let's have the paper." A brown suntanned arm covered with prickly hair reached out into the light right up to its elbow.

"Here's the paper...your orders." The lieutenant stepped

into the module, raised the camouflage net, and threw it into the corner, dragging in after him the smell of a washed and pressed uniform and the scent of talcum powder and cologne. He caught sight of Didenko's pockmarked, scarred, rough-hewn face with its high cheek-bones, full, blue, drooping lips, and bulging eyes. The two spheres cast a grey, gloomy glance at him, and the lieutenant added, standing heels in, toes out, "Everything here...you know.... Yes, some tea wouldn't hurt. And also, Didenko, the sooner you do it, the better."

"Who for?" The ensign bent over, and blood rushed to his neck. He put the orders down in front of him and slapped the paper with his broad, calloused hand, flattening out the dog-eared corners. "What did you do, wipe yourself with it? Heh-heh."

The sun reached the cloven peak. The shadows twitched, then deflated like rubber balls, changed direction, and fell still. The lieutenant's eyes filled with moisture. The window of the module was swimming in the messenger's pupils. A mullah intoned to the sky, for the second time that day. Didenko had missed the first prayer. Somewhere nearby a dog let out a protracted, strident bark. Shooing away the gnats and wiping the beads of sweat from his brow, Didenko raised up his square chin with its blue clefts, overgrown with two days' worth of grey bristles, and lowered his long lashes over his bulbous eyes. "Mother-fucking mullah! Someday I'll knock him off with a grenade thrower. Yeah, and there's no more tea. I have to get to the inn. There's nothing at all in the depot."

He was still diligently smoothing out the piece of paper with his chapped fingertips. The nails were chipped and black from being hit. A brief, musty draught rumpled the hair on his head. Didenko raised his knotty hand and stroked his head. "They're still young, lieutenant, kids.... Ye-eah. But this is the thing. Ye-eah, there's no point in moving that senior lieutenant. I knew him back in the Soviet Union. No one thought he wouldn't last and would cr...die. They really overdid it. Kids, and they're bad, and you must understand that's a terrible thing when you're young and bad. Well, they think we're all jackals. Jackals and that's all. There's more than one side to war, lieutenant. I've been thinking about this all my life. When I was serving under Beria. And with these guys. Ye-eah, some tea, ye-eah."

The lieutenant sat down on the edge of the slatted bed and raised his bony knees. His boots squeaked, and a sunbeam scorched through the smeared windowpane and fell on the toes, lighting up a thin layer of red dust. A smile split his face. A dog with a white muzzle and white circles around its eyes poked its head in through the slightly open door.

"Tsu-tsu-tsutsu!" the lieutenant called. The mullah howled at the sky. The dog ran off, its tail tucked between its legs, raising a cloud of dust and filling the air with yelps.

"I took him away from some privates. The bastards were fattening him up for shish kebab. The dog may be stupid, but it was still a pity. He barks at anything you point at. A stupid dog, but still a pity."

Didenko was standing in the middle of the module, pulling on his pants and trying to suck in his belly. The sun had clambered up to the rocky peak and was flooding it with red, and you could see the blue valley, spotted with green garden plots, mulberry bushes, and, off to one side, a few peasant huts.

"For us, Didenko, here's the thing, we've got to take the senior lieutenant away." The lieutenant put on his glasses and adjusted them with his finger. Yellow balls of sunlight bounced over the lenses.

"You'll take him away. I don't need him. What do I need him for? I'll give you a paper if you like, or you can go to the regimental CO. The whole thing makes me sick. They go on and on about the end, but it doesn't come to anything. You'll die before it's over, lieutenant. Ye-eah, no end in sight. In Stalin's day when they talked about the end, everybody believed and knew that it was the end. That's how it was, ye-eah."

As he walked out, Didenko looked at a beet-red shipping container that had grown into the ground, straddling the barbed-wire fence. A face flashed in a window that had been cut out in it on the diagonal, half a metre square and criss-crossed by two concrete reinforcement rods. The face was unshaven, pale, covered in a green netting of sleeplessness, and with white fuzz on the upper lip. It leaned away, and the black shadow of the frame fell on the forehead. The lieutenant cracked his knuckles and ground his teeth. Didenko heard, but did not turn around. Breathing heavily and glancing at the container out of the corner of his eye, he went down to a long rectangular building that was so old that it had tilted to the left.

"What's this? The morgue?" the messenger interjected.

Didenko merely grunted.

They stopped beside a pit. Didenko sucked in his belly, crouched at the edge, and put his hands on his knees. The wind was blowing through the tarpaulin and bringing up the nauseating, suffocating smell of formalin and chlorine. Didenko threw back the edge and peered inside.

"Ye-eah, it's been hot lately, awfully hot. So get in there and look. I put a tag on him because they were all swelling up. There are three of them. The one at the edge is the senior lieutenant. The others are greenhorns – blown up by a land-mine the day before yesterday. Ye-eah, take them away."

A sweet, heavy stench was breaking through the formalin and emerging from the pit. The lieutenant held his nostrils with two thin, white, pampered fingers. His brow was perspiring, and the lenses of his glasses were covered in moisture.

"Ye-eah. I won't have time today."

"What are you talking about?" The lieutenant was still holding his nose, and the tip was turning red. He watched the messenger expectorating, spitting, swearing, and howling again and again, while beating his thighs as if from frost and pulling out the polyethylene bag with the dead man. "What couldn't they divvy up, Didenko?"

"Who the fuck knows." He was troubled, and he sat there squatting and staring at the edge of the pit, where the wind was rustling a thorn bush. "They were boozing together. You should have figured it out back at headquarters and then issued your orders."

"Do your job, Didenko. You know yourself...and everything will be over soon. I'm telling you as one countryman to another."

"What did I say? I didn't say anything. Only tomorrow, according to regulations, at dawn. Because it isn't allowed."

"Well, we'll see about that. I'll be here at 0400."

On the road Didenko fell on all fours and threw up bile. The dog was running around him, barking, wagging his tail, falling to his front paws, putting down his head, jumping, and kicking up a cloud of dust. Didenko chased him away, vomited once more, got up, and went down the slope to the mess-hall.

In the mess-hall he sat down at a long table with oilcloth tacked on and fixed his gaze on the tiny window. It was quiet in the mountains. There hadn't been any shooting for three days. Sometimes single shots would blurt out, but they didn't give anyone a real scare. Far away, at regimental headquarters, they were thinking something up and waiting. Didenko thought about the lieutenant, how he had held his nose with his fingers, how he had smiled, and then about the next day. He felt nauseated again. His stomach growled, and a bitter saliva rose up to his throat. He vomited it out at his feet.

The sun was a white-hot sphere. It clambered up high and

trembled at the zenith. An eagle's scream settled over the silent tents and the CO's camp and hung in the air for a long time. Didenko went into the kitchen. A woman was sitting on an overturned insulated can and peeling potatoes. He went in quietly, so that she wouldn't notice. A dress with white flowers on a red border was escaping from under her dirty smock. Her left leg was rounded, white, and bared so that you could see the small blue blood vessels. When the woman turned her face, shaded by the metal exhaust, Didenko made an effort to smile.

"I'll be done soon, and then we can go," she said.

"I'm in no hurry. Ye-eah, let's...." He looked at her back, ran his eyes over her round, strong buttock, and slapped it with his chapped hand.

The woman turned around. "Don't be a nuisance. I'll be done soon. You've been drinking all night again."

"It's the job."

"Well, all right."

He was sitting beside the woman, breathing the smell of potatoes in through his nostrils, crumbling a crust of bread, and smiling to himself. If they met when the war was over, it would all be different. He wasn't young any more, old age and liquor and a job that could make you howl like a wolf, but somebody had to do it. It was an inconspicuous job, as long as nobody knew, because if some bastard found out and blurted something out, as if by accident, then you'd understand the whole business. Ye-eah. He stroked the woman's buttock one more time. She gave him a guilty smile. The sun was smearing shadows over the floor and skipping in her green eyes.

"Go on already. I'll come see you."

Didenko wrinkled his brow. "Bring something to drink. I feel lousy all the time. Ye-eah.... And tomorrow's a tough day."

He set off along the road, past the container and the wooden tower, and glanced at the shed, long and rectangular like a railway car, which had once been a peasant's slaughterhouse. The sun stood out at the zenith. He crawled into the module, fell on the slatted bed, and tried to fall asleep. His nausea receded. The sun was striking against the windowpane, and Didenko cracked a vertebra and fell into a deep sleep, thinking at the last moment, "It's all right. It's like having a tooth pulled. At first it hurts, but then it's all right."

The woman came when the sun was colouring the mountains red and purple. The suffocating heat, now powerless, was falling off, and the coolness was coming down into the valley. Didenko lifted his head, and as he lifted it he listened to the muscles cracking in the nape of his neck. Smearing the cool sticky sweat, he looked at the window. There was shooting in the mountains: the thudding of a machine-gun alternated with brief rounds of sub-machine-gun fire. It lasted a good minute and looked like flashes of lightning. Young soldiers think of how it resembles sunsets, yellow and indistinct on the windows of the modules and in the mountains, but this looks so little like lightning, and the recruits feel awkward from it. Only later are they overcome by an unsettling horror, and then the real meaning dawns on them. Didenko thought about this and clicked his tongue.

"My God, how I want to go home, Vasia. If you only knew."

"Ye-eah. Set up housekeeping." Didenko stroked her knee.

The wind splashed sand against the windowpane with a rustle, as if someone had poured water. Didenko undid his fly, pulled up the woman's dress, and threw her down onto the slats. "Well, come on, open up, because I feel sick." He wheezed in the dark, fidgeted about, and then threw himself onto his back. "Yeah, Masha, I can't get anywhere, I've got old. Yeeeah, maybe later." A sunbeam picked out his bulging, bloodshot eye. The woman stood up, pulled down her dress, and put her hand on the ensign's head. Didenko shuddered and pulled his head in between his shoulders.

"It's all right, Vasia, it's all right. Here, have some hair of the dog."

She tore apart a loaf of bread along the fold, white bread with a golden crust, and uncorked a bottle with her teeth. Ye-eah, if you didn't think about it, then everything was fine. Hadn't anybody done that back in the old days? And what had he seen? And what was the use of thinking about it all? No, it was better to think, and then by morning everything would come out normal and take on the right forms, and it would be as if nothing had happened. Somebody had to do it. Who if not us oldsters, who had saved the world once and were saving it now? Or maybe there was something wrong here? Yeah, lieutenant, you'll lose for sure, and we'll all be disgraced, and the whole country will lose for sure. Ye-eah, death is the kind of thing that if you run into it, then you'll always be wearing yourself out with it.

Damn, when had he learned to think this way? Ye-eah, here was a woman with a round ass, and he'd get his discharge soon. He had done his time, and he would grow potatoes and cabbage. The vodka was warm and nauseating to the taste. At first it took his breath away, but then it was fine.

"Somebody's come from the Soviet Union, eh?" Masha stirred in the darkness, and Didenko's sensitive nostrils caught the odours of the woman's body.

"No, it's the old supply. Yeah, yeah, better think about that and drink a little vodka, and it will all go back to the way it was when I was young and wore blue riding-breeches with a luxurious nap. Ye-eah, our young people were allowed to, but now it's the other way around. But it's not our fault, it's the fault of those four-eyed lieutenants, a bunch of greenhorns. And I can tell you, they got scared. Ye-eah, there's never been anything like it. Everybody has headed for the mainland, but here there was this bird. I knew him, that senior lieutenant."

The woman raised her head and turned on the lantern. Her gaze hung between Didenko and the window. "Does this mean anything? Kids to the mainland?"

Didenko didn't answer at first, but belched sweetly and spread a slice of stewed pork on a heel of bread. "God only knows....Ye-eah, only God. They say there isn't one, but you know, Masha, there is something."

The woman took a drink from a mug. Her eyes were two yellow lakes. She was no more than thirty, a civilian. He had taken her away from the quartermaster, who liked boys better, people said. He had acquired the taste in Cuba. Ye-eah Cuba, as much as he had dreamed about it, he had never got out of the Soviet Union, ye-eah. The dog pushed his muzzle through the crack in the doorway and gave a long, tedious yowl. Didenko put his finger in the tin can, went over the bottom with it, threw a piece to the dog, undid his fly, and crawled up on the slats. For an hour he tossed around, licking the woman's breasts. A mosquito was buzzing, first approaching and then flying up to the ceiling. It bit him on the elbow. Didenko fell on his back and started snoring with his mouth open. In the light of the lantern the woman saw the saliva that was running onto his outstretched hand. It was beginning to dawn.

THE LIEUTENANT'S HUNCHED BLACK FIGURE was plodding in front, and his polished chrome-leather boots were squeaking rhythmically. Didenko was trotting behind him, taking in the smell of soap and cologne with his nostrils. Two privates with sub-machine-guns were ambling in his tracks, and the dog was running underfoot. Didenko unlocked the container and led out the arrested soldiers. They crouched down a few times and called the dog, whistling and saying, "Shish kebab, shish kebab!" Didenko wanted to rip off their epaulettes, but the lieutenant motioned that he would not let him, and they went down the hill. Along the way the soldiers joked that they were being discharged, so to speak, because they'd be back in the Soviet Union sooner than the ensign, and generally speaking the way he had put down roots it would suit him to stay here. Without Didenko there could be no service. They lit cigarettes. Wisps of smoke hung helplessly in the motionless air. The lieutenant was now striding at a distance, and the ensign could see the fine sweat on his forehead and glasses and the way his clenched fists had turned white. The soldiers whistled time and again to the dog, which yelped loudly and sonorously and cocked its tail. When they approached the slaughterhouse, the soldiers fell silent, sucked on their cigarettes, and spat the tobacco off their lips. One of them had a low forehead and big ears. His eyes were darting about, and his pupils contracted into pinholes. His legs were shaking at the knees. Didenko prodded him on, and he, limping on both legs, set off after his buddy.

The shed, which was divided by a few partitions, with rusty hooks in the ceiling, smelled of fresh sawdust. Flies were buzzing sleepily. Shooed away by the people, they drummed on the clay walls. One of the soldiers caught a fly in his gaze, and for a long time he watched it struggling in the slanted sunbeam that cut through a hole in the roof. They took one of them behind a partition, while the other soldier, who was shorter, with drooping ears, stopped, stamping in his boots, beside the table on which a water bottle filled with vodka was standing and where the lieutenant had sat down, sticking out his polished boots and flashing his glasses. Then the lieutenant began reading the orders. The soldier started fighting to get free, but Didenko and his private pressed down on his shoulders, bent his arms behind him, and pushed him down to the clay floor, which had turned cold overnight. The soldier cried out, "Pasha, run for it!"

Didenko felt for the round burnished handle of his pistol, set the muzzle against the nape of the soldier's neck, and fired. "You can't do fuck all, you motherfuckers!"

Blood splattered onto the lieutenant's pants, and his face twisted like a baked apple. Didenko was nauseated. He took the water bottle from the table and swallowed a gulp, but felt woozy and went out the slightly open door.

"How do you like that? He said to run for it, really, run for it, there it is. How do you like that? Run for it."

In a minute a wailing started. The door squeaked, and the staff lieutenant ran out, bloodstained and dirtied. "Go in and finish him off. I can't."

Breathing heavily, Didenko walked back into the shed. They had stuffed the first man into a polyethylene bag. The second man was thrashing about nearby in a heap of bloody sawdust. His legs had been shattered by bullets.

"He tried to make a run for it."

"Ye-e-eah, Pasha, it's like a tooth. At first it hurts, but then there's nothing to it." Didenko scratched the nape of his neck out of habit and swore under his breath at the lieutenant. "You're sheep, too. This isn't livestock, you know. It's a human being."

He pointed his pistol; a shot rang out; the body convulsed, and the pants turned yellow with faeces. The body struggled for a moment, raked the bloodstained sawdust with its arms, and then fell still.

The red sun came up. The mullah intoned a long, high-pitched prayer. The dog whined and ran towards the voice.

An Elegy about Old Age

YEVHENIA KONONENKO

A hungry old woman is standing by her apartment window on a sunny spring day and looking out onto the street with resignation. There haven't been any trolleybuses for some time now, and a fair number of people have gathered by the new-style glass bus shelter with the mascara ad. Small children are plodding through the square on the other side of the street, and everything seems to be all right. Even though everything is hurtling into a terrible abyss – all of life, the entire age, this whole city, and this square, which this woman (grey now but just as svelte as before, whom everything in life has passed by) has spent fifty years looking at. But she's not the issue. Life won't be any better for those who are now plodding through the square where her son once took his first baby steps. He's past forty now. And today she turns seventy. Her whole life has consisted of stunning blows and stubborn risings. But now, it seems, she can no longer rise. For now fate is beating not only her, but everyone, everyone without exception.

A few days ago she was walking along an underground passage through the wailing of beggars. Cripples displayed their hacked-off limbs. Drunk old men with neither hearing nor voice tortured damaged accordions. An old acquaintance – she saw him in this passage every time – loudly offered cigarettes to passers-by.

"Ladies! Camel Lights! Just for you!" He pronounced "Camel Lights" in perfect English. He always turned his eyes away when he saw from afar the familiar figure of the svelte grey-haired woman who walked through the filthy underground as if breaking ranks.

"De-ear woman, give me something for a ro-oll, at least," lilted an elderly beggarwoman, holding out an empty tin can. The grey-haired woman had a few hryvnias in her wallet. Shouldn't there be some kopiikas, too? Yes, here's twenty-five. She wouldn't give fifty, though. Both of the old women's hands shook. The small coin fell to the ground. No, she didn't want to demean the beggarwoman by making her bend over for the offering. She bent over herself. Lord, her eyes went dark, and she felt a terrible pain in the nape of her neck. Seventy years old. You can't get away from it, can you? And when she straightened out, her wallet was gone. She thought she'd been holding it in her hand. Or had she put it in her handbag? No, until she had bent over so painfully, her wallet had been in her hand. And then for a moment it was as if she had lost consciousness. And the beggarwoman was still holding out her can, singing, "Go-ood people, give me something for a ro-oll at least!"

She came home without the last of her money. Another two weeks before her pension. And in the meantime she doesn't even have enough left for a little roll. For a few days she has been drinking boiled water because, as if to spite her, her tea ran out. And she's out of potatoes. She cooks gruels out of her pitiful reserves of barley. She found a few wilted carrots on the balcony. She could telephone her son Oleh, of course, but the way she feels every time he offers her another greenback, even death by hunger would be more agreeable. Her son is one of her most painful disappointments. At one time he was a mathematician. What tenderness she had felt for those incomprehensible determinants and Jacobians of his! Now he's a manager at his ex-wife's company. The last time he visited his mother, he told her he had delivered some office furniture for Tetiana, and now he was going to make arrangements for a hall at a restaurant for the next reception in honour of the partners from abroad.

"Everything's all right, Mother, everything's fine! How much do you need? Twenty? Fifty? Nothing for now? Well, give me a shout just as soon as you need more!"

She isn't shouting. She's hungry, but she isn't shouting. Yesterday Tetiana came around.

"Tamara Vladyslavivna, I know it's bad form to be early, but I've come to say happy birthday today because there won't be any time tomorrow. Here's a little cake for you for tomorrow, oranges, champagne. Look, I'm putting it all in the fridge. Lord, it's completely empty! Why didn't you phone? Okay, Tamara will bring something tomorrow. As for you, don't get sick and stay healthy for us for a long time yet!

Tamara Vladyslavivna had raised her granddaughter Tamara. My God, the things she'd seen!

"It's not a life you're living, but a novel," her late friend Antonina used to say.

Yes, she did everything she could do to live a clean and proud life, but has ended up being the heroine of a pulp novel. She has one son, but daughters-in-law – there are two, each of them with one daughter by her son. Her younger granddaughter Olesia has just recently turned six.

"Grandma, how long do I have to wait for you to bring me my doll? What, are you crazy, holding a Barbie by the legs?" This is the way Olesia typically speaks. In the end Tamara Vladyslavivna couldn't stand it and swore – Lord, how many of those promises she had made to herself in the angry solitary silence! – that she'd never set foot in her son's house again.

"You should have said that you didn't want to babysit right

off the bat. Of course it's a lot easier to stand by the window and look at other people's children in the square than to raise your own," Olesia's mother Svitlana had hissed after her.

The older one, who was named Tamara in her honour, is twenty. She raised her practically from birth. And now she's raised.... There she is ringing at the door.

Tamara is wearing incredibly tight jeans and a leather jacket. Graceful, nicely made up, pretty as a she-devil. She carries in bags for her grandmother and hands her three roses. She obviously got them in the underground, where the beggars stand.

"How clean your place always is, Grandma! My place is such a pigsty. It's always go, go, go, no time to clean the house. It's simpler for you."

"Yes, Tamara, it's simpler for me."

"Take today. In the morning it's off to the cosmetician's. Then to see you, that's a must. From here I'm off to play tennis. You know yourself, you have to have a perfect body if you want to meet the love of your life. Then classes. You can't cut today because it's a very difficult lecture. Then what? Oh yes, then I have to go see Mother. There are some Swedes at her office at the moment, and I want to practice my English. For the Swedes and the Dutch my English is perfect. If only it were like that for the English, too. And then at eight I have my personal life. I'm tied up until one. And then it's up at seven tomorrow, and back onto the treadmill."

Gone are those long conversations with Tamara when Tamara Vladyslavivna strove to explain to her that this was impossible. Now Grandma remains silent when her granddaughter briefly explains her philosophy of life, according to which men can be divided into the desirable, the tolerable, and the repulsive. If a woman, especially a young one, can't divide men into a single one and all the others, then you can't explain anything at all to her. Her son and both granddaughters – complete failures, complete failures.

Once Tamara Junior reconciled her with her son. There had been a time when it seemed that she wouldn't be able to look at him, just as it had been with her ex-husband. But after little Tamarochka was born she became a frequent guest at her son's home. She violated one of her solitary oaths. Of course, that maternal pride with all its old elation did not return. But still they sat down at the table as a family, laughing and joking. There was a life, a peaceful and dignified life. And then Svitlana, her present daughter-in-law, appeared. Tetiana wept in her mother-in-law's apartment, sobbing that she had long known about Svitlana. Let the March cat have his fling, she had thought, but look how it had turned out. And Tamara Vladyslavivna told her in a muted voice that her husband stopped existing for her when he found another woman.

"So you didn't love him! But I love Oleh!"

"I loved...Andrii Pavlovych!...very much.... And I never said no...." Tamara Vladyslavivna suddenly fell silent, struck by the fact that she had said what cannot be said even in the most confidential conversation.

"If you love him, then you're fighting for your love!"

"You struggle with separations, with illnesses, and even with death. But not with other women! That's not a struggle, but a nasty quarrel. That's beneath our dignity, Tetiana.... From this day you are my daughter, and he is no son to me."

The women were crying. For the first time Tamara herself told the story of what Tetiana already knew well from both Oleh and Andrii Pavlovych, but the words they used to talk about the same thing were not at all the same.

An anonymous message had arrived showing the address at which her husband Andrii Pavlovych would meet Nina the nurse. The date and time when everything was supposed to take place again were noted. She went in order to prove to herself that it was all a lie. The door of the designated apartment was unlocked, and the horrible depravity of what she saw shook her to the core. She survived. She tore everything up, crushed her own heart, and that same day she moved with her son to her mother's, to this apartment where she is now standing by the window looking at the people at the bus stop and at the square where small children are plodding. Nina the nurse, who had written the anonymous message herself and made sure that the door was unlocked and that the intimate scene was depraved to the utmost, had calculated Empress Tamara's behaviour correctly. But she hadn't expected also to receive a gift in the form of the vacated apartment. Only Andrii Pavlovych had absolutely no intention of marrying Nina the nurse and apologized to the inexorable Tamara. After his eighth attempt he angrily slammed the door and never again crossed the threshold of that room. But Tamara Vladyslavivna did not even want to know whether he had married the dissolute nurse, or was living with her without marriage, or was not living at all. On her own she was raising a son who would also not wish to know his unfaithful father....As before, she made sure that the scarf on her neck matched her handbag and gloves. That the edging on her high collar accentuated her upswept hairdo. That her shoes always shone brightly, and everyone recognized Tamara Vladyslavivna's walk from afar. But after her divorce not a single man – not one! – ever said a word, or made a gesture, that could have been taken for particular attention. And she was proud of this.

She was even prouder of her son. After her divorce she would go to the theatre with him just as proudly as she had gone with her husband. Her son did extremely well at school. His father's son, her friends would say. Mine, she would answer silently. The handsome boy began seeing girls at a young age.

Tetiana surfaced by his second year in university. More than anything Tamara was afraid of becoming a lonesome witch-mommy who insinuated herself unceremoniously into her adult son's life. In spite of herself she was jealous of Tetiana, but struggled with herself: let the bachelor live his bachelor's life. She did not know how often her son sat in restaurants with his father or drove around the city in his father's car, which never stopped at their building. The father and son always maintained their conspiracy.

Tetiana and Oleh's wedding was set for June, after graduation. And when Tamara Vladyslavivna solemnly told the two of them, "It's not worth renting an apartment, this room is so big, even though there's just the one, you can divide it in half with a cupboard or a screen, that was how Andrii Pavlovych and I lived here with my late mother, and those weren't the worst years, and Oleh was born here, for the time being this will do, and later something will come up," her future daughter-in-law said, "Don't worry about that, Tamara Vladyslavivna, we'll live at Andrii Pavlovych's. He has a large apartment, you know that perfectly well."

"What's more, he dumped Ninka a long time ago. Look, Mother, I avenged your honour two years ago." Oleh took a photo from between some books, showing a heavy naked woman. As she grasped later, it was of course Nina the nurse, photographed by Oleh. And Tetiana laughed slyly at all this.

"What different notions of honour we have," she nonetheless managed to utter.

Why did she go to her son's wedding? She had probably wanted to avoid explaining anything to friends of the family and to Tetiana's parents. She sat as if pilloried in one of the places of honour alongside her ex-husband. Once, they had ended up at the same performance at the opera. Her beloved Maria Bieshu was singing; the renowned "Casta Diva" sounded unbelievable. She left after the first act, dragging along her friend Antonina, who just didn't get it: for a long time after she kept asking what in fact had happened and why one couldn't sit in the stalls, if someone or other was sitting in the dress circle. She didn't understand that the huge opera, with all its circles and gallery, still wasn't big enough for both of them. As for Tetiana, whom she couldn't look at after the wedding, but later came to love like her own daughter, and who came to love her, it seemed, she's communicating directly with Oleh, over whom she had wept on the sofa at her place, and then coming to understand that there was only one way to keep her self-respect: never to see him again as long as she lived. Yet how quickly Tetiana rejected what the two of them had arrived at with so much suffering! And what was more, the time came when everything turned upside down. Tetiana started travelling abroad, and then she headed up the company. While Oleh's business hadn't worked out, he had some awful debts that they tried to hide from his mother, but Tetiana helped him get out of that mess, and now he's successfully working for Tetiana, renting reception halls for her and buying office furniture.

"Everything's fine, Mum!"

"What, what's fine? That your older daughter is already a...God forgive me, and soon your younger one will be one too? That you were a fine mathematician and became a poor businessman? That everyone all around is begging and stretching out their hand, and they gave you an old car, a *sekond hend* on wheels, and you don't want to see any of this any more? Why, Antonina died hungry! Hungry!"

"So why didn't you take her anything from us?"

"Yes, I failed her terribly. But back then I was still looking after your Olesia day and night, I was trying to make something worthwhile of her! But the kid won't come to anything! Just like nothing came of you or Tamara!"

"But Mother, Svitlana can't go out to work! And you, when you were coming to our place, to babysit Olesia, then at least you weren't ever hungry! And now – it's a fright to see! That's why you're so angry! Mother, Mother, I had no desire to get on your nerves, on your birthday to boot! Here, let's make something, or at least let's have some tea. Oh boy, you have some Nooyi Svit champagne? And you're complaining about your lot! Your grandmother friends are coming to see you tonight?"

"No one's coming. I don't want to see anyone!"

"So what's the champagne for?"

"Tetiana brought it yesterday. You can have it."

"If you don't need it, you know, I will take it. There's one place I still have to go to.... You know, Mother, Tetiana gets a kick out of keeping me alive! Where's your teapot? God, you don't have any tea either, and you're not saying anything. You're completely senile."

"Thank you, Son!"

"Well sorry, sorry, Mother, but that endurance – that's good in wartime. In German captivity! But in this life you have to act completely differently."

"How, precisely?"

"Well, at least without going on some kind of senseless hunger strike. And your Antonina – what do hard times have to do with it? She had a daughter, but she died hungry! It's her own fault for raising a loser! Her daughter came to us and applied to Tetiana for a job! But why should she take her if she doesn't know how to do anything?"

"And you don't think you're a loser?"

"You can call me whatever you like, Mother, but your assessments are far from being the ultimate truth! But that's enough, Mother, let's have some tea and cake. We'll eat some sandwiches, and I'll be off. And this is for you for your birthday.

A modest little envelope with a modest little greenback. But quite enough for some decent tea."

Her son leaves. And she goes back to standing by the window. Three trolleybuses come up one after another, right away there are fewer people at the stop, and Tamara Vladyslavivna is somehow relieved, as if she had also been standing there, among those people. Endurance serves a purpose only in wartime or in German captivity? She had never been in captivity, but she had been through the war, with her mother. Her mother had worked as a doctor in a hospital at the front, and she, a fifteen-year-old girl, had been beside her the whole time. She and her mother had been very close, delighting enormously in each other. Her mother's jacket with the medical service colonel's epaulettes is still hanging in her closet. They buried her in a different one, a dress uniform. This one she'll have to hang out on the balcony, to freshen it up. Oh, who needs all this? She alone, and no one else. They took her father away in '37. And her mother bore everything, managed everything: she did not renounce her father's memory, and got through the whole war. And raised her to be just as proud and enduring. But she couldn't, just couldn't. She'll die – Lord, if only it were sooner! – and there will be no one left with the slightest idea of what a dignified life is. No one will be the guardian of those truths....

Your words are far from being the ultimate truth. Who said that what you say is right? Your conscience? Are you sure your conscience is a match for the world's? And what about yours, Son? No, not mine. But I'm not out to judge anyone. Judge not, and you will not be judged. You yourself live the way you think you have to, so fine! We respect you. But for our part we live differently. Whatever way we can, that is the way we live! Give us at least a little bit of respect! Still, we don't forget you.

Her son has left the modest envelope with the modest little

greenback on her chest of drawers. What would she do without these handouts? Her mother had always lived on her own money and had died at work. But she had been kicked out two years ago. And she had gone to babysit that little brat Olesia. And for several months now she has been standing by her window all alone, looking down into the street and the square, and this is even her favourite landscape – yes, it's lucky when your favourite block of your home town is right outside your window – but even this has long since stopped cheering her.

The sun is shining exuberantly and joyously; the mad blue of the sky is showing through the black branches in the square, and children are jumping like little sparrows. An unbelievable number of years ago on a day like this Andrii came into this room to wish her a happy birthday. The sun was shining exuberantly then, too. It isn't sunny every year on her birthday. Sometimes it rains. But that year, as today, the sun shone like the very joy of life. Mother said hello to Andrii and ran to the kitchen to her pie. While they looked at each other for a long time, and then kissed. First kisses – they always happen at dusk, in a mist, at sunset. But for them the sun had been at its zenith. That was exactly – yes, exactly forty-five years ago! Then they had had fifteen happy years together. Which is why she was better off not remembering anything at all! And when nevertheless, in spite of herself, she finds Andrii Pavlovych breaking into her memories, she frantically begins dreaming that he'll come to see her, he'll come because he can't do without her, and she will show him the door. He'll plead, but she will be implacable again. The years are passing, and both of them are getting old on different streets of the same city. She dreams passionately of how she will throw him out. But he doesn't come. Yet she still dreams.

"Your door was unlocked, Tamara."

She turns around. Andrii Pavlovych is standing at the door.

Yes, she didn't go lock up after her son. She meant to go and then forgot.

"You have so many flowers. And they're all so lush. My tulips are the humblest of all."

Andrii Pavlovych is leaning on his cane with his right hand. In his left he is holding pink tulips. Tetiana had been telling her: he has been having trouble with his legs. After Ninka he married one more time. But he's been on his own for a long time now. And he lives alone. Tetiana goes to see him sometimes. Tamara Vladyslavivna never inquires about her former husband. Her former daughter-in-law tells her herself.

"Nothing has changed here, Tamara. The same sideboard, the same bookcase with the doors, the same books in it. And you haven't changed. Just as beautiful as you were then."

The street outside the window is teeming. A new crowd of angry people gathered at the bus stop is impatiently cursing the useless trolleybuses. Fast cars are driving past them. In the square across the street, plodding and jumping, are children of all ages, who are born in any kind of times. While a large room on the top floor of an old post-war building is engulfed in a bitter wave of past tenderness. They are both too old to be expressing that tenderness the way men and women do. Silently they move towards each other. He thumps his cane loudly. Her legs go numb. And now he is taking her hand and bowing his forehead down to it. While she silently puts her other hand on his bowed grey head.

Exodus

VASYL PORTIAK

We are walking to the source of Warm Water. We are walking over virgin snow past a stream of black water. Steam clumps above it, and a faint odour hovers in the air. The steam settles on shrubs and sickly little trees in a fluffy hoarfrost, which makes them appear to be covered with abundant apple blossoms. A few measly blades of grass show in bright green in the thawed spots by the water, while we walk over the snow, which is squeaking from the frost, following in one another's footsteps in order to save our strength, for none of us, except for the Old Man, know how far we still have to go.

In the attic, where it had been so warm, where birds had scratched with their feet on the slate roof low above our heads and it smelled of pigeon droppings, when people with harsh voices and boxes filled with scrap iron had broken inside from the cold, the Old Man had said humbly, "The time has come, my children. This little corner is no longer ours." We squatted at the train station for two days, but the police forced us to disperse, and singly we were powerless against the insolent station alkies, who took good care of their worn-in spots. The Old Man went exploring somewhere, came back two days later, assembled us in the washroom, gave everyone a cigarette, said nothing for a long time, sadly scrutinized the broken lens in the

Poet's glasses – two winos had beaten him up the day before – and when we had had a chance to savour the decent smokes after the slobbery and caustic butts, said quietly, "I've been everywhere...."

Everyone fell silent. To a man we were holding our stumpy butts, carefully between our index fingers and thumbs, and shooting apprehensive looks at the Old Man. Only Bova flicked his stub with his lips from one corner of his mouth to the other, leaned his head over to the side, drawing it in like a chicken, and enquired tersely, "Shorted out?"

The Old Man nodded. We started puffing again amicably, burning our lips and fingertips.

"We'll be leaving the city."

"And there?" the Academician interjected. "It isn't summer, you know."

The Old Man, catching his breath after an attack of dry coughing, told us with a trembling voice about a warm nook by the source of Warm Water, which streams through a long ravine in an oak grove to a refinery where he had once been a guard, when he was still "in the world," and which he had now gone to see after fruitless searches in the city.

I began to feel uneasy. I would have gladly left here to go to a shelter like our attic, but the Old Man's words boded something entirely different – a desolate region, backyards, a cold abandoned gully. It even began to seem a pity to abandon this anthill, in which I had pretty much got hold of myself after two days and had grown accustomed to the rhythm of cleaning of the halls and toilets, and mastered the itineraries and frequency of the police patrols and the ebb and flow of the stream of humanity.

I already had some secrets of my own. I had found a spare service staircase you could slip into through an inconspicuous doorway right off the street and have a safe nap or wait for some trouble to blow over. I had observed one little drunk who had stealthily been intercepting jobs from the porters – an hour ago even I had managed it – and now there were fifty kopiikas in my pocket that had barely perceptibly weakened one of the fine threads by which I was bound to my company. I became wistful for all this racket, the booming loudspeakers, even the sweetish smell of the toilets, and most of all the opportunities to go out onto the station square and observe in the smallest detail the now familiar horizon, which had barely changed since our first acquaintance with it (two or three high-rises had grown up on the left), listen to the jarring bells of the trolley-cars on the ring road and the deep muted noise, like even breathing, of the big city.

"One way or another," the Old Man said, "we have to leave this place."

We walked through the city, walking in winter and summer, and winter again, walking through the mournful sounds of the sad melodies that resounded from the loudspeakers, which had appeared on the streets from God knows where. The large portrait above the cinema fluttered pitifully in the wind, and not for nothing either, for no sooner had the sad music fallen silent than people wearing bulletproof vests and helmets came in the night and climbed up metal scaffolding to take it down, but we didn't have time for that because we had a different problem. Walking through the city had become difficult because energetic people with hard eyes were scuttling around places that were peopled and places that weren't, and we barely made it out of the trap that the underground passage on the main street of the city had become. Only the Old Man's foxlike sense of smell saved us, so that the round-up closed behind our backs.

Back then the Old Man was especially dejected. He was not encouraged by the palpable changes around us, nor was he pleased that in the mornings people trickled every which way to work much more cheerfully than they had before, while in the afternoon there were fewer people in the stores. We had gone deep underground to make our way, and following us, like Hercules' shadow after the centaurs, loomed the grim magic number 101.

One evening the Shewolf's pitifully scandalous face flashed before me in the pale neon light. She was being led by two police sergeants, and straggling behind, as if by himself, was her little old husband, his glasses shining meekly from under the sack that he was carrying.

In the morning we left behind in the space between the gate and door the silent Kolia, whose voice I don't think anyone had ever heard. Kolia had lucked into finding a tin of horse mackerel. Mind you, half the fish had been eaten, but Kolia had filled the empty space with crumpled newspaper and brought it to our hideout (there was never a time when he didn't manage to stash away at least an empty bottle or a cigarette butt). The Old Man smelled the leftovers and unequivocally flung the can at the wall. The Academician raised his finger and pronounced meaningfully, "Botulinum, you understand?" Kolia nodded his bowed head in agreement. Then towards morning we were wakened by his cries and moans. The can was lying beside him, empty and clean. Well, the Old Man called the emergency number from a payphone, and we watched from a distance as two orderlies let out a curse and shoved Kolia into the ambulance. The Old Man reached up to his knitted stocking cap and bared his bald head.

"Maybe they'll revive him?" someone said timidly.

"His number's up!" the Academician shook his shaggy hair in contradiction and pronounced once again, solemnly and triumphantly, as if confirming the impotence of science before the scientifically designated circumstances, "Botulinum!"

In the morning the taut waves of a requiem engulfed us once again, and together with the people we bowed down in grief, and our grief was double, but we were able to sigh a little more freely now, as it was safer to go through the city when no one was bothering anyone else, until the flags of mourning fluttered over the city for the third time.

One fine spring morning we gathered together four kopiikas in our pockets, and the Old Man went to a newsstand. Three would have been enough, but the Old Man said that all the same it was better to find out about these things from the national papers, and so we had to cough up one more kopiika.

"A quarter of a loaf of black bread," the Kid sighed dreamily and mournfully. He was the youngest among us, a real youngster, childlike and always hungry, and now sick with a cold to boot.

"Don't piss in your pants, Kid," Bova grumbled. "They'll be opening the health bar soon."

Bova is a connoisseur of the most disgusting eating places, where almost untouched servings of steamed patties and full glasses of murky tea get left on the tables. Many a time this saved us during our march through the city. The Kid threw a grateful glance at Bova and shoved his beak into the greasy scarf that the Poet had lent him. A shiver shook the boy's lean shoulders once or twice, then touched him lightly one more time, and finally he was snoring quietly into his muffler.

"This doesn't have much to do with us," the Old Man said, once we had got through the dense text under the grim headline, "although...."

"The wineries and beer cellars are out," Bova reckoned glumly.

"On the other hand the alkies will disappear from the train stations," the Poet said, vengefully flashing the unbroken lens of his glasses.

"The alkies, like unearned income, are eternal," the Academician said, brushing off any prospects for putting the world in order.

Bova's prophecy soon came true, while the Academician's turned out to be somewhat doubtful, because they started taking in drunks without any provocative behaviour on their part, which some viewed with unconcealed malicious glee, and others with a deeply stifled feeling of solidarity among the not overly united but numerous underground.

The second winter we lost the Kid, whom we had to leave behind with chilled kidneys in an apartment that had been vacated for major repairs and to which shaggy boys with coloured hair and adorned with studs and iron buckles had flocked, attracted like butterflies to the injudiciously lit candle stub, and the metal boys were followed by a police patrol. But the Old Man's sense of smell didn't let us down, and we let the patrol pass us by one floor down, hiding in the shadows in another vacant apartment. This winter, the last one, Bova had to leave our company: his haughty character had got into conflict with the humility preached by the Old Man, and that moral and ethical polemic had ended in a horrible act of vandalism: Bova had peed into the tin can in which the Old Man liked to make himself tea separately from our little pot.

So we had cut through the city, which had been our great road, our great home, and our great mirage all at once, and the Great Trouble that rocked the city when the Bitter Star lit up in the upper current of the river did not concern us. The Academician's perorations were more optimistic than the sedative commentaries of the mass media. The Old Man had said it simply: it is a sin for a drowning man to be afraid of getting wet. The trouble blew over and got covered up in chestnut blossoms and May rains, while we kept going straight ahead.

I walked bodilessly and quietly past places I had once frequented, almost without responding to the distant echoing attacks of memory. Now and then I was stopped by people whom I had probably once known: by the post office a ruddy-cheeked little man grabbed me by the sleeve and spoke animatedly about the new times and great prospects, as my company came out of a little street across the square, stepping behind the Old Man. On their way they came across a wonder that we knew from stories that we had heard – young people were sketching passers-by in the open air – and the company went right through them, without leaving even a trace on their papers and canvases, and I quietly freed my arm and set off with them to a deserted autumn river bank, where we met and took in a whole five quiet and tired people, and another four under a bridge, so that now we are walking along the brim of snow past the thawed spots near Warm Water as a fair-sized group. Still, the Poet, the Academician, and I stick together, stepping in the Old Man's tracks, and the ones in the rear, as if taking an example from us, are also tramping in threes.

A slim athlete, wearing a red cap, on skis, looks in surprise at these four groups with the Old Man at the head. He is speeding along an arc that will cross our paths. He skis a long course, so that when the reddened young men who are going home from work with their cloth food bags set on the Old Man, jostling him and breathing in his face with their liquor breaths, and then, glancing at me in confusion for a moment, knock me off my feet, I still see his red cap for a long time, and then his striped white sweater turns red, and the snow turns red....

"Good," one of them says, with one last kick in my ribs.

"I didn't even notice when the bastard jumped," another one booms as he leaves, as if making excuses to his friends for having allowed some guy to knock him off his feet.

"We should have given it to the other ones, too," I hear from a distance now.

I wipe myself off, and the red calico world takes on its usual colours. I see my company, which has taken off along the creek. There is now a flaw in its strict orderliness. There is one missing from the front threesome, and this seems unfair to me. Although I have no regret about what was done, it does seem to me that it would be more fitting for the Old Man at the front to fall away than one of us, but the Old Man is cheerfully ambling to his source, and the distant skier is still moving along the edge of the field, the edge of the earth, ever farther...farther...ever....

Always a Leader

ROKSANA KHARCHUK

O. O. wakes up out of sorts. In spite of his orthopaedic mattress, his bones are all out of joint. During the night his vertebrae seem to have cut sharp teeth that are faintly tapping out in his body something along the lines of the wake-up tune "Rise up, the Fatherland is calling on its son!" His vertebrae are painfully biting into his muscles. The son of the fatherland turns from side to side. The fatherland becomes silent, and the unpleasant feelings in his spine disappear, but this doesn't make his mood any better. On the contrary, it becomes even fouler. Our hero discerns beside the bed a tiny little newspaper with an even tinier acerbic mention of him – a giant of democracy in the fatherland. It is hard for such a trifle to drive O. O. out of control. He stopped believing in the strength of words and principles long ago, or to be more precise he never believed in them. The giant of democracy wields them. He believes instead in the mastery of matter and the law of profit. In his opinion, truth depends on matter and profit as directly as a feeling of well-being depends on a pair of comfortable shoes. For this reason O. O. takes all criticism, even scandalous, with a smile and a squint.

Nothing more can harm him, only death. His death is far off. And this cheers him up. He palpates his heart, stomach, and kidneys. All his organs are in their places. He listens to them. They are working without interruption. What more can he want? Still his mood remains murky. Revulsion creeps through his digestive tract, floods his rib cage, and crawls steeply up his throat. Tripping on his Adam's apple, it catches on something under his palate and squeezes out a spasm. O. O. belches loudly and feels better. His brain begins working more clearly. His brain cells join together in supple pirouettes of thought. However, despite such neck-breaking gymnastics, not one of them thinks itself out to the end. All his thoughts remain broken off. O. O. can't make himself concentrate on the main thing – he cannot discover the reason for his discomfort. Our hero is not used to discomfort. It annoys him. Outer and inner harmony and a feeling of stable confidence in himself and his surroundings are as much a given for him as air for a grey mediocrity.

And rightly so, for O. O. is not a random specimen in life that fertilizes the earth in vain or gratuitously pollutes the sky. He belongs to the category of, no, not supermen, that smells bad. He belongs to the category of leaders: responsible personalities, engendered by history and the very spirit of the masses – undirected, rebellious, and therefore beautiful. O. O.'s imagination always associates the masses with a headstrong woman who needs to be tamed, but not just any way – delicately. A coarse violation won't do. That is what his intuition tells him. Taming is a delicate matter. It breaks down into several phases: light flirtation, coming together, a promise, and as an apotheosis – a cult of absolute trust. After taming, the script of the hit soap opera calls for apostasy, which has countless shades and gradations, but is always self-justifying. Finally betrayal: not direct, but refined and concealed. O. O. has an especially acute awareness of the womanliness of the masses when he is standing on a platform and they are crowding around below him.

The leader of democracy in the fatherland cannot exist

without or beyond a platform. The absence of an elevation causes him intolerable suffering – chronic sensory torture. The platform is a necessary element of taming. It is not only the brain that produces seductive words that flow like honey or menacing ones that burn with the sacred flame of righteous indignation. It is also the elevation. The platform inspires. And it also conceals the secret pocket in which the leader keeps his supply of masks. O. O. pulls them on with a magician's dexterity to the accompaniment of a recitative "What do you need? Need a pretty boy, a gigolo? I have one! A flirtatious suitor, an unsurpassed seductor? Help yourself! A showman? We can give you one! A steadfast defender, a knight in shining armour and superman? With the greatest of pleasure." Under each mask, however, there always lurks a rapist and a traitor. The virtuosity and expertise lie in the fact that the light-hearted fans of democracy never twig to the rape and treachery. The ones who do remain silent. They don't want to get their hands dirty. And so it should be. Words lull those who are quick to trust. Words warm them and set them on fire, but gradually. In the final analysis, the wonderful, frenzied masses must be put into a trance.

So far, O. O.'s slogan, "Mutual orgasm through mutual satisfaction!", has produced brilliant results. Only some hypothetical malefactor could maintain that this result is a consequence of a sexual culture that is low or even absent among the people. O. O. is an outstanding theoretician. Even more, he discovered the theory whereby words cast from the height of a platform are the bearers of orgasm and the gaping jaws of the masses are its recipient. You may find oral sex disgusting, but in this case mutual pleasure justifies the method. This theory cannot be refuted logically: it is tied not to logic, but to experience. The masses will do anything for a moment of oblivion. They deify the leader who makes them happy the way a penis does.

Politics as a form of sex. To O. O. this thesis is the music of the spheres, the poetry of a new age. He feels the poetry of politics with every pore of his body. Politics is his last, and therefore his most passionate, love. Romanticism? So be it! Romanticism is what distinguishes O. O. from other politicos, who lack not just poetic imagination, but indeed any kind. That's correct, you don't blather about rights, you don't give them or ask for them, you take them. But not with a mortal grip! What for? Dearly beloved, rough terror is long past. These days rights are taken easily and without force, as if in play: without threats or unnecessary fuss – elegantly, sportingly. Not for O. O. machine-guns and cannon muzzles, much less concentration camps. He is a democrat, automatically progressive, and an aesthete to boot. Anything unpolished, uncultured, or atavistic nauseates him. No wonder O. O. has declared war on technological greediness and plebeian tastes on life's every front: from daily life to the social sphere, from the technology of shaving to the technology of atomic reactors. An ad campaign for a civilized way of life has brought about fundamental changes in both the lives and the deaths of the rebellious masses, in their musty psyches and retrograde outlook. O. O.'s fellow citizens brush their teeth with ultrapowerful whitening toothpastes, medicate themselves with soluble effervescent tablets, and wear hygienic single-use clothing and footwear. They say that the teeth of the masses have almost all fallen out, so they end up brushing their gums. They say that effervescent tablets do not relieve pain. They say that the clothing and footwear fall apart after a few tries at intensive wearing. They say.... But that's not the point!

The masses are not supposed to deal with the problem of life. Life does not belong to them, neglected and accidental as they are. Life belongs to the leaders and to those who have latched onto the leaders like leeches. The masses are supposed to deal with the problem of death. The leader knows how to help them. He knows how to relieve the accidental tourist on the road of life of his eternal fear of non-existence. People get stunned by their very existence, as if by a rock on the head. Existence gets poisoned to make them renounce it voluntarily, having acknowledged everything as insane and themselves as losers. A piece of bread is worth something, but whoever grew it and baked it, shipped it and sold it, isn't worth squat. What a downer. There's something to smother your fellow citizens with, to kill those who are fated at birth to be victims. The most effective way is to smother them with their own hands within their own living space. No evidence, and no guilty parties, either. Obliterate the evidence not indecently, but with love, with an appeal to an ideal that, as everyone knows, is never given without victims.

O. O. is a humanitarian and a humanist. He feels the pain of loss and mourns the victims with all his anatomical heart, but he himself has never been a victim and never will be. "Always a leader! Never a victim!" – is another of O. O.'s slogans. Unlike the first, though, it is a product of his inborn nature, and not of evolution. O. O.'s genes are encoded for leadership. That is why, against all odds, our hero has always remained up high or at least on the upward slope. He has never been afraid of heights. He has always dreaded low points. Now he has settled, maybe not on the highest, but on a prominent knoll of fatherland democracy. The mere awareness of this fact and its direct relevance to history, which judges a person roughly, on the basis of an overall result to which thousands of nameless victims contributed, forgetting about such trifles as the leader's personal biography, fills him with pious trembling. A blessed atheist, the very embodiment of undiscriminating history, O. O. clasps his hands for prayer, his eyelids lower sweetly, his lips whisper nearly inaudible words – a prayer for the universal triumph of democracy in his likeness.

It is difficult to hear, but the dominant word "movement" is repeated some ten times. It's clear: he has to move. Where? Why, forward! The leader of the democracy tries to look out into the distances to which he is calling, but his eyes come up against a wall. "No problem," he decides, "there has to be something behind the wall. That's why the people's move, move, move towards democracy is relentless." Indeed, the water-closet is behind the wall. He has to move towards that too, and fast. O. O. proudly raises his head, straightens his stiff legs in a picturesque way and briskly gets up: just a boy, and not a statesman! His feet hit his slippers like a bull's-eye, on his first try. How symbolic. That's how the owner of the slippers hits his foes.

O. O. steps into the lavatory with self-assurance. The sacred ritual of his morning toilet begins. The leader delicately lathers his well-groomed face. It hasn't been trained to suffer – it is always self-satisfied. O. O. can't help admiring himself: what a good-looking man he is, straight off the cover of a fashion magazine. It's a fact. As he admires himself, the leader trains his gaze in the mirror; it's supposed to be gentle, humane, and at the same time firm: not like flint, but like a nut, and his smile – it's supposed to be aristocratically understated, without any cheap tricks. When he shaves, O. O. uses the most up-to-date blades, creams, lotions, and perfumes. It's no wonder his wife jokingly calls him a perfume counter – the expensive smells trail after him everywhere, like the train of a gown: it's not just his hands that are clean, everything's clean. His intentions are no exception. The leader lathers them and rinses them off thoroughly as well. His intentions waft freshness.

The clatter of spoons and coffee things makes its way to O. O.'s ear. The smell of fresh coffee and hot toast makes its way to his nose. The democratic leader can sense the attractiveness of life. He hums involuntarily a song from his distant but unforgotten youth: "Ah, what a colonel he was! Ah, what a man he was!" O. O. is a bit surprised that he is singing in Russian. Democracy, however, respects all national minorities. A matter of principle. There! O. O. delicately dries his physiognomy, which is glowing with pleasure, with a towel fluffy as a cat. One last look in the mirror, and...O. O. stiffens.

A stranger's mocking eyes are moving in on him from the upper right-hand corner of the mirrored surface. A sadistic question is stirring in the eyes: "So, dem-lead, you're all set to purge your plebeian little soul with the help of cosmetics? Why, the plebeian condition has eaten its way into your bones. You live by it. You breathe it. It's your way of life. And no one chooses their way of life. They are born with it. And don't curse your peasant origins, the lack of a proper upbringing, or the poverty you grew up in. What does the poetic village have to do with it, with its unpoetic piles of manure, impenetrable mud, and eternal moonshine? There are people there, too. It's just that you've never been a person. You were and still are manure, the bottom of the pile. There's nothing worse than a plebe who seizes power. Rule!"

For all his aquiline nature, O. O. is not accustomed to such attacks. He convulses, as though from an electrical shock. How disgusting! He hastily shoves his dirty laundry into the washing machine. The observant eyes are gone. Shell-shocked, the democratic leader looks in the mirror. Hallucinations? He's seen those eyes somewhere. Yesterday. No, the day before yesterday. That's it, the eyes live one floor down and belong to a neighbour of O. O.'s – a sickly teacher who has, as the leader rightly noted, unlawful pupils slipping in to her place every day. Private lessons in a private apartment – now there's an under-the-table business, it's criminal! O. O. impetuously wrings the air's neck. He is tirelessly and constantly wracking his high-brow brains for a way of nailing moonlighters like that, pinning them to the wall of survival. O. O. is not disturbed by the fact that his neighbour doesn't get paid for months at a time, even though democracy does in fact provide for payment for work. He demands a full, true sacrifice, not a cheap little fake. His feelings as a secret rapist have been wounded to the core. O. O. cannot tolerate someone managing unaided to obtain even a millimetre of their own uncontrolled living space. And this one – why, she's a big fat nothing, so fat you can't draw one any fatter. They're all spoiled! They think democracy is a private business. They're learning, they're never satisfied. They want to turn the world upside down. They're looking for a place to stand on. Learn, bless you, but there are things that hold this world up that you cannot learn: dexterity, swindling, opportunism, inborn DIPLOMACY! The witch, she must have thought up a way of spying through the waste pipes.

Whereupon O. O. gets a hold of himself, sensing the absurdity of such an assumption. A pause occurs in his monologue. Still, what explanation is there for the paranormal phenomenon that he has just seen? After all, O. O. isn't a mystic or a charlatan, even though he has taken a few classes in hypnosis. Hypnosis in politics, that's the highlight of the show! O. O. is a civilized and educated person. Therefore, first the sources of this strange story have to be found, then the facts have to be arranged in their historical interrelation, and then everything will become clear. The leader saw these eyes the day before yesterday. There is no doubt about it. The exhausted O. O. came home from work. He parked his fancy car, nobly entered the lobby, and aristocratically smoked an unplebeian cigarette while waiting for the elevator. It looks like a real pigsty, but O. O. prefers not to notice this. Puffing on his cigarette, the light kind, for his lungs, the leader got on the elevator. A shadow slipped in after him. At first he didn't realize what it was: there was only one feeble little lamp flashing in the elevator, a night-light in a smoke-filled house. After a while the leader could see the teacher and greeted her politely, blowing expensive smoke in her washed-out face. Whereupon she, instead of giving him a friendly nod, looked him up and down and hissed, "You can tell a gentleman by his boots. What a plebe!" O. O. didn't have a chance to figure out what a gentleman and boots had to do with each other, because the elevator stopped and the teacher disappeared. Once he was home, as he undressed, the leader carefully examined his snobbish white sheepskin coat – not a stain – and gave his shoes a close looking-over too – they shone, as if they had just come from the store – and there wasn't a scratch on his smooth attaché case. "What's this crap?" the leader asked himself. "Why a plebeian? The bitch is obviously out of her mind." Still, the unpleasant incident must have made a painful impression on our hero's subconscious.

O. O. has heard a lot about psychoanalysis and so has figured out the crux of the matter. His subconscious has never been able to come to terms with the fact that democracy, especially the post-colonial kind, smells only too strongly of the plebeian condition. O. O. demands aristocratism and respectability: he does not understand that the main thing in aristocratism was not the external gloss, but the code of honour. Even the bourgeois manner that he adopted back in his youth – first he had been a socialist functionary, and then later a leader in a market society, there wasn't much difference – became his essence, but also strictly externally. For all his moral helplessness, he desperately craves blue blood. The leader is persecuted by the image of his mother bent over her vegetables – a sign of poverty. The stooped peasant woman torments him in terrible, frightening dreams. He fears poverty – he suffers from the complex of a lumpen who has seized power. He identifies power with the full trough from which, as a child, he had fed the hog, sow, and young pig – the family's only wealth. No one, not even his own wife, has any idea of the horrible split personality that has lodged in O. O.'s skeleton. For the very purpose of softening the split the leader bought himself an orthopaedic mattress and an exercise machine for special exercises to prevent splitting of the being, and built a personal swimming pool, not with his own money, of course, but with democratic funds. What a person won't do for the sake of saving democracy! The leader has one other therapeutic toy – a cellphone. Without it, O. O.'s ears don't work at all. There, even now he is spasmodically squeezing the handset, which, as if in spite, remains silent.

O. O. sadly goes up to the exercise machine and even more sadly stretches once or twice. It isn't easy, but he does manage to touch the aristocratic part of his being to the plebeian or rather democratic one. Glumly he heads for the kitchen. For the umpteenth time this morning his spirits fall. In the kitchen the leader openly lets his irritation out, accusing his wife of setting the table in a plebeian manner, not pouring the coffee the right way, and starching the tablecloth incompetently. Although O. O. is in the mood for everything to be wrong, to some extent, nonetheless, he is right. Indeed, the same kind of democratic disorder reigns in his home as in the country, too, whose fate the leader decides. Here there are countless beautiful things, but somehow all of them are mismatched, because they have been accumulated without thought. There is no interest here in beautiful things, which, as a rule, were either given as gifts or bought with easy money. For this reason with time they became ugly. The leader probably can't explain what all these things had been useful for. Unless they're for the sake of self-affirmation. A caricature? But such is a leader's fate.

O. O. hardly has any breakfast: he gulps some coffee, has a

bite of toast, and gets up. He'll finish breakfast at work – in a more refined setting. The leader of the democracy hastily thanks his wife, stores away the witticism on his lips for his future memoirs, and quickly gets away. O. O. doesn't like his home. Not enough of an audience. And then – there's no platform. And so – faster, for his fix. The leader is driven to his platform by the same craving that drives an addict to his narcotics. In his car, O. O. feels confident and upbeat. He lights up, he turns the steering wheel – he's an ace driver – and he's on his way! Out of habit, he presses the knob on his radio. Cheerful sounds resound through the car accompanied by even more cheerful words: "I'm a stylish guy, I have a good time by myself, I don't love anyone, as a fellow I'm exotic, as an egoist a classic." O. O. clicks his gearshift to the beat of the dumb little song. Stupid tears head for his eyes. What a joy it is to realize that ukrainization is taking over the masses through show business. "The show is the future of the whole world," O. O. decides. Therefore, driving up to the luxurious building in which party members once ruled and which now accommodates the secretariat of the democratic party and one of the many mythical charitable funds, ugly hatchlings of the new age, he doesn't turn off the plebeian music. Preoccupied, he doesn't notice that he has gone through a red light and almost run down a man who looks like a pensioner. The man jumps backs to the sidewalk at the last moment. He's not a pensioner, but an opera singer who, unfortunately, hasn't been able to undergo a perestroika because he has no feeling for the needs of the market and doesn't know how to satisfy them and is therefore continuing fulfilling his destiny singing arias. The "stylish guy" cuts the creative has-been's musical ear, but at the same time keeps him from falling under the wheels of victorious democracy. The man sees the boorish car off with a minor look in every register. A rich tenor unexpectedly sings out,

"Plee-ee-eebe!" The opera singer takes fright. O. O. doesn't hear the singing: he is just driving through the automatic gate.

The gate drops at the very moment when one of the plebes sung out in the rich tenor is trying to squeeze through past the car. "Not allowed," the gate tells the "plee-ee-eebe." Who, catching on, turns into the mutt Zhuchka – a pedigreed plebe. Zhuchka yelps cheerfully, wags her tail, and runs to Auntie Mania, who is selling hot patties some twenty metres from the democratic residence. Zhuchka hopes that kindly Mania will give her something, but she is cruelly mistaken. Auntie Mania's activities do qualify as charitable. The profits from the patties are designated for the victims of Chornobyl and thus are also partially tax-exempt, but she doesn't throw the patties around left and right. They are subject to a strict accountability. Auntie Mania gives out free patties exclusively to democrats and herself. While Zhuchka, besides her democratic lineage, doesn't have the slightest notion of democracy. Could that help her soften up democratic Auntie Mania, whom her very own fellow tradespeople call the Monster behind her back? Of course it couldn't.

Going up the wide carpeted steps, O. O. hums "I'm a stylish guy" under his nose, but all the same it comes out "Ah, what a colonel he was!" "Now that's catchy. But why the colonel, and not the guy? Apparently my age is showing," the leader determines self-critically as he greets his supersecretaries and jokes with them: O. O. has gained renown for his humaneness both within and beyond government circles. The secretaries freeze in random poses like models at a fashion show. Faith is responsible for the telephone, Hope – for coffee, and Charity – for visitors. O. O. throws his first instructions at Hope and his second at Faith, while asking Charity to please wait. He pushes open the door to his office energetically, taking his coat off as he goes, adjusts his tie automatically, and smoothes his already perfect hair. O. O.'s every move is reflected in a huge mirror installed along the entire wall of the office. If desired, this office can also be used as a dance hall, a bistro, a casino, or even a public washroom, if, of course, the floor and the other walls are set with hygienic tiles.

O. O. sinks in his chair, lights up, and gets down to business. He looks through his organizer. Like his desk, the leader's organizer is divided into two parts. The first concerns public, government business. The second – personal. Even a dummy like Uncle Fedia, the perpetually drunken little democratic steward who moonlights as a carpenter, locksmith, sanitary technician, and librarian, would notice the obvious disproportion right away. O. O. has seventy percent more personal business than government. However, Uncle Fedia knows that that is how this sorry life is arranged. How can you get around it? A leader of a democracy needs a life too. And a better and merrier one than Uncle Fedia. Fedia needs a bottle. The leader, a hundred. Fedia needs vodka. The leader, cognac. Anyone who doesn't understand this is an idiot. Right on, Uncle Fedia. We understand, don't worry.

While O. O. is poring over his notes, Hope appears carrying a tray in her hands. Moving like a professional waitress, she sets out on the desk everything democracy can offer at this time. There is no need for an enumeration. The citizens know for themselves what their democracy can offer. The coffee break plus breakfast takes place under the searchlight of Hope's radiant inviting smile. O. O. feels it: democracy cannot help conquering. He decides to finish his coffee while talking on the telephone. And here a calamity occurs: reaching for the receiver, O. O. knocks over the cup. The coffee splashes out right onto his trousers. Prominent stains cry out, "Plebe!" The leader of our democracy has an important meeting planned for today with the leader of another democracy, a woman leader to be precise. How can he fall flat on his face in the mud? O. O. looks at his watch: the minutes remaining before his meeting are numbered. He won't have time to send someone for clean trousers. How many times he has thought of setting up a wardrobe at the office, but never got around to it. And now there you are! He summons Hope. Hope, on seeing the stains, almost faints. She swears that had she known, she would have drunk that damned coffee herself, but it's too late now. Hope leaves the leader before he can fly off the handle and let out some not very leaderly words. Instead, Faith appears. That's who can find a way out of any situation! In fact, Faith is holding clean trousers in her hands. In O. O.'s opinion, they are not aesthetically pressed. But Faith insists that the leader will look more democratic in trousers like these. For the pants are the property of the part-time carpenter, locksmith, sanitary technician, and librarian Uncle Fedia. O. O. is reluctant, but he has to agree. He has no choice. Charity reminds him that the time of the meeting is inexorably approaching: the foreign democrats are already at the door. The general mobilization in the house of democracy touches more than just the suddenly sobered Uncle Fedia, who is melancholically pondering the high honour his trousers have attained. His late mother was wrong. Maybe not her son, but at least his trousers will rise through the ranks!

Meanwhile O. O. looks himself over critically in the mirror and decides that for most of the meeting he will be seated behind his desk. He will hide his legs, with their overly democratic trousers, beneath it. But the very next minute he has to get up and go out into the centre of the office – guests ought to be met hospitably. O. O. extends greetings confidently. Ringing in his voice is an unsimulated, but measured, joy that the interpreter imitates to the finest nuance. With an elegant gesture our leader asks the other democrats to make themselves at home. He bestows an elegant kiss on the woman leader's hand, but for some reason she wrinkles her nose. Could she be a feminist? O. O. doesn't get flustered: in an instant he clasps her hand. He even seems to want to give her a friendly pat on the shoulder, but saves this gesture for later, once protocol runs out. The woman leader smiles amicably. For some reason, however, her gaze keeps riding down to the lapel of our leader's burgundy jacket. This disturbs O. O. He pretends it doesn't, very ably, actually. Finally in a brief interval between mutual smiles he manages to have a look at his lapel. He is horrified to see a speck of dandruff on the burgundy background. The speck moves as if it were alive. In a ray of sunlight it is dancing a wild boogie-woogie, chanting, "Plebe! Pleeeebe!" This can't be. Our leader does not believe his eyes, because he washed his hair today using a shampoo with a label that insisted it would rid the purchaser of plebeian dandruff. O. O. grinds his teeth maliciously, but to the point: the other democrats are just asking ours about obstacles to the democratization process on site. The meeting goes into a tailspin: the interpreter can't keep up interpreting our democrats for the others and vice versa. O. O. offers the interpreter a rest. In his opinion, fraternal Slavic languages don't require interpretation anyway: everything is just as clear without words. The meeting is entering the stage of informal socializing. The leader of our democracy offers his guests a drink. Naturally, this is a necessity, not a whim. Why, one has to have some way of easing the tension evoked by the discussion. The other democrats do not refuse. Hope appears in the doorway. She is assisted by Faith and Charity. The modest drinks threaten to grow into lunch, but that isn't on the agenda. The other democrats still have a slew of serious meetings. Ours, a pile of current business. The sorrow of parting is no less warm than the joy of meeting. The distance between the two democracies has become significantly shorter. The woman leader of the other democrats is no longer taking notice of the lapels on the jacket of the leader of our democracy. This is a success. With no exaggeration.

When the last door closes behind the last of the democrats, O. O. can loosen his tie. The next loosening is marked by the next glass. Not a drop is spilled from it. The leader of our democracy groans with satisfaction and instinctively sniffs his sleeve with relish to help the drink go down. The mirrored wall obediently reflects this movement – O. O. freezes, then shrinks back. How many times in the course of the day has the plebe closed in on him! "I'll smash him," he decides excitedly. But the plebe isn't one to scare easily. The reflection curls its lips, sneers, and points its index finger right at the leader: "Government business has been attended to, but what about your own, eh?" O. O. gratefully squeezes his double's hand: he has almost forgotten that he is supposed to inspect several important sites of democracy this afternoon – a cooperative garage, two gas stations, and a pocket-sized nuclear power plant. The latter is a pet project of O. O.'s because, just like the leader himself, it belongs to the modern, new generation. O. O. gives specific instructions to Faith, Hope, and Charity and drives away in the direction of x, y, and z.

The plebe has no unpleasant surprises at the secret sites. Everything goes smoothly. Late in the afternoon, however, O. O. is surprised once more, this time almost agreeably. As he calmly drives up to his building, a fantastic tableau opens before his eyes. Teenagers have jammed O. O.'s courtyard. They are gathered in clusters and talking animatedly. Before the leader can brake about ten airheads with dyed hair rush towards him. They are hailing the leader enthusiastically. O. O. smiles one smile after another. Who wouldn't be moved by young love? But the airheads suddenly stop in their tracks. With obvious disappointment, one of them whines, "It's not him!" What does she mean, not him? O. O. feels wounded. How is he, an old democrat, tried and tested in electoral campaigns, supposed to know that a fashionable recording studio has been in operation for a month now on the first floor of his building and that fans of the country's own show business gather in his very own courtyard several times a week to wait for some pop idol?

O. O. doesn't give up and keeps smiling at his country's youth. But the young people do not react to his gesture of good faith in any way at all. The democratic leader decides that they can't recognize him because it's dark. He takes one more step towards the young people and waves his hand paternally. In answer to which he hears: "Hey man, are you the leader? What do you play – rock, pop, ja-a-aazz?" Without missing a beat O. O. grunts, "Ja-a-aazz!" "Then beat it, pops, that's not our style." At this moment another car rolls into the courtyard. The crowd of fans spontaneously surges towards it. A head pops out of the door. A shock wave of young voices nearly knocks the leader of the democracy off his feet. The crowd is going wild: "Tolia! Tolia! We love you! Give us 'Stylish guy'!" Buttons click on tape recorders; live voices join in. The courtyard starts stamping, shouting, and jumping. The familiar tune booms like a bombshell. The situation becomes clear. No one is paying any attention to the stunned democrat.

O. O. stamps his feet beside his car. He's coming to his senses. A cassette starts playing in his brain: "Find out this guy's name. Put in a rush nomination for a state award. Why, he's doing more for ukrainization than the whole Academy of Sciences! That's when young people will recognize me and give me their votes. Youth is power!" O. O. is thrilled to have coined his next slogan and contentedly lights a cigarette. "Let them have their fun. The plebeians always want bread and circuses. So what? I can guarantee them a show for the rest of their lives.

Easy." The leader of the democracy jostles his way to his door. He did not anticipate that the smoke from the chic cigarette would leave a brushlike plebeian trail behind him. It is a ladies' cigarette.

Karma-Yoga

BOHDAN ZHOLDAK

The thing was that even the ambulance service shock brigade fell into shock. From time to time there are calls like that. What ever won't a person think of in their grief? Or their happiness – what's the difference? There was a fellow by the name of Udchenko living here in the housing project, and his great joy was that no one here knew any Church-Slavic.

However, no matter how much we might want this story to be about that, it is about something completely different. Because the ambulance is already rushing to its call, it's hurrying for real, because the case has turned out to be so incredible that it can shock even the paramedics, especially if any of them are women.

Now that same Udchenko, even though he had never read Freud, nevertheless sometimes personified the part of his name – *ud* – that meant "rod." That is, he sublimated in reverse.

So that one time he went up to a girl he didn't know and began attaching himself to her so politely, and only later noticed how beautiful she was. And that there had never been one like her in our housing project. Because such enchantresses don't live in projects, only in Lypky or downtown.

The professional beauty must have been overcome by grief

or had a bit to drink not even to have noticed that Udchenko was under the influence. Which in fact kept him from coming to his senses when he finally saw what a raging beauty was replying to his raging syntactical pirouettes, reinforced by anti-sublimation.

"Hey you," this was how he began, "why don't you ask me, ask me what my name is?"

"What's your name?" She looked right through him, because men of his build did not have any particular optical solidity for her.

"My name's Kolian. What's yours?"

To her surprise, this man reminded her of her barefoot childhood. They had had someone more or less like that, Grandad Panko, who in addition to being a security guard at a store at night was a goatherd in the daytime, and every morning she would drive Manka out to him by the gate. For a long time, he was the first man she would see every day, until a touring rock band happened into the village.

She almost told Kolian her first, real, name: Motria. Now she was already using the one that was in her new passport: Mary. The evolution towards this name had been rather significant; the previous one had been Maryna.

"You're really funny," she said in unexpectedly flawless Ukrainian and told him her name.

She didn't have to look back at the distant Mercedes. It had been slowly rolling along the streets after her for an hour and a half. Which was why she had chosen the longest route and ended up all the way here, at the project. She knew that the luxurious car had to be there, and that it would be there another two months or so. Until her first aborted pregnancy. Then the Merce would be replaced by a Volvo. And her name would change, from Mary to Marilyn, probably.

At this point Kolian broke into a damp sweat, because he

noticed what a beautiful woman was talking to him, and changed into Mykola. He recovered his senses enough to grasp right away that the luxurious limousine that had slowly rolled right up to their supermarket was tied to his fate.

"And so," he said.

And then he noticed what eyes she had. And practically fell into them, putting a phrase out in front of him in the nick of time:

"There's nothing at the zoo right now. Because they didn't bring any, that's why."

"Didn't bring what?" The girl laughed in a perfectly Ukrainian way because the word "zoo" had reminded her again of the goat Manka. Where was it now? If they hadn't butchered it?

However, she remembered that even back then the goat had been young, that it would still do for two or three seasons and for three or four offspring. What was the best word? Mary thought about this as she took another look at her new companion's eyes. Farrow, that was for a pig, but what would you say for a goat? To lamb? No, that wasn't it. Lambing was for sheep. To kitten? No. One more word from her mother tongue had flown out of her forever. She felt it, and it made her sad.

"That's how they tease people at our liquor department," this lively fellow named Mykola was explaining. "They've fenced it off with an iron grill. Just like the one for the bears at the zoo."

"How are those bears?"

She asked him in an intimate way, because they had to walk alongside the Merce, which was mutely watching the proceedings through its permanently mirrored windows.

That's why she seized Mykola under the arm and pressed so close to him that both he and the Merce flinched.

"Oh, let the bears suck their paws now. I said that" – the

guy couldn't even trust himself, which made him even more like Grandad Panko when he was young – "so you'd know I had a stash."

He blurted this out so joyfully and spontaneously that she almost asked him whether he didn't by any chance have relatives in Sulymivka. But the long list of names that cut her off from her native village, together with the hasty, bungled sale of her grandmother Motryna's house, the grandmother in whose honour she had been given her name, didn't let her wonder out loud.

What else could she have done? When the rock band ran aground and even their sumptuous lead couldn't talk the philharmonic, much less the culture section, into a decent contract. And then the sole object of any value – the Tama drum, bought by chance right from Kobza, disappeared. What she didn't know was that it was Liokha, the bass-player, who had sold that drum, but a new one had to be bought, because rock can exist without a lot of things, even without a Liokha, but not without a drum. Once she had sold the house, she cut herself off from the village forever because, even if she wanted to go back, she no longer had anywhere to go back to.

"And where do you keep this stash?" She pressed up even more intimately with her perfumes because she had seen out of the corner of her eye that the limousine had moved from its spot.

"Well, you see," Mykola hemmed and hawed, "there are places in our neighbourhood that are called dorms. They're buildings where a lot of buddies all live together."

She pressed her palm warmly to his arm. As if to say "I know." To avoid exposing herself by her intonation if she had to talk about residences. Because Banzai had been able to go on tour only because the club at some machine-tool factory could put up the performers in their collective apartments, where they had to take turns watching the equipment. But that's where the Regent had been stolen, because that jerk Liokha had stuck a Korg label on it and some idiots in the audience had believed it. As she found out later, with the help of her new friends, Liokha himself had done that synthesizer in by convincing them that it really was a Korg and even showing them where to kick it. And even though he had to answer painfully for it later....

The car was slowly rolling up, and Mary quickened her step, realizing that she could fool the Merce all she wanted, but she had let herself slip with this Mykola. Actually, he had let himself slip by rolling up to her as he had. In a moment of confusion, so now he himself had to.... She knew perfectly well that this Mykola, whether he had to or not, wouldn't stand a chance against the Merce.

"Are there a lot of you buddies?" she inquired, pressing barely perceptibly with the middle of her palm so that he wouldn't be afraid to augment their number.

Mykola understood this his own way. "All I have there is Makukha. And there's Tolian, too, in 418. But the stash isn't at Tolian's, it's...."

Whereupon he was struck silent. Not because her fingertips turned out so unexpectedly. But because the car suddenly picked up speed.

He pressed her hand under his arm and turned, but carefully, so that by sheer inertia they ended up in the lobby of 418. The same force carried them past the dumbstruck porter, who, as it turned out, had last been naïve on a cadet's bunk at the Frunze artillery school, where he could dream of just such beauties, so that now he could really believe his eyes that she was with Kolian.

They ran down the hall, and Mary knew unmistakably that a men's washroom was coming up. Insofar as all the residences were absolutely identical, the only difference being the names of the cities where they were built.

She had ended up on her own in one like that, without either her friends or any equipment. Because before this they had arranged for themselves a very comfortable gig at a restaurant in Yalta and on her very first appearance one of the visitors there fancied her more, it turned out, than did Liokha. She didn't know at the time that Banzai had also suddenly acquired a new Amati, no mere Tama, but the real thing this time.... Who can convey the feelings of a girl who sits alone in an unfamiliar residence listening to the approaching steps of a man whom she cannot even imagine, because it was he who had given her a really good looking-over on her first appearance at the microphone, when she couldn't even have imagined how this might turn out for her.

"So you live here?" She flashed a smile.

"I do. At Makukha's."

"Who is this Makukha of yours?" She sparkled.

Whereupon Mykola became tongue-tied, because once again he began turning into Kolian. He realized that he had never known what that Makukha had ever been called at all. So firmly had the nickname stuck to the man.

"Well, Makukha, well, he's a friend. Well, he's a stoker. The kind that I don't just live at his place, but I can trust him with my stash, too!" Kolian exhaled as exhaustively on the subject of Makukha as it was possible to exhale.

They went up to the second floor, the privileged one, and to keep her from peering into corners Kolian wouldn't stop. "If you don't have a friend like Makukha, then it's as good as lost. Then you have to switch to cologne."

"Cologne" resounded like a distant childhood dream. How long had it been since she had stopped using it and instead used perfumes, deodorants, aromatic powders, creams, and even scented eye makeup?

They dashed into the room, and both of them gushed with happy laughter at the same time. For now, Kolian felt it too, what mattered was not whether they were in some dorm or not, but the fact that they had got away from the limousine, and for good, it seemed.

He seated her in an armchair. As if he had known when he had pinched it two days earlier from the lounge. And, while she looked around the walls, where Samantha Foxes and Schwarzeneggers were shown in innumerable poses, he quickly leaned behind the cupboard, pushed aside the old shoes, and out of his left cheap leather boot (his only memento of the army!) he hastily plucked, as if from the ancient past, a litre Cinzano bottle with a twist-off cap in which all kinds of other drinks had been splashing around for fifteen years now.

"O-oh," she exclaimed on seeing the familiar label, because Kolian hadn't opened the bottle yet.

"O-oh," she exclaimed once he opened it. But this time the "oh" had the opposite meaning, inasmuch as the emanation from the gullet of the bottle hit her with everything at once: Manka the goat, Grandad Panko, and especially the collective-farm brigade-leader Stop-Stiopa, that is, moonshine.

These particular aromas were all the more particular for having within them a barely perceptible admixture of kerosene and dung – the moonshine had probably been distilled on a paraffin stove in a barn or shed. They hit her so hard that she almost became Motria again, and that was why she went up to the window to take a cautious look. But in fact to make sure that a gulp of fresh air would knock her barefoot childhood out of her head.

That didn't happen. On the other side of the street she saw: the Merce and the Volvo approaching each other.

"There's an hour before they shake down 418. Up to the

fourth floor," she reflected gloomily and reached decisively for her glass.

But her barefoot childhood wafted out of her just the way it had wafted in: this was the first sign that the danger was now only too real. Who could have guessed that the Volvo and the Merce could ever drive towards each other on the same street? And in some desolate neighbourhood to boot.

She felt helpless once more in a residence as unfamiliar as this one, when you're waiting for unfamiliar footsteps and gradually turning from Marichka (a stage name) into Maryna.

While Kolian, who didn't know very much about foreign cars and couldn't have told a Peugeot from a Renault, not to mention a Porsche, reacted completely differently to the "Cinzano." Contributing to this was not so much the fact that he had already been dipping into the stash in the right boot that morning as the rather marvellous changes that were happening to him beside the wonderwoman – he went from chills to sweating and back. And for that reason, to deal somehow with his own microclimate, he settled down with relief to the familiar warmth provided by the bottle whose name was belied by its contents.

"This Makukha, will he be here soon?" she asked with anxious hope, although Kolian had his own interpretation of her perturbed state. And was so overcome with joy that he almost jumped out of Kolian into a Mykola Petrovych.

"No! He won't be coming at all! He's in the hospital now," the fellow almost lied.

Mary had a wonderful ear by now for when a man was lying. This science had started with the Banzai band. Which back then, in her village, had ripped her off for all the songs she had from her grandmother and started playing its own mangled electronic versions of them. She had gone out of her mind when she heard at the club how powerful was her voice, a voice that remained childlike even with primitive amplification. So much so that she hadn't even noticed such an untruth, so fatal, and the first of her short life.

Meanwhile Mykola cut up a snack. With the home-made knife that his friend Rosenkrantz had ground for him as a keepsake before a long trip. Not that they had ever been great friends, only Mykola had never called Rosenkrantz Rosenpotz. His talented turner buddy had found a diesel valve somewhere and had tempered, hammered, smoothed, and polished it for a long time, until he had made a knife that was worthy of Mykola. Later, inasmuch as he never did anything halfway, he had even finished it off on a diamond disk.

Mykola praised that wonder – an end of sausage – and so that the darkness around its perimeter woudn't be visible, he cut it into little cubes, delighting once again in the perfectly sharp blade. And he put the sausage out on the table along with some delicacies: a tin of cod liver.

Having marvelled at the fact that the knife had cut the metal of the tin without even getting dulled at the point, he glanced at the still life and was stupefied by this beauty. Behind which sat an even greater one, who was bashfully touching her fingers to the "facets of knowledge," as cut glass was called in the residence. Here it dawned on him that they had already had one drink and it was only for the second one that he had thought of adding something to eat, and that there was still enough booze for many more drinks, and he praised his army boots, especially the left one. As well as the right one, from which he and the stoker Makukha had taken out the stash in the morning, while the left one he had guessed he should forget. Because, thank God, because Makukha had fallen in his hellishly hot boiler room anyway, because his safety valves hadn't worked. While Kolian, having scared off the assembly-shop girls on the sixth floor, had decided that his condition wasn't worthy of them after all. And so had crawled out into the street. And had been right!

She was observing him trustingly so as not to look out the window, where the mirrored foreign cars had concealed themselves. Whereas the mirroring was domestic. How Mary had pleaded with the Merce not to do it! Because something so cheap doesn't go with a car like that, but he was of a different mind: once he had had the glass mirrored, he could desire her fully only there, amusing himself with the knowledge that the street around him was incapable of seeing through to the inside, where he was taking his pleasure. She wasn't prepared to get used to this diversion, and this turned him on even more.

"You'd do better to emigrate!" she almost blurted out one of those times.

Whether you looked out the window here or not, you still wouldn't be able to look in there, behind the mirrors, to see what he was thinking about just then.

That wasn't the same thing at all as this sweet, trusting boy, all fired up by the happiness across from him. And with everything he had written all over him.

She made a mental note to ask him later whether by any chance he had relatives in Sulymivka.

Anyone who drinks knows their limit perfectly well. And wants to feel that limit even more fully, on a grander scale. But here the opposite was happening: the girl was drinking because for some reason she couldn't start feeling drunk, while he kept getting drunk and then coming back. When they kissed, it all rushed to his head with such a punch that the port from two days before almost came back too. But what was the port? He almost forgot about everything, even the shameful poverty of this closet to which he was embarrassed to bring even an assembly-shop girl. Even if she lived in one just like it.

He pressed his lips to hers once again and fell through – so other-worldly did Mary's lips turn out to be. All the Samantha Foxes, why even the Sabrinas on the walls ended up feeling naked when she undressed. He wasn't even capable of seeing that at that moment she was really very far away.

Because when a Volvo and a Merce suddenly meet on a street onto which not even every Volga is willing to turn, then there's an excellent chance of ending up here in a Trabant....

He tore off his clothes in a hurry, but in too much of a hurry, and Samantha Fox nearly turned into Samantha Smith. Because when Mary suddenly came to be so close beside him and he had to keep touching her to prove to himself that she was not a figment of a military cadet's imagination, but someone warm and resilient, the likes of whom even the most beautiful clothing on Earth could not even come half way to adorning, just one of these shoulders, say, not to mention the knee, and as for the back, well, it was better not even to look at it, because you'd never see another one like it, even in fantasies borrowed from videos, while here you could at least breathe in and breathe out and lean in with your eye, and then open it once more and see what was shining forth from within with a truth that was axiomatic. Such prooflessness exceeded all ideals, even those on covers. It was firmer than an ethereal fantasy, more rounded than a vision, especially on the second floor of residence 418.

Mykola manifested a state of closeness that was even closer than was called for in these cases. Intellectual men have this feeling more frequently, but they know from books that over-arousal sometimes spawns the opposite state and are therefore just as fearful of it as is the turner, who when he was still very young, instead of reading such books, gave up the best part of his youth to the ranks of the army, where he forgot even what he had learned in the trade school, and not just Maupassant, whom he had never read. Because even if he had wanted to, he could not have given over the best time of his short life to the acquisition of either real or bookish sexual experience, given that it was wasted on everything that is so abundant in our highrise neighbourhood reality – because this is other-worldliness, a real reflection of some genuinely valuable way of being.

Mykola darkened inside. Regret and offense at his own self finally exceeded his state of alcoholic and bodily drunkenness. When he felt her, he felt coming towards him everything that had determined the sum total of her transformations from Motryna into Mary. This was so much that it turned out he wasn't ready for it. Even to the extent of feigning an absence of desire. For a moment, it is true, he had the happy impression that from all this he had unexpectedly fallen through the mattress, that was when the vermouth from the day before flew out of him in an instant through the pores of his skin; and deprived of this last point of resistance (the drinking from this day wasn't ready to fly out yet) he found himself again on the mattress, naked and disgraced.

He couldn't stay in such a pseudoerotic state because he didn't know how. It was too late to pretend he was drunk. And time kept dragging on and on. Its end was nowhere in sight.

Once again Sabrina and Samantha proudly stuck their busts out at them. He was shrinking into himself, because he didn't have a one-way-mirrored Merce for times like this, where even in the middle of the Khreshchatyk he could have got his revenge with some heating-system installer, even a thoroughly ugly one, savouring the impunity of the rendezvous. Why, in the present situation even a transparent Zapor, a cheap domestic Zaporozhets, would have been helpful, but he didn't even have that.

However, time wasn't passing from this, but dragging on. He couldn't even help himself along. Things only got worse and worse. As for retreating, beyond Makukha's apartment – there was nowhere to go. He didn't have time to pretend he was crazy, because he jumped up from the bed once and for all, grabbed the knife, and hacked off his disgrace along with his shame.

She raised her eyes in amazement, opened them wide and saw right in front of them a red rose that was moving as it grew. As it bloomed, radiated, and squirted red.

The second stupid thing Kolian did was to squeeze what he had cut off as hard as he could, because he couldn't feel anything in it, and run out into the hall. Where, finally, he was overcome by a raging attack of pain. His entire being cried out.

Louder than any Korg could have done; and Makukha the stoker shuddered in his impenetrable sleep in the boiler room.

The neighbourhood fell silent.

...while he walked down the hall, lighting his way with his own self, squirting over the walls as he went, lifting it up high, step by step, that way, to the washroom, from which there wouldn't be any way out either forward or back, because that was where he did his third stupid thing:

he threw it in the toilet and flushed. And there, exhausted, he fell.

Only then did all the termites of residence 418 swarm out of their alveoli. Everything they saw in the washroom amazed them even there.

All the more so when a girl jostled her way in there, even though this wasn't a women's washroom, from behind their backs, stark naked. Why, if a girl like that were dressed, all of them there would have forgotten about Kolian, so unresidential was her exterior. And this unexpected appearance of hers made all of them realize how profound was the tragedy that had befallen the fellow. Especially when she walked out of there forever. Everyone was struck speechless by it, because they didn't know what to do in a situation like that.

Until the shouting brought the portress running, because it was part of her job to deal with any shouting, wherever it was coming from, even the men's washroom. For a long time she couldn't jostle her way through the throng of residents, none of whom at that moment had any desire to live.

She made her way through just as Mykola finished bleeding. She was going to cry out an F-sharp. But instead of shouting she only managed to open her mouth wide. Then she remembered how it's done and thought of taking a breath first.

"M-u-u-urd-e-er!"

Had she really seen a murder victim there, that isn't how she would have cried out. Yet lying here was someone worse than murdered. That was why it came out even louder than a Yamaha for her.

The neighbourhood believed it.

The stoker twitched once more in his boiler room.

For a moment the Merce and the Volvo became transparent. Then, without turning on their lights, they drove away from each other and disappeared on different sides of the lane.

It was the thumping of the shock brigade that brought her back from thought, especially the authoritative commands of the chief, a Ukrainian woman with the Armenian surname Bohdasarova. So that Mary dared to peer through the windowpane. And saw there not just none of the ill-boding foreign makes, but not even a lousy Zhiguli. This made such an impression on her that she became drunk again, and not from what she had just drunk, but from the freedom that had come her way for the first time in three years. With a stagger she found her clothes. Still staggering, she opened the door and barely missed bumping into Mykola, who was just being carried down the hall. At first she was amazed at how he had aged, but then she figured out that this had to be Grandad Panko, the village goatherd. The stretcher was quickly moving him away, but she managed to get one more look at her aging fellow villager between the attendants' shoulders.

And even though she was wearing a dress, every man in the hall understood that he would have done exactly what Mykola had done to himself. This thought poked every one of them in the back, and they rushed as one to carry out the shock brigade leader's order:

they unbolted the toilet. But they didn't find anything significant there.

Then the best men among them attacked the cast-iron pipes of the washbasins. But it was no use there either. They took apart all the stands right down to the boiler room, but there was nothing there except for the drunk Makukha, whom even news like this couldn't wake up.

Then two of them, Afghanistan vets, grabbed a flashlight from the boiler room, tore off the sewage cover, and rushed to get there in time. Without gas masks they managed to reach the spot where residence 418 poured in with the others. The flashlight barely broke through the gloom of the vapours, and there they saw:

a swarm of rats that had frozen for a moment by the drain. And then let out a squeal and disappeared into the mire, leaving nothing behind.

"I hate rats," the bigger man of the two muttered between his teeth.

Motryna breathed fresh air for the first time and thought that now she'd be able to buy back her grandmother's house from the brigade leader for a song. Because she recalled how much it cost now and was struck by the paltry sum. And she laughed, not quite soberly; everything that her grandmother had earned and spent fit into a rather meagre figure, the likes of which Motryna hadn't been used to for a long time now.

This was so cheering to her that even that first fateful glass of "Cinzano" came back into her head.

Then she laughed drunkenly once again, but differently:

to go back, back to her barefoot childhood, barefoot because there were times when there was nothing to put on your feet besides rubber boots. Except for Grandmother's galoshes.

Physically she felt the morning chill of her grandmother's galoshes, when she would have to get up and let Manka out and not lose the galoshes, if Grandad Panko drove the herd past their gate.

There, among people who always smelled of kerosene? To that house, so defenceless even against mice?

She could buy it back or not. That's what freedom was. She let out a laugh at the thought.

Her next thought was absolutely sober: both the Merce and the Volvo would be in a hurry to claim credit for the atrocity in residence 418. In order thereby to consolidate their positions among other positions. And an opportunity like that was much more important to them than some actual Maryna or Motryna.

Mykola almost came to in the ambulance, because they were no longer applying hydrogen peroxide, but a pad with iodine. The paramedics, who were stunned by him, were talking about "malicious injury to members" in the strict sense of the word. The ambulance swerved on a turn, and the hope crossed Mykola's mind: they do kidnap children for kidneys, they do, it would appear, transplant organs illegally, so can it really be difficult to do this legally?

"But there's no legislation for organ transplants, either legal or illegal!" Bohdasarova raged as she pressed an oxygen mask to the patient's face.

Whereupon everyone all around piped up about the university student who was kidnapped, then had the lens stolen out of his eye and was let go; about the little boy from Obolon who was kidnapped and then thrown out, but with one of his kidneys missing, only he accidentally revived; about the "Kremlin drops," mixed up out of everything they have on hand in the medicine chest, that they give to old people so they won't call the doctors too often; about the Ku Klux Klan that comes to people in comas and turns off the power, because someone absolutely must have an organ for a transplant; about the enormous quantity of donated blood that is used to transfuse drug addicts so that they can start a new life, able then to decrease their dosage significantly; about the orphanages outside Moscow to which they bring kidnapped children from all over the Soviet Union for spinal taps and from which there is no return; that all the children's clinics are now handing charts over to parents, to make it impossible for thieves to select the kids they wanted on the basis of their analyses, and that now that they've thought about it, all adults are getting their own charts, too.

"And here in this nightmare you can find idiots who cut off everything they've got left!" Bohdasarova was furious at Mykola, who decided not to pretend that he was alive.

Finally the police came to 418. Finally the neighbourhood got to feel real horror, for the police began to set a dog on the bloody trail and found the empty room with just the frightening knife lying in the middle, and no one else there. All the residents pushed stools up against their doors. And one deputy who was still living there lost no time arriving at the conclusion that a new stage had begun, new prospects: they'd be catching people and cutting them off. That the mafia, which was as rotten as the whole system, was now capable of the same thing as he was.

"What was the victim's name?" The lieutenant was aghast at the puddle in the washroom. Even he hadn't known that so much could drain out of a human being.

"Kolian," a welder recalled with an effort.

"And his last name?" The lieutenant took out a notebook.

But this the welder couldn't manage. Because no one could remember even Makukha's real name. At whose place that Kolian had been living temporarily. Everyone could still see before their eyes the naked Sabrina who had come to life in order to look at the tragedy and disappear onto a poster. The thread led to the boiler room, however, because the portress remembered that Makukha had had a drink a few times with Kolian to celebrate the new valves that the latter had taken from the factory and through which hot water was now going into all the washbasins, which hadn't been the case for about three years, and now thank God.

The stoker, for his part, couldn't remember anything, inasmuch as his reality turned out to be more impenetrable than his dreams and even police identification couldn't prove to him that they were real, and that was why the police hopped in their car and hurried off as fast as they could to catch up with the shock brigade on the highway in order to learn from them at least some part of the truth.

Cold Medicine

Svitlana Kasianova

It was their third day now in the city, and they had a month to go. There was no way around it. Work experience had to be exchanged, and in keeping with tradition the shop had sent the youngest workers.

Here they were, walking down the street. Only one of the three girls was thinking about half-finished parts, seams, or darts. Although what kind of darts were there on jerseys? But they were going to a shop where work clothes were made, and someone had to be thinking about them. Iryna was annoyed with her own thoughts, especially the fact that she felt lonely. Nelia was flexing her buttocks for passers-by. Iryna could see that men were comparing the girls, but no, she'd never wiggle like Nelia. Iryna glanced at Olia. How good it felt to be walking next to a person composed exclusively of horizontal and vertical lines, without any curves at all. Iryna wondered what Nelia was thinking, but sensed that Nelia wouldn't even let her ask. She had to adapt somehow. Iryna understood her own clumsiness and sensed her alienness.

People who spend their whole life on wheels probably act naturally in a new place. She felt like gazing dreamily through the glass of the trolleybus, but caught herself at it and went back to watching intently for the street names. Damn this city! She wanted peace, she wanted a metronomic life. When would she finally be able not to think about anything?

The workshop had the familiar smell of dust and something else, something Iryna couldn't put her finger on. Milia Yosypovych, the one-legged foreman with the bookkeeper's cuffs, was showing them around the shop. The crackle and hum of machines, the grease-stained patterns: it was all just like home, and Iryna's tension fell away. Then the foreman limped over to his desk, sized them all up from head to toe, said that the next day's work would be more hands-on, and let them go eat.

The girls walked out into the street. Olia set off to look for a hairdresser. Nelia went to call home. "Home, that means Kyiv," Iryna realized only once she was in the store. She went out, caught a breath of air, and felt as if she'd been living in the city for a very long time. But that was only for a moment. The city was still the same. Iryna went back to the residence. At least it was some kind of shelter. Of course the one at the teachers' college was better than the trade school's with its swearing and wild screams. (They had been told about it at the shop.)

Still, the room felt unlived-in. There was something transient about the walls and the cold radiators. If only someone would come visit them. Iryna put on the kettle for tea and wiped off her shoes.

"Irka, you'll die when you see the café I found!" Nelia flew in like a gust of wind. "We're going out for coffee tonight. And then...." She twirled a piece of blue paper.

"What's that?"

"I met some pilots, and they asked me to buy some beer. They're staying downtown, at the Ukraina hotel. We're going to see them. Unless you don't want to? I said I'd bring a friend. There are four of them."

There wasn't any bottled beer in the city, and the girls bought a three-litre keg at the Yantar beer bar.

"What a naïve bunch," Nelia said when they emerged from the suffocating cellar. "They've been transferred back from the Czech Republic, and they have a craving for normal beer. Why, this is swill."

Iryna sensed that Nelia felt superior. Olia declined to go with them, but that was no surprise.

THE CAFÉ WAS DOWNTOWN, near the department store. It was an ordinary summer café, but it was understood that it was only for regulars. Nelia was chatting with the bartender and passing her lighter on to other tables. Iryna couldn't keep up with what was happening. Some guys asked for matches, and Nelia went over to the bartender. Iryna sat tired at her table. She sensed that the men were noticing her, but she didn't want anything just then. She felt just as strange when they were in the hotel room, and she couldn't figure out the rules for blackjack right until the end. There were moments when she regretted she was spending her time off that way, and that was when she envied Nelia. She felt better once she was out in the fresh air. The pilots had hinted a few times that it would be nice if they stayed, but Iryna went along with Nelia, and their coffee, combined with the beer, made them long for rest.

In the trolleybus Iryna realized that she'd never be able to control men. She needed too much time. Nelia, on the other hand, had such a naturally made-up blush and such a smile. Even now Iryna could well have stayed with the pilots, but what for?

The trolleybus was lurching at a stoplight.

"Well, now let them try living in their chicken coop," Nelia said. "Something got to them when they were with the Czechs."

Iryna nodded, because she didn't know what to say. A powerlessness of some sort was coming over her, or maybe it was just coming back.

THE RESIDENCE WAS BETTER THAN THE HOTEL. You could wash your hands and fall on your bed.

"Let's have some tea!" Nelia couldn't sit still. She rushed around the room and turned on the kettle.

"Two creeps have already been here, but I didn't open the door for them." Olia was sitting on her bed, wrapped up in a blanket.

The girls giggled.

"How do you know they were creeps?" Nelia couldn't settle down.

Somebody knocked on the door.

"I've gone to sleep." Olia dove under her blanket.

"We've gone to sleep." Iryna dashed towards the switch, feeling the strength to act within her.

"But they heard us laughing," Nelia whispered.

"Here, put this on over yourself and tell them we've gone to sleep." Iryna felt around for her nightgown and threw it to Nelia.

Nelia opened the door a crack to push a few words through, but somebody held the door open. Iryna couldn't make anything out. The light from the hall shone on Nelia's back, no, lower. She shut the door and turned on the light.

"There. We've all been invited to come over."

"I haven't the slightest desire to go." Iryna sat down lazily on her bed.

"No, look," Nelia said in Russian, sitting down at the table and slurping from her cup. "I won't go alone. Then again…we don't have to go."

Iryna understood Nelia's intonation and realized that

she could either go or not go.

Nelia combed her hair out the way she did every night and sat down in the long nightgown to finish her tea.

"You two won't get anywhere with your fancy men," Olia said half in jest as she got out of bed.

Nelia stopped her with a theatrical gesture. "That's uncalled-for. We weren't even here, you see, but things were already happening."

"Right, right. Let's draw up minutes," Iryna said, banging her spoon. "So, resolved: either all three of us go, or no one goes."

Olia peered out into the hall.

"No, no. I'll be there in a minute."

The girls burst into laughter.

The beer in Iryna's stomach kept settling down and then acting up again. She lay back on her pillow. Her head was humming. She wanted to get out of the city and go to a place where there were blazing fires, delicate smells, and tall people who sang instead of speaking. She smiled and shut her eyes.

"What's with you?"

"Nothing." Iryna glanced at Nelia's hands, remembered that she had some polish somewhere, and sat up to paint her nails.

"It's so cold," Olia bristled, "and you're thinking of going out somewhere." She crawled back under her blanket.

"No! No! Get up."

"I'm not going anywhere." Olia pulled the blanket up to her chin. "I haven't been able to get warm all day. I wasn't invited."

"What do you mean, you weren't invited? Everybody was invited!" Iryna screwed the cap back on her nail polish.

"Yeah." Nelia was putting on make-up in the middle of the room, right under the light-bulb.

Iryna could feel how stupid the situation was. It crossed her mind that back at the hotel no one had made any arrangements for another date or had asked for phone numbers. They had simply had a chat about nothing in particular. They hadn't even asked who was married. Iryna smiled. "Strange."

"Come on. What are you going to sit in the room by yourself for?"

"No-o!" Nelia laughed. "Olia has a reason for wanting to stay...."

"A-ah...." Iryna played along conspiratorially.

"What a couple of pests." Olia got out from under the blanket and pulled on her jeans and black sweater. "I'm coming!"

The girls guffawed.

"I know, I know," Olia said in mock indignation. "I'll have you know that Uzbeks aren't my type."

YURA AND RAF CAME TO GET THEM. Iryna had a look at their long-unwashed track suits as they went up the stairs to the top floor and wanted to go back.

The music in Yura's room was playing so loudly that you couldn't even say or hear anything. The guys were speaking Uzbek amongst themselves. Iryna once again felt like leaving. She just couldn't understand how Nelia had managed to get into the conversation even here. As it turned out, this was pilaf day. There was no vodka on the table, but when Marat, with a huge ring on the middle finger of his right hand, sat beside her, Iryna caught a whiff of alcohol. But Nelia was laughing and coaxing the guys to have some pilaf. They responded with strained smiles. Iryna felt strange among these short, swarthy guys with their narrow, wide-set eyes. They glanced out from under their dark brows and occasionally exchanged a few throaty words. Iryna couldn't imagine any one of them being a Russian teacher.

The music was so loud that Iryna couldn't hear what the guy next to her was saying. She nodded and looked around at the walls. People were going in and out of the room and passing cassettes and books across the table. Iryna wanted to leave, but had forgotten her neighbour's name.

They pushed the table out of the way and started dancing. Iryna went up to Nelia and yelled in her ear, "I've had enough!"

Nelia nodded.

Iryna looked around at the already unfamiliar faces and started making her way through the swaying crowd, with its smells of cologne, alcohol, and cigarettes.

The beer inside her revolted.

Iryna went out into the deserted hall. The guy who had been sitting next to her at the table caught up with her by the stairs.

"Leaving already?" he asked in Russian.

"Yeah, I'm tired." Iryna waved her hand goodbye.

"It wasn't supposed to turn out like this." He was shorter than Iryna and probably younger, too. "Those other guys came. We just wanted to sit and talk, but they wanted to disco." He seemed rueful, but Iryna wasn't paying attention any more. "Come on, I'll show you something." He pulled her along the hall insistently, although not forcefully.

"I don't want to." Iryna was feebly trying to shake her hand out of his square palm.

He pushed open a door into a dark room. A muffled thumping of music was coming through the wall to the left.

"There's no light here. Have a seat! There was a candle somewhere." He started rummaging through the nighttable and then looked behind the blind. "Oh, there's a lamp shining right in the window here." He pushed the blind away. A street lamp peered into the window. "Tired?"

Iryna nodded.

"You can lie down."

"No!"

They sat in silence.

Iryna stood up. "I'll be going."

"Where are you rushing to?" He came up to her, put his arms around her, and pushed her down on the bed.

Iryna hadn't been expecting this. A feeling of disgust and filth rose up inside her. She pressed her elbows against his chest. "Take your hands off me!"

"Or else what?" He nipped her neck with his mouth. "What are you afraid of?" He bent one of Iryna's arms behind her back, but couldn't get hold of the other one.

"Let go! You're hurting me!"

"Okay, then. Let's not argue. Okay?"

"Okay."

This was too much! She pushed his chest in indignation, jumped up from the bed, and rushed for the door. In the half-light she noticed an empty bottle on the table and clutched it in her hand.

"Open the door!" she shot out in a low voice that wasn't her own.

"Fool!" He got up and stuffed his shirt into his pants. "Open it yourself."

Iryna couldn't find the lock. A switch made a dark spot on the wall. She pressed it, and the light went on.

"There's no light?" she asked caustically.

The guy collapsed onto a chair. "I think we'll meet again."

Iryna opened the door, her hand trembling, and threw the bottle on the bed. "I doubt it."

She slammed the door and walked heavily down the hall. She went down to her own floor. A feeling of outrage was thrashing about in her chest. Iryna swallowed her tears and walked along the dimly lit hall to the washroom. She washed and then, leaning her hands on the sink, listened to the drops rolling down her face. Her stomach turned, and she closed her eyes and threw up, first the pilaf and then the beer. A good thing it was dark. She stood there a long time, pressing her cold, wet hands to her cheeks and rinsing her mouth.

HER LEGS WERE GIVING WAY under her as she walked into her room.

"Where were you?" Nelia was getting ready for bed.

"Washing." Iryna felt feverish.

The girls said nothing.

Iryna pulled back her covers and turned out the light. She breathed in noisily. She tried to calm herself, but her head was roaring and her heart was pounding. When she pressed a cool hand to her chest, tears rose up in her eyes. She could hear Nelia wheezing in her sleep and Olia snoring. She tossed in her bed but couldn't get warm. "I should have stayed. He would have warmed me up," she tormented herself. Her stomach ached, and snatches of noisy music were getting mixed up in her mind with the clatter of sewing machines. How cold she was, God, how cold!

"Children. Today we are going to learn Nekrasov's poem 'Tom Thumb.' All together now: 'Once upon a cold winter day...' Brr, it's cold. All together now: Brr, it's cold. No, children. 'Once upon a cold winter day...'"

A grey dawn was breaking.

Nelia was sitting on the edge of the bed. "Ira, do you feel sick?"

Iryna opened her eyes. "I'm cold." She knitted her brows, trying to figure out her nightmare.

Nelia felt her forehead. "You've probably got a fever. Put my sweater on, and I'll go ask where we can find a doctor." Nelia threw Iryna her sweater and started to get ready.

Olia turned on the small kettle.

"That's all I needed, to get sick." Iryna felt feverish. She pulled the sweater over her nightgown. Olia covered her with her own blanket. Iryna was dozing. She could feel the perfume from Nelia's sweater infiltrating her. Nelia was dressing, trying not to make any noise.

"Does anything hurt?"

"No. I feel feverish."

Nelia went out quietly.

Iryna heard voices in the hall, Nelia's usual laughter. She bristled and was overcome by fever. In a frenzy she threw back the blanket and tore off the sweater. "I'm even colder with it." She covered herself with the cool blanket.

She spread herself flat on the bed, smiled, swallowed her thick saliva, and closed her eyes.

"And now, to sleep. To sleep."

The Day of the Angel

YURII VYNNYCHUK

"Here's your coffee, Mr. Hrushkevych!"

The secretary's thin voice startled him. For several minutes now Mr. Hrushkevych had been watching from his office window a small dark figure running over the wet autumn roofs, jumping up comically and waving its arms. The rain had stopped and the sun had burst out from behind the clouds, and that was when he had turned his head to the window and noticed the extraordinary being. Maybe it was a person, although it was doubtful whether a person could skip over the roofs so easily. Mr. Hrushkevych's company was on the fifteenth floor, and you could see a wide panorama of the city from the window. He had never seen anything like it. Although there had been other bizarre sights. They had started not that long ago, when he had been hurrying to a very important meeting and his car had skidded on a turn and thrown him into a ditch. Mr. Hrushkevych came out of the accident safe and sound, suffering only a serious concussion. But afterwards he felt an astonishing change in himself. Out of nowhere he developed the gift of foresight.

His infallible guessing of the next day's weather was a trifle that is not even worth mentioning. Mr. Hrushkevych could now foresee much more complicated things, like the calamity that was to befall his neighbour or the illness that would strike down a company employee. And sometimes the image of someone's death would run through him like an electrical charge. "This person is going to die tomorrow!" would suddenly flare up in his mind, and he would barely be able to restrain himself from rushing to the doomed person to warn them of the calamity.

Hrushkevych's gift of foresight soon had a great effect on his company's fortunes, for he managed to cut a few deals so successfully that the company increased its capital by a factor of ten.

It wouldn't have been so annoying if his new state of consciousness had been limited to predictions. He would have gazed into the future randomly, without the slightest interest in one person or another. But other astonishing images would appear that he did not know how to interpret at all. Sometimes he would suddenly see in a person's face some sort of duplicate features, as if one face were showing through the other, but the second one was monstrous and repugnant and grimaced at Hrushkevych, too, or stuck out its tongue. Sometimes it wasn't even a face, but the muzzle of an animal. Inside his interlocutor he would see a whole clump of snakes darting about nervously and swaying their heads.

A few days earlier he had ventured to tell a psychiatrist he knew all about it.

"If I didn't know you, I'd think this was an ordinary psychiatric disorder and everything you're telling me was raving," Dr. Kovalyk had said. "Some people fill their heads with such far-fetched things that it makes you want to laugh. But still, there's nothing I can say to console you. You've become a kind of psychic, and all this is a gift from dark and evil forces. At first they endow a person with miraculous powers and give them the power of foresight, but not without a price. In time he will start meddling in your life and force you to submit to his will."

"Who are you talking about?" an astonished Hrushkevych had asked. "Who is this 'he'?"

"The one who has endowed you with extraordinary abilities. For the time being he seems to you to be just an innocent projection of your consciousness, but soon he will take on a real form and show himself to you somehow."

"What should I do?"

"Don't submit to him. Don't reveal your powers to anyone, don't make any use of them, for yourself or anyone else. There are people who can't pull themselves together and go into a frenzy and throw themselves into curing people of hundreds of illnesses. They don't understand that they are serving Satan. It is Satan who blesses this whole flock of pseudo-healers, so that they can win over as many innocent souls for him as possible."

At first Hrushkevych hadn't believed his ears. What Satan? What did Satan have to do with it? But Dr. Kovalyk clearly hadn't been joking. His voice had been trembling with emotion, and he had lowered it, as if afraid that someone was eavesdropping.

"How am I supposed to live with this?"

"Just keep on living. Maybe he'll see that he has no power over you and will leave you alone. The main thing is not to give in to temptation."

"But I already have. I used my gift in the interests of my company. And that brought significant profits."

"Don't do that anymore. Try to let your mind wander and don't concentrate when you're making a decision."

"One time I hypnotized an executive from another company, and he signed some papers for us that he would never have signed in a normal state."

"You see, you're already in his clutches. You have to understand that your life is in danger. It isn't too late yet to wrest yourself from his grip."

"It isn't? But how am I supposed to learn not to see what I see?"

"Think about something else. You're due for a rest anyway. You didn't go anywhere this summer, did you?"

"No. Once I took this position, I just couldn't get away."

"Find a way," the doctor had insisted. "I can also recommend sex. You know, that's the best cure for stress, depression, fatigue, and so on. Sex is a release. Your nerves settle down, and stupid ideas blow away. Do you have a mistress?"

"M-m, not at the moment." Hrushkevych had blushed. "Ever since I became chief executive of the company, there doesn't seem to have been time. And then there was that accident...."

"But do you feel up to it?" the doctor had asked with a slap on Hrushkevych's back and a loud chuckle.

Hrushkevych had answered with a laugh and thought to himself that the doctor really was right. A mistress would rescue him from this stupid situation.

Hrushkevych took a sip of his coffee and thought it tasted strange. It was salty and viscous. Like blood. When this comparison came to mind he cast a horrified glance into his cup. But his coffee wasn't red. It was its usual dark colour.

He was overtired. It would be worth getting away somewhere to have a rest. Autumn wasn't the best time for it, but things couldn't go on like this anymore.

His gaze slid back over the dark wet roofs. The strange figure was sitting on a chimney now, swinging its legs. Or maybe it was a chimney-sweep. Thin wisps of smoke wrapped around it and seemed to stretch it and lengthen it and transform it into something menacingly gigantic.

Hrushkevych remembered that a few days before he had already seen something similar, but then it had been over on that factory smokestack, too far for him to distinguish what it was. At the time he had thought it was a bird, but some bizarre kind of bird: it had flapped its overly long wings as if it were trying to take off, but it hadn't taken off, as if some force had fastened it to the smokestack and wouldn't let it go.

The chimney-sweep finally jumped down from the smokestack and, stretching out his arms awkwardly to keep his balance, set out along the peak of the roof. By this time the figure could be discerned as a human being. It was just that its arms were disproportionately long, or maybe it dressed in some rag with long sleeves like that. Its clothing was black, and it looked like a raven.

An incomprehensible sense of alarm came over Hrushkevych as he watched the man coming towards him.

When he got to the edge of the roof, the chimney-sweep shifted from one foot to the other hesitantly and then suddenly flapped his arms, jumped up, and landed in an instant on the next roof.

Hrushkevych stiffened and felt his diaphragm seize up convulsively. He drained his coffee nervously and decided not to look out the window anymore. To hell with that numskull!

His secretary's high-pitched giggling reached him from the reception area. Dumb cow. He had no feelings for her. He had inherited her from his predecessor, who liked jelly doughnuts. Nobody knew whether he had had anything going with her. Probably not, because the old fart could hardly have been capable of exploits like that. The only liberty he had permitted himself was to paw Virunka where she was softest. And she had to be really soft there, because she bulged so deliciously in all directions, but especially backward, that your hands would head for this treasure on their own. How was it that he had never made a pass at her? In the six months that he had been chief executive, this was the first time the thought had crossed his mind. He had never paid his secretary any special attention.

Why was her luscious little bum coming to mind now? Probably because nothing else about her was of any interest. Except maybe her breasts. Because Virunka's pink little piglet's face with its tiny smeary eyes attested only to the fact that in the not too distant future she would turn into a swollen lazy sow fit only for grunting sleepily beside her husband. If, indeed, anyone would take her.

Hrushkevych's wife had left him, and for a few years now he had been making do with rather dubious affairs, but had not yet found anything worthwhile. Now he recalled that his secretary had often teased him playfully, made eyes at him, pouted, and taken every opportunity to offer him her fantastic ass.

Something forced him to turn back to the window. Slowly and intently the chimney-sweep was crossing one roof after another, approaching unrelentingly and looming ever larger before his eyes. Why was he running over the roofs? It started raining again, and a grey quilt of mist settled on the city. But even this could not hold the stranger back. It seemed that even thunder and lightning couldn't have stopped him, nor gunshots. Nothing could stop him in his stubborn forging ahead, ahead to some marvellous and wild goal that could very well have consisted of a void, an abyss.

Hrushkevych thought to himself that if this oddball ended up slipping and fell head over heels from a roof, he would feel relieved. As it was he felt a vague influx of alarm that squeezed his heart and brought out a sweat on his brow. A premonition of some unpleasant event oppressed him and filled him with fear. But whom was he supposed to fear? This oddball of a chimney-sweep? Or his very own self?

Now the stranger was making some sort of signs at him, but because it was too far away for him to be able to understand anything, Hrushkevych felt only anger and irritation. What the devil did this madman want from him? Why was he jumping up, bending down, straightening up, and waving his wing-like arms? Now he was climbing onto a smokestack, sticking his head inside, and holding still, letting the thick smoke blacken his face. The smoke billowed even thicker than before, but it was some kind of very white smoke, like a morning mist. Strange figures appeared in the rising billows, stretching and spreading awkwardly in the grey boredom of the sky.

Hrushkevych pressed a buzzer, and Virunka floated into his office. Before she got to the door she had managed to turn on the friendly smile on her face, and now, all aglow and animated, she filled the office with an unbelievable *joie de vivre.*

"Happy name-day!" she chirped, placing a vase filled with flowers on a table in front of him.

Only then did he remember that it was the day of his angel. In the past his friends had reminded him of it, but now he no longer had anyone to remind him. Chief executives don't have friends.

Hrushkevych's gaze slid over her body, dove into its most secret depths, and brought to the surface something terrible. Virunka's days were numbered. A horrible incurable disease had lodged in her body and was consuming it with an omnivorous rapacity, and death was stepping up closer and closer. Why had he never seen this before? Why only now, when it was no longer possible to do anything about it? Virunka herself obviously didn't suspect a thing. She probably hadn't had any signs yet of the disorder in her body, but any day now the frightening moment would come when pain would wrack her body and burn up her youth, her health, and all her hopes.

"What's wrong?" she asked, seeing the worried look on his face.

What could he tell her? That he saw her imminent end? What ever for?

She came up and stopped beside him. This was still a

plump and tempting body with animal instincts and a yearning for love. She probably liked pain, slaps on her bum, bites, and savage growling in her ear.

Without a word he drew her closer, and Virunka not so much sat as dropped into his lap with all her lush weightiness. He put his left hand on her waist and pulled her towards him as he placed his right hand on her bosom. Virunka was so happy she half-closed her eyes and mumbled something inane and indistinct.

Hrushkevych was kissing her on the neck and running his tongue over her throat, and her rapture made her open her full lips the way a fish does when you throw it out onto the shore.

Bolder! Hrushkevych gave himself an order, and now his hand was fondling her rounded knees. Were these stockings or pantihose? His hand crept along her thighs. How big they were, how voluminous, powerful, and hot inside! Stockings they were. Now his fingers were touching her ultrasmooth skin, under which he deduced a thick layer of fat. They raced ahead, like bold guardsmen and, coming upon the silken barrier of her panties, they resolutely pulled them away, in order finally to get to the burning hot lips, gurgling with lust, into which he longed to plunge both hands, just as, when he had hunted crayfish as a boy, he had slipped his hands carefully into the dark caves of their dwellings and oh so quietly moved his fingers, feeling for the concealed prey.

Virunka was moaning and oozing juice. There was no way of holding off anymore, and Hrushkevych, bending her over with her breasts on the desk, tore off her dress, and entered the snow white softness, nearly burning himself on the irrepressible heat that radiated from her as from the crater of a volcano. Ejaculation could only have been seconds away when some demon made him turn his head to the window and his gaze fell upon the idiot who was walking over the roofs. He was standing on a chimney now, close enough that his face could be seen at last, unnaturally white and crumpled like paper. There was nothing to this face except laughter. Who was this idiot laughing at? At him? Could he actually see everything that was happening in the office? Now he was straightening out his exceedingly long arm and pointing his finger. At what?

Hrushkevych turned his head and tried to concentrate on the young woman. But her little white bum opened up before him a whole terrifying panorama of pathogenic processes that had just blossomed with particular vigour in her system. The act seemed to be stimulating and speeding everything up. A red cancer tumour that looked like a bright branching coral began to grow before Hrushkevych's stunned gaze. Its tentacles crept in all directions, taking over an increasingly larger territory and destroying absolutely everything in their path. Cells were bursting and popping like tin cans; vessels throbbed and, plugged up like water hoses from a sudden burst of pressure, broke away from their settled locations, and blood started splattering in all directions at a crazed speed, as if somebody had taken a powerful pump to it.

Virunka was oblivous to all this and was peacefully squealing with pleasure at every thrust, managing to sway the walnut desk onto which more than one generation of executives had channelled its sensual problems. A heavy marble paperweight slipped off the table with a thud. A marble inkwell like it, with a pen stand, flew off after it, shattering from the blow. Then papers and files fell off the desk; pencils rolled off, and the telephone crashed to the floor and, after letting out a pitiful squeak, fell silent. It seemed that not just the table, but the whole office was rocking, and with it the whole building with all of its offices, reception areas, rooms, stairs, elevators, and countless people who didn't suspect a thing.

He'd found a fulcrum and shaken the world apart.

Hrushkevych laughed as he pressed against Virunka with increasing force, until her good-natured squeals finally turned into a deep growl, as if she were saying goodbye to life under a heavy butcher's knife. The knife went into her smoothly and softly, pumping blood, air, and ardour.

"Caw! Caw!" a clamourous cawing of ravens suddenly hit the windowpane. Hrushkevych's startled gaze darted towards the window and caught just the black flapping of a wing.

The white-faced chimney-sweep continued his journey, only now he was running, not walking, and flailing his arms in a comical way. He was also yelling something, yelling it to him, putting his hands up to his mouth over and over again, but his cries dissolved in the noise of the rain and Hrushkevych's ears caught just a jumble.

Enough! It was time to finish up this exhausting love-making. Virunka, however, was showing no signs of satiation. It seemed that she could keep on playing that way until she died.

But the damned chimney-sweep on the roof wouldn't let Hrushkevych concentrate. The mere feeling that someone was hurrying towards him, yelling out some message that could actually even be important, constrained him and took away his pleasure. Oh, the devil with him, I don't want any more. With that thought he tried to let Virunka go, but suddenly he realized with horror that she wouldn't let him go. He pulled back with all his strength, pushed her buttocks away with both hands, but it was no use. Instead he heard a quiet maliciously gleeful giggling and Virunka's head slowly turned around a full 180 degrees on her neck. O Lord! Her smiling face, its teeth bared, turned to him and splashed out laughter. No, this was no longer a gentle and humble young lady, faint with satiety. This was a real devil in a woman's likeness, the brilliant fires of hell flaming in her blazing pupils.

He kept trying to tear himself away from her body and put

all his strength into the effort, but he could feel her pulling, sucking him in like a quagmire, and there was nothing he could do about it. His eyes sought salvation outside the window, where the chimney-sweep, the one who had irritated him so much such a short time before but was now his only hope for salvation, was running and jumping from one roof to another.

"Ha-ha-ha!" Virunka laughed in a coarse manly voice, and Hrushkevych's hair stood on end.

An incredible force was sucking him into her body, and he could feel an increasingly strong heat that was raging inside her. His legs pulled away from the ground by themselves. Bent, knees first, they crawled to the place from which there was no return. His legs disappeared, and now he found himself up to his waist in a wet, hot concoction that burned his skin. He filled the office with spasmodic screams.

The roof runner could see now that he was late and once again tried to give him a message using signs, waving his arms like a madman, but Hrushkevych couldn't understand anything and just kept pushing with his hands as best he could, while his legs dangled and had no hard surface to set on. How was it that he could foresee someone else's demise, but had overlooked his own?

The force that was sucking Hrushkevych into the young woman's body was indomitable. He jerked and twitched, but despite all his efforts he kept plummeting deeper and deeper. Then, when only his head was left on the surface, a dark shape suddenly appeared in the window, and in it he recognized the oddball who had been running over the roofs. The shadows obliterated his face, but he was visibly beating against the window like a moth, and instead of arms he had broken wings, and he was all black only because he was covered in soot, because he had flown out of some factory smokestack. Now a strong and joyous downpour was washing the black soot off him, making his entire form gradually become lighter, and the last thing Hrushkevych saw in this world was a figure with broken wings, but white and clean as snow, white and bright.

Falling into the hot interior, he saw below him a swirling red stew in which heads, legs, and arms turned over at a frenzied speed. One last cry, and he plunged into the concoction, gasping from the scalding hot liquid.

Virunka gracefully hoisted up her panties, fixed her hair, and, turning to the window, stuck out her tongue.

Necropolis

TARAS PROKHASKO

A gift for Olenka

I.

Marcus Mlynarsky was writing: "It may turn out for all of you that the sense of your existences and of all being is recombination. The creation of a text by way of a series of enduring genetic recombinations. Recombinations that through countless attempts, an infinity of uncertain displacements, should lead to a concrete structure that someone has conceived. Perhaps that is how God's Epiphany (Manifestation) is supposed to occur. Or it could be that the most essential recombination is rhetorical. Perhaps in the end, too, there should be the word. And we select it, adapt to it, pronouncing and rejecting texts that are not it. The same with plasticity. We change space; we replace one space with another as we move. It is not known what movement or what deed may turn out to be decisive, what selection of simultaneous world movements will create the space that will stop everything, so that the stasis of eternity may endure in such a configuration."

At this point Marcus himself should have stopped, but he kept writing, violating his own calculations: "The only problem is becoming conscious of the totality of recombinations, connecting and joining simultaneous discrete tropisms into one (really single) system, a closed system, where the cause of anything is not just anything else or the combination of the two, but the unembraceable state and juxtaposition of all the other elements not just at a discrete moment in time, but also in their stratification, their accumulation since the beginning of time itself...."

Before this Mlynarsky had not written anything other than a philosophical treatise that could not end. Actually the treatise turned into a chronicle – along with contemplation of utterly concrete daily events were distilled such abstract ontological reflections that only Marcus himself would be able to recreate what had been done on the basis of the chronicle of what had been pondered.

It is true that besides the treatise he also had a diary that lay on the desk beside the window that looked out on the enclosed courtyard, in which Marcus wrote only what he saw in the course of the day through that very window. (Despite the almost complete inactivity in the yard and the absolute absence of what the man in the street calls living nature, as well as Marcus's strict taboo against recording in his diary any reflections or associations that would somehow lead away from the space delimited by the buildings closing in around the courtyard, Marcus nonetheless saw so much every day that work on his diary deprived him of a bit of the time when he already felt very much like sleeping; some of the entries therefore had something of a somnabulous flavour; thus during one nocturnal drinking bout in the kitchen Mlynarsky undertook to make his daily entry in the presence of his friends, telling them about the nature of his diary and even reading a few fragments – not the ones he liked best, nor the ones he thought were the most interesting, but opening the notebook a few times with his eyes closed; his friends were taken not so much with the entries as with the very idea of pinning down the mutability of changelessness and modelling a variety of interesting variations at length, and then they imperceptibly moved on to other topics, but when they gathered a few days later without Mlynarsky, they agreed in all seriousness to use various discreet means to bring about at least some kind of events in Marcus's courtyard, and even though the game did not last long, at that very time there appeared in the diary such chimeric realia, each of which could evolve into a story, that Marcus decided to write a novel, unifying them with some sort of plot.)

The novel Mlynarsky conceived was to be titled *Necropolis* (city of the dead). Let's say a group of people who don't know one another buy at an auction plots in an as yet nonexistent cemetery. These people have long since lost any interest in normal life in the city, lost their friends and acquaintances, are left without their families, all of their real ties to the city have worn away, they are lonely, poor, superfluous, they are barely alive, they don't want, nor do they know how, to live like most people, while the majority has a fierce dislike for their primitive life style, once they break down the majority simply stops taking any notice of them, which is actually why they have all taken such a bold step, to ensure at least the external forms of this world for their other-worldly life. Having taken the step, however, they are afraid both of what they have done and of themselves – perhaps it is precisely this fear, combined with a secret wish to make it even stronger (one way or another, it is still a life experience, a heightened existence) and with a striving to wrest themselves from the Rule of Fear here at least, that forces each of them to come to the cemetery once, then again and again, hiding from chance witnesses and later from one another as well, gradually getting used to their own plots, their own land, gradually taking there more and more of what binds them to life – they are already secretly acquainted, it is an odd form of socializing, but already an intrinsically valuable one: avoiding and yearning for one another, watching and hiding, studying drawings, plans, itineraries, habits, directions, customs, and preferences, finally declaring yourself, knowing you're being watched, possibly from several viewpoints, pretending you don't know, but in such a way as to let them understand that you know more than is even possible, entering the increasingly complex intersections of this widely acknowledged game – it will then inevitably happen that somewhere, sometime two will not pass by each other, they open up to each other, for them this is a happiness that has an intolerable effect on anyone spying on them, they unmask themselves and they unmask others, the most timid ones – they start to establish their places and in time it is more like a cooperative building common, and finally the semantics of a cemetery wears off; they carry their habits over here, they themselves move, for the first time they cultivate a niche of some sort for themselves, suiting only their own tastes – they are convinced of their mutual affection and compatibility – more and more means of communication appear – but they are still destructured as personalities, each of them burdened by habits that, until recently, were an imitation of sense, they are deprived of the kind of experience that would go beyond the limits of their own experience of emptiness (experience of their own emptiness), they haven't kept up with the development of terminology and nomination, it is important for them to think with words and concepts, their feelings exceed significantly the opportunities for expressing those feelings – somebody concludes that they need to become a chamber orchestra – instruments are distributed according to the seating arrangement in the orchestra, but they sit according to the layout of their plots – trading plots (certain constant pairings have emerged, and circles for which the question of being immediate neighbours is of fundamental importance), and trading instruments, but that doesn't matter, because in the beginning no one knows how to play anything – they now occupy themselves mainly with uninterrupted rehearsals of funeral marches – they are sufficiently emptied and sufficiently avid for something better to gain fairly quickly a dilettantish mastery of their instruments (even considering all their trading of them). For some time the marches satisfy them, but before long that turns out not to be enough. There is among them one composer manqué, who is in fact the one who conducts the orchestra and trains the musicians. He is charged with writing something appropriate. For the composer this is the first real event, his first chance to become a real composer, and he tries long and hard to compose, but the world of the cemetery is ephemeral, and the composer is good and refined, whereas his talent is illusory, nonetheless he brings some music. It's Mozart, a symphony, which the composer has copied out by hand at the library, containing only the parts for the instruments they have in their orchestra. Everyone really likes the music, and everyone has learned their part with no difficulty, yet their joint performance is appalling. They all lack lightness, abandon, and a capacity to hear intonations. They all lack freedom.

Mlynarsky decided that his novel would not have any concrete time framework or any overly specific characteristics of any period of time. Even the genesis of events would have to be eroded in time. There would be no features of everyday life that could belong to any one single decade. Nor any stylistic markers in the writing that would hint at any decade any more persuasively than designation of a year. No clear or detailed psychological portraits beyond the deeds of the protagonists. And the logic by which the novel would unfold would be the logic of the inseparability of the next deed on the basis of those previously done, with the next ones determined by the previous ones only in such a way whereby the previous ones repeatedly block off the ways of choice, simply filling up any free moves. This irrational logic is the logic of accessible possibility. He would love this weakness of his characters. He would break off lines to return to them after some time in order for this time to pass by; in the lines there would be drops, unevennesses, and gaps behind which it would not be possible to trace in which ones anything could have happened. He wouldn't know much about his protagonists, and he'd have to make things up to fill in what he didn't know. They would have to talk to themselves. He would introduce into the text a few microscopic viruses that would take advantage of the unforeseen possibilities of his text to pull them out of the text and reproduce, rising up on them as who knows what once they were outside the text.

Mlynarsky had even thought up a very elegant ending for his novel. He would introduce himself into the text and become one of the plot owners, one of the musicians in the orchestra. He would remain himself with all his efforts to tell this very story, and the novel itself would then be the author's story of his writing a novel about events in which he was an equal participant. And at the very end he would reveal himself to be author-observer, that is, the real Mlynarsky. This would, of course, be a directed virus. And a very interesting virus that would be able to alternate variously the view from the novel, the view into the novel, and the view within the novel.

It was around that time that the first musings on recombination turned up in Mlynarsky's endless treatise. And the day that in the courtyard (according to his diary entries) the rain began, with the chestnuts and the chrysanthemums that had been thrown to the ground starting to wilt from their lower petals, that day Marcus was writing: "The main indication of all combinations is their limitlessness. The classification lists of the components of a particular combination, as also the separation of the combination itself, are conditional. Combinations are open systems into which any adjoining elements can be introduced infinitely. Everything can be reduced to one combination."

Mlynarsky wasn't in the least troubled by his disordered phrases. He was delighted to give half-accidental, half-weighed expressions the opportunity to draw unexpected and unforeseen motifs, associations, and chips off nearby constructions into the text. In this way the phrases reminded Marcus of the circles on the water when you drop in a stone. Only in Mlynarsky's imagination the film of his vision was projected in reverse – the circles came together from the periphery towards the centre, increasingly dense and tight, until the stone burst out from under the water, bringing up with it a whole sphere, rising up in a flowing trajectory, losing its aureole of moisture, and visibly drying off. At this point Marcus cut off the vision to allow for multiplicity in the last stage of the trajectory.

Marcus Mlynarsky was all the more shocked by the course of the spontaneous recombinations with which his conceived novel had meanwhile come to seethe. He noticed odd changes in his concept once, then again and again, and in time he had to admit that all his variants had turned out to be lethal (they weren't even capable of being refined). Instead one single line had come to dominate, one that was not an involuntary expression, but the result of uncontrolled recombinations of separate fragments, phrases, sketches, spoken lines, features.... Marcus agreed to follow all the ins and outs of its logic.

But the logic held fast to one dogma: the residents of Necropolis could not be buried in their places, Necropolis should not become a cemetery. They would therefore all have to be taken from the city and killed. This would be almost impossible, because they had not left the city even individually practically since childhood. All that was left was a hot-air balloon. (This was a very important turn. It was only here, reaching the turn time and again, and returning to its start, that Mlynarsky became convinced of what finally led him to the definitive *Necropolis*. It's true that the definitive *Necropolis* took place much later, but for the time being Marcus understood the meaning of fate, chance, relativity, and everything connected with them.

A passage from the treatise: "The essence of both fate and chance is one and the same – the accumulation of the sequences of the recombinations produced by the very process of recombination. And this is irreproducibility....")

It was just this kind of irreproducibility that the balloon, the montgolfier, turned out to be. They were now on their second flight. The first time, their irrational orchestra had flown in order to play its Mozart there, on a small patch of uncertain *terra firma / firmament*, in a state lighter than air, rid of all its earthly fears, complexes, habits, manias, neuroses, and doubts. Existential music. Naturally, they succeeded, naturally, only once, only there. It is clear how aroused they were when they returned. It was an ecstasy, a euphoria, an explosion, a shock, a trance, a dissolution, and a condensation. Of course they had no interest in the panic that had engulfed the city, the perturbation of the authorities, the work of the experts, the introduction of a curfew and martial law, the patrols in the marketplace, the guards on the roofs of public and government buildings, the posts at the exits from the city, or the ban on public gatherings. Nor did they know anything about the city's biggest sensation – a few of the most up-to-date cannon had been brought into the city.

The second and last flight was even more understandable. The music that came about as they flew could not be recreated on earth. Therefore the second flight was one of despair and hope, a new dimension, a last chance, revenge, and scorn. It was a physiological dependency.

It was entirely to be expected (and there is nothing symbolic about it) that they flew off without an anchor, with no ballast (the little bags of sand had been thrown out back at the level of the lowest trees), loaded with musical instruments, and the only indication of any foresight at all was an uncorked bottle of cherry brandy. It was also justified for the commodore of the outermost cannon outpost to give orders to destroy with fire the odd, incomprehensible flying machine that hung at the edge of the city in a westerly direction (having flown over the city beforehand at a height from which nothing remained inaccessible to special optics), and from which spread sounds that resembled broadcasts on a closed radio frequency. The only mistake that the special commission found was the complete destruction of the machine, which made it absolutely impossible for the experts to arrive at any conclusions....

Mlynarsky was almost convinced that no one in the hot-air balloon had had a chance to notice either the cannonade or the actual hit. Unless the Composer, who was a good composer, was able to sense how badly their orchestra needed a percussion section, which everyone had rejected as a sign of being uncultivated.

The hot-air balloon had been assembled haphazardly, with one part of the largest basket being matched up to another in the attic of the two-story house that was the home of the only woman among the owners of Necropolis. Lacking any notion of practicality or technical imagination whatsoever, in assembling the balloon they had created a few times something so absurd that it was initially taken to be an apparatus for performing very specialized and secret operations. But when the balloon finally happened (and that was what was lying disassembled in the trunk), no one had to say a single word in order to draw up a common indisputable plan.

The house had once belonged to a well-known traveller and describer of flora. Every year he would wander by himself, taking the riskiest routes, leaving his little daughter behind unsupervised. He would return when the first snow fell, loaded down with dried objects, and he always led or carried home with him a variety of lizards, birds, and animals, while losing or leaving behind a portion of his expensive gear because he was so loaded down. He would spend the whole winter sitting in his study, elaborating the materials from his expedition. His daughter would bring him breakfast and supper, empty his ashtrays, water the flowers in the solarium, and feed every living thing. She was allowed to look at anything in the study, laboratory, library, and attic, where collections were stored, along with equipment for the next expedition, which he would buy up when he drove out at lunchtime to a restaurant. In time she became more and more immersed in the object of her father's research, helping him compile lists and copy-editing what he had typed. By the last years she knew everything, even the details of his planned routes. Nothing else was of interest to her. She was sure that her father had not become a collaborator. He had simply refused to give up his travels and academic activities upon the arrival of the new regime. She realized how abnormal her feeling of guilt was for that spring trip to the coast, during which her father, having submitted the report from his last expedition for publication, was arrested, released, and buried, and not saved in the best hospital. Since then she had been on her own. No one interfered with the house, publishers sent money, and no one came to see her until the orchestra's second rehearsal, which she offered to hold at her place. After that they never looked for any other place to rehearse; somebody from the orchestra would often stay late, somebody would spend the night, sometimes they would come individually, or in pairs, sometimes they would all be there, coming one after another, and then they would disperse in the most varied possible order.

She did not live in poverty, she lived amid a luxury that was completely useless. But those accumulations of things – books, clothing, tools, instruments, plants, weapons, equipment – made up an exotarium that could exist as a separate world, and in it one could exist autonomously from the world, without feeling a lack of impressions, phenomena, enumerations, names, secrets, or adventures. There was not even enough time to do an accurate classification of that world. On the other hand there was too much space – walls, stairs, halls, doors, inside windows, furniture, and paintings comminuted the space of the house into an interminability of sub, para, super, trans, and interspaces that did not lose their capacity for flowing into one another, or out of one another, and that were unclosed, did not have a solid border, and changed from the slightest rearrangement of objects.

Now the animals did not lend themselves to any kind of training. They simply loved her and needed neither cages nor restraints. She recognized them by the way the floor squeaked – the length, weight, and speed of each animal's steps brought its own melody out of the hardwood. This was made more complex by the fact that every single floorboard emitted its squeak according to a pattern that also belonged to it alone, often not concurring with the direction in which a body was moving along the floor and being more reminiscent of studies laid out on a chessboard. She recognized each of them by its hypertrophied likeness in the shadow that passed on the ceiling of the study, which was transformed into a sphere by the play of insufficient lighting, seeping through the frosted glass into the hall. She would lose the most significant part of her consciousness when she had a cold and her sense of smell was out of order. She experienced the sweaters she found in closets like flirtations, like chance, fleeting contacts. Sometimes she would light up a pipe in order to cover the smell of the room's memories with the aroma of one of her father's tobacco blends.

Now when Mlynarsky situated her on the terrace – a chilly rain was falling, she was sitting in an armchair of ice, wrapped in a winter coat, squeezing a cup of grog between her knees, and not flicking the ashes from the cigarette in the hand that hung over her lowered book (the cigarette was not touching the book, but still a brown mark appeared on the paper from the heat) – he sensed that he had never been closer to anyone than this woman. He had never yet given anyone so much of his knowledge, his secret knowledge, and his most thoroughly verified and most distinguishing habits. He had never been so generous. Or had experienced such gratitude. She immediately acknowledged the inevitability of his habits in the quest to bring the desired ordering of the world as close as possible to the natural, chaotically normal one.

Mlynarsky gradually gave her almost all his external experience; he even ran out of known things. She demanded new experiences as she experienced the unlived. Most often she didn't notice the weight of Marcus's experience in what Marcus gave her at all, perceiving it as continuously shared. This woman arrived at the fragment on the terrace herself.

Mlynarsky came to be afraid. He was not afraid of being emptied, he was not afraid of self-denial or self-destruction. It did not frighten him that she rendered anything else impossible, nor that everything he did at any particular moment was her whim – anticipating associations that would be brought on by recognition – the day before, Marcus would consciously insinuate himself in events the experience of which he needed to give her. Marcus was going through certain experiences, rendering lawful what had been previously named – the possibility of naming forced the facilitation of happening. Meanwhile, the whims were straying increasingly farther from the dominant of rationalism, good, beauty, and intellect, and coming closer to an acknowledgement of the intrinsic value of being. And Marcus knew that her unfathomable ability to posit causation as the ultimate cause would lead her out (even if in the course of accidents) to essentiality. Only then would neither *Necropolis* nor the balloon be accidental.

Marcus was not even afraid of responsibility. He was simply afraid for her. Everything changes from a change in something – Marcus would save (or destroy?), save her by not being with her. And Mlynarsky stopped writing his novel.

There was a thaw. The leaves that had been lying on the ground since autumn freed themselves from the snow and were falling again, caught up in the warm wind that had become stronger and had blown in snow clouds that had been gathering somewhere off to the side for several days, and from which snow had already begun to fly, melting at a certain height in the warmth of the wind, and, landing on the ground as a cold rain, were covered in other leaves that were significantly slower.

In the treatise, Mlynarsky noted: "Being is, actually, co-being. The simultaneous existence of everything with everything and the coexistence of everything."

In fact, at that time Mlynarsky was interested only in problems relating to the further fate of *Necropolis*. He understood that the outline of the novel was already a text, was something out of everything, it was already coexisting, it was a reality. The concept of the novel was already equivalent in everything to Mlynarsky himself and was capable of being the start of independent chains strung onto the presence in continuous being of all the possibilities of all the ensuing moments and the possible arrival of those very moments.

Necropolis was a reality in a world where there is nothing unreal at all, only various forms of reality. Revealing the form of reality in *Necropolis* and including it in a series of forms that changed into one another – that was what Mlynarsky had to complete. Here a situation arose that was similar to the status of Mlynarsky's treatise. The treatise was the transposition of Marcus's everyday existential experience into the experience of philosophy, the experience of realization. The new form or structure of *Necropolis* should then become the modelling of imaginary experience – the experience of imagination – according to Mlynarsky's philosophical schemes. As always, a recombination had appeared unexpectedly – in that case *Necropolis* was a reflection of a reflection, a system of mirrors that could be extended further and further (Mlynarsky was sure that they were not Venetian mirrors, but even older ones, silver and dusky, that lose an image perceptibly as they cast it from one over to another, and even the first mirror gives a clear reflection only if a certain focal distance is maintained).

It was then that Mlynarsky felt a frenzied calm (the feeling of calm threw Marcus into a frenzy, he shook, froze, and spoke badly as he became conscious of the essence of his calm) from one indefinite thought. Calm engulfed Mlynarsky to the extent that he did not need to crystallize the thought; he felt the calm of the harmony between the world and his own understanding of the world (he knew that everything rested on this and that his only purpose in life was to elaborate explanations of the world that would harmonize with the world, he knew how infrequently such explanations occur, how all-embracing they seem at that moment, how short-lived their effect is, what an illusion of sensefulness and of not being in vain they create, what satisfaction from an obligation performed they grant, or relief, how they justify the entire preceding period, and what hope they give for the coming period), while it was his understanding of the mechanisms of this calm, superimposing itself on a continual repetition of the thought, that drove him into a frenzy.

It was possible to apprehend this thought by juxtaposing entries in the treatise and the diary. There was no doubt that they were about the same thing. "For all its diversity, uniqueness, and infinity of variations, experience ultimately comes down to a few things, a few feelings and states, the measure and the circumstances of manifestation of which are nonessential by comparison with the fact that it simply was. Thus, they are made equal by experience and are not greater or lesser, but other." (Mlynarsky then goes on to arrive at recognition as the thing to which absolutely everything can be reduced, the sole and ultimate structure that does not even distinguish humans from all living beings. Still farther, we come across a thought that would seem to contradict the very first one, but is really a reiteration of it, if the imaginary cube of the space of cogitation is turned over onto another side: "The measure of only one phenomenon (fear, hunger, risk) can also be a reading of experience.")

And in his diary: "The snow was deep. There were tracks in it, and there came to be more and more of them. Then the snow melted and froze several times, deforming the traces of melting and fixing the deformations by freezing. And every morning the strange relief was different, the chimerical topography changed, closed within itself, with only three degrees of freedom at its disposal – the primary snow with its original prints, melting, and freezing. Knowing this (and the number of repetitions, too), it is certainly possible, through an application of effort, to return through the thicket of recombinations to the fundamental principle, the authentic tracks, and then to the perfect inviolability of the surface of the snow."

It was this recombination of Mlynarsky's reflections on recombinations in the snow that turned out to be decisive for the course of recombinations with *Necropolis*. Meanwhile

Marcus was creating variants of his constructions of *Necropolis:* according to one of them, *Necropolis* was a concise and lyric short story that told an urban story (the reality of such a story is something particular, such stories are integral, inviolable, and self-sufficient regardless of whether they are more or less full of details, and only consistency is of any importance here) that the author heard while visiting some city, the text of the short story was read by a script writer, the script he wrote made *Necropolis* more effective, the writer rearranged stresses, added dialogues, and emphasized individual portraits, certain scenes that were so clear that they were not even mentioned in the short story were worked out in great detail, second by second, the script was read by the director, who made extensive comments, additions, elaborations, and notes (it was this text, almost a director's journal, that was given), straying even farther from the spirit of the short story, the director would send them by mail to his cameraman, who ran everything that was written down through an imaginary camera, reality changed according to the possibilities of the lens's way of seeing, the cameraman's interior monologue followed the text, the last fragment in the chain of texts was the shorthand record of the whole group's advice regarding the film, with additions and inventions, pinned down and layered on – limitations by the lighting and special-effects technicians, the sound director, the designer, the makeup artist, and the costume designer, and this text was monstrous, that is, it had the beauty of an uninhabited structure, but the ruination of the short story was so pathological and blasphemous and the fantasy of the project so ugly and unrealizable that the director, not wanting to lose a fine plot, undertook to write a new script himself, freeing it from all ramifications. Naturally, the text of the script turned out to be the absolutely unchanged text of the short story (which the director had not even seen and about which he did not know), concise and lyric, and the director decided to make an animated film; another variant of Mlynarsky's would have been a headache for the printers, because the text of *Necropolis* was supposed to be set on the sixth line of a musical staff that would already have the music of Mozart's marches and of avantgarde jazz printed on it; yet another was a separated text – the first chapter contained portraits of the dramatis personae, the second – painstaking descriptions of the smallest details, the third – just all the dialogues, the fourth – the appropriate musings, inner states, and monologues of the protagonists, the fifth was reminiscent of an encyclopaedia composed of excerpts of eclectically compiled geographic, historical, technical, physiological, ethnographic, and linguistic knowledge, and only did the sixth reveal the bare scheme of the plot, the sequence of actions; and in keeping with one plan *Necropolis* was written on a divided page where, beginning with a first common phrase on one of the halves each sentence differed from the analogous one on the other in only one word. And many many more other variants of *Necropolis*.

Later it got hot, summer baked the city, and Mlynarsky started to get depressed (thinking up variants took several months and drew Marcus into an invariable state of constant lightness of being). He left for the country, drank linden tea, ate wild strawberries, bathed in the river, and every evening read his treatise from the very beginning, no more than a few pages a day, recreating the images of his own life according to each entry.

Mlynarsky's reading took him up to the March entry about the deformation of snow only towards the end of summer. And evidently he was sufficiently prepared by his treatise and his summer impressions of being without impressions because he was capable of experiencing afresh that thought, that state, reviving the whole alchemy (Merab Mamardashvili calls this "falling into thought," by way of comparison – "falling into being"). More than that, its continuation turned out to be obvious: knowing the ending of still the selfsame *Necropolis* (and Mlynarsky considered the real ending to be the discovery of the hot-air balloon and the decision to go on a flight), knowing those people and their city, and having gone through all the recombinations of their actions (which pertain and – it is this that is the very main thing – do not pertain to the plot line), it would be possible to restore all the states, the state of each person at the moment when they came to the auction where the plots at the future cemetery were being sold. Only in this way could one explain what makes up *Necropolis*. Who makes up *Necropolis*.

All September Mlynarsky worked twenty hours a day, drawing up an uncomplicated list, a description of the scheme of recombinations. For his fundamental structure he chose the action, the verb. The investigation looked like an enumeration of the most numerous variations of actions that branched out from a few determinant ones to increasingly more refined and more contrived ones, to increasingly more detailed ones; from one verb to whole expressions, with subordinate clauses that characterized the most specific actions (for example, the chapter "Smoking" was segmented by several dozen planes into several hundred subchapters, such as smoking a pipe, smoking thin cigarettes, smoking tobacco rolled in newspaper – this according to one plane of segmentation, but according to others – smoking in the mountains, smoking indoors, smoking in solitude, smoking one cigarette after another. And so it was divided down to the ultracomplex notions "in bed toward morning smoking her cigarettes, so refined-tasting that the smoky smell is almost imperceptible the ashtray on the breast sometimes ashes fall on the sheet turn into a grey spot from overly forceful flicking it lasts longer than usual only holding the cigarette prevents falling asleep however what is spoken is now in fact a delirium consciousness agrees with the measure imposed by the direction of the coordinating axes of the position of the cigarettes").

Most complex of all were the descriptions of planes that emerged with the congruity of irregular figures – subchapters. This, now, was a topology, a geometry of uninterrupted planes. From any arbitrarily chosen point at all, without detaching oneself from it for a moment, it was possible to pass from one point in the register to another, to another elementary chapter, and then either to a more generalized subchapter in the same group or to an equivalent one in an entirely different group. And so, wandering along curved horizons and verticals as far as the primary word "to recognize" and finally as far as the hot-air balloon. By October Mlynarsky had completed his huge map of being (with help from his friend, a computer pirate). All that remained was, limiting himself to the real possibilities of the protagonists of *Necropolis*, to draw the fantasmagorical curve of the way from the balloon to the auction. But there is nothing strange about the fact that Marcus lost interest in his project. Why, first, he had very little left in comparison with what had been done, and second, the moves of *Necropolis* had lost all their value against the background of this universal and totipotent code. Mlynarsky considered *Necropolis* to be an interesting and fertile period of his philosophical creativity, his life, and the sum of his experiences and impressions. Finally, he was grateful to the people of Necropolis.

In December, not long before Christmas, a theatrical festival took place in the city. It was a holiday; Marcus spent entire days talking with friends and acquaintances who had come from out of town, made love to actresses, saw all the performances, wrote articles for various newspapers and periodicals, partied and hosted receptions, spent his nights in the most diverse gatherings, and took part in a seminar where he delivered a superb lecture on the philosophy of the theatre. Meanwhile, actors from a theatre of plastique dance had moved into his home with their choreographer, the brilliant Spanish Arab J., who had been a friend of Marcus's for many years. J. was a hermit, and he could be seen only at the theatre and only on days when his group was performing. He spent the rest of his time sitting around in Mlynarsky's apartment, taking advantage of the opportunity to be alone with Marcus's papers. He knew that Marcus was deliberately staying away from home, egging him into a calm examination of what Marcus had recently been writing.

Among the papers J. found the map of being. It made such an impression on him that reading anything else became impossible; it got under his skin for a long stay. For the first time in his life J. copied out passages from a text. A year later J.'s theatre brought its own programme to the city. Among other plastique compositions it put on the premiere of *Necropolis*, a plastique construction based on motifs from the idea of M. Mlynarsky, who was taken aback and accepted the invitation to the premiere with pleasure, even promising to say a few words from the stage after the dance.

The only evidence of these events is a mention of a few paragraphs in a newspaper: the atmosphere at the premiere was faerier than throughout the entire festival of the previous year and a veritable artistic bacchanalia went on for two hours in the foyer, in the stairways and corridors. Among the guests there were many whom it had never yet been possible to lure to the city. Mlynarsky did not speak, because after the performance, which ended triumphantly, he was nowhere to be seen.

In the morning a woman friend of Mlynarsky's came to J. and told him that during the first act Mlynarsky began having an excruciating headache, lost consciousness and raged, and left the theatre together with her. The fever lasted all night, she gave him compresses, then she fell asleep for a while, and by morning Marcus was gone. On 2 January J.'s theatre left; on 7 January Marcus returned; on 20 January J. came to meet with Marcus, but Marcus had left for the mountains on 19 January; on 23 January J. forbade recording the movements of *Necropolis* in any way at all – either photographically or in any other way; on 1 March Mlynarsky went to see J. himself, they were seen on all-day odysseys through cafés, wineries, bars, inns, taverns, and pubs.

Mlynarsky's relations with J did not suffer. *Necropolis* was playing for the last time in November. During this whole time Mlynarsky almost rudey avoided any questioning or talks about *Necropolis*.

Gradually everything was forgotten.

Thus ended the letter received by Dr. Vynnyk, the author of the most widely read biography of Marcus Mlynarsky, just as he was preparing the second expanded edition of this bestseller. Granted, there was also a poetic postscript. First the author noted that he had been told the whole story several years before by one of Marcus's closest friends, then he explained that he had tried to mention as much as possible of what he had been told, but preferred to drop some of what he didn't remember clearly rather than make anything up or strain to remember (Vynnyk sensed something of Mlynarsky's spirit in this), and in the last postscript he swore that he knew absolutely nothing more, couldn't add or relate anything in any more detail, and for that reason was remaining anonymous. Vynnyk, who had elaborated Mlynarsky's biography exceedingly thoroughly, was hearing about *Necropolis* for the first time. He would have been interested to learn more about that friend of Marcus's who knew something like that, but the second edition of *The Unending Changeability of the Unchangeable* came out without any reference to the secret of *Necropolis*.

II

AND YET IT WAS FOUND. And yet he was found. At least one person who knew about *Necropolis*. Had even been involved in it. In a hospital for forced treatment of alcoholism, in Mlynarsky's native city, Vynnyk found a completely broken-down seventy-year-old cellist who in his youth had played in the orchestra of the city theatre. He remembered well almost all the themes of various ballets, operettas, and vaudevilles. He remembered playing *Necropolis*, too, when some theatre had come from abroad. The scores were theirs, but he couldn't remember the music at all. Vynnyk sat in the unnaturally clean physiotherapy room with the old man until midnight. He rolled one cigarette after another for him, listening to the fantasmagorical tales of the life of a theatre musician. He even cooked up a fairly decent hot wine in the autoclave, using contraband wine, at the risk of being expelled from the hospital. It loosened the cellist's tongue. He no longer had the strength to put off the story of *Necropolis* (it had seemed offensively unwise at the very beginning to talk about just one single episode), and Vynnyk got what he was waiting for.

There was one woman and six men. They were the ones who danced. Although they not so much danced as made various motions. Generally the woman would do something with one person. The others would either be on stage doing something of their own or would leave. Sometimes there would be the woman and two, three, four, or five men. She looked well on her own, too, and a few times they were all together. The stage as a whole was divided by the most diverse shapes into a large number of spaces. On the stage there were windows, with weavings, strings, and synthetic film hung to mark the separations. There were lamps shining in various strengths, attached in various places. There were lamps and special bulbs and ordinary ones, table lamps and projectors, and flashlights, turned on and left lying around just anywhere. In addition, a technician manipulated a complex system of lights directed at the stage. Various levels. Scaffolds, swings, cubes, benches, candles, and candle holders. Water was flowing. From taps, from pierced spheres, from tipped dishes. The water flowed out or collected in the next dishes. Animals wandered freely over the stage – dogs, cats, snakes coiled here and there, porcupines hid. A few animals slept peacefully, some were tied up and tried to break away. Birds perched, butterflies flew out of somewhere, very many butterflies, wasps, moths. Insects flew into streaks of light, streaks of smoke. Because smoke was rising from cigarettes left in ashtrays and papers were burning. Housewares were being thrown about. There were many plants. Ivy fell; pots, tubs, and vases with plants and flowers stood about. A mixture of smells came from broken bottles and jars of perfume, spices, and brewed coffee.

A whole army of worker shadows went in and out carrying furniture, assemblies, plants, and books. They rearranged objects on some tables. They rearranged pieces on chessboards, poured drinks out of bottles into goblets, mixed them, and poured them out or drank them. They rearranged paintings and moved sculptures around. Someone settled on the piano and lived there, not touching the floor. An operator changed the slides that were projected onto all the surfaces. Workers chased away dogs, looked through telescopes, microscopes (one girl was constantly changing the preparations on the microscope stage), and binoculars, ground leaves and grass, and pounded roots in a mortar.

The ones who danced appeared in different costumes each time. There was such chaos that after a certain time all the ones who had performed could no longer unravel their way out of it and did not what they would have liked, but what was dictated by the strict order of the chaos. On top of that from time to time phrases, verse, and fragments of prose were recited in various parts of the theatre.

Every time the music for the ballet (the cellist persisted in calling this a ballet) was performed it drove the musicians to throw down their instruments, unable to endure the psychological overload from the parts they had played, and they would run out of the orchestra pit. The music was insane, pathological, and insuperable. It would not release one up to the very moment of ejection. No one knows why one or another musician would go mad from it – whether because of fatigue or because of some previous impressions, or perhaps because of their entire past – but, starting as a whole orchestra, they would play to the end, losing some combination of instruments and not paying any attention to their absence.

The cellist had made it through all of them, but now he was sleeping. Dr. Vynnyk had walked over to his hotel and was also asleep, although he remembered what to think about when he woke up – about the fact that he had to tape-record what he had heard in the hospital, that it was possible to write *Necropolis* by superimposing a plastique register on Mlyanarsky's schemes as described in the letter.

And what was strange: on going to sleep, always forgetting overnight what he had been thinking about, but not needing anything in the morning to keep on thinking the same way without obstacles. And nothing is forgotten overnight.

Vynnyk's archive did not turn up anything anywhere near *Necropolis*. Once demolition of the house had begun, and half of the orchard had been chopped down, after removal of the last bundles of empty frames, the doctor's friends pointed out that a dull reflection of the car light ran over the tree that was closest to the balcony in a thin, strangely tangled broken line. It was an audiotape flung onto the crown, immovably attached here and there to the branches, at times stretched to the limit, but for the most part free, blown up by the wind enough for the streaks to curve beyond the imaginary contour of the crown, changing the configuration of its profile.

In the process of being taken down the tape tore in several places. In one place it had got so tightly tangled up that the branch had to be broken off.

The tape was completely mutilated; it had nearly become one with the sap circulating in the tree. Some pieces had completely lost their colour, others had become coated with dust, covered with Irish moss, a few spots had been gnawed by moths (they must have become disoriented and flown out to the tree through open windows), the tape was marked with streaks of ant acid and snail slime, fragments of it were covered in petrified glue, like amber, bark beetles had frequently eaten through it.

An audition of the tapes produced a dissection of time. Beyond the ultrasounds of bats and mosquitos, beyond transfusions in capillaries, the application of radio interference (this can all be explained only by the influence of the constant magnetic field from the relative positioning of powerful antennas) right away behind the orchard emerged excerpts of free verse spoken by Vynnyk. A synchronic interlinear translation built up an indubitable *Necropolis*. As it turns out, the voice was copied only by the genotexts of our being, because a repeated audition gave duration only to a wasteland of wear and tear, openness, cleanliness, and waiting.

I, Milena

OKSANA ZABUZHKO

On the surface everything seemed fine. That is, everything was indeed fine, or so Milena assured herself as she hurried home from the television studio those dark winter evenings (her face still stiff under the stage make-up she hadn't taken off yet and the feeble – at the thought of her husband, *I couldn't wait for you to get here* – smile of tenderness that of its own volition puffed up her lips into the little pipe of a kiss – *ah, you, my kitten* – breaking through the make-up, as if through those wafers of ice on the asphalt that you had to watch out for all the time in the dark, even if they weren't there). Mincing cautiously over the invisible skating rinks, she would approach the building and, before going in to the courtyard, would sometimes walk under the chestnuts that separated the building from the street and turn up her head to search out her windows with her gaze and by determining which of them was lit to find out what Puppydog (Pussycat, Cottontail) was doing just then, not suspecting the joy of her approach. Most often the light was on in the bedroom – a washed-out spot of blue on the lower part of the curtains: Cottontail was watching television. As he would jokingly put it, he was growing a tail: for some reason he would start to get an erection in front of the screen. And he would also say that he was watching for his sweet Milena.

Everything was fine as long as Milena was working in the news department. Twice a day she would appear before the camera with the moist light of "oh-what-a-joy-it-is-to-see-you-again" in her eyes (because the viewers must be loved, as the director was always saying, and Milena knew how to do this; sometimes she even knew how to do it with her acquaintances, as long as she wasn't very tired) and read a text prepared by someone else, but that she occasionally improved upon, if not with words, then at least with her voice: Milena was unsurpassed at this or, to be perfectly honest, brilliant, and anyone who has heard her and remembers her from the screen will confirm it, so I'm not making anything up. With a voice like Milena's you could topple governments and parliaments in the evening and return them to their places of work by morning, and without any opposition from the electorate at that: her voice sparkled, shone, and spilled to overflowing in every possible hue and shade, from a warm chocolatey low-pitched intimacy to the metallic hiss of a snake, with an emphasis on the "s" (assuming that it is not just in stories that snakes hiss, and that it is true that anyone who hears that sound must die). It even had a few shades that no one knew yet to be possible, for example, the ozone freshness of dewy lilac at the start of the morning news (at half past seven), or ironic cinnamon spiciness (Milena had a particularly rich scale of ironic tones), or the kindly toastiness of a crust of bread that was reserved for government announcements, and if anyone considers everything I've been saying to be a metaphor, then they should try for themselves to pronounce after a day's training "President Kuchma met with the prime minister today" so as to make it sound sincere and even emanate domestic warmth, and then they will surely grasp why Milena, a woman who was on the whole as helpless as a sparrow, was fundamentally feared by her colleagues and her bosses alike and why, even though she never took liberties and always tinged the news with the colours she was expected to (Milena had always been an A-student, both at school and at university), the sweetly painful richness of her voice stubbornly pressed to the surface, radiating out onto her face barely discernible, coquettishly-secretive mimicking little grimaces, which naturally made her especially attractive, but which did not always agree with the text that she was reading, so that it could appear to someone who had just awakened, for instance, that she was thinking of sneaking in a snort of laughter in a thoroughly inappropriate spot, which she wasn't really thinking of doing, or else some other utterly stupid thing like that. In short, Milena was feared and even considered a good journalist, and so someone in some oak-panelled office had taken it into their head to give her her own show. And this is where it all began.

Actually, suspicious symptoms had appeared earlier, too, in her news-department days. Insofar as the news was broadcast on channel thirty-something, Puppydog (Pussycat, Kittycat, Cottontail) had nailed on with his own hands a specially acquired antenna (forty-five dollars, not including installation) outside the window, so that in the evenings he could watch his sweet Milena, because the building's common antenna got only the first three channels. Since then, lots of "nice shots," as Milena's photo-journalist husband (who puffed himself up into a "photographic artist" on his business cards) called them, had started to appear on TV, and he was now in the habit of spending his evenings in the bedroom with the door closed, as if he were in a darkroom – only the lighting there was, if you looked at it from the street, a ghoulish blue rather than red – picking over the buttons on his remote and hopping from channel to channel like a bank manager calling up subordinates on the intercom, and when Milena would poke her head into the half-light of the bedroom to ask him what to make for supper, he would show her his teeth, from the bed, coloured by the glow from the TV screen. After this they would often start making love. (Milena would turn off the TV at the critical moment.) Then her husband would go to the bathroom, and Milena would lie there face up and listen in wonder to the continuity of her life, thick as caramel, slowly moving around her in space.

And so one time when she came in from the cold, and straight from the hall into the bedroom, before she had even caught sight of the illuminated teeth, Milena heard a man's baritone greeting her from the TV screen with a booming "Good evening, love." It turned out that some atrociously-dubbed Brazilian soap was playing, and she and her husband had a good laugh at the surprise. Not long after, something similar happened to Milena's mother when she came for a Sunday visit. The two women's senseless jostling and tripping around the kitchen with their pots in an absurdist arrhythmic dance and their equally senseless jumpy conversation, all loose ends of interrupted sentences, cut off, dropped, and never picked up again, would tire her husband out quite quickly, and he would run off to the bedroom and lie low in front of the TV until the visit was over. Well, this time, his kind-hearted mother-in-law, who was looking for him in order to enlighten him (she'd just thought of it) as to the proper way of sharpening kitchen knives (on a step in the courtyard), headed for the bedroom herself and, just as soon as she had pushed open the door, from the twilight diluted by flashes swimming as if in an aquarium, a hysterical screen falsetto unexpectedly screamed at her, "Get out of here! Get out, I'm telling you! Do you hear me?" His mother-in-law forgot about her knives on the spot (then remembered them on the way home and telephoned from the streetcar stop, just when her daughter and son-in-law had turned off the TV because the tail, as its bearer had claimed, had grown quite big enough). And possibly the very next day, when Milena, worried because her period was late, pressed a button on the remote in the bedroom to take her mind off things, an unbearably brash little cartoon frog croaked out to her from the screen, "Don't cry, little girl, let me sing you a so-o-ong instead," and a cheery little tune poured out, and an hour later Milena's flow started. It was then that she had her first evil suspicion: someone had taken up quarters in the TV set.

She didn't know yet who it was exactly, and later, too, she only thought she had found out, because, as I've said, this was all happening back in the news-department days, before Milena started her own show, which did so extraordinarily well in the ratings so quickly. If anyone has forgotten, let me remind you: Milena talked with jilted women. There were old ones among them and young ones, pretty and ugly, smart and not very (Milena rejected completely stupid ones): a peroxide-blonde translator – fat legs, a short skirt, a plastic doll's light eyes – talked about how many men were fighting over her just then, while a Ph.D. in chemistry, whose profile could have been called Akhmatovian if she had known how to carry it, aggressively insisted that at that particular time she was completely happy, and only at one moment did her eyes tear up out of the blue, whereupon she pulled a handkerchief out of her handbag, fell silent, sniffled, and stuffed it back in again. Milena didn't cut those shots (not least out of some vague hope of moving the chemist's ex-husband to pity, in the event he was watching the broadcast). She had started with her girlfriends' friends – their classmates, hairdressers, and cosmeticians, friends from the nursery their children went to, and there's no end of occasions when women indulge in female confidences. Later, when the show was better known, the heroines came *en masse* themselves, just for the asking, and Milena simply marvelled – sincerely at first, and then in a dull conventional way, in conversations for the most part – at the insatiable lust for publicity human suffering carries within itself, and aren't we all so afraid of death because that is the one thing you can't share with anyone? She was proud of the fact that she was helping all those women to recut and resew (well, at least to rebaste) their own suffering into a style they could wear, sometimes even quite smartly. This had happened to her on one of the first shows, which had subsequently brought in a whole cartload of letters. An awfully nice little woman, dark-haired with barely a dusting of grey, mother of two boys and boyish-looking herself, her hair almost in a crewcut and her shirt probably borrowed from the older one, a librarian, in other words, with no money to speak of, but with a classy sense of humour, went on, spreading out something invisible in her lap the whole time, about how she would be raising her boys from then on so that they wouldn't grow up to be like their father, talking in a calm and measured way that made the camera operators convulse with laughter behind their cameras, and it really seemed that the father was a real asshole if he couldn't appreciate a clever little woman like that. Granted, everything didn't always turn out so well, sometimes quite the contrary, and in ways you'd never even think of. Milena couldn't sleep for two nights in a row and took corvalol and valerian with water when she found out that an ambulance had taken away one of her heroines because the day after the broadcast the stupid woman had gone and opened all the gas valves in her apartment. Everyone had a good scare that time. The director had even rushed off to consult someone about getting a certificate from a psychiatrist just in case, because you could tell the broad was a neurotic right off the bat, and her upper lip twitched on the right side, the camera brings out things like that like a microscope, there's no denying them. Here, evidently, Milena had got stung by her choice, but thank God, the whole thing had worked itself out. The dumb cunt had spilled her guts, who the hell wouldn't dump her? And why would you try so hard to get on screen, the producer spat out in puffs of smoke, if you can't even look in a mirror without your meds? Ahh, stupid broads! Milena took quiet joy in this gracious verdict, that it was not she who was being blamed, and then immediately felt ashamed of that feeling, and felt ashamed all day until her shame melted away. On the whole Milena was a woman of scruples, no matter what anyone said, and who would know better than I? So there.

That's what Milena's show was like, and she put it on, I'll say it again, with scruples. That is, she remembered well how she'd been taught at university that journalists must show not themselves, but their subjects, and if they wished to revel, if they wanted to all that badly, then not in themselves, but in their subjects. And she really did have a genuine interest in all those women and in peering over the fence into the abyss. As if to think what would happen if she ended up in their position herself, if her pussycat took off one day and left her for good, which was somehow unnatural, even stupid, for her to think to herself, much less imagine, as if your legs were unexpectedly to seperate from you and scurry off down the street on their own, and leave you sitting on the sidewalk on your legless rear end, but still, what then, what would she be like then, and how would she feel? To try something like that on for size in her mind was so alarming and terrifying that it made her dizzy (like when you were a child and listened to stories about robbers while cowering under your bedclothes, or like violent erotic fantasies, when you imagine being raped by a platoon of soldiers). Milena's pupils would dilate hypnotically on the screen, which, physiologists assure us, is in fact the main guarantee of attractiveness, and she'd cast spells to boot with her luminous voice, which ranged from the calming sensitivity of a sister of mercy *(tell us, please, tell our viewers and especially our women viewers...)* to the angry low-pitched rasp of solidarity of a fighting sister *(and you put up with all this for so many years?)*, although sometimes she could not manage without the stealthy purring cajolement of the temptress when a broad would suddenly close up and wouldn't say another word, wouldn't reveal any more secrets, and she'd have to crack her shell as best she could. Why, sometimes Milena would even let out one of those lascivious low-pitched giggles of encouragement, practically indecent, as if in love-making, brusque and irascible, as if to say, oh yes, my dear, oh yes, I've been there myself, well, and then what? That was usually how the most delectable bedroom morsels were got out of the heroines, after which the flood of letters and calls would rise to life-threatening levels. Milena didn't really like herself when she resorted to tricks like that, but the tainted feeling was more than compensated for by the lamps of professional triumph, all lighting up at once – look what I've done! – in which there were both beads of joyful sweat between her shoulder blades and captivated and envious looks from her colleagues – well, kid, you're an ace! – and that swelling sense of her own power, which comprised the main high, like the gymnast's from his absolute power over his own body: this way and that, I can do it any way. When she happened to be watching the show with her husband at home, then in those most drastic spots Milena, her sparkling eyes fixed on the screen, would unseeingly squeeze his hand white – *there, right there, there's going to be a tour de force in a second, listen!* – and, nervous and aroused, would giggle at every felicitous word that came from the screen, and he'd chortle, too, pleased and proud of her success. Their professional ambitions didn't overlap, and he had never photographed Milena, except well before they were married, back when they were dating, and even that was more as a pretext, because the static Milena was at a great disadvantage: her voice, her mimicry, the glint of quicksilver – that was her element, and not under any circumstances a stiff portrait, and Puppydog preferred to take pleasure in her live. For that matter he took pleasure in her portraits, too, and generally considered Milena a beauty, which was, of course, an exaggeration, even though there were others besides him who thought so, especially when Milena got her own show and nothing seemed to foreshadow any trouble.

Now they were planning to buy a satellite dish and install it on the balcony. This would come to about three hundred dollars, but it was worth it, because, although Milena conscientiously watched almost all her colleagues' shows, of course, Ukrainian TV couldn't satisfy her. Not that the Russian was any better, three-quarters of it ripped off from American models, while Milena was a patriot and always said that Ukraine must follow its own path. In fact it would be worth buying a second set, because her husband preferred to look at "nice shots," and there are more nice shots, obviously, in movies, and he would mumble a recap of their storylines, in two or three quick sentences – who's who, who's with who against who – in Milena's ear, up to the point at which she had come and snuggled at his side. His eyes glued to the screen, he would pull the duvet over her, gropingly tuck her in and gather her up to himself, tickle her cheek with his lips, and mutter, "This one here, the blond guy, he was abducted by aliens, but now he's come back." "Why did he come back?" Milena would ask absent-mindedly as she pressed against him, staring by now in the same direction, and so, after a little more fidgeting, they would fall silent and, lying side by side, would sink their eyes in the screen, and the third person in the room and the apartment was that Panasonic, so that as time went on the idea of buying another TV even began to seem a bit awkward and bizarre to Milena. Wouldn't it be just like splitting their bed or apartment? "After all, intelligent people can always find a compromise, can't they,

Pussycat?" Milena would say (which was to say: Pussycat would watch what interested her with her, and the rest of the time he would be free to amuse himself with his nice shots as he pleased), to which the smart Pussycat would call back cheerfully, like a soldier, "Yessir!" and just as cheerfully and resonantly smooch his sweet smart Milena: compromise had triumphed. But late in the evening Milena herself didn't mind watching something more entertaining and thus distancing herself from the many faces and many installments of women's misfortune with which she now lived out almost all of her waking hours.

Altogether, that misfortune was quite strange indeed – made-up, dressed up, and coquettish. (Some of the women plucked up the courage for such a forced familiarity in front of the camera that she was embarrassed for them. When that happened Milena would yell out a categorical "Cut!" to the camera operators and, muting her voice, would spend five or ten minutes "chatting" the overly emotional young lady down to a more or less normal state.) And yet, and this is what is interesting, every one of them was genuinely suffering, sincerely and unaffectedly, and Milena had even thought at first that slighted women went to these tapings mainly in the secret hope of bringing back their ex or at least getting revenge on him. For there were those who asked Milena whether it was all right to address him directly, and then in millions of evening apartments there would resound from the screen ever so movingly, "Sasha, if you can see me now, I want you to know that I've forgiven you for everything, and I hope you're happy." Whereupon Milena herself would get a lump in her throat: at that moment she could actually physically feel the choral, gurgling sob of the female half of the nation spreading out in space – crescendo, crescendo – and a dark wave of public anger, rising up (as if to smash an oppressive regime, as Russian TV used to say), swelling up, surging up at the unknown Sasha. "Bastard!" millions of lips would whisper; millions of noses would sniffle, and for a fraction of a second the country would stiffen in an orgasm of human sympathy. And this was all her doing, Milena's: she edited out the rest of the speech, because the speaker herself had not managed to stop with this exquisite opening. She had visibly been tossed about, like a car on a slippery road, and irresistibly drawn into the ditch – "Of course, you hurt me, and very badly, I still can't see how you could have been such a jerk, and after all I did for you" – throwing out ready-made phrases ever faster and faster, seething, rattling, and almost foaming from her bottled-up rage, predatory flames in her eyes, the hair on her head looking as if it would stand on end any second now, like that of a witch taking off in flight. In a word, the ultimate effect was completely opposite to the initial one. Milena's power was in presenting those women the way she saw them herself (better, of course, better!), and when she was unanimously chosen "show of the month" and in her own interview she said (focussing her attention on making sure that, God forbid, this didn't sound condescending) that to her heroines she was at once a girlfriend, a psychiatrist, and a gynaecologist this was, clearly, the absolute truth, which none of them could have managed to contradict. And yet Milena had a vague feeling that this was not the whole truth: something still remained unexpressed, some exceedingly important ingredient, like yeast in dough, had been left out. And so, something similar was probably happening to them, too. Even as their single, all-devouring intention of calling out one more thing in their ex-better halves' tracks drove them into the studio, somewhere at the bottom of each of them there still stirred, as an amorphous dark spot, a far more incomprehensible urge: they were flying towards the light of the screen like moths on the porch at the cottage on those humid

July nights towards the luminescent blueness of the old black-and-white Slavutych set, so that up close you could clearly hear the dry crackling of electrical charges or sizzled little wings. Did they (the women, not the moths, although who can know for sure what a moth thinks?) perhaps dream that by crossing over into that space beyond the screen they would get back the soul that a man had taken from them, and not just get it back, but get it back completely renewed, enormously enriched, basking in the glow of fame and raised up to unreachable heights above the lives they had lived until now, merged forever with the fantastic coloured shimmering of all the TV movies at once, so that Santa Barbara, Dallas, the Denver dynasty, and the snow-white villas on the shores of tropical seas would all become their own, something that had happened to them, since they were there too, on the other side of the screen, and their everyday existence would be filled with perhaps even a kind of divine meaning? Milena knew only too well from her own experience this magic of the screen: the spellbinding effect of your own face in the frame, unrecognizable in the very first instant, multiplied by itself a hundredfold in all its barely perceptible movements, and how it envelops you in a ticklish warmth, like a foam bath, and you soften, you develop and expand, warmed by the energy streaming from the screen, unexpectedly so much larger than life that you are prepared to believe for a moment in your own omnipotence.

"An energy boost," Milena's husband would say. "Just go and read about lepton fields." (He would clip articles from popular magazines and put them in a special folder.) "Why do you think that back at the turn of the century the Inuit would break ethnographers' cameras and run away from them as if they were evil spirits?"

"A camera is different," Milena would fling back, her face still flushed and her eyes flashing, sensing that if this comparison were taken to its logical conclusion she would end up as an ethnographer and her heroine as an Inuit. There was no way that could please her, and so her husband would silently and agreeably switch to a different channel, one with reruns (all the more so as on Milena's they were already running the last commercial), and the TV would aim at them the typical squinty look of a Soviet secret policeman, a chekist, and, as befits someone from the NKVD, he would say with paternal warmth in his voice, "I'm looking at you, and I can tell you guys are really good sports!"

Somehow both of them imperceptibly got used to the way the TV had gradually become an active participant in all their chats, why even, not infrequently, a counsellor and a referee, and they stopped bursting out laughing when, for example, during an argument in which Milena, irritated not so much by her husband's imaginary jealousies as by the fact that she wasn't allowed to relax even at home, kept shouting (still flattered) that that Italian, the one her husband said she'd been making goo-goo eyes at over dinner all evening, wasn't worth a fig and that all she needed was some Italian, as it was she could barely drag her feet into bed, at that very moment an elegant, well-built gentleman was coming into view on the TV (which they now had turned on almost all the time) and saying judiciously, "My dear man, these days most Italian men are homosexuals, so this isn't going to give you much mileage," after which the argument fizzled and they started kissing (noticing occasionally out of the corners of their eyes that the same thing was happening on the screen, only now lying down). Most of the remarks on TV showed it to be noticeably more cynical than either of them. It would jabber perfectly calmly, as if it were talking about something self-evident, about things that either of them would admit to the other only in a fit of self-reproach. This was highly salutary, they both thought, because once you've heard something like that from the screen, you no longer have to be ashamed and to pretend. Milena, for example, would never have noticed on her own, or even if she had noticed, then not anytime soon, that her husband, even though he was listening and nodding patiently, was beginning to tire of her constant complaining about the studio head, who, although he wasn't finding fault, because there was really nothing for him to find fault with, was still probably the only person who had never once openly shown any kind of enthusiasm or at least approval for Milena, whereby he greatly shook our A-student's courage, you could say he simply hobbled her, until she began to suspect that this demonstrative disrespect, as she saw it, concealed a behind-the-scenes intrigue, sabotage, a secret plot to take her show away from her, whereas Pussycat, on the contrary, expressed the assumption that the studio head simply had the hots for her and had chosen this way of keeping her in constant suspense, and so they kept dragging out this subject dully, always on the same point, and would perhaps have kept dragging it on until Pussycat lost his mind, until one evening the TV broke into a frenzy instead of him. No sooner had Milena started in on the studio head in the doorway, "He gave me a lift home, and what do you think, not a word about yesterday's broadcast, not a single word. No, I can't keep working like this," than she heard, "So unzip his pants and give him a blow job." The cool advice came from the TV in two languages at once, French and Ukrainian, from an awfully vulgar floozie. Stunned almost to tears, Milena had shut up after that on the subject of her studio head. Moreover, the TV seemed to intercept their thoughts even as they thought them, to abbreviate and edit them, sometimes even before they themselves set about thinking them through or elucidating their own true wishes to themselves. "Shall we hit the sack?" Milena's husband said as he put his arms around her and slid his hands down her back to her buttocks. She resisted a bit. "My script for tomorrow isn't ready yet." "E-ekh, my dear!" the TV intruded brashly, in the guise of a seasoned old broad from a Russian backwater. "How are you going to hold on to your husband if you don't keep putting out for him?" Hey, maybe that was true, Milena thought in alarm (a bit offended, though, at its being put so coarsely, and for Puppydog's sake, too: is a guy some kind of rabbit, heaven help us, for nothing else to matter to him?), but who can figure men out, no matter how long you live with them, you never know for sure, and so she finished that thought stretched out on her back, with her legs bent at the knees, as he was going into her heavily, without any rhythm somehow, and she wasn't getting anywhere, until she opened her eyes at last and gasped: rivetted to her with the lower, mobile half of his trunk, he was leaning on his arms and supporting the upper half in order to see the screen over the bedpost, bursts of colour running over his face, as in a discotheque, his eyes glued to it with a wondrous glassy look, and sweat sparkling on his upper lip. What? What is it? Milena wanted to shout, crushed by the weight of his body, which suddenly seemed to have tripled, coming down on her from above, by this humiliation, destructive as a steam roller, all the more destructive for its unexpectedness. Who was he with? Whereupon he moaned and came down, went limp, burying his face in her, now undeniably in her. Stunned, with mixed feelings of being laid waste and robbed, of sadness and reproach, she drew her trembling hand along his back, as if she were trying gropingly to put back in place the reality of her life, which just a moment before had vanished, disappeared into nowhere. "Who were you with?" she asked quietly, to avoid asking, what were they showing? because that would have been a direct complaint, almost a quarrel, whereas she was waiting for an explanation, a reconciliation, and apologies. But he didn't understand the question. He raised up his joyfully damp little mug in astonishment at her, glowing in full colour. "What do you mean, who with? What's the matter with you, Milena? With you. Who else would I be with, girl?"

Milena tried to forget this incident, squeeze it out, thinking that maybe she had really imagined it, like the studio head's intrigues. After all, immediately afterwards, turning over onto her stomach, she had begun watching a very pleasant police drama with her husband, with lots of female corpses, and when he trundled off to the kitchen to get something to nibble on, as he always did after they had made love, and then came back and asked her something, she mumbled in response without listening, and twice, when he was too persistent, she even snapped at him, "Don't bother me!" In the end then, even if she had had to stand up in court, for example, even she couldn't have sworn with one-hundred-percent certainty what had taken place in bed and what had taken place on TV. All in all, this sort of thing happened to them rather often. In fact, the TV not only interfered in their lives, but lived its own life, too, and an incomparably more vivid one at that, more festive, uniformly bright, and saturated on all nine channels at once, while the two of them each had maybe three or four (work, parents, friends) and only one joint one, and all of them, of course, were working in a slower and more boring way, with breaks, dark abysses, floating streaks of unnecessary moods surfacing from who knows where, and ghosts. Moreover, unlike them, the TV always had everything in order, and it was in an invariably chipper mood: each of its stories, however terrifying and bloody, always got a logical resolution; it never dropped anything in midstream in the cowardly hope that somehow everything would shake down all by itself, and it didn't leave behind any loose ends (relations that were not completely cleared up, unavenged life defeats, unrealized ambitions, unburied dead people, or any of the other baggage you take on in a lifetime!). It managed to put absolutely everything in order, to set out accents, and to insert titles and subtitles wherever they were necessary, so that it was actually a pleasure to watch.

There was nothing strange about it, then, that when Milena's husband had sold some wealthy magazine all the negatives he had shot in one lot and then the bastards had started dealing in his photos, and with no thought of sending him anything back, and he, like a pouty little boy, was telling Milena for the umpteenth time how he had once again seen a photo of his that day there and there, he had to repeat this speech umpteen times before Milena managed to tear her unconscious look away from the screen (on which a very nice Canadian newspaperman was just deciding to sue his boss, who had cheated him) and noticed at last that her husband and the TV seemed to be out of sync with each other and were even almost contradicting each other, and kept asking, "What? What?" The dialogue that continued between them may have sounded something like this:

Husband: I'm saying that they swindled me, that's what!

Milena: So why don't you take them to court?

Husband: What court, are you kidding? On what grounds? Why, they paid me over and above my contract. They threw me a bone, and now they're raking in as much as they want! (Milena steals glances at the TV.) With the taxes we pay if I were earning according to my contract, you and I would have been collecting bottles outside supermarkets long ago!

TV (in English and Ukrainian): There are no hopeless situations, man. We'll get the union together, we'll put our material in all the newspapers, we'll teach the beasts to respect the law!

Husband (confused): What trade union? What newspapers? What law?

Milena (shrugs her shoulders and turns back towards the screen).

And that, once again, is why it wasn't strange that neither of them noticed – and by the time Milena noticed, it was too late – what Milena's mother was the first to sense – and, as it turned out, the last – only, in her usual manner, she interpreted it the way she wanted to, and what she, who was still incapable of comprehending that a threesome in a home was, however you looked at it, a full set, what she wanted, naturally, was a grandchild. And so one morning she phoned and asked, with a happy girlish excitement in her voice, "Milena dear, I was watching you the whole time yesterday. Are you by any chance pregnant?"

"No," Milena said in surprise. "What gave you that idea?"

"Mmm, you seem to have gained weight. You were sitting there so nice and plump, and your face looked a little puffy or something."

For the second time in one day Milena, alarmed, weighed herself on the floor scale in her bathroom (a procedure she performed every morning) and even wondered whether the scale was broken, because her weight was, of course, stable – just like the day before, and the day before that, and the year before, and the year before that, and, after all, if she really had put on a bit of weight, who would have been the first to tell her if not Puppydog? Just in case, Milena decided to wait for Puppydog. (He would disappear until noon into his darkroom, and Milena would leave the house in the afternoon, so for the most part they wouldn't see each other until evening.) In the meantime she rushed to review the tape of the previous day's broadcast – with an elegant financier/economist, winning in every way, with a peppery dark Spanish beauty, who talked about how since her divorce she had been banging (she clung to this word insistently) only younger men and what a positive effect this was having on her self-esteem. Only this time, as soon as

Milena saw her all-conquering financier appear in the frame, she fast-forwarded in irritation, greedily picking out just herself, especially the close-ups: could that idiot operator have screwed something up? (Milena knew that in three-quarter profile her face seemed wider and rounded in a homely way, and in front of the camera she usually didn't forget this.) But everything seemed to be the same. And yet it wasn't. Even if she was neither puffy nor, God forbid, plump, the on-screen Milena was nevertheless in some ungraspable way different, as if her bones had thickened and the shapes that were emphasized by her homey pose – her arm on the back of the chair, her hip turned up from the way she had crossed her legs, and her skirt pulled taut over it – had jointly weighed down into a grotesque, Toulouse-Lautrec-ish monumentality that the delicate Milena had never ever had. It was somehow over-free and irritating, maybe even arousing in its own way, but only to a taste that was indeed very plebeian. What's more, things were even worse as far as her face was concerned, which conspiratorially switched expressions in unison with what the irrepressible financier hadn't even stated or rather hadn't finished stating. From a professional point of view this was an extra-classy job, of course, insofar as it set the viewers off in the desired direction (for which the off-screen Milena, moved and shamed, could not in fact congratulate herself). At the same time, though, there were moments when it demonstrated an almost indecent satisfaction – flowing out satedly in a half-smile, the eyes ready at any second, it seemed, to get bleared (which only Milena's mother, obsessed with her own idea, could have taken for the distant "wandering" look of a pregnant woman!), until, as if she were really pouting, puffing up either with herself, or because she was pleased with the way the talk was going, or, perish the thought, at her own and the financier's delectation in the muscular torso of her young bodyguard-chauffeur-masseur. Something dark and impure was looming in all this, its saturated slime poisoning the charge that Milena would usually get when she watched herself on screen. Her voice rocked, like thighs swaying, an aroused hoarse little laugh, a ticklish maculacy. What had happened to her voice? Where did this vulgarity come from that was poured into it, dammed up like a stale breath? "What a slut!" cried the off-screen Milena harshly, as if slapping her hand, suddenly sobered, as if she had been drenched with water, by the sound of her own voice that had thus been renewed, and to this very same sound the on-screen Milena slowly turned to her that insolent mug of hers, shamelessly beautiful, blazing drunkenly from the studio lights, with its kiss-swollen slit of crimson lips, and winked arrogantly, even almost triumphantly, flashing a grin as if to say: and so, what did you think?

Breathing quickly and for some reason holding onto her pulse with one hand, the off-screen Milena pressed "stop" and then "rewind" with the other hand. This time the on-screen Milena, turning her full face towards her, stuck out her tongue at her, and between those dark glistening lips it really did look completely repulsive – pale, as if it were naked, and even twitching at the end. The off-screen one pressed the pause button to catch the wretched woman with her tongue hanging out: let her sit like that for a while! But she missed: the frame went by, and the on-screen Milena, suddenly brought to a halt, froze and gaped in surprise like a tarty doll feigning offended modesty. She even pouted her little lips for a "tsk-tsk," as if she were on the verge of saying: bad kitty, you've hurt your sweet Milena! "Hey, you're teasing me!" hissed the off-screen Milena, stung to the quick, covered with a slimy scaly cold. "You just wait a minute, I'll sssssssho-o-ow you!" She clicked the buttons, almost to the rhythm of her own accelerated heartbeat, forcing the on-screen Milena now to revive and expire by turns, now to twist and twitch in a cheery marionettish shaking, now to move in slow motion like a sleepwalker, forcing herself to raise her hand, as if under the pressure of a hundred atmospheres, but none of it was any use – the other Milena did not reveal herself in any other way and turned into a very ordinary screen representation, persecuted for who knows what reason, so that God knows how much time passed before the off-screen Milena, who was already prepared to drop her schizophrenic pastime (that is, agree with the other whore that she had really dreamed everything here in front of the screen), heard the ringing of the telephone from a distance, as if through a layer of water, and picked up the receiver, also in slow motion for some reason, overcoming with that one movement the pressure of all hundred atmospheres at once.

"Hello," said an unfamiliar man's voice, clearing his throat, pushing onto her from the depths of the receiver like a storm cloud. "Hello, I need to talk to Milena." Now she felt a chill inside, too. This was how it had been in the dreams about a bear that she'd had as a child from which she had always awakened with a cry of terror: the bear was coming nearer, giant and dark, and covering her with his shadow.

"Speaking." She tried to defend herself with her voice, reflexively switching on a silvery secretarial timbre.

At the other end, after a thoughtful pause (as if he were aiming for a precise hit), an answer, with feigned awkwardness: "Listen, pussycat…Here's an offer for you. I'm tired of looking at you just on TV. In other words, call your girlfriend, the one from yesterday, and let's set a time, I'll come around. Don't get hung up about the price, I won't haggle."

"Who? What? How dare you? Who are you?" the off-screen Milena rattled off in outrage, at the same time as she was noticing with even greater outrage how the on-screen Milena, who could no longer sit still in her chair, had tensed up her whole body and started to play again. Her eyes flashing, with the impatient vibration of aroused giggling, she called out to the on-screen one, right in her face, in despair, just like an idiot, "I'll call the police!"

A nasty, authoritative laugh came out of the receiver. "No you won't, you fool. Better think about it, and I'll call back. I know where you live. And talk to your girlfriend. Don't worry, you'll like it."

"Go away!" the off-screen Milena shrieked, her voice completely squeaky now, but the receiver had been hung up anyway (whereupon she heard from who knows where snatches of the first few bars of Beethoven's "Für Elise" in an incredibly cynical, mockingly dance-like rhythm: pa-pa, pa-pa, pam, pa-ra-pa-pam! gurgling out, as if they were drunk, then someone very seriously grumbled, "Sorry," and the dial tone started dripping noisily, like water from a leaky tap). The receiver lay down quietly on its rest, and the off-screen Milena, just as quietly, in a voice that was white with rage, said to the on-screen one, "I'll kill you," obviously with no idea of what she was saying.

Because really, well what could she do to the other one? Even in the unconscious fever of the first hours – run somewhere, explain something, and argue every which way, saying, take a good close look, that's not me at all (make a statement on air! even as absurd an idea as that had crossed her mind, imagine!) – Milena stayed lucid enough to be coolly aware the whole time, somewhere deep down: the other one, even though she was itching to tear her off herself, like mangy skin, was still far from alien to her, and not just in her external likeness. In her own way, that other one was even very effective, far more self-confident than the first Milena, less restrained (that's for sure!) and, on the whole, ideally suited to her purpose. From a professional standpoint, it had to be acknowledged, she could not be reproached for anything at all, even though pent up inside Milena was a painfully vague recollection, lowing from the effort of trying to break out, that back when she was just starting the show, she had imagined her screen image to be different somehow – warmer, more radiant, or something. The kind of sincere women's sessions that go on in the kitchen nearly until dawn on the once-grasped and never again released crystalline-singing note of ever-deepening spiritual union: sister, sister, the pain is subsiding, you're not alone in this world, your children are sleeping in the next room, and life goes on, we'll be wise, we'll be patient, these are precious moments, like music, like love, because you do in fact love her at these moments to the point of stiffness, of numbness, your head reeling a little from the intolerably burning height of her suffering. Here there is tenderness, and pain, and pride in our brave and silent woman's endurance, and a beauty that is unspeakable to the point of tears, and that later glows from both of the women in the conversation for a long time yet (until the crowd on the bus rubs it off): that's what Milena, who had known no small number of such evenings in her lifetime, strove to obtain from her heroines and from herself. In one of the very first scripts (someone had later cut these lines without leaving a trace) this was called helping-the-Ukrainian-woman-find-herself-in-our-complicated-time. Well, and what had come of it?

On the way to the studio (she didn't stay put to wait for her husband after all: she needed to be in motion, she needed some kind of action) Milena covered her head with her hands and moaned: a sticky and, most importantly, undeserved feeling of defeat was festering in her. After all, she had done everything the way she was supposed to, she had made an effort and put herself out like a mad-woman, overworking herself so much that Puppydog had been reproaching her (recently, it was true, he had fallen silent), and now that odious creature was sitting in the studio, winking and hinting at something filthy, and, what was most important, no one, had noticed the difference! Well, yes, over the time of the show Milena herself had learned many new things, had grown professionally, as everyone said of her, and would no longer make fun, the way she used to, of her news-department colleagues, for really coming to life only when there were catastrophes, fires, or killings, and preferably atrocious ones. Even an idiot knows that if you want people to hear you amid all this wild noise of ours and not switch channels, then you have to either cuff them or tickle them in some intimate spot, and do it so masterfully, too, that they won't get jaded, that is, by changing your technique, and whoever says that's easy is simply envious and a failure, but!...There was, all the same, a "but." As the thought of that obscene complacent mug on the screen (oh, to smash it in!) washed back over her, Milena was blinded, as by a stroke of lightning, by a long tremor of hatred, very much like love, that ran down the whole length of her body. "What should I do now?" She mumbled to herself, ever so quickly, unconsciously speeding up her pace and digging her fingers into her coat collar, as if it were her enemy's throat: Milena was scared.

"Caw, caw, ca-a-aw!" she suddenly heard the cries above her. Milena raised her head: way up high, about halfway to the raw and empty sky that with springtime was already farther away, bare branches of trees were swaying in a feeble attempt at a Japanese drawing, a flock of startled ravens circling over them. "What a beautifully composed shot, and right to the point," she thought. "It's precisely on topic, and it doesn't need any editing." And so, from that moment, everything around her began unfolding smoothly, as on a TV screen, as if she had stepped out of herself into the space behind the screen where nothing more needs to be decided, just watched. In the corridors at the studio no one paid any attention to her, her preoccupied acquaintances hurried past, goggle-eyed and unseeing, and even in the stairwell not a living soul was lingering over a smoke. Here Milena remembered, with an instant unpleasant chill of humiliation, that she had dashed out of the house in a rush without her makeup, without even putting on lipstick, and she felt embarassed, as if she were in her bedclothes. At the same time she was glad that so far no one had intercepted her and she could surreptitiously slip out, dash home, put on some makeup there, and then come back with a respectable face, to meet the cheerful hubbub of greetings and noisy commotion of work switching on as usual as her appearance, starting with the guard by the turnstile down at the entrance, and then racing like a flame along a safety fuse to the elevator and up, up, along the corridors, running along loops into offices. The strangest thing was that for some reason the simplest and most obvious solution hadn't occurred to Milena, namely, to drop by the makeup women and to rattle off to them, panting, "Oh, I've been running. As you can see I've completely lost my face, so put some Indian war-paint on me, please," and even to visit with them a bit, smoke a cigarette, it was nice to take a break like that before starting work, especially because the girls liked her, followed her show religiously, and one, who was divorced herself, even boasted that she unplugged the telephone when the show was on so no one would interrupt. However, nothing even close to that dawned in Milena's confused mind, and she wandered through the corridors like a sleepwalker, an apparition, towards the service stairs: somehow she had decided that she just had to escape by the service stairs. As she walked she glanced into open doors, keeping her own face in the shadows, as if it were burned or something.

Suddenly the director charged out of a doorway right into her, his face distorted, and mumbled or hiccuped, in Russian for some reason, "Ex-excuse me." He wafted a sulphurous burning smell: a match, Milena gathered, noticing that a curl of grey smoke was unfurling above him as he fled into the depths of the narrowed perspective of the corridor. "The poor fellow's going to burn out some day," she thought, beside the point and without regret, for somehow she lacked not only regret, but any feelings at all, as if the light-bulbs meant for them had been unscrewed, leaving only the speed at which frames were changing or, rather, she was advancing involuntarily from frame to frame, through a flashing tape. There was no way she could stop, she had to keep moving, while any feeling, this she remembered quite lucidly, necessarily requires stopping and dropping out of the stream. Therefore, if one of them did by any chance come to life like a spark or a fidgety little flea, then she would immediately shake it off without stopping, letting it fizzle out all by itself and turn into ash in mid-air. Indeed, people sped this way and that, like comets, in intersecting sparkling cascades of tails as they burned out – more luxuriant behind some, more sparse behind others, whereby a constantly raised working temperature was maintained on the premises, and there collected over the years that fine, barely perceptible bluish-grey coating on the walls, faces, and floor that studio guests sometimes take for a sign of plain smokiness, when in fact even though it is a smokiness of sorts, it is however far, far from being that plain. What a wonderful job I have, Milena thought with pride or, more precisely, with an embryo of pride. The embryo of pride flared somewhere behind her back like a firefly, brushing imperceptibly against her cheek, and sizzled up on the floor, without developing into a thought. Milena carried her gaze ahead of her rapidly, like a camera: the corridor was running onto her, constantly breaking in unexpected turns, and flashing increasingly goggle-eyed faces to meet her, but the main effect was based on the fact that it was as if the camera were hidden, because no one saw

Milena. Actually there wasn't any time to see her, either, because the film was advancing faster and more jerkily and everyone was jogging or even galloping instead of walking. There now before Milena's eyes, that is, in front of her camera, the studio head's secretary, a long-haired blonde who was becoming short-haired as she went and then a brunette, miscarried, evidently a baby conceived just a minute earlier, which, with a gurgling froggish croaking that Milena found vaguely familiar, slipped out into the ashen twilight of the corridor and instantly disappeared, as if it had tumbled into the fourth dimension. "Could it be the studio head's?" Milena scribbled a question mark in her mind, the way she would have in the margin of a script, more for the sake of form, because she really wasn't in the least curious, and so the question took off after the wretched foetus that everyone had forgotten about. Milena did remember, though, that she was supposed to go out onto the service stairs and could only wonder, if the word is at all to the point here, why looking for them was taking her so long.

Suddenly the director popped out of a doorway again, now with a beard, using both hands to jostle ahead of himself, like a cart in a supermarket, two fat wenches, joined inseparably, as if they were making love, from which Milena concluded that one of them was in fact supposed to be her new jilted heroine, and the other quite the opposite, the rival homewrecker, and again she put an approving exclamation mark in the invisible margin. To liven up the show, it was a great idea, as long as they didn't get into a fight in the studio, although right behind them, wiping out any traces of them, there thundered past, in a fierce gallop, a sullen herd of men in identical dark grey suits with identical badges on their lapels. Milena didn't have a chance to look at them more closely. Some of the men were running, bending under the weight of banners with text that was running together in a blur, and the last one was actually carrying no less than the red-and-blue flag of Soviet Ukraine. But then dashing victoriously right after them, making echoes resound, came athletes melted together into a yellow-and-blue whole, only the first one, it seemed to Milena, who was by now a bit dazed from the onslaught of faces, was racing with a lit Olympic torch, and so the impression she was left with was cheerful and life-affirming after all. But here a shot of the grey sky and ravens was suddenly wedged in again: caw, caw, ca-a-aw! The branches swayed up high. Where had the ceiling vanished to? She had got a double exposure, Milena managed to grasp, and forgetting about her unmade-up face she grabbed the first prop that came to hand, a door handle that gave way at a light push and revealed in the doorway none other than Milena's own familiar studio: deep inside, cameras were all set for taping, and two chairs, lit up from all sides, stood on the set. One, for the guest, was still empty, while sitting in the other one, covering herself with the lid of her compact for one last look to check herself out, was some awfully familiar broad dressed in crimson, her knees roundly pressed together and put out ahead in a no less familiar way from under her skirt, like a shield. "Where have I seen her?" Milena fretted, noticing at the same time that the backdrop in the studio had changed, which is to say the show's logo, too: something like an ad for Revlon lipstick, with huge, moistly parted lips that promised either to surrender or to swallow you whole in one gulp, was hanging there now. And there was something else looming behind the chairs, in the unlit background, like a low couch or something, as in a psychoanalyst's office, but that she didn't get a good look at, because just then the woman in the chair took the compact away from her face, and glancing at Milena was her own face, that is, not hers, but that other one's, from the screen, only this time it was somehow improbably, simply not even humanly, even terrifyingly beautiful, as if from the days of silent films: the eyes flamed in dark rings; the lips blazed; the witch's eyebrows met on the bridge of her nose in a swallowtail, and her skin, matte with makeup, disdainfully immovable in the glaring light of the lamp, breathed with that heavenly peace that only the screen can really feign. "What have they been feeding her here to make her look like that?" Milena thought in the doorway, bewildered and still numb, while the other one looked at her in dissatisfied wonder, as if asking who the intruder was and even planning to clap her hands from her luminous height for someone to throw the pest out the door. "But this is my studio, and this is my show!" Milena almost cried out, on the verge of tears from the humiliation, and especially from her own looks, so out of place here, so plain she might as well be invisible, that instead of trying to argue with someone she could only run away, crawl into a hole, and not inflict herself on anyone's sight, because it was enough just to look at the two of them right now to say with certainty which one deserved a place in the studio – surely not this slattern by the doorway! But still, how did that scum dare, and where was everyone looking, the director, the studio executives, the viewers, after all, since when did she have all the rights around here?

On this last thought Milena had to step aside to make way for a procession crawling in from the corridor like a wedding: the director – now clean-shaven again! – the camera operators, and looming somewhere behind them not one but two makeup technicians at once, and other dark figures. They were all leading, or almost carrying, a young blonde, barely conscious from emotion, with a pageboy haircut, with delicately raised cheek-bones and a delicate sharp nose on which drops of sweat had soaked through the makeup. The blonde's eyes were still and glassy as if she were in a trance. They did not express anything themselves, only reflecting light from outside, and

Milena, I have in mind, of course, the one who was standing by the doorway, was stung by a vague recollection of having seen eyes like that before, in someone close (familiar, warm), and of that moment being connected to something extremely unpleasant. The blonde pageboy was stepping unseeingly, as if her legs were folding under her and she was on the verge of crashing down on her knees, stretching her arms out ahead of her with cries of ecstasy, because she was breathing quickly and her lips were moistly parted, practically like the ad on the backdrop, but it wasn't the backdrop that she was staring at so unblinkingly, like a calf at the sacrificial flames, but – Milena herself went numb, too, following her gaze – at that other one on the set who was now poised to meet her, like a panther about to leap, and was luring the new arrival with a smile so greedy, so evil, and yet so lush playing on her lips: come on now, come on, closer, closer – as if she were drawing her to herself like a spider, step by step, along an invisible gluey tautly-stretched hair, until Milena could hear it humming. Or maybe it was the hum of the switched-on equipment, hastily filming the blonde, who had already been caught by her blouse collar on the hook of the microphone, as she neared the set and raised up to the voracious witch in crimson – a crimson at once vibrant and fluid, as if it were filled with blood – her prayerful, incredulous hands, "Ave, Caesarina!", and as the other one leaned down with an impetuous twist of her torso, to hold her up, "Come to me, and I will soothe you," literally to snatch her, suck onto her because the poor thing was reeling, was ready to fall to the ground at the feet of her deity from a surfeit of emotion, no, she was really going to kiss her on the hand! "Music!" someone called out breathlessly, running past Milena in the dim light and just missing pushing her into the plywood cubes, boards, and other rummage stacked up against the wall. "Don't forget the music in this episode!" "Fuck off!" answered a nasal voice clearly out of the dark. It was this sound that made Milena suddenly realize that something horrible was about to happen on the set, something so unthinkable even to her own imagination that she just had to switch channels immediately. And, turning over in her mind like a mill-wheel the mindless phrase, "What's going on, what's going on, what's going on?" Milena lunged through the doorway back into the hall.

"She's going to slaughter her." The next thought caught up with Milena on the run in the middle of the hall. "She'll simply lay her out on that couch and slaughter her, chop her into little pieces with a knife, and that foolish woman will expire with a humble smile on her lips. All of them in there, have they gone mad, can't they see what's coming?" She ran through the whole production in her mind and hardly had any more doubt that things were really heading towards some kind of ritual killing that had to be brought to an immediate stop. According to the script Milena was the one who had to do it, and that was why she hadn't managed before to find her way to the service stairs: now that it had been wound up, the plot was evidently unfolding according to the strict logic of TV. The revelation could not help inspiring Milena to decisiveness, even enthusiasm, and she tried to return to the terrible studio, but this turned out not to be all that simple. Once again the interminable corridor bored into her view, breaking out in dark flashes of turns, and people were running about. Suddenly she ran into the noisy throng of a whole company, leading Kyiv actors, all of them in wheelchairs for some reason. They jostled her and pressed her with her nose up against a brass plaque that was cold to the touch (and covered to boot, like a windshield with breath, with a greying sticky film of that TV ash) and on which Milena, forcing herself to lean away, just from an instinctive revulsion, unexpectedly read, to her great delight, the words "Studio Head."

"Why, of course, that's who's supposed to put a stop to this outrage!" With renewed zeal she managed to feel her way to the door knob and burst in. The secretary wasn't in the reception area, she had probably stepped out for another abortion, the door to the office was unlocked, and the studio head really was in. Milena saw him from behind, with his back turned to his desk, a very wide oak table, about the size of a Soviet Khrushchevera vestibule, grandly authoritarian, at the very sight of which Milena and, let it be known, not she alone, had always experienced a vague erotic arousal, marvelling at the same time how authority can be so sexual even when represented by a table. At the moment, however, it was not the table that had her attention, but the studio head, to whom something strange was happening. Black netted wings, folded like a grasshopper's or a dragonfly's, were growing straight out from the stiff shoulders of his suit jacket. They were moving, preparing to spread, and the grey suit was jerking between them, comically flapping its rumpled vents. The next moment the wings moved decisively, letting out at the ends something that looked like bird beaks, and turned right before bewildered Milena's eyes into two outstretched woman's legs in net stockings and black pumps with pointed heels. Milena must have made a muffled sound because the studio head made one too. He looked behind him and froze in his unfastened trousers at the sight of Milena. Meanwhile, opening up to Milena behind the studio head was an entirely different sight that caused her to think, for the first time in her life, in a very agreeable way, "Hey, I'm going mad, nothing to be afraid of, it's even interesting." At first, a crumpled spot, a familiar crimson, flashed through her mind in a single strident smear, then something horrible flashed by in stripes, naked and hairy, and when she had a good look, it was her own unrecognizable face. She, that bitch from the studio, was now ensconced on the studio head's table with her legs triumphantly thrown up in a V-for-victory worthy of a rally, waving one of them in the air as if she were conducting an inaudible orchestra and watching Milena with no expression at all by now, as if she were an insect or something.

"Excuse me," Milena muttered stupidly, and the studio head, too, holding up his trousers, moved his lips in mirrored obedience, echoing her, but then he was impatiently pushed by a swinging black-netted leg with a heel, and a harsh cry rang out, like an execution order. Milena had never heard herself make such a sound as long as she had lived. "Well, what are you stopping for? Give me more! More! More!"

The head ohhed, twitched, and coughed up his half-swallowed "Excuse me" over his shoulder in Milena's direction, and again two netted black folding wings squeezed and pinched him from both sides, and he obediently resumed trotting to that savage, unrestrained whoop of "More! More! More!" Also shaking, with a repulsive, dry shiver from deep within her gut, Milena shuffled blindly out of the office and shut the door tight behind her: an utterly futile gesture, because the whoop was not in the least silenced thereby, but kept roaring in her ears, and the ceiling collapsed into oblivion from it, and there, flying up above the swaying black boughs, cawing, were the ravens. There was really nothing more to be done at the studio.

Just as soon as she understood that, right away Milena found herself on the service stairs: now the gigantic multistorey digestive tract of the TV studio spewed her out easily, without any resistance. And the sleepy, very sleepy thought stirred heavily that maybe it was for the better (on the stairs for some reason Milena had started getting terribly sleepy). Maybe that's how it should be, why, that other Milena (now she was finally agreeing to recognize her, calling her by her very own name for the first time), that other one had gone farther than she herself, without her, by nature, would probably have dared. No, she certainly wouldn't have dared to act this way (her thought was interrupted by an exhausted yawn so wide it drew tears) – stopping at nothing, with no scruples, taking on all the dirt. She felt a relaxing warmth embrace and rock her: let, let someone caring and strong do everything for her, and then she...later...later...later...), and now fully a queen and no longer the perpetual A-student, like *some people* – she reproached herself for this in the tender grumbling tone her husband used – and dissolved into a smile, blinking her way out of her insuperable, deathly fatigue: to sleep, to sleep, pressed up against Puppydog, his broad barely-furred chest, one sleepy hand feeling its ticklish growth and the other cradling his warmly swollen tail, Puppydog would put his arm around her, mm-m, sunshine, my golden pussycat, calm her with the touch of his lips, a last bedtime kiss, "I love you," Milena would say to him from the far shore of sleep, and all the others, well, to hell with them and all their games, their shows, and all their insane broads. And that was what Milena dragged herself home with.

It was dark at home, and only a low, bluish-grey light was seeping through the new stained-glass bedroom door into the front hall. Milena was astonished momentarily by the new door (when had her honey had time?) and by the whole ungraspable, disturbing feeling of unfamiliarity that one's own home evokes after a long absence (how much time had passed, anyway?), reached for the knob in the usual spot, was astonished once again, in the very skin on her palm this time, when she found it on the other side, groped about, and finally went in.

And saw.

That is, heard.

That is, simultaneously both saw and heard:

Milena: (from the screen, still wearing crimson and her legs in the same victorious "V"): Give me more! More! More!

Husband (on the bed): Just a moment, Milena, hang on, love, hang on....

Milena (from the doorway): No! Get out! What are you doing? You're mine! He's mine! (Undecipherable from that point).

Milena (from the screen): Well, look at that! Look! Look! Oooo, what a turn-on! See? See? And now you do me, come up and do it, use your tongue, hear me, girl? Use your tongue, they all do me that way, all those manless broads, and they all rave from it, right on the air, the highest rated show, two million letters a month. More! More! More! Use your tongue, I said, your tongue, there's no other use for you anyway. More! More! More!

Milena (from the doorway – she comes closer, takes the remote, and turns off the TV).

Husband (rabid): What? Who? Who are you?

Milena: I am Milena. Your wife.

Husband: Fuck off! (Grabs the remote and turns on the TV.)

Milena (from the screen, sitting in a chair raised high on the studio set): My beloved! My dearest, my sweetest viewers, and above all my women viewers, my brothers and sisters, I turn to you once again – I, Milena! I am the one who comes into every home to remind you that there is no earthly woe that cannot be conquered by the great force of our coming together! I am with you, my sisters. Anyone who feels lonely and abandoned this evening, cheated and hurt, come to me, and I'll satisfy you! I'll let you have a bite of my flesh and my blood, my sweet flesh and even sweeter blood, and your hearts will be filled with great joy, and you will be avenged on those who have hurt you, they will gnash their teeth and gnaw the earth in their impotent rage, for as long as they live they will never know the joy that is yours and mine, sisters! Here she is, my beloved sister who will be in the studio today with me and with you, here she comes now, come, my dove (a church hymn starts playing), come, my sweet, my body is waiting for you, loving you, as no-one-has-loved-for-thousands-of-years, oh come!

But she has no body, the other Milena suddenly thought, and it seemed that she had cried this out loud. "She has no body, do you hear me? This is all an illusion, a terrible fraud. This really used to be my body, and still is even now, and there is no other nor can there be." And, as if she were looking for proof for herself, she grabbed a knife, her husband's beautiful pocketknife, a Swiss knife with a tiny pair of tweezers and a bone toothpick in the handle that was lying open on the night table – but then it was possible that she was simply in great pain at that moment, realizing that she, too, had been jilted, the impossible had happened, dreams had come true, and she was finally united with the throng of all the countless women towards which she had been heading so unswervingly from the outset, and therefore unconsciously lunged to outscream one pain with another, louder, but easier one, as people often do when they thrust even rather different objects in themselves. The blade laughed blindingly in the teleblaze, its teeth wide open over the naked forearm, and then from the forearm there streamed, and ran, and even began to drip something inky-dark, the colour of a blank night-time screen and with a shine like that of a metallic, greyish oily film, which crackled with sparks sputtering...

And that, my beloved viewers, is the end of Milena's story, and it's almost time for us to say goodbye. May I remind you that I'll keep looking forward to your responses and that the authors of the most interesting ones, that is those of you who suggest the most captivating, boldest, most dramatic stories for us to look at from your own lives, will be invited to the studio to take part in our upcoming broadcasts. The show goes on. Don't miss your chance! I am waiting for you – I, Milena.

CANADA

ORANGES

BARBARA SCOTT

In my grandmother's kitchen there are no Ukrainian Easter eggs, their geometric lines poking fun at perfect ovarian curves, no Orthodox icons in a sensuous riot of colour mocking any attempt at strict asceticism. There are no traces of Ukrainian costume; those glorious colours and streamers are never seen, not even on special days. It was all my grandmother could do to trade in her pilled-over brown rayon pants and green acrylic sweater for a sagging green wool skirt and a navy cotton shell before heading to bingo on Wednesday nights.

On the sideboard in my grandmother's kitchen, children and grandchildren are framed in cardboard, grey, navy, and black. There are no shiny appliances on the counters, no spots on the speckled linoleum. No wooden plaques with rhyming kitchen prayers on the walls, no coiled throw rugs on the floor. It is a kitchen marked by absence, bare of decoration, bare of colour, bare of all that could be called bohunk.

The strongest surviving presence in my grandmother's kitchen, now that my grandmother is no longer there herself, is the smell of food – the holubtsi, pyrohy, sausage, sauerkraut soup, and borshch that we heated up yesterday. She had enough food in the fridge, freezer, and pantry to take care of her own wake. She would have been proud.

The wake was yesterday. Today, my mother and I inhale the fading aromas and finish washing up the dishes. The chrome sink gleams; the dishtowel, folded neatly in thirds, not in half, hangs with edges trim under the sink. The last time the three of us were here together, I watched with open mouth as my grandmother elbowed my mother aside, "Out of the way, Karolka, I can do it better myself." The source of tradition, a piece of the puzzle locking into place, the same words ringing down long years of my childhood, but from my mother to me. This kitchen is also where I learned the source of another tradition: my habit of slicing potato peels so thin you can see through them. It is a custom born in the Depression, and useless to cling to now, but I remember my pride on the day I first held a slender shaving to my own kitchen window in Vancouver, first saw that murky glimmer. My grandmother's smile.

My mother sits at the kitchen table, peeling an orange, breathes from the clear green plastic tube that coils from her nostrils and hooks her up to a black box twenty feet away. It chortles and chugs and keeps her oxygen levels high enough to sustain life. We have been looking at photos; the cheap plastic cases are spread over the table. "When I was young..." she says. And I lean my elbows on the table while my mother talks past the phlegm in her lungs and mouth, past the tubes in her nose. "When I was young," she says, "I loved oranges even better than candy. You couldn't get them more than a couple of times a year in Kelvington during the Depression, and even then my family could never afford them. I didn't taste one until I was seven, and I thought it was the most wonderful flavour in the world. Later on, though, I discovered tomato sandwiches."

WHEN HE READ THE FIRST TEN PAGES of the family history my mother wrote for the Kelvington town history book, my husband Leon, who is at the funeral parlour settling the last few details, said, "I don't know. It's just a bunch of detail with nothing *behind* it. I don't get a sense of where you come from, what your background is, who your people were." My people. Sounds like Bostonians with several generations of gracious living behind them, not like the Ukrainian immigrants who scratched out a living in the dustbowl of Saskatchewan. This is the kind of cliché my mind slides into whenever I think back to the rare and infrequent stories my mother has told me. They scroll before me in black and white or sepia, not like those art movies that load every shadow with meaning, but like the photos on the table – flat, with a scratchy finish. My grandfather is Henry Fonda, with jutting chin and stoic bearing, my whole family stiff with peasant dignity – the Joads, but with Ukrainian accents. They stare into colourless sunsets and angle park by the drugstore in clouds of grey dust. In my mind the drugstore always has faded wooden boards curled by the dust and dry heat, and, inside, my mother is always thirteen, wearing a scratchy flour-sack dress. She is also in black and white. But the tomato sandwich frozen halfway to her mouth drips red juice and one yellow seed onto the arborite counter.

WHEN LEON SAYS "YOUR PEOPLE," so pat, so easy, I see a family history whole and entire, custom wrapped and handed down like an heirloom, something rare, to be handled reverently, with love. When Leon says "your people" I see *his* people, and I think, "Easy for you," coming from that long line of born story-tellers. My family hand down nothing whole and entire. Like the photographs, they offer to the world and to me only the smooth face of an eternally trapped present. But occasionally the flat surface buckles and tears, occasionally it lets things slip, so that my history is something I have had to put together piece by piece, segment by segment.

SPIRALS OF ORANGE PEEL wind over my mother's knuckles, drop over her wrist to the arborite table. She has lovely hands, fine-boned with delicate nails. Her skin, loosened by age, sits so lightly on those bones you could almost believe yourself capable, if you dared, of peeling it away in pliant sheets, of tracing the bright red pumping of arteries, the blue tangle of nerves.

"The first time I ever tasted an orange," she says, "was in the late part of the Depression. When your grandparents were running the store on main street with your great-uncle Mike and his wife, my auntie Daisy. Your grandma's sister, she was. I wouldn't have been more than seven. They kept a canning jar on the top shelf for spare coins. No one ever took money out of that jar without all four adults agreeing to it. It was a communal jar, and all decisions made concerning it had to be communal. This was mostly your grandfather's influence of course, coming out of his commitment to Marxism.

"Anyway, there I was in the grey wool bathrobe that was all I had for a winter jacket, and the rubber boots that were all I had for shoes. The boots were so big I had to wear three layers of your grandfather's grey work socks to keep them from falling off. Of course, there were care parcels from the Red Cross, but somehow the stuff inside never made it from the English families, who all knew the railway worker Mr. Thomas, to the bohunks across the tracks.

"December first, a box of oranges arrived at the store. A kind of miracle, especially at that time of year. They cost ten cents each. More than a loaf of bread. Mrs. Thomas came in with her daughter Jennifer in their fur collars and button-up boots and ordered a dozen. Your grandmother watched them leave with the oranges, and then she looked at me. All week all we had eaten was baked potatoes with the skins on and some home-made cottage cheese. She did what she could to give the meal extra flavour by sprinkling it with the dill that she kept layered with salt and frozen in a jar by the back door. All the same, I was staring so hard at those oranges my stomach hurt. And she gave me one. Paid for it, too, by stealing a dime right out of the jar."

AND I CAN SEE IT ALL, pint-sized canning jar, with a red rubber sealing ring and glass lid and the raised letters in bubbles of glass on the sides. The pile of coins, their slow and painful pilgrimage towards the rim. Pennies mostly, from bright coppers to greenish-black lumps, but sometimes a nickel or even a dime flashing a defiant silver from beneath layers of tarnish. I see the oranges, each in its wrapping of tissue paper, the smell a wild and sweet possession. Her mother packs them, one by one, into a brown paper bag, and the other woman scoops the bag under her arm, handing an orange, carelessly perhaps, to her daughter. The door opens and slams; a wedge of light and a cold blast of air cut across the worn floorboards and are gone. My mother's rubber boots scuff the bare wood floor; her eyes, wet with longing, are fixed on the fruit's warm glow. She is the little match girl staring through a frosted pane, Lillian Gish locked out in the snow.

Her mother's face like ice when it has frozen too fast and cracked. The lines waver, shift, harden. She reaches one hand for the jar, the other resting at her lips to keep her daughter quiet. The ring of the till, the rustle of sweet-scented paper. And then an orange is smooth and heavy in a fine-boned hand; tangy and sweet on an urgent tongue. And for a moment, quick, before it vanishes – I am there too, awkward in the grey wool bathrobe that is two sizes too small for me, reaching for the peel drying in the sagging pocket. Never quite touching.

"FOR THE LONGEST TIME whenever I tasted an orange I could see her hand reaching for the jar." My mother's eyes are fixed on the orange, her fingers toy with the scraps of peel before her. "Your grandfather was very angry when he found out, her going behind his back like that." She pauses. "They were never really suited to one another. He was an intellectual. She loved to garden and can and had no time to talk. She and I would spend all day in the kitchen, making pyrohy." There they are, cutting out perfect rounds of soft pyrohy dough with a glass, pressing a mound of warm potato mashed with cottage cheese into the centre, then crimping the edges to form warm, soft pillows. "Then your grandpa's friends would come over at night and eat them with melted butter and onion. I remember sitting at the table with your grandfather and his friends, listening to them talk politics, government, revolution." Feel the fists banging the table, see the golden butter drizzling down their chins. "Sometimes they let me eat with them – back then I could eat twenty pyrohy at a sitting, for all I was only five feet tall and just out of the San with one lung lost to TB."

My mother adored him, you can see it even now in the slight tremble of lip, glisten of eye. There she sits at the table laden with food, sits not with the men but slightly off to one side so that she can stare undisturbed at his animated face. They are freedom fighters, firm of chin and stern of eye. And she glows with their reflected glory like Ingrid Bergman, all misty with emotion and soft light. And my grandmother? Perhaps that is her at the stove, with her back turned. Or maybe that is her in shadow, watching from the doorframe.

My mother lifts the pale green hose from her nostrils briefly, wipes at them with a Kleenex, returns the hose. "Your grandmother never really wanted to marry your grandfather. She wanted to go to high school, she was only fifteen. But they were living in a two-room house. A shack really, I've seen pictures of it. There simply was no money, for food and clothing, let alone for school. She was the oldest of four children. It was just easier for her parents if she got married. And so she did. Of course, your grandmother didn't tell me any of this. Auntie Daisy told me. She thought I should know."

THE LAST TIME I SAW MY GRANDFATHER he pulled me on his knee where I perched awkwardly, afraid to let him bear my full weight. I was fifteen. He was crying. He had not seen me for three years. Over and over he said, "Honest to God I cry, Blane, honest to God." Sometimes I can still feel the scratch of his beard against my neck. But then I only wanted to get away from the crush of his embrace.

THE ONLY TIME I SAW MY MOTHER CRY was on the long drive home from Kelvington to Calgary after my grandfather's funeral. We stopped to see my grandmother on our way out of town, and as my mother told her about the service, my grandmother's face was all bone. Nothing pliant to shift or waver, nothing to see behind. Two hours out of Kelvington my mother pulled over and stopped the car, crying into the steering wheel with the hoarse sobs of someone unused to crying, "God, doesn't she feel anything? I'm so afraid I'll end up like her. Dead. Just dead." But when I put my hand on her arm, she snatched it away and started the engine, scrubbing roughly at her face.

"HE WASN'T A BAD MAN," my mother says, more to herself than to me. "But times were so hard then. My aunt once told me that when they first got married your grandma used to paint *pysanky*, Ukrainian Easter eggs, that she had a whole basket of them, all in beautiful intricate designs. And one night Auntie Daisy brought Mike over to introduce him to her sister. They had just started going out. Well, Mike had brought a bottle of vodka with him and one thing led to another and pretty soon your grandpa got into one of his tirades, ranting about the revolution and how it would smash these old customs and religious rituals once and for all. The opiate of the people and all that. He got Mike going pretty good too. Daisy tried to get your grandmother to go with her into the other room, let them get on with their drinking and raving. But your grandmother shook her off and stood there looking at your grandpa, arms tight across her body and lips carved shut. He yelled at her to get out, and still she stood there, completely expressionless. Staring. And then he stopped yelling and picked up an egg and held her eyes while he hefted the egg in his hand. And still fixing her with his eyes he threw the egg against the wall. Your grandma didn't even flinch, not once, as one after another he smashed them. Every one. Some of them just exploded into fragments, but some of them hadn't been blown; green and brown slime ran down the wall. And still she stared at him. Auntie Daisy said she didn't even make a sound, just mopped up the slime and bits of eggshell with an old rag. But the stench of rotten eggs hung in the house for days. And she never made another *pysanka.*"

I clear my throat. "Why didn't she go home to her parents?"

My mother hesitates. Swallows. "It's so hard for you to understand. The way things are today. The things we had to do back then, just to stay alive. Dramatic as that sounds, I know." She smiles briefly. "I think she did try to go back. I think that's why we didn't see much of my grandparents when I was growing up. But what could they do? They had other children."

THE PHOTOS AT MY ELBOW are of my great-grandparents, whom I never knew. They are dressed in traditional Ukrainian costume, which I have never seen on any of my relatives. The photos, which we found at the back of the bottom drawer of the sideboard, are in sepia, the colour drained, the intricate patterns of the costumes barely discernible beneath the yellowing and cracking. There is something preternatural about the grimness of their expression. Their stoic bearing. Their impenetrable silence. No wonder my grandmother locked them away.

WHAT I WANT TO SAY IS "What else did he smash?" The night he counted the money and found one dime missing and the smell of orange on his daughter's breath. Is there a point in this story when the crack of eggshell shifts to the crack of bone on bone, when bits of coloured shell cower beneath splashes of bright red? And you, Mother. Are you there, somewhere in this story, somewhere I cannot follow, hiding, with your hands over your ears? There is no frame large enough for this story, no filter that will help me see what, in the end, I do not really want to see. And for this, I want to say, I am sorry.

Some traditions are too strong. I say nothing.

My mother rubs weakly at the smudges under her eyes. I think she would like me to touch her, to hold her even, but her body looks too brittle. I can't brave the attempt. And then I think, perhaps it is I who am too brittle. Too well-versed in lessons from a tomato seed, a scrap of warm dough, a bit of rind in a bathrobe pocket. As my mother has said, and probably her mother before her, we do what we must. But I will dare what I can. I reach towards her, take the orange from her hand and section it carefully. I offer one segment to her, place another in my mouth. Then we wait for the flavour to burst upon our tongues.

Myna

MARY BORSKY

Myna is up to ladies' girdles when Lester comes back in. The noise of the pump pours into the room, then muffles a bit when he shuts the door.

Myna chooses the girdles almost at random, flipping the pages of the catalogue as she places her square finger quickly in turn on each one she's picked. With the brassieres she takes longer. The models are lined up sideways and overlapping, like the ribs of a fan, displaying a rainbow of available colours. There are scientific-looking cross-sections of some of the features available, padding, wiring, bone inserts. Some of the brassieres have little trapdoors, that can be unlatched to feed a baby. Myna stares at these, but when she chooses, she chooses the strapless black from one page, the low-cut lacy apricot from the next.

"Do you ever play this?" Myna asks Lester. "What you do is, you pick one thing from each page. One item per page, period." She flips to men's shirts and slides the catalogue across the table-top toward him. "Here, you try it," she says, grinning up at him.

Myna's smile is her best feature; Miss Kay, her typing teacher had said so when Myna was still in school and still in Miss Kay's typing class. Miss Kay was young and pretty and from England. She hardly ever yelled at the class, although once she'd gone three days without speaking, writing instructions on the blackboard only. Sometimes she stayed after school to talk to the girls and gave them tips on what to do at a dance if you weren't dancing (smile), how to make yourself look thinner (tuck in your pelvis), or what to do when you're smarter than your boyfriend (don't let him know). For example, if your boyfriend got his car stuck in the mud, you should say, "This silly car!" and not blame him, even if it was his fault.

Myna was happy to have these tips. Herself, she probably would have got out and pushed. That's what her mother did. Myna was glad to be tipped off.

Miss Kay had said Myna had good bone structure and should walk as if she were carrying a basket of cherries.

Myna would rather have been small and delicate. Her ears were delicate, though. Buddy had said so. "You've got ears like a china doll," he'd said. It seemed a shame to have her good looks wasted on her ears.

Lester shifts in his gumboots inside the door, but doesn't move to sit down with the catalogue. The toothpick in the corner of his mouth moves out, in, out again.

"I was thinking," he says above the noise of the pump, then stops. He pushes the peak of his cap back with a finger. His face is red and lined, but his forehead above the line of his cap is pale, blue-veined, almost private-looking. "What I was thinking," he says, one side of his mouth clamped on the toothpick. "Come on to town. Pick what it needs. Shirt. Pants. Hat. Maybe." He looks at her with his pale blue eyes, then quickly down at the floor. He rubs his hand over his mouth and chin.

Myna stares hard at the calendar on the wall beside Lester's shoulder. She is thinking about how Lester noticed without seeming to notice, and about whether that makes him sneaky or polite.

Finally she stands up. She guesses it's not exactly a secret now. She feels settled, like she has folded something, and put it in a drawer, for the time being at least.

"Diapers," Myna says, steadying herself on the edge of the table. "It needs diapers, pins, and some of those little matching outfits from the Red and White."

The pump shuts off. The silence in the room is sudden and heavy, and there is a faint smell of kerosene.

"Wee-el!" Lester says. He wipes his mouth on the top of his hand and grins. His toothpick bristles up like an exclamation mark.

Myna changes to her best, which she's glad now that her mother threw out on the road, that night she'd figured out about the baby. The dress is not home-made. Myna bought it herself at the Red and White with the money she'd saved up from waitressing. It has a blue velvet top with rhinestone buttons and a flowery satin circle skirt. The large blue flowers on the skirt are flecked, as if with dew, by glittery blue sequins. The dress is good enough to wear anywhere, although up to now Myna has saved it for Saturdays when the girls dress up and walk with each other uptown past the Co-op and the Red and White, the barber shop and the beer parlour, then past the Elite Café, looping back down on the other side of the street past the pool room, Ikie's garage, and the Roxy Theatre.

Myna can get the dress over her head now, but the zipper at the side won't do up. Then she remembers the stole. It will cover the zipper. It's June, but it's early, and the mornings are still cold. Why not go in a real lady?

Buddy gave her the stole, a fur, he called it. White fox, he said, and it was in fact slightly yellowish, the way a winter rabbit can look, running across a field.

Myna had worn it to school with a straight purple skirt, seamless nylons, black spikes, her stomach sucked in and her hair bobby-pinned into a French Roll. The Grade Twelve girls in the washroom had said it was a fake, but they were jealous. Buddy was really cute with wavy black hair combed back into a ducktail. He didn't dress like the boys in high school though, with plaid shirts and bluejeans or work pants. Buddy wore dress pants and dress shirts with the sleeves rolled up to the elbow, like the other businessmen in town. He was through with school, ran the Angeline Rooms, and drove his own car, a two-tone yellow and black Pontiac.

Lucky for the stole, Myna thinks, and twirls around as best she can, watching the skirt circle and glint blue sparks around her.

Lester has the horses harnessed by the time she gets out, and an extra blanket on the seat. The seat is so high and the ladder so steep, he has to help hoist Myna up.

"Hang onto the seat there," he grunts. "Now put your foot on the other rung! Hang on!"

"Don't go getting a heart attack," Myna says, settling herself.

Lester climbs up beside her and takes the reins. The horses strain and brace themselves because the water is heavy and they have to go slightly downhill to the road. The dripping wagon creaks and lurches, and Myna grabs the rail in front of them once or twice because it feels for a moment as if they might tip. Pretty soon they are down on the highway, which is bumpy with gravel, but level.

Myna checks her hair with her hands, straightens the stole, and arranges her skirt around her, puffing it up so it glints and sparks in the sun and you can't even tell about the baby.

The air smells fresh and leafy, and the road is lined with green weeds and yellow dandelions. Birds are clothes-pinned out along the telephone wire and call noisily to one another. Not too far off a woodpecker is hammering away. Myna thinks it was a good idea to come. Lester's place in the bush is fine, especially the front room with the big red Chinese lantern, but how long can you play cards and listen to the radio? She's been at Lester's for over a month now.

This is the same road Myna had been on that first night she came to Lester's, but it had been much colder then and almost dark. She had been going to the highway to wait for the bus. It had been muddy and although she'd tried to walk mostly in the packed-down tracks in the centre of the road, mud still oozed over the tops of her shoes. Whenever she heard a car or truck approaching, she moved over but kept walking. She didn't want to talk to anyone. Then another car whipped past, not bothering to slow down at all, splattering her with mud. Her clothes, her arms, her legs, even her face and hair were spattered with tiny gobs of mud. That's when she'd started to cry, sitting on her cardboard box at the side of the muddy road, her nose and fingers freezing, her feet cold and rubbed sore.

She was crying because of the mud. Not because her mother had screamed, "No better than an Indian!" and had thrown her clothes onto the road, ruining Myna's powder-blue Ban Lon pullover and matching cardigan. Not because her brothers sat silently over their supper of pork sausages, mashed potatoes, sauerkraut, and peas, one of them with his hand clamped over his eyes, crying, and the other one not crying at all. Not because her father had stood on the front steps, moving his lips soundlessly before he'd finally said, "You made your bed and now you gotta lie on it," and gave her thirteen dollars, or thereabouts, a ten, a two, and some change. Myna had been thrown out before, but never with her clothes and thirteen dollars.

As she sat, weeping, on her box in the mud, she thought she heard the creaking and banging of a wagon and a team of horses coming down the road behind her.

She stopped crying, waiting for them to pass, but then she heard the horses stop slightly behind her, jingle their harness, snort their surprise. Finally, they pulled up alongside her.

Myna didn't even need to look around, although she did.

There was only one person besides the milkman who dragged around town with a team of horses.

"Go away, Lester Mulhoon!" she yelled, lifting one arm to wipe her nose on her sleeve. "Get out of here and leave me alone!"

Lester Mulhoon, the water man, lived in a tar-paper shack behind the Stampede Grounds. Buddy, who had gone there once to get a tow for his car, claimed Lester lived right in the same shack as his horses.

"I jest not!" Buddy had said to the men drinking coffee in the café. Buddy had held up his hand as if taking an oath. "The self-same shack! I kid you not!" Buddy's mother and sister were schoolteachers and some of their way of talking had rubbed off on Buddy.

Lester sat on the seat of his water wagon without saying anything. Lester hardly ever said anything. Lester's father, Old Man Mulhoon, who used to drive the water wagon until Lester took over, had been the same.

After a few minutes, Lester cleared his throat, as if waiting to be paid for a barrel of water. Finally, he said, "Hey there," a kind of question.

"Hay's for horses," Myna said, folding her arms for warmth and looking straight ahead. She was wearing her muddy powder-blue sweater, which possibly she could get clean with a bar of Sunlight soap if she got a chance to do it soon enough.

"Want a ride?" he said.

After a moment Myna answered him. "Oh, why not," she said, and climbed up, hanging on to her ruined and muddy box.

"I'm going to the highway to take the bus," she said, over the sound of the wagon which had begun to move again. The thirteen dollars was more than enough to get to Peace River, where she would buy new nylons and a wedding ring, then get a waitressing job. The bus would pass along the highway at one AM or shortly after.

The water wagon creaked as they bumped and splashed along the road. Everything on the ground was getting dark now, the road, the trees, the horses and themselves, but the sky still held the light, and a skinny moon was coming up straight ahead.

Lester didn't look at Myna or talk to her or bother her at all, and Myna liked that. She liked moving along in the dark like that, under a still-shining sky.

"My husband passed away," Myna said, as much to herself as to Lester. It was easy to practise her story in the dark like this, and although Lester was silent and facing straight ahead, she slipped her muddy left hand under the box on her knee. "Hunting accident. The gun went off with no warning whatsoever."

Her story sounded much finer and sadder out loud than she had expected, especially as she thought of herself now going to wait alone for the bus on the dark road. She touched the side of her cheek with the heel of her hand.

Soon she saw the dark shapes of the stands at the Stampede Grounds come up on the left, and she knew they were getting close to Lester's place, which was back off the highway where she would wait for the bus. The moon was shining a steady pale yellow now, and the sky was the colour of the ink they had to use at school, blue-black. They were not allowed to use Mediterranean Blue, Sea Green, or Red, although these colours were prettier and the drugstore sold them for the same price.

"If you would kindly get me a flashlight," Myna said to Lester, for she would need a flashlight to signal the bus.

"Bus isn't for awhile," Lester said, then stopped. Then after she thought that was all he meant to say, she heard him clear his throat and add, "You could wash up."

"Listen to the pot calling the kettle black!" said Myna. Feature that, she thought. Lester Mulhoon, who sleeps with his horses, telling *her* to wash up!

The wagon lurched as they seemed to go up a level, and Myna hung on. The road was so dark and so far down and she was having a good time up there on the wagon. She made no protest as the wagon cut off the main road onto the side road that led to Lester's shack farther back in the bush.

That was the end of April, and now it's June, school's almost out. Myna guesses she's failed Grade Eleven, which is not what she'd planned. She'd planned to finish Grade Eleven and go on to hair-dressing school. She hopes she never has to see the report card saying, *Failed*, or possibly even, *Expelled*. Three boys got expelled last year for skipping math to play pool, so she supposes she could be expelled for doing what she's done.

The horses are pulling hard but steady, and early as it is, Myna hears a truck come up behind them, then pass. It's a green Fargo pickup, Elmo Perry and Elmo Junior. The truck slows right in front of them while the Elmo Perrys talk, stare, grin; then they spin their tires, shooting gravel out behind them, and leaving the water wagon in a trail of dust.

The horses try to veer into the ditch.

"Bloody sons-of-bitches, stupid blockheads," Lester says, but in a soothing way for the horses, which he holds to the road.

Before long they're passing the dog catcher's shack under the bridge, the dairy, then they're into town.

With each stop Lester has to get off, undo the hose, drag it to the waiting barrel, while Myna waits on the wagon. Sometimes people come out with a pail or a pot they want filled. Some people pay Lester on the spot, others owe him. Lester wears a pencil behind his ear but doesn't write anything down.

"Lester," Myna calls out, "Is the H^2O always such a hit?" She sees Mrs. Cook holding back her kitchen curtains to watch, and Old Lady Kopko squinting at them from behind her front gate. Myna doesn't mind people getting an eyeful. She's high up on the wagon and she's wearing her best.

The stole is too warm now and Myna has to drape it off one shoulder, taking care to cover the side where the zipper won't do up. She strokes the stole with her free hand. It is hot and silky, like a dog in the sun.

Next they pass the baseball diamond beside the school. There's the flagpole where Edmund Cox froze his tongue in Grade Four, there's the parking lot where the older boys fought at noon hour, rolling furiously in the dirt, then shaking hands at the end.

Lester was one of those boys, she remembers in surprise. When she'd just started school and was coming back at lunch, she would stop and watch the older boys fight, a privilege the bus kids did not have. She remembers seeing Lester, red-faced and old-looking even then, pale spiky hair, rolling in the dirt, his arms punching like pistons.

"I remember you," she says, "You ripped Arthur Rudd's shirt, and his lip was bleeding. You must have got the strap."

"No. I dunno," says Lester, rubbing his face as if tired. "It couldn't've been me."

Usually boys were proud of the lickings they'd taken in school. Myna had never seen anyone not at least get a good story out of it.

The deliveries beyond the school take longer than Myna expected, and she wishes they had a radio up here. Then they cut across a few streets and are suddenly on *her* street, near *her* house, the house where she's lived for her whole life, except for the last month.

It seems to her the horses slow almost to a stop in front of her house, although her mother has a well of her own and never buys water. Sometimes her mother lets the neighbours use her well, and other times she cuts them off, if they've done something wrong like stepping on her flowers or spitting in the yard.

Myna looks at the little house with its brown, brick-patterned siding, its wire fence, and the flowers between, dahlias, not yet blooming, marigolds, asters, baby's breath, columbine, and bleeding heart at the side. There is a wash, freshly hung on the line, and rags spread on the side bushes to dry and bleach in the sun, but no movement anywhere.

As they move past the house, Myna sees her bedroom window at the side. Her white bed is in there. It has a padded vinyl headboard and is a double, so large it takes up almost the whole bedroom. She'd wanted twin beds, like another girl she knew, but her mother said no, double is better, she could take it with her when she married. Her mother was saving family allowances too, so that when Myna married she could buy a chesterfield and matching chair. Why should she feel bad, Myna thought, about the white double bed, already bought, and the chesterfield and chair, as yet unbought. Why should she care about her mother planning and saving all these years? I didn't ask her to, did I? Myna tells herself. Who asked her to do that anyway?

The water wagon crosses the main street by the clinic and Lester delivers to the Elite Café where Myna used to waitress. Although you could eat whatever you wanted except the T-bone steaks, Myna hated waitressing. People always wanted something. Tea, even if the coffee was closer, raisin pie with their coffee, or ice cream with their Jello. They complained if the crackers came after the soup. Myna thought they should eat what they were given.

When they pull away from the Elite, Myna suddenly realizes where Lester's going next.

"I'm getting off," she says, lurching up and almost over the rail in front of them.

Lester catches her by her arm and steadies her, but by then the horses have pulled up outside the Angeline Rooms.

The Angeline Rooms are a wooden, two-storey building, painted blue. There is long grass in the front, and the smell of cats. The grass and road in front are littered with broken glass, cigarette butts, even the skull of a cow that has been in the weeds beside the steps as long as Myna can remember. The sun catches on a few bottles that have been left in a line at the side of the road, and the glare hurts Myna's eyes.

Lester doesn't pull off to the side like Myna is one-hundred- percent sure she's seen him do before, but stops right out front and is already dragging the hose off to the side.

Here I am, Myna thinks, stuck up here like a clipped chicken. She looks ahead at first, hanging onto the stole on her shoulder. Maybe no one will pay attention, she thinks, it's just the water wagon and no one ever looks at the water wagon.

After a time it seems safe to look inside, and she can pick out the men sitting and smoking in the dark lobby. That's Pete Symington with the cowboy hat, Stan the barber, little, almost bald, with no hat, and Alvin Shanks with the greasemonkey hat he always wears even in the rooms upstairs. She knows they're smoking, not saying much, and tapping their cigarettes into the monkey ashtray or dropping them on the oiled wooden floor.

She doesn't see Buddy, but he could be there; he could be sitting on the stool behind the counter right now. She would like to see Buddy, except for knowing that he doesn't want to see her. She'd put things so poorly. "Take your time, Myna," Miss Kay used to say when they did their practice job interviews in front of the class. "Think before you speak." She'd forgotten that advice when she'd needed it the most.

What she'd said was, "I'm in trouble, Buddy, and you're the one to blame." Then he'd hit her.

Buddy had started to change before that, though. He'd started not being there when she delivered sandwiches from the Elite; he never invited her to their upstairs parties anymore where they smoked, played cards, and drank whiskey and Coke from paper cups.

She's glad she never gave the stole back, even though he'd said she had to, that it was his sister's.

"What a sad tale to tell," she'd said when he asked, and dropped the three hot western, two ham, and three turkey sandwiches on the counter in the lobby. "Too bad. It's mine now."

She'd started throwing up in the mornings and had known she was in trouble. Either that or she had cancer. If she gave the stole back everything was over. Her mother had had such a crazy fit about it in the first place, how could she give it back now?

Someone inside says something, and the men cough and laugh a little. Someone spits. Probably Alvin.

"Got the time to step in, Myna?" someone says, low and gravelly, but she hears it, and hears the bit of laughing after.

A wave of hotness passes over her, leaving her dizzy. Her dress feels all wrong. It's too small and pulling across the chest, and the sequins look like ordinary things, not like dew at all. Sweat trickles down her side under the stole. She wants to jump off the wagon and run.

Then Buddy is there, standing in the doorway. His furry arm is in the bright sun, but the rest of him is scissored off by the shade of the doorway. It is so bright she can hardly look up, but when she does, he is just staring, like a stranger through a bus window.

"The fur," he says really quiet, without moving. "Take it

off. Take it off and throw it down."

Lester is rolling up the hose, and in sixty seconds they'll be gone, fifty seconds, forty seconds. She is counting backwards to herself.

What is Lester doing? Myna can't believe it. Everything looks dark around the edges. It seems to her that Lester is moving very slowly, like a picture on a movie screen when the projector jams.

Lester walks back toward the Angeline Rooms, stands there a moment before he sits down sideways on the unpainted front steps. He takes off his cap and rakes down his pale hair with his fingers, then replaces the cap.

He reaches down and picks a stone off the ground, shakes it between his hands like a die, then – quickly now – throws it at a Pepsi bottle that is standing in the line of bottles on the edge of the road. The Pepsi bottle breaks, and Lester picks up another rock, shakes, throws again. This time he hits a beer bottle, breaking off the top. It is very quiet and bright.

The men inside sit without moving. Buddy stands across the doorway, his feet apart, his arms across each other. He rocks backwards and forwards, from his heels to the balls of his feet.

Lester scoops up two more stones, larger ones this time, and hits another beer bottle. He breaks the Five-Star whiskey bottle last. It shatters loudly, scattering across the road like ice.

Lester stands up and climbs back on the wagon. He settles with his elbows on his spread knees, picks up the reins, and the horses pull away easily, their load lighter.

At the corner, the horses, knowing their route by heart, turn left without a pause, heading for the Red and White. Leaning with the turn, Myna looks back along the straight grey road. The Angeline Rooms are far back now, a duller, flatter blue than the sky above, which is bright and very high.

There is still someone standing in the dark doorway, but it

is hard to tell for sure who it is, because the horses are moving quickly and the road is rough. A fresh breeze catches them rounding the corner and, looking back, Myna sees the water trickling from the wagon, flying back in threads of silver.

The Lost Winters of Emerald and Silver

RAY SERWYLO

We are – all of us – we are *kumy*. Godmothers and mothers, fathers and godfathers. It's what in the south they call *compadrazgo*, and so we're all family. We all belong together. We're cronies, gossips – it's true, in the Old Country they always say, *The godmothers gab with the mothers and the pigs have uprooted the carrots* – but it's true too that we are good and intimate friends. This isn't to say that there are not those among us – there's Mrs. Lushchak, poor woman – who are childless. Yet it is the very children shared among us that form our bonds, that make us *kumy*. Some of us are both – father and godfather, mother and godmother – but that does not have to be. Some have the child, and some, like Mrs. Lushchak, are chosen. Because she herself has been christened and is not the mother of a child, because she herself has achieved the age of reason and is not a heretic, neither a declared excommunicate nor a deposed cleric, no one can stop her. There are some of us who privately recite the public phrases we believe are at once judgment and law, *Not if she's pregnant, Not if she doesn't want to lose the godchild, Not if she doesn't want to lose her own.* But none of us knows for sure. We can only guess, and use other proverbs to try and understand why her husband, the car not yet a year old, locked it in the garage, left it running, and has never been heard from since.

Now, we *kumy*, we were not born in this place. But we treat it as our home. It is where we have started to die. It is where we have begun to bury ourselves in the cemeteries that *we*, and no one else, have started. *All Saints*, *Holy Ghost*, there are three or four in a stretch past the city's perimeter, between the river and highway leading to the locks and the turn-off for the white sand beaches where several of us now own cottages, or just empty property lots. As far as any of us can remember we came to this city at the same time, dealt here in one quick hand, fellow citizens of a camp near Nuremberg. And a few before that were already neighbours, from villages near the junction of the Prypiat and the Uzh.

If you could look far enough along a straight line from our new city you would eventually see the towns of Dibrova and Dytiatky in the Old Country. Yet we knew we had been carried by a flash flood of history and deposited like sediment in a foreign land. Most of us, our behaviour – well, we did like the animals. But in the early days, except for Mr. Lushchak and for quite a different matter, we could judge none of our group. Some simply continued the emigration, never becoming immigrants here, never letting this place be a part of their memories. Vlodko and Halia Zhuk, they stayed for only a year before they followed the sun across a warmer sea until they reached the eastern shore of still another world. To live, as some of us still foolishly believe, where there are black men. In huts filled with snakes. It was they who lived with the Lushchaks, it was Mrs. Lushchak's responsibility to flood their child's soul with sanctifying grace, even if across salt waters pulled by the moon.

Others, after a few years and like Muscovy ducks, returned to the Old Country. Then left it. Then left here again to return once more. Like Lionik, to one of our villages caught in Poland. We think he has forsaken it for the last time. *Adieu*

Polonia he tells the woman who lives upstairs, and he shares with her the vodka he has brought to Mrs. Lushchak's. But we know: soon he will weep and vow to return to that border once more.

Of course there were those who became infected and feverish with this new land and quickly revealed the deaths they had brought with them. Those for whom *we*, and no one else, began to create the cemeteries. We will all be dead – it is a fact. But there were these – Semenenko in the year before the great flood, when planes brought food even from England, and Buriak in the days when we were frightened to even whisper the word polio. There were the others too, whom we sometimes forget. But never Doroshova, her curses as she gave birth; this new place, we knew, begetting that death. The winters, already too cold.

The rest of us, we stood our ground no matter how severe and long the winters grew. But even here, of this group there are those who adapted and thrived, who own hotels and motels, who are on the boards of SUMK and Plast and UNO and KUK and our many many church councils. We will reap fine pensions and host large weddings for our daughters where two, three, four hundred people will dance *kolomyikas* and drink good whiskey. But there are those, and again we speak of Mrs. Lushchak, who have slipped into a lazy torpor, a hibernation. As if she believed she could live off the fat of her memories, waiting, but not even at her window, to smell the spring blossoms of the old world, of her past. We have feared witnessing her slow disappearance.

YOU SEE, IT IS FOR WHAT HAS HAPPENED to Mrs. Lushchak that we *kumy* cannot truly forgive her husband. Oh, of course nothing among such a group can be unanimous. There are those of us who cannot deny that in the contexts which excluded his wife he cut an attractive figure. Like Lionik, he drank and drank, yet always looked the youngest of us all. A boyish face, a smile. The almost Mongolian eyes that saw only pleasure. We could no longer distinguish whether he had been drinking or not, for he always seemed to act the same, and no one really remembered what he had been like in the Old Country. At his house he would always be offering us new bottles of whiskey, *Five Star, Plainsman, Hudson's Bay.* Never the same one twice it seemed. And then he would begin in his fine tenor voice the songs we have all brought with us and could sing automatically, the choruses, *Oh oh, my old man, my oh my, my old man—oh oh, my old man, oh he was a drunk.*

And Mr. Lushchak loved to dance too, and he could be found Friday, Saturday nights, every weekend, down in the basement club of UNO on North Main, waltzing across the small floor with the widows who came there to sip rye 'n' Coke. Or with the occasional not yet middle-aged woman – they appeared once every five or seven years – whose family, a brother, a third cousin had, as we say, *pulled* her out of the Old Country. With small movements, for Mr. Lushchak was in essence a quiet and unobtrusive man, he would lead these women around the dusted dance floor, a respectable shuffler in his suitcoat and pants which seemed every year to grow larger, a grey-brown colour. He would suddenly clap lightly, delicately, and point out, *Sunamagun, it's a good orchestra,* and ask the woman if she would like another drink. He would sit with these women and make them laugh, buy them ryes 'n' Coke, and before the evening was out, he would be dabbing at his eyes with a rumpled handkerchief at their tables. Telling them that there was too much sadness in this world, no matter where you lived. In their own great pity they would agree with him, dabbing at their own eyes. Widows who had decided that there had been enough mourning throughout the week – this one alone for twelve years of such weeks, that one for five. It's been enough.

Mr. Lushchak used to offer these widows rides home too, for he was one of the first among us to buy a car. And it was a good one, a Chevy with the three round lights on each side at the back, not the mere double lights of the cheaper models, the Belair, the Biscayne. No, he got the Impala. Oh, he was proud of that car and seemed to be ever celebrating the event. And of course that was his problem. He lost his licence first for only two months, but the second time, within a year, it was for much longer. The widows stopped accepting his proffered rides home, and his still-brand-new Impala began to spend as much time in the garage he had built out back of his house as it did on the road. The last time was the worst. He lost his licence good that time. He's lucky no one was killed. It was at a christening far out down Pembina Highway, for the child of the son of one of our *kumy*. You can see how our family has grown. And at the end Mr. Lushchak would give the keys to no one in the son's house. He would drive himself home, he insisted, and he didn't care who came along with him. Amongst ourselves we still analyze that event, and we all conclude that it was foolish for Mrs. Lushchak to go with him, and more foolish still for that son of one of our *kumy* to sit close beside him as he drove home, thinking he could grab the wheel in an instant if he had to, reminding Mr. Lushchak all the way of the curbs, the corners, the colour of the lights. It was lucky no one was killed. The car skidded on the ice, slowing and finally stopping in the centre of the intersection. A police car had been following them for several blocks. He lost his licence for four years. For him it was forever. It was a few days after his case went to court that we began to believe he was gone, that no longer would he ever be a member of our group.

None of us can say, not with any certainty, if we ever saw Mrs. Lushchak ride in the Impala except that one time. And now it was hers. Parked in the garage in their backyard. A garage built specially with Mr. Yulich, like a shrine. He was the group's carpenter, and most of us had hired out his hammering hand, the two joints missing from separate fingers. He had asked all of us if we had any old pieces of lengthy metal. Old bed springs, or bed frames, or whatever. To bury in the concrete base, to make sure it would never shift and crack in the brutal winters. The floor upon which the car sits is still level and firm, seamless and without sags. For the first few years after his disappearance, we wondered whether Mrs. Lushchak would sell the green car or whether she would learn to drive it. She has done neither, and it still sits where her husband left it, now over fifteen years ago, parked at a slight angle in the centre of the garage.

A neighbour was the first to find it. He turned off the ignition and handed the keys to Mrs. Lushchak. He told her it was likely the tank was empty. Mr. Lushchak had left the engine running, and walked out of her life.

THOUGH THE CHILDREN that once brought us all together – through whose births our bonds of *kumstvo* were forged – have begun to move to cities and continents whose names are foreign to even our twice or more translated tongues, we still remain *kumy.* And though our own years have flown in different directions, we yet remain *kumy.* Because our kinship is spiritual it cannot be torn asunder. *Let what God bringeth together....*

And yet we are no longer one. Perhaps we should have seen our disintegration in the very beginning when already Vlodko and Halia Zhuk exorcised their child of godparents just as those parents had exorcised the child of Satan. But now there are few of us who have not abandoned the other. Who have not been misunderstood. Who have not been lost in the white darknesses deep in the winter snows.

There is the mother of two sons whose own teeth have all rotted along with her memories of the place where she was born, a woman with an island-shaped birthmark, the size of her palm, beneath breasts her children have forgotten. The older boy is now a man himself, with his own children christened, but his godmother has forsaken his spirit. She sits alone in her softness in the cigar smoke of her ancient father's house on the banks of the city's other river. Her body ever on the verge of tottering. The imbalance of her stance. Her lips gentle, her words always the end of endings. The swirls of gold hair no longer tight. And there is that son's godfather too, a face and voice formless. There have been the years we have caught a glimpse of him boarding a bus on the same street in which he lives with his Germanic wife, taller than him, the two of them living in a house that is still not their own and has the indignity of a fraction in its address. They too have remained childless, like Mr. Lushchak who has disappeared from his home, and Mrs. Lushchak who has disappeared into it.

And of course there is Nick Shymertiuk who perhaps has been abandoned by us all. We remember him for the silver tooth which shone in his mouth, a magical talisman which allowed us to live at times in our old-world dreams. His face was very dark, even in winter, for he was one of the Odesa Slavs who for generations have been burned by the southern winds off the Black Sea. And that tooth shone like the moon on the surface of those waters where the *haidamaky* had centuries ago sailed and sung and slaughtered the Ottoman lords. As soon as he came to this land he knew not to make it small like the village he left. Some say his father had ended their final embrace with gold coins, and others said he knew which pieces of unwanted property would soon be valuable. It was not long before, like the tooth in his mouth, diamonds shone on his fingers, large square rings on the smallest fingers of a man himself not tall among us.

Nick Shymertiuk was a good friend – perhaps the best friend – of our *kumy* who left the city as soon as their children were christened. It was at the same time that Nick left for what some believed was Pennsylvania and others Alaska, and maybe it was in one of those places that he really made his fortune. But no one knows for sure. All we know is that he rejoined our group, his face darker and his magic tooth brighter, and there were few to whom he did not lend money. One hundred dollars, two hundred dollars. The first sums which were needed, great sums then.

He remained all the years a quiet man, his words gentle cello strokes, nodding and smiling that tooth smile, his voice speaking further and further from us. Some began to say he had lost it all. That debts were unpaid, debts owing to him. A hundred dollars to this man and his wife, a hundred dollars to another. A down-payment on a house, a down-payment on the hotel across from the abandoned limestone quarry. All, they say, was eventually lost. It was a silver silence. For him there was nothing loud in this land. We still sometimes see him at our funerals. But he stands distant, as if at another's grave, at someone else's burial.

THOUGH WE WERE AT OUR WITS' END wondering what sort of consolation we could offer her, we were not entirely relieved to see that Mrs. Lushchak did not take the loss of her husband poorly. Mr. Lushchak has still to this day not been seen or heard from. We doubt that he could have returned to the Old Country. No. Most likely he just continued to some other unknown place in the emigration which we all started in one shape or form – together, more or less – almost thirty years ago.

But, as we say, Mrs. Lushchak took the whole mysterious

business rather well. We knew that her husband had taken the dog but none of the cats, and when she could begin to talk about such things, which did not seem too long after her husband was gone, she told us too about the eight albums which were missing. His entire stamp collection. We remember him often asking each and every one of us for the large and frequently triangular, messed-image stamps that we all continued to receive from the Old Country. We thought he would have had enough of his own, but no, he wanted ours too. And he asked Nick Shymertiuk for the stamps of the Queen which he received from Vlodko Zhuk, and which were almost identical to the stamps of the Queen that we ourselves used here. But talking to Mrs. Lushchak we soon exhausted the possibilities and began to repeat – each of us our own – pet scenarios describing the disappearance. And Mrs. Lushchak only sat there, embarrassed by our deliberations.

Of course, on her own, she was even more flustered than she had initially been during what were becoming too infrequent visits. And none of us ever received her in our own homes now. Oh, she was invited a lot. But we believe she never left her house at all, actually. She was lucky the Roykos on Arlington still took orders over the phone and delivered the groceries even in summer. To the occasional party or Sunday dinner which was held she did not come. And what no one could understand was her refusal to join us at the weddings of our children and godchildren, at the christenings of our children's children, and the burials of our compatriots.

It did not take long before we realized that none of us had talked to Mrs. Lushchak for months at a time, even though we visited our own married children who lived not more than three or four city blocks from her Norman Street house. Those who did drive up to the front of her house, unannounced, would see the curtains beyond the veranda windows part and close. Or if there were those for whom she had no choice but to open the door, they would hear her over and over condemn herself, her voice croaking – a bark – the scraping of ice crystals unused to the spaces filled suddenly with other people. She would always wipe her hand down the front of her dress along the huge blooms of dark flowers, trying to remove the folds and stains of her hibernation. *Oh, I have no food, there is nothing to drink*, and she pats at her hair but doesn't know what she is trying to achieve. She would sound on the verge of hysteria, on the verge of reality. She had an energy that could sparkle, but in stops and starts, the hesitancies of a revel long forgotten. There was always the *studenets* she could offer from the fridge, the pigs' feet wobbly in the grey and unset gelatin. Many of us remember the unkindness of Mr. Lushchak. *She gets the hooves from the devil*, he would laugh, *and they'll never freeze in her jelly.* We could never say it, even amongst ourselves, but she did not cook very well.

At last we *kumy* began to believe that Mrs. Lushchak was crazy. It was nothing to worry about. A stupid craziness. Not the kind where she had to be taken to Selkirk, to the hospital – heaven forbid. No, she wasn't insane. You see, we thought that even she didn't take it seriously – not much. That it made her comfortable to act out her lunacies, lunacies that were no different than most of our own. Only hers were constant and unrepentant, brushing off suggestions that she come out of her house, that she visit us in our homes. At times like these she would promise to send a wedding gift to, say, Lionik's daughter, but of course she never would.

We could not understand her. She still seemed to have a nervous wonder at what was happening out there, in the surrounding white of this weather. But at other times it was almost as if, even though he has been gone now for so many years, she expects her husband to return at any moment, and punish her for the loss of his beloved Impala, sitting in the garage out back. We could see the regret in her eyes, for a love grown old and cruel, for a man whose face remained ever young and unmemoried. Which still must have glowed before her like that emerald green car, or that lone silver tooth in Nick Shymertiuk's mouth.

The First Lady

LIDA SOMCHYNSKY

Jacqueline Kennedy Onassis died a few weeks after my mother. Both had cancer. Jackie's death gave me a strange sense of consolation during my initial months of mourning. I could see them together in the "great beyond." Having feverishly read various life-after-death accounts after my mother's death, it made immediate sense at the time. Their initial meeting would be somewhat awkward, but after a while they would find their common ground. Perhaps my mother and Jackie would engage in pleasantries, sitting side by side at a loom, weaving intergalactic tapestries. Mama would enjoy that, as she'd enjoyed knitting original patterned sweaters for me every Christmas. Given their places in the world, Jackie would most likely be the loom design supervisor – with Mama at her side.

OVERNIGHT MAMA HAD BECOME a great admirer of a specific neighbour next door – the First Lady of the United States. Not that she had previously had a fascination with anything American. Reading biographies of European royalty had always been her evening pastime.

The transformation came quickly. Whenever a special occasion came up, Mama took to wearing the pillbox hat, which Jackie had introduced. Just as Mrs. Kennedy spoke and adored all things French, Mama resolutely set out to do the same. Instead of hearty Ukrainian dishes such as pyrohy and cabbage rolls, she would serve the family exquisite French delights. My dad and I would search through cream-laden sauces to find out exactly what we were eating.

Monet and Renoir prints appeared on the walls beside reproductions of Ukrainian poets and Cossack victories – much to the consternation of my father. Mama took evening French language and literature courses, graduating with top marks. Bookcases began to be filled with French classics. André Gide quotations neatly printed on scraps of paper served as bookmarks. We were waiting for the moment when Mama, à la Jackie, would begin horseback riding lessons. Whenever there was a high school French test, I would be drilled incessantly. Most of the time I did well. Soon I was wearing a beret; four different-coloured ones to go with the seasons.

MEANWHILE, MY FATHER WAS TRYING to instill in me lifelong Ukrainian patriotic zeal. I took Ukrainian Saturday classes, Ukrainian dancing classes, and went through a revolving door of endless Ukrainian concerts. He believed that all this activity would culminate in my wanting, along with other young Ukrainian Canadians, to free the oppressed homeland. My father was troubled about whether French would gain ascendancy over my Ukrainian consciousness. I tried to give both equal footing. He rationalized his wife's French obsession by placing it within a larger historical context. My mother was of mixed Polish and Ukrainian ancestry; the Poles' fascination with France had obviously seeped into Mama's way of being.

* * *

The night I received that long distance call, spring had arrived, after a particularly harsh Alberta winter. It was an evening when I had been feeling unusually content. My video research proposal on youth and ethnic retention had been completed well before its deadline. Snuggled into the couch, I was surrounded by a blanket of newspapers and monthly publications. Usually when there was a lag in my current affairs reading, panic would set in. As a fledgling documentary film-maker, I needed to be in touch at all times. Methodically, I began sorting all the reading material into what needed detailed concentration and what could be skimmed. Tonight, once again, I was accompanied by my faithful partner of the last year – the TV set. With everybody buzzing about the Olympics, I chose to watch the women's solo skating championships

GATHERING AROUND THE TUBE to watch the Olympic skaters had long ago become a family ritual. Mama would commandeer my father and me into the living room at the appointed time. We would pay dutiful attention to her favourite skating ballerinas. Father would dryly inquire if Jackie was watching the same events. No response. Mama was out on the ice, dancing. Occasionally we could see her holding back the tears – usually when one of her favourites landed unceremoniously on her backside. Once we filled the living room with a unanimous cheer. Mama's favourite had become the world champion.

MEMORIES ENVELOPED ME as I watched the skaters. Oksana Baiul, the young *wunderkind* from Ukraine, entranced everybody. A TV newscaster intoned, "She's a mere seventeen-year-old orphan who yearned to be a ballet dancer. Grandparents recently died due to the Chornobyl radiation disaster." Oksana's rosy, fresh face stared at me. Those blue eyes radiated nervousness. Before gliding out on the ice, she made the sign of the cross and with the grace of a swan began her dance.

MEMORIES JUMBLED ONTO THE SCREEN. Mother attempting to make me into the next Anna Pavlova. The best ballet instruction that our suburban town could offer. Studio classes in a dank, dingy church basement. Seven years old, quaking at the barre, trying to master a pirouette. Stern orders of "Straighten that back; feel the rhythm; toes pointed out."

I despised ballet and begged to take riding classes, once again appealing to Mama's admiration of Jackie. The response was a categorical no. "Soon, you would want one as a pet." Did she think I was going to house the animal in the family rec room?

And so for three consecutive years, at the year-end ballet concerts, I was cast in the role of a motionless tree – which would occasionally shudder out of boredom. In my final year, I moved up the ranks of the ballet corps to become a male guard protecting a crudely rendered canvas-painted castle. Near the end of the performance, I improvised what I thought was a subtle although somewhat shaky pirouette. The ballet teacher was not amused.

IT WAS WHEN OKSANA EFFORTLESSLY TWIRLED into a triple axel that the phone rang. I decided to let the answering machine do its job. A strangled panicky voice filled the room.

"Anna...you there?"

My mother. It had only been in the last six months that I

managed to convince her to leave messages. Many times in the last year, after my father's death, her voice would be filled with suppressed loneliness. I thought of her quick hand darting through still jet-black hair; I decided I was mellow enough to talk to her.

"Hi, Mama. It's me. How are you?"

"So, you saw her."

Brevity on my mother's part; this was long-distance.

"Who?"

"Again this year you didn't watch the Olympics."

"Now how do you know that – maybe that's what I'm doing this very minute."

"Yes, but you probably missed her *Swan Lake* dance last night."

I had learned over the years to do exactly what pleased my mother and do it very well. Too well, a therapist once told me.

"I've been glued to the TV set for the last week. Food supplies are getting low, but it's okay – there's cat chow."

"Doesn't surprise me, anything. You never liked to cook."

Teasing is a frivolity, especially when it's long distance. In the last few months, I had finally succeeded in having our long-distance telephone conversations extend to the eight-minute mark. But I knew enough to get to the topic at hand.

"Mama, Oksana's fantastic! Her axels are far better than Katarina Witt's."

"For sure. Just think, only last year she was standing in line for food. That is how character is built." She choked on the words.

"Yes, she has great will power."

"So, Anna, have you finished with the cigarettes yet?"

"Cutting down – you know, she really looks like a swan when she flaps her arms. They're doing a replay of *Swan Lake* right now." I reached for a smouldering butt.

"How many cigarettes now?"

Sinking lower into the couch, sliding into a fetal position, I responded with a lie. "Only five."

"Anna, I went today to the doctor."

"That's wonderful! You're finally taking advice from your daughter. See, Ma, we're moving into a new phase of our relationship. We're listening to each other; communication roadblocks are being removed."

I had been trying to convince her for years to go for a checkup. Mama's response was that the two miles she swam every day at the community pool was proof enough of impeccable health.

"Doctor says cancer. Dark shadows everywhere on the x-rays. I'll call you when it's time to come." Her tone was matter-of-fact, heavy and tired.

"Mama, I'll fly out tomorrow." The words and their meaning belonged to someone else.

"No, I don't want everybody wandering in the house just waiting. Nothing can be done."

The conversation was over; Mama had to go. Hopefully to Mrs. Davidson, her next door neighbour. After thirty-five years of living side by side, they had slid into a friendship based on loneliness, as both were widows. That night, I called my best friends and sought comfort. As I cried myself to sleep, I prayed for Mama's health, repeating in Ukrainian, "Our Father who art in heaven...." The belief in prayer came back to me just as it had when I was eight. Then I had prayed for the power of learning how to float on my stomach. My wish was granted to me at my swimming class the following morning.

I FLEW HOME THE NEXT MORNING. Emergency surgery was prescribed for Mama that evening. Each hour she slipped further away into agony. Aside from asking for ice chips to soothe her thirst, she said nothing.

Every few hours, I ran out to the hospital parking lot and huddled on the floor in the back of the car, fortifying myself with a bottle of Jackie O's favourite Beaujolais wine. That gave my drinking dignity. And then I would return to her. Watching helplessly, I stroked her hands and whispered over and over how much I loved her. In her silence, I understood that I was speaking for both of us. I mumbled on about plans I had looked into (but had never told her about) for the two of us to go to her favourite museums in Paris. With tears streaming, I thanked her for everything.

Three days later she was gone, in the middle of the night, while I wrestled with dreams of horses running. That day the robins arrived, perched as always on the huge boughs of the spruce tree in the front yard of the family home. Their chirping seemed innocently cruel. I wanted a downpour – heavy black rain.

TWO MONTHS LATER I returned to my old neighbourhood. There was additional business that required looking after.

Mrs. Davidson had organized a luncheon in honour of my return. Walking up the driveway, I stared at our former family home. The FOR SALE sign swung in the breeze, creaking an eerie welcome. The realtors had kept the front and back yards in the same immaculate condition as my mother had. Asters and mums stood in even rows, as if on guard, paying their respects.

Standing on Mrs. Davidson's front steps, I stared across the yard, to where my life had been lived for eighteen years, and where it had continued intermittently for another twenty. The voices of the neighbourhood women floated through the screen door.

"I remember the time Eleonora was coming back from grocery shopping...why she was lugging three bags in each hand, as if it was nothing. So I called out...hey Mrs. Marchinsky...you know it took us about twenty years to finally get on a first name basis...did you get some good deals at Loblaws? I come rushing out to give her an hand – didn't think I was intruding or anything. Well, she's got the biggest smile on her face – you know when she smiled – the whole world lit up."

I heard the other women clucking and cooing like doves.

"So I take a look in the shopping bags and they're all filled with books – French books. Mind you, I thought they were Spanish or Latin, but of course she set me straight. So I says to Eleonora – well, I didn't know you knew this language too, because I swear I think she spoke something like eight or ten languages. I lost count."

Again the women murmured. I recalled how Mama had laughed over Mrs. Davidson telling the neighbours that Eleonora knew ten languages. It was actually four. Ukrainian, Polish, German, and French. Not to mention English, which she'd started learning on the boat to Canada, after the war. Word got around very quickly, and soon distant neighbours would appear at the doorstep asking for translations. She loved the work, did it for next to nothing, and managed to keep it hidden from my father for a few months. He discovered her secret life when an Arab woman showed up. She had heard about the translator on the block. His thunderous response had been, "No need for a civil engineer's wife to be working. Don't we have enough money? Do you need as many mink coats as Jackie?" Her short-lived career was gone.

"So I ask Eleonora, why would you be wanting to start to learn French? And she looks at me, as if I was just born yesterday, and says, 'Why, it is the most beautiful language in the whole world – Jacqueline Kennedy speaks it, you know.'"

Finally another neighbour got in her two cents' worth.

"Oh yeah, but when she found out Jackie was marrying that Greek tycoon...well that didn't make her happy. I mean really, after a president, should a woman settle for a...well you know...let's face it...he was nothing but a gangster with lots of bucks. Eleonora kept saying, 'Where was her dignity?' and I totally agreed with her."

These words brought back images of the proud, solitary lady who reigned on this tidy street where all the lawns were neatly and identically manicured. Never one to engage in the neighbourhood gossip, or be bothered to clip coupons and indulge in over the fence garden exchange, Mama was proud of the fact that some thought she was a snob. She liked it that way.

Mrs. Davidson regained her ground, her voice rising above the others.

"But you know, Eleonora had that something about her, didn't she? I would say she was the first lady of Maplehurst Avenue. You know, I had this print that I picked up at a garage sale some years ago. Anyways, one afternoon she came to the back door, kind of shy like, to borrow an aspirin. Would you believe it? It was her third aspirin in her life! Anyways she saw the print and before you know it, I'm getting a history of French art. I think this guy was called Rebet, or Ronot...."

It was then I decided to join the women for the luncheon.

"That was Renoir," I said, turning towards them. "One of her favourite painters."

The brood of women, decked out in their finery, greeted me, but I was elsewhere. I thought of my mother, Eleonora, floating way up there, maybe with Jackie, no, Jacqueline, at her side, sipping Beaujolais and crowned with pillbox hats.

The Still-Boiling Water

CHRYSTIA CHOMIAK

By the time I arrived, they were already sitting around the kitchen table, drinking wine and laughing. The long dining room table, had been set for twenty-four, and the house was full with the sweet smell of beets cooking with wild mushrooms, bay leaves, fresh dill, peppercorns, and just the right touch of tomatoes and carrots as the Christmas borshch slowly simmered on the stove. The kitchen counters were covered with cookie sheets holding tiny pockets of transparently thin pastry filled with a mixture of wild mushrooms and onion, ready to be boiled. They had finished their preparations for Christmas and had started their stories. Each one of my six aunts talks louder than the other, and they all laugh at the same time. Their first stories are always about their boyfriends and husbands, old and new, and who's coming with whom that year. Then they go back to the small two-bedroom house that they grew up in, and the stories become quieter and the laughter slowly stops. And that's when this story is told.

"When I was three years old," my aunt Maria starts, "I fell into a large canning pot of still-boiling water, which my mother had left on the kitchen floor. When I was finally pulled out of the pot, pieces of my skin remained on its sides. After this accident, I stopped speaking for three-and-a-half months – for my entire stay at the hospital."

My baba interrupts. She is always the first to tell the story. This is her story. She begins by talking about her suffering, about her poverty in Canada, about the constant numbing work of raising six daughters. Then she talks about the accident and how she could not stop crying, how she almost lost her daughter Maria. She turns to me, looks me squarely in the eyes, and says, can you imagine losing your own child, watching her die?

She recounts the day's events – preparing the fruit for canning, preparing the jars for canning, preparing the shelves for more jars. She spends considerable time describing the size of her canning pot, the weight of the jars, that she had no one to help her, that while she canned she also looked after her six children. She adds that she had to can in order to have food for the long, cold Edmonton winters, and that it was very hard for her to provide for her children.

She says that she was tired that day, that all morning Maria and Natalia had repeatedly called her and that she had told them not to bother her anymore. She repeats this point a couple of times and tells me how she had to run up and down the stairs, from the basement to the kitchen, each time they called her. She adds that there was a newborn in the house, sleeping in the upstairs bedroom.

Then she says that when she heard her children calling her – still yet another time – that that time she decided not to run upstairs but to finish her work instead. She adds that when she finally went upstairs it was she who plunged her hands into the still-boiling water and pulled Maria out. It was she who wrapped Maria in blankets, carried her to the cab, and went to the hospital with her. After a pause she describes – with some amazement – that during the whole ordeal, Maria did not cry, and that instead Maria tried to comfort her and kept asking her to stop crying. "Maria did not cry," my baba repeats and they are all silent, waiting.

Then she describes the scene at the hospital: how the doctors placed them on adjoining beds, how they instantly connected them – by tube – one arm to the other – one life to the other – no questions – how they lay there alone, she in her house dress stained with peach and plum juices from the morning's canning – giving blood – giving life – again.

She describes the visits – the daily visits for three-and-a-half months – to the hospital. Daily, walking the seven blocks to the bus stop – every afternoon – taking the bus to the General Hospital, staying just a short time – "I had children at home – little children," she says – and then returning. From the house to the hospital, from the hospital to the house, every day. She adds that Maria stopped talking after the accident, and that she feared that Maria would be mute for the rest of her life.

Then she describes the afternoon, at the hospital, when Maria finally spoke. It was when she came to the hospital with an old friend, an emigré doctor, Maria's godfather, just days before Maria was to go home. He gave Maria a ring, she says, and it was then that Maria finally spoke for the first time in three-and-a-half months: "And where is my bracelet?" At that point my baba finishes her story, sits back, shakes her head from all the remembering, and smiles.

Then it is Natalia's turn. She begins her story by crying. She begins by saying that it was not her fault that Maria fell into the pot. That it could have been her. That Maria had done the same thing to her. Then Natalia stops.

At that point, Maria asks her, "What happened? What were we playing?"

"Tug-of-war."

"And what did you do? "

"I let go of my end and you fell into the pot. You were

standing too close. You had done the same to me," she adds. "You had let go of the rope before and I had fallen. It was your turn to fall. You started it."

Then in great detail, Natalia recounts how she tried to pull Maria out of the pot, but that the water was too hot. She describes how Maria was stuck to the pot and that the pot was too high for her to reach into. She repeats how she ran up and down the stairs, several times, up and down, all the time afraid to leave Maria alone, all the time calling her mother for help. Natalia recounts how she could not explain to her mother what had happened, as she ran up and down the stairs, until finally her mother understood. Then Natalia adds that it was she who went next door and asked Mrs. Parks for help, and it was she who called the cab that took Maria and my baba to the hospital.

Natalia describes how she stood by the front window of their house waiting, all afternoon, not moving, waiting for her mother and Maria to return. She describes how she told her father what had happened, when he finally came home from work. She adds that all during that time she did not move from her spot, in front of the window, until her mother finally returned, late that night.

Then Natalia talks about the long months that Maria was gone and how she had been told that Maria could no longer speak. She says that she could not understand what this really meant, but that deep down, all the time that Maria was gone, she felt guilty. Then Natalia adds that when Maria finally returned from the hospital, she wore a new cream-coloured satin dress, with smocking on the front, and that she gave Maria a new doll, but that Maria said nothing to her.

ONLY WHEN THE OTHERS HAVE TOLD THEIR STORIES does Maria tell hers. She starts by describing the day. She talks about its warmth and that she wore a sun dress. She talks about the jars of canned fruit that her mother had prepared, how they glistened when they were set on the table. She adds that her mother told her to stay away from the pot, that it was too heavy to lift onto the table.

She talks about the fun Natalia and she had that morning, how they laughed and played and how delighted they were in their disobedience as they called their mother, all morning, just for fun. Then she adds that she does not actually remember falling into the pot, but that she does remembers calling out for help. She describes the commotion, the panic around her, but repeats that she felt no pain. She adds that she tried to comfort her mother during their drive to the hospital.

Then she recounts arriving at the hospital and how she expected everyone to be dressed in white, but that they were all in green. She says that the only things that she remembers from the first weeks in the hospital is her mother's blood flowing into her in the emergency room, how warm it felt, and then the repeated elevator rides – going up and down and up and down, and rolling along corridors while lying on a bed. She describes how the doctors examined her and looked at her skin and talked about cutting skin from one place and attaching it to another. She always adds that they talked to each other as if she were not there.

When she was feeling better, Maria says that she was placed in the infant ward – infants who cried all day – and how angry she became because she was not an infant. She was three years old. She describes the constant noise of the bottles, being brought in and out, day and night, and the revolting smell of the diapers all around her and that she could not sleep there. She adds how long and hot the afternoons were in the hospital and how lonely she felt, alone in that ward and how she cried, silently, every afternoon until she fell asleep.

Maria tells us that at first she pleaded with the nurses to move her, but that they did not or would not understand her. "They shouted at me to be quiet." She states that she also asked her mother, again and again, to move her to another place – away from the infants – but that her mother did nothing about it. My baba says that Maria is making this part up.

Maria recounts the afternoon when she became hysterical with desperation and how the nurse came and yelled at her, but that she still was not understood. Maria says that it was that afternoon, after the nurse left, that she finally knew that no one could hear her and that was when she decided not to speak anymore.

She tells us about the next visit of her parents and how startled they were when she did not answer them and how they called on Dr. Michalchan, the only Ukrainian-speaking doctor at the hospital to examine her, but that she would not answer him. "I remember all of them speaking to me, all of them, but I just didn't answer."

Lastly, she repeats the story of her godfather's visit and adds that he spoke directly to her and promised her a gold ring and a gold bracelet when he returned. Maria recounts her godfather's return, and that just as he had promised he gave her a gold ring and how happy she was. She says that she waited until he was about to leave before she asked: "And where is the bracelet that you promised me?" She adds how excited they both became when she spoke and how her mother laughed her deep throaty laugh and how beautiful she looked.

Finally she describes the day she went home, how she rubbed the new dress her mother had brought her against her cheek – smooth, creamy satin. She describes how beautiful it felt, and how proud she was, riding home in it. Then Maria adds that when she came home, Natalia pushed a doll into her hands and that all her sisters stared at her as if she was from another planet.

Green Sundays

PATRICIA ABRAM

My father grew up in a skinny house. A row house only twelve feet wide on Niagara Street in Toronto. Nearby was a Laura Secord factory. At night he'd slip through the odd unlocked window and steal chocolates with his friends. The factory is gone now. He tells me this as we drive through the architecture of his past.

It is a grey November afternoon. He points out the haunts in his life as we turn the corner to a road that leads to a dead end and a driveway with a building. That's where the slaughterhouse once stood, where his father used to slice the tender necks of calves or smash the heads of squealing pigs, spraying a lace of blood on his clothes, the smell never washing from his hands. My grandfather, my *dido,* as I would have called him had he lived to see me, was lucky to have that job – he couldn't speak English, only Ukrainian. Couldn't even read or write in his native tongue. At age ten my father taught his own father how to write his name, Yurii Stephans, in English. Before that *Dido* always signed an "X." I heard this story often as child, as though my father wanted to remind me of where I came from and how far I had come.

But over the years my father told me little of his life as a boy. I never knew my grandfather or grandmother. My father's only sibling, a sister three years older, died of pneumonia when she was twelve. I often flip through the old family album with black dog-eared pages and stare at the brown and white photographs of the girl named Magda. A girl with the same eyes and round face that I had, as a three-year-old, a girl who would have been my aunt. There aren't many pictures of her; most of them are static poses shot in a studio – Magda crisp in a white dress and black shoes, perched on a stool between her parents, a frown on her face, her hands clawing the dress. But there are three candid snaps of her. One with my father, where they are both in woolly sweaters and Magda's eyes peer out from under a knitted tam that almost swallows her face; my father's cheeks are pudgy dough, his tongue curled between his lips. In another shot, she leans by herself against a wrought-iron railing of what looks to be a bridge, her hands by her side, legs straight, only a hint of a smile on her face.

It's the third picture that lets me "feel" her. She is standing outside the front windows of the house. It must be summer, she stands behind a rose bush in full bloom that frames her lower body in shadows. Her face and torso shine in sunlight. You can tell she can't stop smiling; she couldn't hold it in if she tried. It bursts from her face like the sunshine itself. She looks about seven in the picture. I can't help wondering when this photo was taken. Was it before that awful day? I can't imagine her ever smiling like this again after that day. A day my father didn't tell me about till I was in my late teens, and even then he told the story in little snatches, small bits of words left behind like bread crumbs or pebbles strewn on a path. Broken words left for me to collect and piece together.

MY FATHER DIDN'T HAVE A MOTHER from the time he was four years old. I was four or five myself when I learned this, as well as the startling fact that my father's family came from what he called "the Ukraine." This announcement was a treasure like the pink quartz stones I hid in a tin box under my bed. To have a father whose parents were from "the Ukraine" was exotic – different from the white-bread, WASP families of my street and school. I always begged my father to speak Ukrainian, to teach me the words of this other land that flowed in my blood. But he didn't speak them often – his father had died in 1954, and like him, my father had never learned to read or write Ukrainian. It's the written language caught on a page that keeps the words whole in your mind – not broken on the tongue. Besides, my mother was of British background – upper-crust English on her mother's side and Scots-Irish on her father's side – and she never felt quite at home in the confusion of my father's ethnic customs and language, though she did learn how to make cabbage rolls from his aunt.

As a child the only time I saw the Ukrainian language in a written form was on Green Sunday in June when we made the yearly pilgrimage to the cemetery. All my father's family, cousins and aunts and uncles, would gather in the graveyard starched in their best clothes, the women in gloves and veiled hats, the men in hats and ties. Everyone would pay the priest to bless the gravestones with holy water. Except my dad. My *dido* never believed in doing that. In fact, my dad had never attended the Ukrainian Orthodox church as a kid, never attended any church. I think my family participated in the yearly Green Sunday because it was a family outing, a coming together of the clan. Later I learned that this special day was a time to remember and commemorate the dead – ancestors are sacred to Ukrainians. My father still had that strong tie to those buried in the cold earth, although he had no religious belief. Compared to the staid and plain style of the Baptist church I attended, the white and purple robes of the Orthodox priest, his tall crown adorned in jewels and gold, and the strange words he spoke as he sprinkled that special water on others' headstones were magic.

I remember throwing maple keys in the air, watching them spiral, the smell of cut grass, staining my white socks green as I slid to catch those twirling helicopters. And I remember our family tombstone. Granite polished like black ice on one side with our name "Stephans" carved in English. On the other side Cyrillic letters cut the stone. Some looked like those I recognized from the English alphabet, but others looked like ancient symbols that held a code to my past. I'd trace their shape – my finger always fit the curve of cold rock, knew its direction as though it were in my bone. Although my father couldn't read them, he knew the words recorded his grandfather Mykhailo's birth and death, though only the year was given for his birth. No one knew the exact date, not even Mykhailo knew it when he lived. He was born in 1852. Strange to have lived your whole life without a day to celebrate your birth, but I guess he had different things to worry about. He was born in the village of Perehinsk just after serfdom had been abolished. He died in 1938.

Further down more Cyrillic letters appeared, but plunked in the middle were English letters that I read over and over.

HIS LOVING GRAND-DAUGHTER
MAGDA STEPHANS
BOURN 1927, AUG. 13TH TORONTO, CANADA

I wondered why they spelled born with a "u." I wondered what it would be like to die at twelve – I was only eight myself. And I wondered what this girl Magda had been like. It was hard to think of her as "my aunt" when she had died as a girl – I thought of her more as a sister. I loved her name and wished it were mine, not the plain English one I had, like all the other girls in my class at school – Susan, Anne, Carol,

Debbie. I wanted that exotic touch, that otherness. I wanted to know her.

The rest of the Cyrillic letters told the story of my grandfather Yurii's birth and death. I knew my grandmother had died too, but we never talked about the dates of her birth or death. She had a strange and beautiful name: Valeska. There are only a few pictures of her in the old family album. One of her with Yurii and Magda at age three, and one of her dressed in her Ukrainian costume. Though it is a black and white photo, I know the waves of beads that spill down her chest are red. She wears a crown of flowers. Long ribbons fall below her waist, embroidery cascades down the puffed sleeves of her blouse. She holds her arm out, bent at the elbow, hand on waist, as though purposely displaying the craft she has recorded on her sleeve – ancient stitches and patterns that speak of her ancestors. This picture always filled me with pride, identity – I wished I had a costume of my own. There is another picture of Valeska. With my father when he was four. They are outdoors in a park. "Little Marko" wears knickers and suspenders, his blond hair tossed to the side, his feet splayed, his mouth curved down, eyes staring at the camera. Valeska stands beside him but does not hold his hand. She is a big woman and wears black pumps and a fall coat. A hat casts a shadow over her plain, round face. She holds a clutch purse and does not smile. This is the only picture of my father with his mother – it has been ripped in half and taped together. As a child, I always assumed that her name and the dates of her birth and death were hidden there too in the mystery of those Cyrillic words that broke the hard stone of our family marker.

TODAY MY FATHER WANTS TO VISIT the cemetery after we have seen his old house. I steer the car left onto Niagara street. The row houses are attached red brick, some painted to hide the years. There is an empty square of dry, dead grass and weeds clawing at a wire fence. "That's where the lead batteries used to be thrown," my father says. Years ago there was a battery factory and old used batteries were dumped on the grass or buried under the ground. He tells me that in the 1970s, long after he had left, people complained the land was poisoned with lead and demanded that the city clean it up. The factory was torn down and the soil washed like an old potato that had sat in the dirt during the dark winter months.

When I park the car where my father has told me to pull in, I glance at him and realize how hard this must be for him. He hasn't been here for years and years; he is doing this for me, for my desire to arrange the past like bricks laid in ordered rows. To see the structures that stand under me, the foundation that has made me. I gather up my purse and watch my father get out of the car, his silver head bending, his squat, short body twisting. He doesn't have the belly he used to. Not since the triple by-pass he had two years ago and the low-fat diet my mother put him on. But he looks older now, with the flabby skin hanging round his neck, the wrinkles webbed around his eyes and streaked across his square Slavic forehead. He puts money in the meter. His hands are large and sprinkled with liver spots that look like islands on a map. His index fingers curve to the side – he always says this is from playing baseball as a boy, the hours he spent throwing the ball, carving a shape to his hand. But I have the same curve, the same structure in my index fingers, and know that it's in the bone.

We walk down the sidewalk a little ways, my father slowing to a standstill. He points to the second house in the third section of row houses, number seventy-one – it belonged to his father's brother Ivan. My father points to number sixty-nine and says, "This is where I lived. Old sixty-nine." His eyes are wet and I touch his jacket sleeve.

He says he is fine, that the house really hasn't changed that much, that those are the original windows, he can tell. Paint, the colour of eggshells, peels on the second-storey windows. And yes, the house is skinny. The brick is still red, not painted like the others. There are six houses in the row; four had been owned by my grandfather's siblings. The front yard is barely a patch of grass, and there is a tree, tall and twisting with naked branches that look like veins – in the summer they would be covered in green leaves. My father remembers that tree being a tiny twig. He remembers the hot summer nights, pulling the mattresses onto the front lawn and sleeping in the city heat and drone of cars and clatter of trains.

I look at the house, and remember when the phone rang one afternoon in March of 1976, when I was seventeen. A gruff voice said, "Is Mark there, it's Freda."

The voice hardly sounded female, scarred by years of cigarettes. As I heard her take a long slow drag, I imagined smoke curling out the tunnels of her nose.

"I'm sorry, he's not home right now. Can I take a message?"

"Yeah, tell him the rent cheque's in the mail."

"Are you sure you have the right person?"

"Yeah, for Mark, the rent cheque for sixty-nine Niagara."

I still didn't get it and said nothing.

"You mean to tell me your father has never told you about sixty-nine Niagara? It's his house, I rent it from him." She laughed, full of throat, and something else I didn't like.

"I'll pass on the message," I said and set the phone down softly.

Later I questioned my mother about the call, and she told me that my father still owned and rented out the house he grew up in. She also told me that when she married him, she didn't know he had the house. Didn't know about it till they had been married for four or five years and Slavko, a cousin of my father's, blurted out the secret at a family party. I couldn't understand why everything was so hush-hush about a house. Why my mother had never told me until now. Or my father. That's when my father dropped another bit of his broken history – his mother, he said, had left his father. Left her children. Left to live with another man. When my father was four and Magda was seven.

His words were a bowl slipping from a hand. Images, scenes, reeled inside my mind. I wanted to know more, to mould the story. But he would give me no more details, just those few sharp words. And the fact that she had died some years after Magda had, as if the guilt Valeska felt about Magda getting sick and dying of pneumonia killed her. I couldn't imagine a mother leaving her children. Leaving to live with another man. Women just didn't do that back then. Who was this woman – my grandmother? I wanted to know more about her. But my father would not speak – "I didn't have a mother," he said flatly. And I had to be satisfied with the broken pieces I had been given.

Five years later I graduated from university and was in the midst of packing my belongings – I was moving away to another city to work in an art gallery as an assistant curator. I remember being in my parents' bedroom looking for something, but I can't remember what. My hands searched through the top drawer of my father's dresser, poking about. Probably for loose change, now that I think about it. He always had a few spare coins scattered through his stuff, and ever since I was a child he'd let me "borrow" this money when I needed it. I must not have found any change near the front because I pulled the drawer out farther than I had ever done before. And there in the back corner sat a small box, the colour of avocado flesh. Without thinking, I lifted up the lid. I found rusted clips and old coins, ribbons, the faint smell of something I didn't know, and a square of paper faded along the folds.

Even now, fifteen years later, I still remember the crest stamped in crimson ink, this moment of opening into knowledge. The letterhead: *Fort William Asylum* and words pencilled in Cyrillic letters. It was cursive writing, swimming in little streams on the page, not like the square sculptured symbols on the family gravestone. I couldn't read a word on the paper, but sensed that it had to belong to someone my father knew. Then my father was there behind me, snatching the sheet from my hands. He fingered the creases on the page, but said nothing. "Who wrote the letter, Dad? It wasn't your father, was it? He couldn't write." I spoke tentatively, trying to hide my curiosity, but respectful of the fact that I had been rummaging through his drawer.

"It was from Valeska. To my father." He stared at the faded, pencilled words.

"But it has a letterhead that says Fort William Asylum on it." I was practically whispering.

"She went there six years after Magda died. Cracked up. Broken woman. She used to be in and out of the mental hospital here on Queen Street, but then that man she lived with finally had enough of her. Had her committed to the asylum up north in Fort William. She died there." His fingers rubbed the creases on the page, his eyes still didn't meet mine, but I was standing there, not wanting to break his words, the spell he was under, rambling off this history that I was so hungry to hear: my grandmother had died in an asylum. I conjured up visions of her hair matted and straying from her head at odd angles, her mouth screaming silent words as she slumped in a hall, other patients locked in their own trances. My life had been so middle-class, so mundane and boring. And here was this turbulent family history hidden in a drawer the whole time.

"She wrote to my father. Begged him to take her back. But

he would have no part of her." His words severed my thoughts.

"You've got to be kidding me," was all I could mumble.

"No, I'm not. And he was right to do that. What she did was wrong. You don't know what it was like, what happened."

How could he be so hard? I thought. It all happened so long ago – couldn't my father just let it go, forgive his mother? He seemed to carry this wound in his flesh as if it were fresh, he seemed to carry it for his father.

And then he told me about the day she left.

IT IS 1934. Valeska is stirring borshch on the stove, the smell of beets and carrots curling through the air. Marko is four and plays on the floor, pulling a string as though something were attached behind it. Maybe a dog or a pony. Magda bursts into the house and sets her school books on the table; she bends down to Marko. Only then does Valeska grab her hat and coat and kiss Magda on the cheek, telling her to be a big girl, to take care of her brother. Valeska kisses Marko and closes the door behind her.

At first Marko and Magda play a game of hide-and-seek, tearing around the house, knowing that Mama won't be there to scold them for knocking over a lamp or a bowl. But as the day wears on and the borshch boils dry in the pot, burnt beets staining the air, Magda begins to wonder when Mama will return. They are hungry. Marko cries, his round face a fountain of tears she can't stop. They huddle in the corner by the stove, trying to gather warmth from the coal, dead and cold now. Where is Mama? *Mamo*, Marko sobs. His small body heaves up and down like a bellows, Magda thinks. She does not cry, she has to be brave – can't let her brother see her cry. Soothes his forehead and whispers that she will take care of him till Mama comes home.

Night spreads over them, broken only by the shifting patterns of streetlight. Finally Marko heaves into sleep, his body limp in her arms. *What happened to Mama?* she wonders. *Is she hurt? Is she lost? Where is Tato? O Tato, please come home from work.* She twists a strand of hair round and round her finger. The clock on the wall ticks as the pendulum swings back and forth, back and forth.

Then Yurii is home, flicking on the light, running to the stove, to the smell of singed beets, yelling, "*Valesko, Valesko?*" He sees them, cradled beside the stove, Marko's sleeping face flushed and swollen, Magda staring.

That is what Magda can't forget: her father's face. The way it sagged like an empty sack. That and her mother's back as she closed the door.

Magda can't understand why Tato spits on Mama's clothes. Why he won't talk of her when Marko asks for her. Only says over and over that they have no Mama now – she's gone. Gone where? Magda wonders day and night. She knows Mama will be back. She will come back. She wouldn't leave them, leave her children. She loves her *dity*, Magda knows this, just as she knows she loves Mama. But Tato says, "No, that woman not love her *dity*, or why she leave?" Still every night Magda holds onto the hope that Mama will return, holds it as if it were the embroidered bookmark that lies in between the pages of her Bible, the bookmark Mama made her and which she treasures more than anything. Marko just cries and asks for Mama.

During the next few days Magda hears her aunts whisper about her mother, their words brittle snaps. They always stop when Magda enters the room. Marko spends his days at *Titka* Larysa's house while Magda is in school, but she watches him on the weekends. It's important to give him a chance to be at home, so she can teach him English. Tato tries to speak

English, but his words fall like the heads of the calves he crushes with a hammer every day at the slaughterhouse. Marko will be in school soon, and he will need to know this language too, Magda keeps telling Tato. She knows how hard it is to sit in a classroom, strange sounds spitting from her teacher's lips.

A week later – on Saturday at noon – Magda places chipped bowls on the bare table. The kitchen is small and cramped with the table and four wooden chairs and a black coal stove used for cooking food and heating the entire house. There is a white tin sink with a cupboard above it and pipes below it. A straw broom leans in the corner.

Marko sits on the floor playing with that single string. Magda drags a chair to the stove and stands on it to stir the pot of boiling cabbage. This past week she has been trying to be a big girl and help Tato as much as she can. She has always tried to be a *chemna divchynka,* helping Mama by sweeping floors, making beds, playing with Marko. She never liked to see Mama sad, that dark line of her lips turned down, breaking her round face in two like a crack in a bowl. Magda used to see Mama like that when she washed the dishes or cut up cabbage or when she sat in the armchair by the window at night, waiting for Tato to come home. But there were times Mama did smile and hum Ukrainian songs. That was when she washed the laundry of the boarder who lived in the back room, scrubbing his white shirts and heavy pants, hanging them on the wire strung across the backyard, the sunlight circling her kerchiefed head. He paid her money. Magda knew Mama liked to buy pretty things – a brooch or a flowered shawl. Tato never had money for those things.

"*Kapusta* ready, *Marku,*" Magda says, grabbing a bowl from the table, just as Mama bursts into the kitchen. Instantly Magda sinks her face into her mother's roundness, the new dress she wears. It feels soft, like petals on the pansies in the school garden. "Oh, *Mamo,* you come home. You come home."

Marko jumps up and hugs his mother's leg. "*Mamo, ty vdoma! Mamo, ty vdoma!*"

Valeska reaches down to pick him up and hugs both her children, crying, "*Moi dity, moi dity.*"

Magda pulls away and looks at her mother, her new dress, the pretty hat on her head. That's where Mama went, she thinks, to buy a dress and hat. "*Mamo,* you bring new dress for me?"

"*Moia Magdo, dobra Magdo,* Mama bring something better. Mama live with new man. The boarder from upstairs. He buy big house. He have chocolate and money. Here – taste." She takes a dark square from her purse and places it on Magda's tongue. The richness pools in Magda's mouth. She has never tasted such sweetness – thick and smooth like honeyed mud. "*Ohhh Mamo. Tse dobre.*"

Marko tugs on his mother's sleeve. "Chah...co...late." He struggles to speak those English words that seem to bring such pleasure to his sister. Valeska pops a piece in his mouth, and he too breaks into smile. "*Ohhh Mamo.*"

Valeska laughs, her grey eyes fill with tears. "*Marku,* Mama come to get you. Take you with her." And she squeezes his pudgy body.

"We go to live in big house?" Magda asks. "What about Tato?"

Valeska puts Marko on the floor and bends down. "Oh, my Madga. The man say I can bring only one of you. He tell me. Only one. And Marko, you know, Marko is little. He need me. You big girl. You stay here, take care of Tato." She points to the stove. "You cook dinner. You big girl now."

The bowl in Magda's hand slides from her grip and smashes – pieces scatter like hard snow. She grabs that dress, the fine cloth tight in her fist, crushed like petals. She will not let go, she will hold onto this dress.

Valeska pulls away from her daughter. Her eyes are wells. "*Magdo,* Mama can not take you. The man say. Only room for one of you. Cannot take you." Then she wipes her eyes with her large hands, her lips hard now, that dark line fracturing her face. "Be big girl for Tato."

Magda stares at her. This is not her mama, no, her mama would not leave her. Magda pushes her mother away, that fat belly. She spits on the fine dress. "You go. You not take Marko. He stay with Tato and me. You go." She shatters another bowl, shards cutting her leg, blood weeping down her skin.

Marko sobs and Valeska scoops him up like a sack of potatoes. Magda grabs the broom and waves it at her mother, chases her out of the kitchen. Valeska struggles with the weight of Marko in her arms, as she pushes out the front door, calling, "Mama no can take you. The man say."

At night Yurii finds Magda sitting on the floor, in the dark, a piece of dirty string and fragments of a bowl in her hands.

MY FATHER ALWAYS SAID his sister had a temper. He remembers that spit so well, and the broom, Magda swinging it in the air, smacking Valeska. I can't comprehend what it would have been like – that child's moment of knowing what her mother meant to do: leave her behind. The pieces all fitting together and at the same time scattering, breaking apart, never to be whole again.

But for my father the breach came a week later, after he had spent a week crying in the big house "the man" owned. Valeska tried to soothe him, but he wouldn't stop his noise. Finally the man had enough. Told Valeska to take her son back, or else she had to leave. The next afternoon she left my father in an alleyway. Near the slaughterhouse so Yurii would find him. And she ran back to the man. My grandfather found his son wandering up and down the dirty pavement, sobbing for his mama.

And now I stand here in front of the house where it all happened.

How could a mother leave her son in an alleyway? What would have driven her to that? There must have been something else in her life that pushed her to leave the house, to go with that man. Who was he? What hold did he have on her?

I turn to my father and ask him if he still has that letter – the one Valeska wrote from the asylum. I haven't seen it since the day I discovered it in that avocado-coloured box. He says he just threw it away the other day when he was cleaning out his drawers – the day after I asked him to visit his old house. But he did keep his father's passport and Valeska's too, and would give me those if I wanted. And the family photograph album.

After all these years, he has thrown away that letter. I wonder why he ever kept it in the first place, and why he has let go of it now. The letter is something I would have grabbed onto – a piece of my history. A connection to my grandmother. Her side of the story. I crave some kind of knowledge of her, and those words on that page might have given me that. And he has just discarded it. But I say nothing. Instead I ask him when Valeska died, what year it was.

He stares at the house, tells me these row houses can never be torn down. Ten years ago the city planned to erase them, scrape them from the face of the earth, as if they had never existed. Something I can imagine my father wished for often, something he tried to do in his mind over and over. The city wanted to build an apartment complex on the land, he says. But the historical society had the houses classified as Heritage Properties. During the 1800s they had served as quarters for the officers at Fort York. Now they can't be torn down.

He looks at me and says, "She died in 1973."

"You mean she was alive till I was fourteen years old? And you never told me?" I watch years of Ukrainian tales, red beads, her Ukrainian costume I could have worn, fall like leaves from a tree, colours fading, drifting in the wind, branches left bare, wanting. How could he have not told me? How could he deny me a grandmother?

"I couldn't tell you," he stresses, his large hands open. "The house was in her name, that's why I never sold it. My parents never divorced. She didn't know my father was dead when she wrote that letter in 1956. If her family had ever found out about the house, they would have wanted her to sell it for the money. And my father made me promise that she would never get this house. Never. I finally sold it the year after Freda called our house – my mother had been dead four years then, everything had gone through probate and I could sell it."

I register somewhere in my mind that he has said the words "my mother." But I can only mutter over and over, "I had a living Ukrainian grandmother and you never told me."

"Your mother always wanted me to tell you about her. To go up there and visit her in that asylum after Slavko blurted everything out. But we could never go up there. If the people at that place knew she had a house they'd have told her to sell it so they could have some money to pay for her keep, I know they would. And if you saw her, you might have let it slip out that *Dido* was dead. Kids are like that. No, it was best that no one knew."

I realize now why he never told me the dates of her birth and death that I thought were carved on the family gravestone. "Where is she buried?" I ask.

"Here in Toronto. They shipped her body down." He bends his head, pauses. "She's buried in an unmarked grave."

I can't believe I own this history.

"The people in the asylum wanted me to pay for her grave," he whispers, "but I refused."

I can see his shame now, the sweat on that square forehead, his blue eyes avoiding mine. And I realize the magnitude of what he has done, keeping this history from me all these years. But I realize too the magnitude of what he has done just now. For me. Here in front of this house. This house that can't be buried. That stands here defiantly as a reminder of other things beside officers' barracks. Other lives. The structure of *my* heritage. I touch my father's hunched back.

The sky is dark. He says it's time to move on. He still wants to visit the cemetery where his father is buried. He hasn't been there in twenty years and it's time now to make peace with all his ancestors.

The Children of Mary

MARUSYA BOCIURKIW

I wanted to go to Lourdes and swoon, soft and gauzy like Jennifer Leigh in *The Song of Bernadette*, black and white and flickering with visions on the movie screen. I dreamed of going to the very place where Our Lady appeared to Bernadette, and glorious rays of light descended upon her bowed, veiled head. Me, my weird sister, my angry ma, my deadbeat dad, we'd be a perfect family, travelling to France together; we'd learn French before we'd go.

My sister and I joined the Children of Mary at a time when we were needing way more drama in our lives. Junior High was not the thrilling experience I had thought it would be, and the 70's were definitely passing us by. There were hippies camping out by the river, kids our age smoking dope, eating brown rice, and selling love beads downtown. There were protests and riots burning through the TV screen, there were free schools that we'd heard dim rumours about, where you could take subjects like astrology and creative writing all day long – but those were distant, unattainable rebellions. Children of Mary was Kat's latest idea, something she thought up one boring Sunday – *What the hell*, she said, when I told her she was nuts, *it's a way to get out of church faster.* The Children of Mary always filed out first, like business class in an airplane, and, if you played your cards right, sucked up to the nuns and sold enough crocheted bedjackets and baby booties, you did get to go to Lourdes, right to the grotto where Jennifer Leigh had had her vision, and holy water perpetually squirted from the ground. The most goody-goody girls got a bonus trip to Rome to see the holy skeletons in the catacombs and the petrified bones of St Peter, encased in a sacred glass tomb.

Besides that, there were crocheting and macramé lessons, and the fact that Kat usually got me to do whatever she wanted. She said I had to join, because in addition to being sisters, we were part of the larger Family of Our Lady. She was so full of it. The rosary wasn't all that hard to memorize, though Kat actually whispered the words in a theatrical sibilant murmur, instead of just mouthing them. Always having to go one step further than everyone else, out on an edge. I had to be there, make sure she didn't fall.

According to Kat, we now had to do Sacrifices all the time. Not just giving things up, she informed me in a smug, teacherly way – after all, we were used to *that*. Sacrifices, she insisted, meant *willingly* doing things we didn't *want* to do. Ma was suspicious of Children of Mary – they didn't have them where she was from. *Pfft*, she said to me, *your sister with her stupid ideas, takes after her good-for-nothing father*, but she definitely liked the concept of Sacrifices. On Sundays, Kat volunteered both of us to stay in and do housework. Kids' voices droned through the open windows of the bathroom while we piously scraped at grout and scrubbed the bathtub ring. Saturday would have been even more of a Sacrifice, but I drew the line. A couple of times, Kat had us do housework in Silence. This wasn't an official Children of Mary thing, it was something Kat had seen in a movie, *The Nun's Story*, starring Audrey Hepburn. Once, we managed to not speak for about five hours, until Ma got mad and said we couldn't have supper until we started talking again, she said we were just being smart alecs.

There were Mortifications, too. Lying on your back all night, not moving, hands crossed over your chest. Eating dry bread or drinking water with vinegar in it. Beating your back with a hairbrush, or a stick, or the end of a small whisk broom. And worse things: stories of female saints with bloody wounds blooming like flowers on their pale, delicate hands.

The big Sacrifices were the ones Sister Paraskeva, the Children of Mary leader, alluded to in her dry, husky voice. Not Having Relations. Ever. Not marrying or having children. You could become a nun, but you didn't have to – just a Lay Person, with a lot of medallions around your neck, under your sober, buttoned-up blouse. For Life.

The problem that torments me I place in your blessed hands. Remember me O Blessed Mother in my Hour of Need.

I WAS THIRTEEN and Kat was going on fifteen, the year we got religion. Children of Mary took a lot of concentration, and quite a bit of time. But it was something different. It was more appealing than we cared to admit: more meaningful, more glamourous than ordinary life, a dark, humid place inside your head where, if you prayed all the time, everything would be OK.

Sometimes, I could almost hear Our Lady's voice, so sweet and kind, blending with the whisper of poplars and the hum of the river outside my bedroom window. I had a lot of questions for Her. Like, how were we doing? Was there a bonus for the grey wood-and-stucco bungalow we lived in, two bedrooms for the three of us, yellowing acoustic tile in the livingroom, no rumpus room? Our Ma being a cleaning lady and always calling Kat stupid and me self-centred, was that a kind of Mortification? A dad somewhere in Alberta or Saskatchewan, who sent us a Christmas card every year. Ma always looking for a folded-up cheque inside the card, but there never was one.

Once – she took him to court – I heard her say he was a *kurvyn syn*, which I later found out meant "son of a whore."

Thinking about this stuff made me feel like I was crazily suspended in Purgatory, my Immortal Soul caught between heaven and hell, no landing place. Did suffering make you go to heaven faster? Did being happy slow down your Salvation?

ONE DAY, ABOUT A MONTH AFTER we had joined Children of Mary, Kat claimed to have a Vision in the parking lot of the Liquor Store. We were waiting in the car for Ma, stuffed inside with bags of groceries and spooky second-hand clothes Ma had picked up at a church basement, windows rolled shut like Ma told us to. I was reading my latest Nancy Drew book, *The Password at Larkspur Lane*, and stretching out my gum to see how far it would go. Kat had her face pressed, sweaty, red and moody, against the glass.

Sonya, there she is!

Who? Irritated at the interruption, I didn't even look up from my book.

Mary!

Mary Woschinski?

No, stupid! Our Lady! Over there by the alley!

This got my attention. I squinted hard. The sun was streaming through a break in the clouds, backlighting a lilac bush behind the store that had long since lost its blooms and the old drunk guys who sat out there most afternoons, giving them haloes. *Glories from heaven*, just like at Lourdes.

Like a magician, Kat pulled a rosary out of nowhere, and whispered a Hail Mary with short, hurried breaths.

HolyMaryMotherofGodprayforussinnersnowandatthehour ofourdeath...

I just hoped it would all be over before Ma came back to the car.

I WAS IN A PERPETUAL STATE OF EMBARRASSMENT. A membrane of shame surrounded me like a blue, watery amniotic sac. Too fat, too smart, too mouthy for a girl, I always wanted to disappear. But every time I thought I was starting to blend in, Kat would blow my cover. Insisted, since joining Children of Mary, on being called *Kateryna,* which no one at school could even say. Decided we should be excused from school January 6, Ukrainian Christmas Eve, which our family never really celebrated anyways, but all the other Children of Mary did. We spent the day at the shopping centre following Ma around, getting on her nerves. I missed Theatre Arts class, which I loved, and also had to put up with a certain distance from the popular crowd – led by pert, slender girls with names like Cindy and Mindy. After that, I thought I heard the word *bohunk* whispered in the lunchroom one day, but I couldn't be sure.

Still, Children of Mary wasn't bad. It was comfortable. It was easy. Everyone was Ukrainian, all of us felt snubbed by the popular crowd. Sometimes all we'd do would be to talk about "the swingers" while we crocheted table runners and bed jackets out of Banlon wool for the church bazaar, and Sister Paraskeva scratched prayers onto the blackboard. It wasn't good to be a swinger. It meant you were "Insecure." The comfort felt dangerous, even then.

KAT ALWAYS HAD BIG DRAMATIC IDEAS. This one was no different. It was Good Friday, no school. There was a cold, pale grey sky, like the inside of an eggshell. We went with Ma to get fresh cream and eggs from Mrs. Boychuk on the farm outside of town. There didn't seem to be anything moving or growing, except for the pussy willows by the edge of the road.

We weren't allowed to have dairy products till Sunday, and today, because of Sister Paraskeva's suggestion, Kat and I were fasting. By afternoon, when we had to go to church, the hunger pangs had been replaced by a pleasant giddiness. My body felt swollen with the sweet, hot agony of Jesus.

The church was full, mostly old ladies dressed in black, kerchiefs on their heads, crying uncontrollably because Jesus had died on the cross. The Children of Mary in the front row, crisp blue robes, doilies – what I called them behind Kat's back – bobby-pinned to our heads.The front of the altar, usually a wide, soothing expanse of deep red carpet, was dominated by an oversized black coffin. On it was a life-size, life-like painting of Jesus In His Agony, with all His Bleeding Wounds. There were five, and you had to kiss them all after Mass was over. It was creepy, but you had to do it, especially if you were Children of Mary.

Children of Mary went first. You had to kneel and then hobble alongside the coffin on your knees, trying to be graceful, trying not to gag, kissing each wound, glazed over with years of people's saliva, one by one.

Now and at the hour of our death...

Kat had tears running down her face.

When we got home, Kat took me behind the garage. She said Our Lady had given her a Message.

I was in a daze. I said yes.

Neither of us could believe how much blood there was.

I almost swooned.

SISTER PARASKEVA WAS SUMMONED BY PHONE, by Ma, to see the wounds. My body felt interesting and dignified with the gauze bandages covering the stigmata on my hands and feet. We were sent to our room. Sister Paraskeva and Ma talked in the kitchen. We could hear my ma's voice slicing through the thin walls, sharp and afraid: *What kinda things you teaching them there, makes a girl go and cut her little sister with a kitchen knife?*

It seemed like a reasonable enough question, given the circumstances, but I figured we could kiss our trip to France goodbye. I lay on my bed and looked at the ceiling, throbbing hands clasped behind my head, feeling like a man on Death Row. Wisely, Kat kneeled by her bed and said the Rosary. We would need the extra prayers.

Ma grounded Kat for a month, which included Children of Mary. I went a few more times, then quit, out of loyalty or guilt, I didn't know the difference. So much for Lourdes.

The popular girls swarmed me during the long school months after Easter. Either they wanted to save me from Kat, or they wanted some of her notoriety. I did go to some of their sleep-over parties, with their hard-to-figure-out rituals of gossip and seances and Ouija boards. I had to talk Ma into buying me a sleeping bag and a frilly nightgown. I had to act giggly and have secrets to tell. Once, at Julie McNiven's house, we sneaked red wine from the McNivens' liquor cabinet in the rumpus room, at three in the morning. I got a bit tipsy. The other girls, who were Roman Catholic where they only had wafers for Communion, made me show them how Ukrainian Communion was made. They got white bread out of the fridge, a goblet from the cupboard. Julie was the priest, she pretended to be Ukrainian, but she sounded more like Boris Karloff, it was embarrassing.

Kat stopped talking much to anyone, and she didn't talk at all to me. On her fifteenth birthday she went to the river bank across the field from our house and stayed there all day, by herself. I went looking for her, found her asleep on the cracked, dried-up mud, a rosary entwined in her fingers, and pale spidery slash marks on her arms. I woke her up and got her to come home to a birthday cake and our ma's thin good cheer. I never asked Kat about the scars, though later, of course, I wished I had.

Kat became best friends with Louise Thivierge from school. Louise was French, from St. Boniface, she wasn't one of the popular girls. She had long thin blonde hair and pale bluish skin, and she was brainy. I thought people were only nice to Louise so she would help them with their math or their French.

Kat and Louise were ready for a change of image. After the month of being grounded was over, they would go to Louise's house after school, leaving right after the bell so I wouldn't follow them. Kat would come home looking totally different. Coloured poodle barrettes holding back the sides of her hair. White lipstick, dark-blue mascara, and avocado-green eyeshadow, which Ma would make Kat wipe off.

Kat never went back to Children of Mary, and she stopped making me do the same thing as her. After school was out for the summer, she started hanging out by the river with some of the guys from Grade Twelve. I knew, but I didn't tell. The secret was the only thing I had.

Mostly Kat and the Grade Twelve guys smoked, just one cigarette passed between them. Sometimes they sat on the riverbank and drank Mateus wine from a paper bag, quite a daring thing. One of the guys, Randy, strummed guitar and sang: *Stairway to Heaven, Me and Bobby McGee.* Kat would sing along in her sweet soprano Children of Mary voice, and Louise would try to sing harmony, which never really worked. I often parked my bike behind the lilac bushes, to listen, and to watch out for Kat. She had a new laugh with a harsh, practised ring. I wanted to ask her where it came from. I had never experienced a loneliness this difficult or sickly-sweet.

That summer, I got sent to Baba's for a month, to get separated from Kat. It was not a place I ever wanted to go. Kat got sent to Dad's, who had resurfaced in Regina. He said he had a nice apartment, Kat said she wanted to visit him, and Ma didn't say no.

Baba lived in a trailer court outside of town. Nice garden, even managed to grow sunflowers, but still a trailer, aluminum, not even painted. She insisted on giving me her bed – I didn't even want it – and she slept on the couch. Baba's bed had gritty sheets that smelt like baby powder and mothballs. There was a large crucifix over the bed and a rosary on the bedside table, which I never touched.

There wasn't anything to do. Mostly, I pretended I was somewhere else: playing with Kat in the field by the river or down along the railroad tracks, like we used to, years ago. Sometimes before I went to sleep I'd comfort myself with a big scenario about going to Lourdes with Kat and Dad. We would visit the Grotto, and we would bathe in Holy Water. Everything would be forgiven; everyone would speak French.

Baba cooked a huge supper every night, it took three or four hours, Baba lurching from cupboard to counter to sink. Overcooked roast beef, mashed potatoes from a box, gravy, peas from the garden, which I had to shell. Often, while we were eating, Baba pulled out old photographs from a box on the floor by her chair, and would arrange them absent-mindedly on the table, like a game of solitaire. Once, she pulled out a picture of her mother, my great-grandmother, dead in her casket in the Old Country, her jaw hanging open like in a horror movie. It sat there, in the middle of the table, all through dinner. Afterwards, I threw up.

IN SEPTEMBER, Kat started dressing kind of slutty. Wearing her new white Bonne Belle lipstick to school, and the white vinyl go-go boots and pink hot pants from Dad; Ma didn't stop her. Kat also bought a set of steam hair rollers with her saved-up allowance, and started flipping back the sides of her hair Farrah-Fawcett style, using Ma's hairspray. One night when she was out I searched her dresser drawers and found: cigarettes, Cosmopolitan magazine, razor blades, a picture of Dad from when we were little, some prayer cards, and a box of condoms.

What explained some, but not all of it, was that she had secretly started dating – Randy, from the evenings by the river, who was English, and a high-school drop-out to boot. Kat told me she was dating, but that was all she said. She was always out late with Randy and sleeping in weekend mornings, patterning her movements in a counterpoint to mine. So that we were totally in synch, totally out of each other's way.

Sometimes, in the morning while Kat was sleeping, I would lie on my side and observe her face. The tiny flickering movements of her eyelashes, the twitches in her mouth. Occasionally, as an experiment, I'd lean across the narrow space that separated her bed from mine, and I'd place my hand near her face, to see how close I could get without waking her. I could feel her warmth and smell her sour apricot smell. Kat never moved away when I did that, which reassured me.

I started dating too: tentative, agonizing liaisons at movies and school dances with a boy I never touched. You couldn't enter a dance with your girlfriend any more; you had to have a boyfriend, limp and mute, at your side. Besides which, I thought it might give Kat and me something in common. But it seemed like the minute I agreed to go to the junior high semi-formal with Terry Woschinski, Kat dumped Randy and joined the Women's Liberation Movement. I had to go to the semi-formal anyways, and afterwards, on the sidewalk outside my house, under a streetlight that stood in for the moon, Terry kissed me with a mouth like a cool, damp washcloth.

Kat was always one step ahead of me, but now I couldn't

keep up. Not long after school was out, Mrs. Woschinski saw Kat downtown on Main Street, barefoot, no make-up, wearing a long Indian dress, her hair all loose, holding hands with another girl, also in bare feet, both of them smoking that *mar-ee-wa-na.* Mrs. Woschinski told Ma, and then she told everyone else. It was the bare feet that had the Ukrainians in North End Winnipeg talking for months.

I was impressed. Ma wasn't. It was the last straw. She and Kat had a screaming argument. Ma called Kat names I didn't know she knew, like *pervert, whore,* and *slut.* She hit Kat in the face, there was blood, I saw it on the towel Ma stuffed into the laundry hamper after Kat ran crying to her room.

Kat didn't call me until about a month after she ran away from home. It was the first time I had ever heard my sister's voice over the phone. It sounded tinny and young.

Kat wanted to know did I want to meet at the Windmill café for a coffee or something. I never went to the Windmill and I didn't drink coffee, but I said yeah, OK, for sure.

For the week until we met, things I wanted to say buzzed inside of me, flies caught in a house. What it was like since she'd left: Ma was being nicer to me, she didn't want me to leave, too. Letting me stay out late on Saturday night, turning a blind eye to the dating thing. How it was having my own room: OK, but kind of weird. I didn't mind at all if Kat and Ma made up and Kat needed to come home. And questions I knew I wouldn't ask: was she really a lezzie and a drug addict, and how come she had changed so much, so fast.

I got to the Windmill early. I brought my book, ordered a Coke, tried not to look shifty. The waitress kept a sharp eye on me: girls didn't go alone to a restaurant in those days unless they were in some kind of trouble. Kat was half an hour late. I didn't mind. When she walked in the door, I spilt half my Coke on the table.

Still as clumsy as ever, eh? said Kat, with a fake cheerful sound in her voice.

I didn't like that, it was condescending. I was already fourteen.

Kat ordered coffee and pulled out a pack of cigarettes. I didn't know she was smoking in earnest.

How ya doin'? she said, and didn't wait for an answer.

I'm not really a homo you know, she blurted out. *I'm just having fun with this girl in my commune, her name's Angélique, she's Métis. You'd like her. She can speak French 'n' everything. We're gonna go travelling. It's all women living in the commune, men can visit but they can't live there. We all take care of each other, we cook together, it's so great, just being with girls, with... women...*

The waitress arrived with the coffee. Kat's voice trailed off, then came up again, but in a smaller, flatter way: *I hope you're* OK. *I mean, it must be kinda weird for ya, being on your own...*

The stuff I wanted to say flooded out backwards, and all in a rush.

If Ma lets you come back, I don't mind sharing my room again, I mean, it's nice having my own room, but if you came back –

It was like Kat was waiting to get mad, and any comment would do.

Forget it. I don't ever want to come back. You always try to make me stay the same. You always take her side. You always did.

There was about a minute of silence, but it felt longer than that, like a car ride through the prairies. Everything looking the same, everything changed.

It was the very first breaking of my heart.

KAT'S FLING WITH ANGÉLIQUE became public information. Sister Paraskeva saw them necking in the park near the church, in the middle of a school day, and wanted to call the police, but Ma talked her out of it. I wasn't sure what they were most freaked out about: Kat kissing another girl, or Angélique being Indian. As usual, I had to take the rap for Kat. Ma said I wasn't allowed out late on Saturdays anymore.

One day when I came home from school, Ma was talking in the living room with Father Melnyk. I hung around in the kitchen. I couldn't believe my ears. They were talking about performing an exorcism. They were planning to corner Kat and hold her down, sprinkle her with holy water, the priest scaring Satan away with his crucifix, as though she was Linda Blair in *The Exorcist*, which had come out a couple of years earlier. It was a time of cults and runaways, of teenagers being lost to Moonies and Hare Krishnas, of missing children pictures on the milk cartons. Furthermore, Ma was never one to admit defeat.

I told Ma I was going to study at Terry's, and then took the long winding bus ride to the commune in Corydon where Kat had told me she lived. Pouring rain, a ten-minute walk from the bus stop, I was soaked by the time I got to the house. Door wide open, a welcoming wedge of yellow light like a scene in a TV commercial.

I called for Kat from the front hallway. I could hear muffled voices, laughter. Went upstairs, opened a door.

Kat naked, with a man lying beside her. Her face turned towards the wall. A gasping sound coming out of her mouth.

I stood in the doorway for a moment, love and revulsion churning in my stomach like milk gone sour. Then I closed the door and ran out of the house.

Ma went through with her plan. One night, she barged into Kat's house with old, scary, drooling Father Petryshyn who'd apparently had a slew of successful exorcisms in the Old Country. He sprinkled holy water in the hallway while Ma went into the kitchen.The commune was having supper, and finally, Ma could see what was really going on. Men, women, macrobiotic food. Probably sex. Kat asked them to leave, said to Ma was she crazy, told Father Petryshyn he was a pervert and he should get a real job. When Ma described the scene later, she made the food sound like the worst thing of all: brown lentil stew and brown bread, the kind of food you had to eat when you were poor.

AFTER WOMEN'S LIBERATION, Kat joined the Trotskyists. On Saturdays sometimes, I saw her downtown, in front of Eaton's, selling newspapers. Once, I walked up to her, just to say hi. Kat stared at me for a moment. Then she turned away and said to a girl I assumed was Angélique, *Man, it's my friggin' family, on my back again.*

By then I was working at the drugstore after school and on weekends, saving up to go to college like Ma wanted me to. Being busy filled in the sore gaps of Kat's absence, but not the ache of what she had become. I tried going to some of the Women's Liberation meetings, like a detective looking for clues, but the meetings reminded me of Julie McNiven's sleepovers, with all their self-satisfied confessing and revealing. I was always too quiet; I never had secrets to tell. It was after I'd been four or five times that I overheard one of the women talking about Kat: *She's fanatical, brainwashed by the Trots. Says feminism is counter-revolutionary. White trash from the North End, telling* me *about politics.*

I quit Women's Liberation, took up yoga instead.

By fall of that year I stopped seeing Kat outside Eaton's anymore with the other newspaper sellers. Angélique wasn't there either. I built up the courage to talk to one of the men, a big bearded guy with a British accent and trembling smile who said his name was Full Moon.

Full Moon shrugged and said Kat had left the commune,

he wasn't sure where she had gone, but why didn't I come to one of their Tuesday night potluck dinners and maybe someone there would know. He stroked my arm, offered me a joint, and gazed at me with soft, girlish eyes.

I told Ma, who got mad and wondered her usual thing: Where Did I Go Wrong.

I got busy working overtime during the Christmas season and never went to the potluck. I didn't know what I'd take, anyways, or what I'd ask. On my days off I'd take the bus downtown, peering through veils of snow, eyeing every long-haired, long-skirted young woman I saw. They all looked the same – no mittens, no hat, walking slowly even in the bitter cold – but none of them was Kat. After a while I stopped, it was too depressing.

The problem that torments me I place in your blessed hands.

It wasn't until Christmas of that year that Ma got worried enough to call the police.

WHEN I GOT OFF THE BUS FROM WORK I could see the cop car in front of our house, red lights on, glowing through the falling snow, like votive candles, like a sign. It would be OK, Kat had probably just been caught shoplifting, please Jesus, thank you Mary, it was going to be OK.

There were two cops sitting at the kitchen table, clutching their hats with big, apologetic hands. The table was empty, not even a pot of tea. Kat wasn't with them. It was like a tableau from a school play, where everything's really literal and obvious, and then and there I knew Kat was dead.

Ma sat up very straight in her chair, stroking the bare table cloth, sweeping off invisible crumbs. She gave me a long, hollow look. She said my name in Ukrainian, with the added suffix that made it an endearment, *Soniechko,* a private code.

Then she got a grip, switched to English, and told me the facts, as though I was a newspaper reporter. Kat's body had been found by the side of a highway just west of Fort McLeod, Alberta.

The who, what, when, and where, but not the why.

My life split into two pieces that very afternoon. Everything that happened before, and everything that happened after, like a paper torn down the middle. Caught in between was me, and everything I wanted to become.

The cops asked me a bunch of questions, I don't remember what. Full Moon and some of the other commune members were questioned, and then got busted for marijuana and hashish. They took Angélique in for questioning, after they found her working in a bar in St. Boniface, but she and Kat hadn't been together for over six months. I didn't understand why they were investigating everybody when it just looked like a simple car accident, but I was too full of confusion, like a room too full of furniture, to say anything at all.

It was in the newspaper, and I still have the clipping. They used an old picture from Children of Mary, Kat in her robe and doily from when she was still fourteen. Ma gave it to them. That was the only way she wanted to remember Kat.

There was a funeral – all I remember are odd fragments. The food, tons of it, the kind Kat and I would have made fun of, pretending to put fingers down our throats: cottage cheese and cling peaches salad, Kraft Mayonnaise Waldorf salad, macaroni and ham salad, Polynesian pineapple salad, lime Jello aspic salad. A million pyrohy and cabbage rolls. Everyone eating tiny bites with pursed lips, as if they wanted to say, "I told you so," but didn't.

It wasn't long before the rumours started to pile up. Nobody wanted to believe it was an accident, everybody wanted made-for-TV drama. Suicide. Pill overdose. Slit wrists. The wrists rumour was the favourite one, seeing as everyone vaguely remembered the Good Friday episode from a few years ago, except they remembered it wrong, that Kat had slashed herself, instead of me.

We got the autopsy report just after the funeral. No alcohol in the blood. No suspicion of wrongdoing. Just a hit-and-run driver, the cops didn't think they'd ever find him. My ma's averted eyes, when she told me this. Mrs. Woschinski's face, all sucked in and blank, as she stood next to my mother. My face in the mirror afterwards, sulky and heavy: I hardly recognized myself.

And a lingering set of unanswered questions that would always ring between my ears, like an obscene story I couldn't believe I'd heard.

Toronto, 1980

Ma didn't want me to go, of course, and Mrs. Woschinski said it was truly a Mortal Sin to leave my poor mother all alone like that. I was young enough not to care. I had waited until a year after Kat's death, a year that felt like a century.

Mary Woschinski had just moved to Toronto, and for lack of a better idea I followed her, even though we had never really been friends. I slept on the futon couch in her tidy, tiny apartment near Yonge Street for a month, until I found a job and a place of my own, a basement apartment on Roncesvalles. Worked in a photocopy shop and then in a same-day photo shop. Took a government training course, and by my third year in Toronto I was a ward clerk in a university hospital, a good job with a dental plan.

Ma tried to get me down for Christmas or Easter every year, but I always had the excuse of not being able to get more than a long weekend off work. Then after I said that, I'd say that Ma was welcome to come to Toronto. It was the wrong order to put things in, and Ma, with the attention to detail that lonely people have, would say in a small, strained voice, *No, thank you, I can't get away.*

We were so mad at each other for the longest time. Being mad was the only thing that made it halfway bearable.

EACH PERSON I MET IN TORONTO led me into a new point of view, a strange part of the city, connected only by the subway line's narrative thread. This was a city where I could be someone different, someone brighter and more upbeat, someone *into being positive*, a *people person*, leaving my sulking face behind like a worn-out skin.

The glimmer and rush of the subway excited me, you could go anywhere you wanted, the names of neighbourhoods flashing past like a slot machine: Ossington, Dufferin, High Park, Jane. Movies, plays, cafés, strange, dark downtown streets, or the ghettoes lit up like carnivals, the part of Church Street they said was gay, the strip of Gerrard that was just like India.

One of the first things I joined was a peace group downtown; it was a time of huge anti-nuclear marches pretty as Easter parades. You could fit in easily, just by holding a placard and wearing brightly-coloured buttons that said things like, *One nuclear bomb can ruin your whole day.* I went to women's peace actions at Litton Systems Canada in the suburbs, where they made cash registers and cruise missile guidance systems. We wove coloured wool into the wire-mesh fence and wept as women climbed the fence and got arrested, as they spoke of doing this for children they'd not yet given birth to.

Through the peace group I met some Latin American refugees, desperate, charming men from El Salvador. Victims of recent changes to immigration law, their only way out of the bureaucratic maze would be love, marriage, and a baby carriage. One of the Salvadorean men told me he loved me, after I had coffee with him a couple of times. I started volunteering as a tutor at the literacy clinic he attended. My guilt was everywhere, then, my activism a band-aid on a sore: mine, not his.

Like the outlines of bodies we drew in chalk outside of nuclear power plants, like the the dead we remembered at rallies for El Salvador or Nicaragua, shouting "*Presente!*" as their names were called, Kat's body was invisible, unimaginable, and darkly present everywhere I went. It changed shape, but it was always there: grotesque, bruised, covered with tire tracks and mud; waxy, smiling, and gaunt as a mannequin in a store window.

It had been, in the mincing words of the funeral director, a "closed casket ceremony." At the time I was relieved. But now I felt deprived of a body to remember, to forget her with. I wandered through a huge city, looking for a place to bury the dead weight of my grief.

I HAD BEEN IN TORONTO FOUR YEARS. My world, from work to home, was comprised primarily of women. I hadn't planned it that way, didn't even notice it. There were women I met at the peace rallies who used words like "woman-centred," or "gynocentric," a fairy-tale land where everything was run by women: all the buildings would be soft and curved and there'd be no wars. I didn't buy it. I still remembered the ladies of the church, Mrs. Woschinski's remarks about Indians and Chinamen, my mother's sniping ways.

Women's Liberation had evolved into feminism, which involved huge meetings that sizzled like oil in a pan, women from all over the city, from trade unions and socialist feminist groups, health collectives and Trotskyist cells. I only went once or twice, but several of the women in my co-op attended each week, coming home late at night saying things like, *Can you believe what that woman said?* popping the tabs off of beer cans, leaning their elbows onto the worn kitchen table with exaggerated fatigue, as though they'd just come from working in the fields. A couple of my housemates organized marches past the porn theatres on Yonge Street, or through the hookers' neighbourhoods. I went to some of their slide shows, where larger-than-life pictures flicked onto the wall: women being gagged or tied up, or even just having sex with each other or with men. Except for the time I caught Kat in bed with a man, those pictures were the very first images of sex I'd ever seen. My eyes adjusted immediately to the dusky illicitness of it all. I was always sorry when the lights came back on.

My room-mates dragged me to all the marches, like parents herding a child to church, where I stood on the sidelines, warming my body with all the heat. I knew they had fun too, these solemn, ponderous women, and like some kind of anthropologist, I wanted to find out exactly how, and where. One night, Lisa, one of the women from the peace group, took me to a women's bar called the Chez Moi, hidden in a side street near Yonge and Bloor. Lisa had got me high, and I kept thinking half the people were men, but they weren't, of course. We went together several times, and then I started going on my own.

It was exciting at first, an expensive, forbidden fruit I could finally eat. Something I'd always wanted to try but couldn't, because Kat had done it first, and it had been so bad.

Was it like this for Kat? This floating in the city, this half-life, this *demi-monde* where you were moth-like, visible and invisible, beautiful and repulsive, at the same time? *Had Kat felt this?* This heat in your body congealing into a secret hardness when you came home on the subway early in the morning from the bar, the metal edges of the city pressing against you, flattening your undercover passion, your hidden, pulsing heart?

And always, this defiance, this sense of derring-do. Looking at women on the subway, not even seeing the men. Coming home and peeling off the dress, the pantihose, even the bra. Jeans, a T-shirt, a subway ride to the Chez. You could feel political, even if you weren't. And most of the women weren't. They talked about TV shows, their cats, their bosses, what kind of music they liked. Women like me, from smaller cities and towns, working stiffs, coming to the bar as though to a new world, which always self-destructed on Sunday night. Except for the one-night stands or the one-month affairs, I never saw these women outside of the bar.

Once, a woman I danced with asked me out for lunch. No one from the bar ever did that, which was how I knew she was one of the more political ones. We had lunch in a downtown fern café she chose. I could tell from her eyes she wanted to sleep with me but couldn't say it, so instead she talked politics non-stop.

Patriarchy, sexism, classism. I didn't really know what classism was, so she told me. I had a flash of remembering Kat outside of Eaton's with her Trotsky newspapers. Kat, who never wanted to admit that Ma was a cleaning lady, and then suddenly was proud of it, overnight.

Zoe, the woman I had lunch with, said lesbians were invisible. Made invisible by the culture, was how she put it.

I was surprised to hear that. I had never felt so visible, so looked at, in my life.

BY MOVING TO TORONTO, I thought I could forget the worst things. At first it worked, but eventually Kat came back, in dreams and waking flashbacks like a light left strangely on in the daytime. And the kind of women I was attracted to. Not so fucked up as you'd notice right away, except when you were in bed with them. Then you'd see the slash marks on their arms, or a week later they'd tell you how their family in Northern Ontario completely ostracized them since they came out and now they were really depressive, and they secretly drank.

She was always with me in that space between being asleep and being awake, at either end of a dream. She was the beam of light at the bottom of a tunnel, waiting for me. She would be wearing her blue Children of Mary cape, but with white lipstick and avocado-green eyeshadow too. And I would think, *Oh, she's alive*, but then I'd think, *Oh, she's crazy, too.*

Sometimes, I'd linger in the tunnel a little too long and when I finally moved towards daylight she'd be gone or I'd wake up. One or the other.

WINNIPEG, 1987

I WENT BACK IN THE MIDDLE OF SUMMER, six years after I had left. It all looked so beautiful, in a way I didn't remember, a picture postcard, the ugliness airbrushed away. Canola and wheat fields for miles, as you come in by plane. The land divided into circles and squares, every shade of blue and green. All that sky.

Ma's new apartment seemed small, but she said it was just what she wanted. Starting all over again, like me. Ma took me for supper to Alicia's, the Ukrainian restaurant in the North End, figured I'd want Ukrainian cuisine first thing, and she never was much of a cook. She ordered the Perogy Platter and the Cabbage Roll Combo and couldn't understand why I hardly touched my food.

Everyone acted the same as always, and I became what they saw: my teenage self, except that the outline of Kat's body beside me was empty. *Who's your boyfriend?* they'd say to me, and, *When's the big wedding?* Mrs. Woschinski came over for a visit and said, *Ooh, dat Toronto, a bad place, you be careful, my Mary, she never liked it.* Nobody asked me about my job or how I lived. Nobody mentioned Kat.

The third day I was there, I borrowed Ma's car and drove to the cemetery. It was pouring rain, the first time all summer, Ma said. When I got to the grave I stood around some, kicking at the grass. And then, maybe because of the rain, maybe because it was so strange being back, I cried for the first time since the funeral. It didn't feel good like they say in the self-help articles of the magazines, *just let it all out you'll feel better.* It didn't feel better.

It felt like anger, not just at Ma, but at Kat too. It felt like a gash of pain and blood down my arms, down my chest, across my back. It felt like the stigmata we had learnt about from Sister Paraskeva. *Made invisible by the culture.*

And it felt like relief. Not relief from crying.

Missing her was the sweetest part of loving her.

I GOT BACK TO MA'S APARTMENT in time for supper. Baba Woloshyn was there too, She was too old now to help with cooking, so she sat in Ma's La-Zee Boy recliner and thumbed through an old photo album, going, *tsk, tsk.* Ma asked me where I'd been. I said, *Visiting Terry, my old boyfriend.* Baba said, *Do you remember, Soniechko, the time you came and stayed with me in the summer, such a nice time we had?* Ma said, *Yes, she begged me and begged me to go, finally I let her.*

Ma was preparing roast beef and mashed potatoes. She said, *Remember, for a while, Katya was into that, what do they call it, that* vegetarian.

Ma's voice started out playful, then it changed. She almost

whispered: *Katya made me supper one night, everything so heavy with the beans and that brown rice. Such craziness.*

Mama continued, her voice tight and thin, unable to stop herself: *Oy yoy, I thought it was just a passing phase, they always have their phases. But she was different, always went to the extreme. I should have been more strict.*

Baba said, *Shh don't talk like that. It was God's Will, what can you do: nothing.*

I set the table. I could feel my adult body floating above me, everything I wanted to become.

Before dinner Baba said a prayer in Ukrainian. I only understood the last few words.

Remember us O Blessed Mother in our Hour of Need.

Ways of Coping

MYRNA KOSTASH

I. Haidamaka, *from the Turkish, meaning "warrior" or "robber," and* **Haiduk,** *from the Hungarian, also meaning "robber."*

To the Poles, the haidamaka *was a runaway serf with only one means of survival: the sneaky, lawless, fugitive plunder of the property of his former master. To the Bosnians and Serbs, the* hajduk *was an escapee from the Turkish military press gang, who sought sanctuary in the hills and woods, descending to the highways to plunder and kill the Turks. Legend has it he distributed his booty among the poor. It is impossible to confirm this.*

I am excited by this transgression, the violent male in the prime of his physical prowess who chooses to quit the plough, the field, the labour for another man's bread, and heads for the hills and the sphere of morally dubious action (theft, arson, assault). In his courage against the enemy, he acts for me: I am mired in necessity, repetition, inevitability; he creates his own activity. He has no ideology, no blueprints. No matter. Onto him I will project the drama of the people's liberation I have worked out in my head while scrubbing the bedlinen of the master's household.

Introduction to the Idea of Atrocity

In May, 1768, a band of seventy *haidamaky* under the leadership of the Cossack Maksym Zalizniak headed north from the Motronynsky Trinity Monastery near the right bank of the Dnipro with a manifesto for the peasants through whose settlements they moved, hoping for recruits.

The ruins of the monastery, old ramparts and a dilapidated church, have been overcome by the uncontested growth of the forest; the townsite now lies unremarked under a field of honeyed wild grasses. But this was once the fief of Princess Motrona, whose husband, being medieval, was frequently away from home on campaigns of war. The town came eventually under Polish jurisdiction in the seventeenth century.

The *haidamaky* prepared for an uprising by rallying under cloak of darkness at the monastery, digging up their caches of weapons and untethering their fattened horses. Then they set out, northward.

By June, some two thousand peasants had joined up and the rebels were in control of entire provinces, or "liberated zones." Then they came to Uman. And the horror.

Red Banquet

All the bells of Ukraine rang forth.
The *haidamaky* cried out:
"Die, you lords, die!
Die."
Medvedivka is the first
To heat up the heavens.
Smila burns, all of Smila
fills up with blood.
Korsun burns, Kaniv burns,

Chyhyryn, Cherkasy;
It all blazed up along the blackened road
And blood watered the land
All the way to Volhynia.

Ukraine, the Summer of 1768

Burning, smouldering, whole villages collapsed into mounds of fiery embers save the gallows bearing the burden that swayed by the neck above the charcoal heaps: behold the traitors. Dogs and crows feasted at the crossroads, gnawing on the bones of gentry. All the men were dead, while women and cattle were herded off into the *haidamaka* camps. Children wailed at the city gate. Blood flowed into the river. Three times the bodies of the enemy were tortured – blackened, bloated corpses suspended from rafters were chastized even in death. Three times they must be tortured so they may never rise again but lie cursed in eternity. The chieftain Zalizniak filled up his cup with wine and drank to their souls.

And then the army reached Uman, boasting that it would fleece the Polish landlords of their own soft, white, powdered skin.

The *haidamaky* surrounded the town. After the Ukrainian Ivan Gonta, an officer of the Polish commander's guard, went over to the rebels with his entire unit, the town surrendered, including gentry, clergy, leaseholders, and women and children who had sought refuge within the walls. Thousands – perhaps many thousands – were massacred.

What is a massacre like? We may imagine the scorched Gothic ruin of the Catholic church, the black cloud of carrion crow, and the jackals leisurely feeding on the bodies of the dead, among whom, in the democratizing light of the fading day, it is impossible to distinguish Pole from Jew, priest from leaseholder, youth from elder.

"The Poles froze," writes the poet, "while the Cossacks warmed themselves in the flames."

And Gonta cried: "Where are you, cannibals? Where have you hid?"

This fury does not exhaust the *haidamaky.* They make themselves a feast in the central square of Uman, dance and drink themselves into stupefaction, feeling for a few hours the relief of having discharged into the body of the enemy the toxin of revenge.

It's no use, of course. They will soon be routed. Their Cossack leaders will be mortified in a variety of ways and the rank and file, the rabble, will be sent back to the baleful estates, there to be routinely tortured to death at the headquarters of the Polish commander of the forces sent against them. They had their fling, and now they are cast back into obscurity and their unacknowledged, unredeemed toil.

How They Died

According to Taras Shevchenko's notebook, Gonta was taken in chains to the Polish camp near the Baltic Sea. B, the Polish general, ordered his tongue cut out so that he would not say anything against him, then had him stripped, lashed until the skin slid off his back, and fastened to a bed of heated iron bars. The dying Gonta opened his eyes and glared horribly at B. With a wave of B's hand, the executioners set upon Gonta. The parts of his quartered body were distributed throughout the kingdom and nailed up to posts at important crossroads. Zalizniak, on hearing how fearfully his comrade had suffered, "broke down and wept, fell ill and died. The *haidamaky* buried him on the steppe by the Dnipro, and then dispersed."

Gonta Has the Last Word: Another Version

He came out on to the place of execution with a joyful face and in peace, as if he were approaching his godparent at his baptism. The executioner, armed with pincers, tore off a chunk of his flesh and blood spattered about, but the *haidamaka's* expression never changed. He ripped off another piece. Then Gonta, turning to the crowd, spoke. "They said it would hurt," he whispered. "It doesn't hurt a bit."

II. The Cow Stories

My mother was raised in a little house on the edge of the city limits. It was her task as a girl to take the cow out to pasture on the railroad embankment; she would do this after school, tethering the cow and flopping down in the grass with her English textbook. She would memorize poems, odes from Shelley and Keats, and declaim them out loud to the wind and to the nonchalent Bossy chewing her cud. Thus to my childish mind there was an inextricable connection between the cow and the intellectual advancement of the Ukrainian-Canadian female.

It was the Depression – that mother lode of my parents' tales – and thus the point of the oft-repeated story was this: "As long as you have a cow, you won't starve." It's the story of a working-class family threatened by poverty ("Look," said my grandfather to my mother the schoolgirl, turning out his empty pockets, "this is how much I have for your schoolbooks") and how it was saved by the cow. How grandfather, unemployed and useless in his catatonic reverie under the apple tree, could not help his family, but how grandmother and her two daughters, milking, separating, churning, and curdling, sold milk and cream and cheese for pennies around the neighbourhood, especially to the "English" families, who, of course, did not keep a cow.

The same message was in the stories that drifted in from the homesteads, of families imperilled by the loss of gardens to early frost or brush fires, by the ravaging of crops by locusts or drought, by the unseasonable death of the patriarch or his disappearance for months and even years, into coal mines in the foothills or extra gangs pushing track through the Rockies, families being saved from starvation by the miraculously unextinguishable flow from the udder of the family cow.

They told the same stories in Ukraine itself, although we would hear of them only much later. They came from the clandestine lore of the Great Famine.

Vasyl Makarovych Indenko, born 1922, village of Poharshchyno:

"We would all have perished if it hadn't been for our cow. She supplied us well and saved us from a death by hunger. Often we went hungry so as to feed her with whatever: beets, a handful of oats, rusks of corn. She lived in the house with us like a real person. Without her, we would have vanished from this earth."

Image Bank: "The Best of Unions – Husband and Wife"

The canvas is dominated by the figure of a cow. She has an enormous head, short yellow horns, and a sweet, doe-like expression, and her four splayed hooves seem to carry her floating above the grass, as though she were ethereal, tethered to the earth thanks only to the short length of stout rope in the hand of the husband. At her flank walks the wife with an expression of proprietary satisfaction, leaving no doubt that the "union" is trilateral: man, woman, and cow.

The painter is Mykhailo Popov, born in 1946 in the city of Kharkiv. What does he know about cows?

Yet here's another one, a black cow with red udder, almost indiscernible against the twilit landscape, looking toward two foregrounded figures, a mother and child standing in the penumbra of their haloes. The title of this painting is "The Annunciation."

Perhaps this is now her role: totemic, heraldic, as her function as real cow diminishes on the farm. In the early 1960s, when the soon-to-be dissident mathematician Leonid Pliushch was a teacher in a village school sixty kilometres from Odesa, he noted in his memoirs that one of the reasons for the villagers' immiserization (one-third suffered from tuberculosis, and the school principal, along with some senior students, from alcoholism) was that they had been forced to turn over to the collective farm the milk from their own cow whom they kept stabled at the back of their house. It has been downhill ever since.

A FARMSTEAD WITHOUT A COW LOOKS LIKE A HOUSE WITHOUT A MISTRESS. – *old Ukrainian saying*

A cow story: a Ukrainian peasant makes his way imperturbably along the King's Highway, the oncoming company of German soldiers parting, like the Red Sea before Moses, to let him pass. For he is leading a cow. O unimpeachable beast!

III. The Young Master Visits the Ancestral Estate

In May, 1990, the Russian-Canadian writer Michael Ignatieff, took a trip to the village of Krupodernytsa, 180 kilometres south-west of Kyiv. The reason he was visiting this godforsaken place at the end of a rutted washboard road was to see for himself where his family's story had begun.

It is not just his story – but he doesn't know I'm in it.

In the 1860s, Mr. Ignatieff tells us, his great-grandfather built a great house in this village and dispatched his family to it from Moscow for the summer holidays, "with all the servants, baggage, tutors and nannies," alighting at the family's very own train station. The village church, needless to say, is also great-grandfather's. I can imagine how refreshing it was to take one's leisure in the "Little Russian" countryside while Muscovites broiled in the stinking heat of the pre-revolutionary summer.

Now the great-grandson visits, the first of the family to do so since the Bolsheviks took over the place. They turned it into a collectivized village on a collective farm, but still Ignatieff recognizes everything. He has seen the photographs taken by the English nanny and observes that the "peasant huts are exactly as they were in the photographs of 1913," that is, still largely without electricity and running water. It is difficult to tell whether this is to his satisfaction or dissatisfaction.

This ambiguity persists in his account of his meeting with the villagers. His tone is elegiac yet somehow also equivocating. Are we meant to be moved by the picture of the old woman in a kerchief who "steals up" to him and suddenly kisses his hand? Or appalled? "Then she leans against a tree and begins to cry." Why does she do this? Why doesn't he find out? He visits the tomb of his great-grandfather, an impressive monument of black basalt and white marble that is strewn with flowers by villagers who have paid their respects here as well as at the village war memorial. What is it they are honouring – wealth? reputation? Or do their flowers celebrate a "good riddance" to an eclipsed landlord who once listed them among his property? And when Mr. Ignatieff describes the priest with the Homburg on his full mane of hair, carrying bread and vodka from a shopping expedition, "big, ruddy," with a capacious belly and stained cassock, are we meant to feel queasy, as though stuck inside a Gogol short story? or are we meant to laugh?

But no, "It is normal," he writes, "how things ought to be."

Those are *my* people in that "normality." This reunion he is enjoying so much is a convocation with Ukrainian peasants: the comic priest, his wife in slippers and a house dress, the collective farm worker at the bus stop, the barefoot children.

Those also were my people who had helped his family unload their baggage into the brougham at the private train station, who had tended the ornamental gardens, prepared tea, given suck to the nobleman's brats, and brought in his crops. In bonded labour until 1867. Now the young master stands among their descendants in the warm glow of fellowship. This is "normal."

It is not normal, apparently, to make a peasant war, to burn down the manor house, turn the patriarch's tomb into an abbatoir, hook up the village to the national electrical grid, and send the kids to school.

I cannot bear the old woman in the kerchief who kisses his hand and bursts into tears. I want her to hiss. I want her to stick her tongue out. I want her to lick her lips and sink her brass teeth into his left pinky.

IV. The Eternal Triangle

Imagine a painting with two focal points of light. In the first a Polish gentleman, a *pan*, along with his slim-ankled bay mare, his red velvet riding coat, his golden braid looping his right shoulder, glow warmly in the spotlight as though on a stage where the backdrop, the villa, stands in a discreet subtextual shade. In the second, a fainter spotlight illumines a fur cap, a muscled arm, the white shirt of a young peasant, his round moon face with moustache, its sallow luminescence. He looks directly out at us as though to say the picture is about him: his youth, his strength, his audacity, rather than a display of the *pan's* property, himself included.

For the *pan*, this is a representation of bucolic plenitude and of European civilization, which extends eastward from the villa out over the fields as far as the thatch-roofed serf's cottage squatting in the gloom of Galicia. For the peasant, it is about the tension, even excitement, of knowing something his master does not know: the Cossacks are coming, from the east.

Not in this picture but behind the villa in the washhouse is the woman. She too knows what is about to happen. She stands flat-footed in bare feet, her overskirts tucked up under the broad sash that winds several times around her waist just under her fat, rosy breasts. Her white thighs are as sleek and sturdy as gateposts. Her braids are loosening. She licks the sweat off her upper lip with her quick flat tongue.

She is scrubbing her master's bedlinen, scouring its uncleanness in the hot water that has reddened her small hands. That morning she had hauled it off his bed while he shaved at the window, and the faint antiseptic aroma of his shaving soap mingled confusingly with the musk of his naked body seeping out from the sheets. He sleeps naked, she knows this, or at least he is almost always naked when she comes in to get the bedlinen for the wash. While she yanks at the sheets and pulls at the pillows she can "see" him standing at the window, pouring out a basin of water from the pitcher she has filled at the well, his legs akimbo as though securing him to the floor. Once she had peeked at him through her eyelashes, had seen the brown sac swaying between his thighs. He splashed at his groin, then rubbed himself dry and tossed the cloth at her as she stood with the linen piled in her arms. She was looking sideways, at the bedpost.

She is thinking of Pavlo in the fields, of his thirst on this hot day and the sweat caking the fine warm dust of the wheatfield to his neck and feet and forearms. The *pan* is pleased with Pavlo's labour, the way he musters the lumbering oxen, wields the whetted scythe, rebundles the loosening sheaves more careless hands have bound. And for praising Pavlo from the cool verandah of the village, shouting out to him as he trudges home across the common, rake on his shoulder, the *pan* is pleased with himself. But she knows what Pavlo is thinking: he wants to kill the *pan*.

He dreams of running away, far east of here, to the emptied lands of Rus scourged by the Asiatics, to join the other runaways – the serfs, the defrocked priests, the army deserters, the town adventurers on the lam – known as the Zaporozhian Cossack Host. They live at the bend of the sweeping Dnipro inside a wooden palisade at the rim of the western empire just beyond the reach of landlords, tax collectors, and recruiting officers. They hold the line against the raiding Tatars and Turks who regularly loot, burn, and ravish Ukraine, and drive their living plunder in herds to the slave markets of Smyrna and Crete. To the west, in the lands the Cossacks had deserted, their kin still live within the thrall of the Poles but they, fugitives, squatters, brigands, mercenaries, and warriors, live in the "empty, wild East" known wistfully to the Poles as the "divinely protected zone of freedom" as though the Cossacks act out for them the drama they no longer dare: emancipation, far away from home.

And now the Cossacks are gathering all across the steppelands, arming themselves and their peasant recruits and followers, untethering their ponies fattened on wild grasses, and boasting of fleecing the Polish landlords of their soft, white, powdered skin. They are on the warpath.

She has heard this. She is excited. What excites her is the transgression of the violent male who, in the prime of his physical prowess, finally quits the plough, the dumb field, the sweat for another man's bread, and lights out for the territory of rape and murder. She is mired in necessity and repetition and cannot create her own activity, but he can, and he does it for her. She has worked it out in some detail while bent over the washtub. The steam slicks her neck as her arms plunge in and out of the water, the damp bodice of her shirt clings around her puckered nipples, and her buttocks sway rhythmically with each lunge of her arms. She can "see" the *pan* at his window, watching her.

Soon she will surely hear the scrunch of his boots on the courtyard pavement, sniff the mansmell of him as he approaches her, feel his heft as he positions himself behind her, his groin pressed against the bunched-up cloth of her skirts over her hips. He leans forward on her curved back, his mouth in her unravelling braid, his hands pulling at her shirt. He kicks at her thighs. "Wider," he whispers. He too is hot and wet and bent to his task. He groans and gasps and weeps. When he slides his finger into her mouth she sucks it as though to pull him down her throat.

She is condemned to repeat this, over and over; even her pleasure is part of the necessity that traps her. Her Cossack mate will live beyond the eastern horizon, out of earshot, planning revolution.

NOTE: The poetic stanza (my translation), "Red Banquet," comes from Taras Shevchenko's epic drama-in-verse *Haidamaky.* The edition I consulted was illustrated with drawings from which I drew much of the description of the massacres.

I came across the Famine images and anecdotes in issues of the illustrated weekly *Ukraina,* whose editors, evidently emboldened by the relatively permissive atmosphere of *perestroika (perebudova* in Ukrainian) in late 1980s Soviet Ukraine, published what had been forbidden knowledge up to that time.

The Michael Ignatieff article appeared in the *Globe and Mail,* May 30, 1990. Another version of this visit appears in his book *Blood and Belonging.*

Another version of "The Eternal Triangle" appears in my *Doomed Bridegroom* (NeWest Press, 1998).

Two Triangles

MARTHA BLUM

My mother can't cross the room. Fifty people sit on suitcases and bundles. We speak to each other in sign language, hands, eyes, and bodies. Ghetto doors are locked. What we know comes through the air, window, keyhole. Information flows, fed by rage, hope, caught by antennae on our skins. Through the windows we see the trucks leave. No one believes their eyes. It can't be true.

Resettlement. Palestine. Ukraine. Life somewhere. I am pushed around by my neighbour, who polishes his dentistry gear, totally oblivious to events. He is concerned with a space of ten centimetres. Secures ten centimetres with growls and shoves. Polishing and straightening out and counting his drills. He is going somewhere, he knows. My dentist is unaware that God is not answerable to Job. Or to him. A room full of dentists, fighting for ten centimetres. Doors fly open. Romanians behaving like Germans, masquerading as masters. Bad theatre. Romanians. They are no masters; poor and earthbound, they are serfs, slaves, underlings. Brothers in arms with a bulldozing might, they take on like all slaves the trappings, the forms, the show of the master. Here and there you will see one Ian or Petru do it well. Rarely. They are so ill-suited. A twinkle in their eye, they do not cherish murder. Too messy. Orders? Commandments? Not really. Romanians do as if....They do not obey orders easily. They like wine and women, and here and there men. Bow to the powerful to save their own necks. And sometimes also ours. So, they come up, in the middle of all that desperate chaos, a chaos of immediate hunger, thirst, and the sudden loss of simplest civility, they, the Romanians come up with a proposition to the *Oberkommando*: use these people before they die. It is not new, of course. Built into the system; Nazis did it anyway. But here it is new. Doctors, pharmacists, and engineers selected, separated, and retained for other uses than transport.

My yellow star clearly displayed on my white coat. We are requisitioned – my father and myself – to a hospital for work. I serve the German boys. Shot, amputated, delirious, young, they die for a madman. The Jewish team works silently. No sounds exchanged. The holy words are not pronounced. Who dares? My boss, hero, victimizer, German doctor, enters the makeshift laboratory. We are short of everything, have to invent, improvise. New transports from the front. Boys with bullets in chests, arms, bellies. No morphine injections. We make solutions of whatever we can find, sterilize it in stages, not to destroy the tender morphine – which can't stand high temperatures – and hand it as a usable injection to the master, the doctor in charge. We are as good as any I. G. Farben research laboratory, he says, coming very close to me. *Sleep with me tonight. You'll have dinner, cigarettes, and wine, and I will let you rest in my quarters for a day. You are clever and you know me now well enough, you know I will be good to you.* Yes, but may I respectfully ask for a favour: bring my fiancé out of the ghetto, and I will.

Walking between two strapping SS guards, dogs at the side, I think the Lord's Prayer, lighting one on another like a chainsmoker. It serves me well. From the Latin *Pater noster* to the Romanian *Tatal nostru*, with the *Vater Unser* and the *Notre*

Père, I speak them wordlessly as I did at the first hour of each school day, when we rose to the teacher's entrance, starting the day with the *Lord's Prayer.*

Rumours are that the ghetto is emptying fast. Whispers carry messages; they travel on underground paths, from ear to ear; are heard by those afflicted, those whose days are numbered, who glean the truth from horror-tales with the finest of sieves. And numbered days infuse a strength beyond your own, an inner tuning of the finest discernment, a high alert. So you hear what no one else can and your body makes decisions in seconds.

The ghetto soon to be annihilated. Poor sweet Max in there. I have his release, I have the letter. This sweet idiot of my teenage years, walking in long strides, shoelaces trailing.

In my hand I carry this letter and pray he somehow heard the rumour, that Dr. Bauer succeeded in granting his release. Just prayer, no thought, a trance-like suspension, a dip into our adolescent years together, when love is undefinable, a vague waiting and melancholy. Our Father –

I'm made to hasten my step. March, the two SS men say, March. The dogs look more human. But solace returns with oblivion, prayer and past. Oh, the sweet, sweet boy under my window....

MY NAME IS MAX, he said, and ran as if stung by a tarantula. I saw him hiding behind an eaves trough of my school principal's house, day in and day out, until one day I crossed the road to ask him his name. A slight slap with the back of my hand brought him back to this world. Max, he said, and ran. Oh, the sweet boy, lanky, gauche, not yet grown –

We were both fifteen or sixteen, and one high summer day I took his hand and said let's go to the river. Down the ill-named, ill-fated Saint Trinity Street, leading to what is now the ghetto, down the Train Station Street, the *Bahnhofstrasse*, into the river valley. Through ripening corn, high standing, golden-stringed hair unto the endless stretches of sand, pebbles, and tall, tall grasses. The river was almost out of its banks, after a stormy rainfall the day before. I felt reckless and more so because of the tender timidity of the boy, who hardly touched me as we stretched into sand. Let's go swimming, let's swim down below the bridge. No, he said, no, I do not know how well you swim. It is too dangerous, especially beyond the bridge, where the river falls with crests of white foam, spiralling, pulling you down. I smiled. Of course he'll go, he loves me, he stands for hours under my window, just to see me come out of the old gate. Come, I tell him while gliding down the high bank. Come! And in my summer cotton I dip into the mountain stream. Not as clear this time. Swollen, cloudy with debris, the stream took me fast beyond the bridges to the falls. Water in ears and throat, I can't fight the river, my feet caught – when I feel jostled and then carried on Max's back to the lower bank. He had seen me sink, kicked his runners off and jumped to rescue me. Breathless, we stretched upon heated stones, when I heard him say, in a very ordinary everyday voice: Will you marry me, Süssel? I smile. I will have to, because you saved my life. Yes, of course I will.

But we were more like brothers. Wandering along the river dunes or the seven kilometres to the Cecina mountain, in one day there and back.

As we hiked up our mountain, resting on stones near the thousand springs, he would take his steady companions – pencil and paper – and show me how simple truth can be, a shape like a triangle, a circle, or a rhomb. And talk about Galileo or Copernicus – the Polish father of astronomy. Or his adored Johannes Kepler. Without magic, he says. Without magic. The truth is here, I will show it to you, Süssel, without incantations or priestly swinging of myrrh. Just beauty in itself. Forever. Then he smiled: Unless modified and changed by the moving times. Yes, I said, I'll marry you. You're too beautiful to leave. And we blushed without kissing, holding hands and straining up the mountain. Give us this day....

Our town at the foot of the Northern slopes of the Carpathians, nourished by fertile fields and by the waters of its springs, fed us with a myth of being chosen. All mountains touch the sky, as does the Olympus of Greece, the Sinai of the Law, and as does our Cecina for the little people at its foot. Next to the Gods. And sweating up, stone by stone to the top, just to get the sight of the river valley, the Pruth, looking out at German and Ukrainian villages and further ranges on the horizon. I wanting to put my hurting feet into the springs, listen to the rush in the grasses, and rest after an hour's march, and he would come down to me, throw the rucksack onto the ground, and say, look I want to explain this to you: and he goes on about Johannes Kepler, who made a living as an astrologer – pure nonsense in Max's view – yet laid down the most basic truth about the revolution of the earth around the sun.

No, I do not think we could marry; oh, it would not work, but he looked at me with such longing that I took his arm for support. When we descended, almost rolling down that mountain, the stars were up and we hurried away. So he remained my fiancé. A contract-brother – his face of fear and abandonment in the ghetto crowd – forgive, forgive us our trespasses, as we forgive.... Dr. Bauer will take me and I have no way out.

FIFTEEN. Sitting on my fountain of fear. Horror of Ahi's encircling arms giving me goose flesh still. I lean against this many-armed body of cool iron, resting on the fluted spouts. Ahi's arms. The Turkish henchman's powerful arms, spewing water. Do not sit there, Ileana screams, do not sit there, Ahi will grab you by your hair from the back, encircle your body and shout with joy when you drown. And no frog-prince will kiss you in a thousand years. Father, as we forgive –

Towards evening, when all piano and homework was done, I sneaked down, waiting with the exhilaration of danger for the copper arms to move. I touched a fluted arm as if calling for water, when it fell by its own metal-weight and I was left holding it, the end-face grinning. Too frightened to cry, I ran into Ileana's lap. Stories are true, Ileana says, you defy them at your own peril. He'll get you next time. He knows you're Süssel! Let's fix the damn thing to give him his arm back. I do not like his anger. Dear, dear, it's hard to work for Jews, they have to prove everything, they don't believe the simplest thing. If people say Ahi lives in that fountain, for me he lives there. And it is dangerous to play with it. If you need water, he'll give it to you, but do not play with it. What a naughty, naughty child – who trespass against us.

After that I would not go near it until I was fifteen. But now I feel grown, adult, above superstition. I sit on the rim, touching the slate with washed toes – a deep green slate. I sit there, legs trailing, loving the fountain. The way it occupies the crossroads between the Archbishop's Residence and the Evangelical church and, cutting across, binds Holy Trinity Street to Gallows Hill. The henchman in the middle, Ahi. The multi-armed Turk, who can string up three men at the same time, swings the knotted rope around one man, holding the others with new arms sprouted from his body. Three he can hang at once, cracking their necks, making music almost, Ileana laughs. Do not go near that hill, Süssel. No grass grows there, no tree, the earth refuses seed, for all those tears have salted the earth and made it barren. Do not go near it, bad girl.

Father, lead us not into temptation, lead us not....

But at fifteen I do. Up the hill without fear, or just a little horror in my veins. Up the cobbled road, vaulted houses from Turkish times, dark, menacing – close to the ground and almost around the corner from our uptown palaces – low, arched cellars, the poorest live there. Ukrainians and Jews. Speaking a Yiddish-German, Ukrainian sounding. Proverbs and wisdom of the Slavs. A singing sound, crying and laughing. A local code of understanding and cheating. Merchants of coal by the piece, winter vegetables, and kerosene. Poor, very poor. Selling lighting or heating oil with ancient measuring means, the Dame-Jeanne, a huge-bellied lady – green-glass or tin – the *Damigiana*, as Ileana called that crazy bottle. All these cellar merchants, reeking wet-pounded earth. Here and there a winter-apple shop, a little more respectable, sporting shelves, apples, and dried fruit. The east side open, precipitous, with a view of the chestnut treetops.

Up and up the hill. No blade of grass there, no moss, no brush creeping, no hazelnut bush, no tree. A small gust lifting surface earth, the salty taste of tears covering my tongue. The air remembers, carries its truth to those tuned to hear. No gallows to be seen. Yet all there. Not to be erased. Just for a short moment, my eyes graze the valley, a German village, orchards – and I run back home. Enough, enough. Deliver us from Evil, Father, deliver us from Evil.

TWO TRIANGLES OF CARDBOARD covered in yellow cloth, juxtaposed on my white coat. I am preparing a makeshift autoclave to sterilize syringes and needles. I am in charge, I run a medical lab: six prisoners, my father under my command. Hungry and trying to smile, he looks young. Our hospital has been evacuated to accommodate hundreds of wounded

German boys from the front. They come on trucks or tanks, shot, shelled, or in shock. It is my father, who invents *ad hoc* anaesthesia, some chloroform, some ether *pro narcosi* or just a soluble barbiturate. He distills water in a contraption made of two Jena bottles of neutral glass and an end of rubber hose, sterile enough to inject. And Dr. Bauer, Major Hermann Bauer, operates. I am under Dr. Bauer's command, so to speak. Six prisoners looking after all these young German lives. We are too bruised, broken, hungry to think of sabotage, of poisoning them all, or setting the hospital on fire, or fleeing. Slaves do not think – we jump at the raising of an eyebrow.

New beds to improvise, barracks to be built. Jewish prisoners from Moghilev arrive to put them up. I recognize my uncle Jacob. My light-hearted, singing, printer-typesetter uncle, the youngest, called Jankel. Tell us a story, Jankel, tell us the story when you set a whole page of the *Vorwärts*, our socialist daily, with wild Jewish stories of ghosts, dibbuks, possessed, screaming brides, and dancing, exorcising rabbis, instead of the news of the day. How you got drunk with your buddies, draping yourself in the red flag of the "party," playing revolution, got fired and rehired, for there was no other typesetter of your quality and speed. Tell us. Tell us! He is stricken by typhus, he can hardly move. None of the thirty *muselmen* – Jews at the end of their strength – are able to build anything decent. But triggers are loose, and they do what they can. I approach Dr. Bauer cautiously, humbly, to see if I could be permitted to requisition that particular Jew for the cleaning of our latrines. No, he says, not from that team. They are full of fleas and typhus.

Rumours are that in Moghilev four incinerators with some thiry-two creusets from the *Firma Topf und Söhne* have been installed, to deal with the disposal of corpses and typhus-diseased flesh. Not from that team, he says. I'll keep your father and I'll keep you. But watch out. And he pokes me in the ribs with his *Reitgerte* – a small sharp leather whip – and then bangs it rhythmically against his own leather shank, in front of prisoners and patients about to be operated on. Yes, we know who is God, no need to enforce it. No rebellion, just knowing.

It is *so* funny. A Jewish child, pious, singing to the Lord and hearing His voice in reply, in fetters now. Total corporeal confinement. Yet with an end of muscle left in my face, the smile is there. It is there for the sudden pleasure, the removal, the absence of our daily companion: guilt. It just isn't there. Everything seems acceptable, feasible. The law, the centripetal law of living amongst one another, is gone. Could I smile undetected, I would. Of course, I will keep my deal. He has freed my fiancé, my so-called fiancé. He stands, across the street from the old house, hidden by an eavestrough's overhang, waiting for me. We sit on the Ahi fountain and chat, as fifteen-year-olds, tackling the big questions: existence, search for God, intellect versus heart.

Dr. Bauer expects payment. Passing my father, still so young, a picture of himself as a young officer in the Austrian army, *Zwicker* (pince-nez glasses) on the nose. Moving among his test tubes, touching me sideways with his flared coat.

I am the sole woman among the six prisoners. Head Jew foreman, coordinator between lab and ward, my whereabouts are uncontrolled. Or so I think. But not really. In a tight hungry universe everyone senses the life-level of the other. Silent anonymity is best. Nose to the ground, guts at high alert. They all know: I sleep with the boss. And I find myself in a state of hilarity. Guilt? Where has it gone? Just theatre. Absurd theatre. And this total abolition, the absence of it, gives me a strange freedom: no law! Nothing matters, not one of the ten! Maybe the fifth, honour your father and mother. For the surge of blood to my face, seeing my father at work, looking like a very young man, and his silent acceptance of the cigarettes or chocolate which I smuggle into his lab-coat pocket, makes me still human. The only thing.

I make a deal. Dr. Bauer has offered me a day of rest. This first day in total seclusion is the first day of my life! Windows covered, warm water in a tub, apricots, chocolates, and dry prunes in small dishes, and a field-bed in white linen – his barrack is fifty metres from the hospital, somewhere in heaven. He said he would not come until I had rested. I sleep countless hours. When he enters he watches me, takes me like a child to the tub, scrubs with surgical brush arms, legs, and back, cuts with medical scissors nails on toes and fingers, says nothing, until: "You have beautiful hair." I smile, of course. My head is bare and so is the mound below my navel. At the last de-lousing, all that has gone. I smile at Dr. Bauer. In linen, he takes me to his bed and leaves me there. He returns to wake me at four-thirty in the morning, my sterilized prisoner's garb in his arms; he had operated with the help of two *feldschers* all night. There is coffee, bread and butter, and Vitamin-complex chocolate. We share it. Five o'clock, I am on duty, through the wards, stern face, machine movements.

During my absence a shipment of gauze, bandages, potassium pemanganate – the purple disinfectant of old – and live mercury has arrived. Intense joy pervades my team – to feel human, to work with purpose. All seems forgotten: hunger, sleepless nights, the occasional strap, and the eternal rush to the latrine with loose bowels. Only one thing matters: to escape into purpose. My father gets at the live mercury, commands everyone around to find some vehicle. He'd like pork fat, wool fat – he settles for third grade Vaseline. Fashions pestles out of wood, constructs a tub to mix it in. To start, equal quantities of mercury and Vaseline are needed to achieve a homogenous mixture – mercury runs away on you otherwise, partitions itself into millions of small silver balls. Slowly he incorporates the rest of the Vaseline. There is a good scale rescued from the Jewish hospital, and he and all of them glow at the achieved mercury ointment. It combats everything, including venereal disease.

It was a good day. They were rewarded with soup from the hospital canteen and they all fell to their bunks, oblivious of the world. Guilt? Funny what people can think of, when they are warm and their bellies filled with bread and butter.

Dr. Bauer appears at the ward. Shaven now, rested, he drops his key into my white coat pocket. The new *feldscher* takes over, and I go into the night. Not really hoping but expecting Dr. Bauer to be there. He is not. I undress. There is warm water in a bowl, an old-fashioned ceramic bowl, red tulips, blue tulips looking at me with strange eyes. White tulips on white on my mother's damask covered table. Where? When? Flowers blooming everywhere. On bottoms of Ukrainian bowls, more tulips, and green leaves on the handles of the pitcher next to it. Dry prunes, dry apricots to chew. One chews here.

Key in lock. Dr. Bauer enters, sausage fried, sauerkraut in an army covered dish and the smell of bread. It is to loose one's mind. One camp chair for Dr. Bauer across from me on the bed. I eat little and none of the cabbage. A slave knows her moment. She does not have a morrow. It is all now: If there is food she eats and if there is warm water – well, it is simple. What plans, what design, who sees you, where is the all-seeing eye, laws to follow and laws to transgress, where are those small loose bricks at the foot of the moorish wall, to swindle yourself, a secret mystery?! What mystery – where? It is simple.

Dr. Bauer inspects me for lice and fleas, says *sotto voce*, a voice one never heard on the ward, your hair when grown again will be beautiful, and leaves me to my apricots and prunes, to the sucking of their pits like the comfort of a baby's thumb. At four-thirty, he appears with coffee. No word spoken. At five o'clock I am out in a cold that feels like minus forty degrees Celsius. Lab and ward.

After three days he comes and stays. Four o'clock in the morning. Undresses fully, kneels by my field-bed with coffee in his army tin mug. Sweetened with thick milk; and a light-aired slice of loaf. The crusty sort. It falls in crumbs. He collects them with his mouth. For the first time he touches my skin. Rises to put away the cup, and, also for the first time, I see him naked. He is unaroused. Funny to watch. A dog's tail, between a man's legs. No wonder Germans call it *Schwantz,* meaning just that. How he handles every object from coffee cup to scalpel. Knowing fingers. All tipped with brains of their own. They know things. Perceive and move, seemingly undirected. Innate elegance, singly and in the palm, hanging from the wrist. I had watched these hands sever legs from knee or hip, sewing and suturing, pushing bones into place. All with the tenderness of strength, joints moving on their own, yet in unison. I have seen beauty of such nobility in Johann Sebastian Bach. And I see it here. I watch those dangling, glorious fingers as he approaches my bed. Still unaroused, he kneels by me. And raises his left arm to cover my eyes, forehead, hairline, with his whole flat hand. Fingers, imperceptibly moving, close my eyes, as if for the last time. With his right arm he moves across my body to press my left arm and with his body he holds my right one. Stretched and stilled now along hip and flank. Limp all muscles, limp as in death. No breath audible. Breasts fall in. Mine were never there. They are negative breasts. They make hollows and go the other way, inwards. I saw my face in his shaving mirror a few days ago and a boy's was looking back at me. A hint of pink hairline, cheekbones moving up and green of eyes all over the face. My father at eighteen. A young man, gaunt.

His breath is closer now, barely touches my nipples, warms

them and brings them out of the hollow, with lips as clever as his hands. Taking time, his hands move down, calling for stillness; fingers entering the hairless sex to find the labia. A sharp stroke, repeated without gentleness. The thrill of small death. Tears rising to the throat.

It's almost five o'clock. Hundreds of Soviet prisoners have arrived, he says. Do not go near them, they are full of typhus, lice and fleas. There is no facility to delouse so many. I have to keep what I have for ourselves. They huddle on the outer side of the compound against the shed, on the frozen earth. They will die soon, and, if they do not, we'll help them to it.

Out into the night. To the job. Sucking prune pits. Some for my father. Guilt? Avert your eyes, oh Lord!

THESE ARE THE DARKEST DAYS, between November and February. Stalingrad raging. Russian prisoners flooding in, not enough guards, food, or water. Machine-gun shots – rhythmical savage dancing – as I emerge from the barrack of my true lover. I love him furiously. His face, his duelled sharp Schmiss across his right cheek, distorted upper lip, eyebrows, celestial arcs, are with me. Everywhere. Fed and rested, I can love. With my team for sixteen hours of the day, I am pursued by this face.

In a deputy role again, self-imposed, I order everyone around, fearing for my life. They'll get me somehow. They'll stab or strangle me, they'll poison my tea or catch my foot in an iron trap. And he'll rescue me. Mad, mad. I love him. Afflicted.

He has come to me fully aroused, one morning at four-thirty, and taken me without warning. The key in my pocket the night before, I came to cold meat and red wine prepared for me. Drank and ate at a small pine-box table he had improvised, army towel with crest for tablecloth, washed in the tulip-ridden Ukrainian bowl, saw that my hair had filled in a little, smiled at his shaving mirror, put on his army shirt and stretched limbs, long, stiff, free of muscle as he wants it. And was wakened by the sharp parting of upper thighs and a brutal entrance. Catatonic as he wants me, the thrill will ring through my life. He came upon my navel, lying in his juice like a newborn from the womb.

INDOMITABLE SNOW STORMS, elemental blizzards of the Ukraine steppe as far as the Urals. These were bitter days. A small commando stripped the prisoners of war of their good heavy coats and covered the bodies with snow. Their coats we used as extra blankets. Boots piled high. Here and there a ring no one had seen before turned up on a German finger. These were dark winter days, with typhus the ultimate equalizer.

We were unspeakably lucky. My father and one other no-name-Jew chemist had devised a sulphur volatilizing chamber, where coats and woolens of the dead P.O.W.s were deloused, and we all wore them, Jew and German. There was now total dependency. Without us the German soldiers would simply die of shock, bullet wounds, and gangrene. They knew it and we knew it and our régime changed. There was more collegiality and banter, and we ate from the same pot. Always hungry, none of us or them had enough. But latrine cleaners and Jews brought in from Moghilev for rough work had nothing at all. They died under our eyes. Recovering soldiers took over some chores, trying not to return to duty. I caught them rubbing their thermometers under the blankets with fingers or linen to show high temperatures to get another week away from action. Boys. Hardly any beard. Children almost.

The six of us holding their lives gave us the stature of parent, almost love. It operates on simple laws, irrefutable. We were the masters for a moment. Or a kind of master. Or just a role, changes in a classical play, in the unity of time and place. This was still January, the famous month with two faces of God. Janus watching the gates of Rome, looking both ways, inward, to keep order in the city, and outward into the world for approaching danger. This was our January, where every day had to be lived and none could be jumped. Lived through, bitten into, as the hours stood still, all limits set. Our bodies moved with destiny. This was our January of 1943, a date just for the record in history books. This was *our* January, that stuck to our soles like Russian mud in spring. Heavy, black, and sinking. No time-feel.

Yet, one incomprehensible day in February, orders from Command. Strike the set. Most of the prisoner-Jews shot at dawn. Dr. Bauer, one midnight, calling in my father only and not me. Orders us to run in groups of two. Three times two, at intervals. He will be on duty. There are no dogs any more. My father: The sick German boys? They will be shipped on trucks, tanks, and on foot. Dr. Bauer: None of your concern. My father: It is my concern. Dr. Bauer: It is not. Look out for yourselves. Here is a small rucksack with what I could spare. Take your daughter. Take the Russian coats, fur hats, and boots. In thirty minutes you move silently in twos, out of the compound, direction south-west. Hurry. One moment more. Shake my hand – I have never seen a war hero of your stature – and he buried his head in Father's shoulder in a moment's embrace.

Walking at night. Sleeping or lying in hollows by day, not to be detected by friend or foe. Two unlikely figures from a strange unlikely world. We rationed ourselves to eat the absolute minimum of biscuit and sausage, a little plum brandy and prunes, to snack out of that rucksack. And matches, thank God for matches. I found a spade under the snow somewhere. Everything can be done with it – snow piled into heaps for protection; if the earth permits, a fine bed fashioned, branches brought down for a fire in a hollow.

On the third day a huddle of houses or huts, still and dark. With roofs above and sheds at back. Small, almost square Ukrainian windows. A kerchiefed figure in one window frame. She seems to be there, part of the winter landscape, and moves away to open the door. A gesture so natural and simple, as if for expected guests who arrive just a trifle late. She looks at these two ghosts. No questions, just: Go down into the cellar, there is straw and sheepskin. You'll find soured milk in two open trays. Eat your fill. She comes down to us with heavy black bread, resembling her own earth and sticking to the palate, two bowls, and wooden spoons. She says, "Eat, my babes, may the Lord be blessed, that I can help those that have less than I have." And she makes the sign of the cross. "Sleep, sleep," she says, "my children." We stretch into the straw and I fall upon my father's breast. Tears streaming down our faces with the warmth of the sheepskins and the blessing.

Lunch Hour with a Soviet Citizen

Kathie Kolybaba

I can smell her when I enter the house. I can smell the perfume, the sausage frying on the stove. I put my briefcase down in the alcove, step past her boots, and enter the hallway. I can hear her voice, the guttural sounds chopping the language I love, the language of my dreams, my memories, and all of my desires. She speaks well, but the tone is sharp, abrasive. My spine is rigid, my heart shouting, wracked within aching bones. I hear the syllables of English harsh on her tongue, see her mouth open beside the plastic of the phone. "I have every right to stay here," she says, "every right. I am here from the Ukraine, and I have – how do you say it – suffered; you have enough for me. I am educated. I speak English. On the bus yesterday I saw all kinds of people – Asians – how is it that you allow them here but not me? It is absurd. I deserve to stay here, and I will. I will have fine things, and money, I will."

There is so little gentleness, so little grace here: my house bleeds cacophony. All my edges are out; I am strung as tight as a fretful kite, riding high winds. My body collapses inside itself, and I cannot speak in clear tones. I want to run down the stairs and hide in the basement bathroom and weep, want to balance salt on my tongue. I cannot bear this shriek of voice in my ears, this other body. My husband comes towards me sipping coffee, smiling; the rough texture of his expectations – that I can live gracefully with this imposition – makes me look away. This girl, Olga, streaks past me, hungry only for my money and my food; I cannot bear the smell of her body, this perfume like dust, everywhere in the house. I walk slowly into the kitchen; the sausages fry in grease on the stove. Tomatoes ooze juice on the counter. Olga enters the room through the other door, parading in front of me, cutting bread. Her elbows jut out; one hand grips the loaf, the other saws, splitting the air with crumbs. She pours herself the last bit of coffee, takes her plate to the table, hunches over, and eats. I am home looking for my children and there is only this girl eating and my husband smiling. The smell in the house is thick, sickening. I feel as if I have entered someone's dream, in another country.

I AM LOOKING FOR MY CHILDREN. There is too much noise here and I retreat, slide out of the room, move up the stairs. They are wide and gorgeous in this old house, the bannister smooth with age and generations of hands beneath my own small palms. It is quiet upstairs, but I find my sons sitting on the floor of their room, colouring. They look up, and I look down at their small faces, see the relief in their eyes. And then they jump up, and Nicholas chants, "We're hungry mommy we're hungry." Both he and Michael are still in pyjamas, though it's noon and school is soon, soon. Nicholas starts spinning, hugging, pulling me down the stairs; Michael following, mimics everything. It's noon and my eyes hurt already with fatigue. They pull me down the stairs, into the kitchen; their bodies clutch me, and then expand. I see the empty coffee pot on the counter; remnants of food clutter everything, and dishes are stacked haphazardly on every single available space. Olga drinks coffee, picking lazily at strawberries, talking on the phone, the plate of grease pushed in front of her.

"Well, I do not want to work – how do you say – in a restaurant. I was a teacher in my country. I am an educated woman. No. I will not go back, I will stay here, I have every right to stay here. This is an easy country – why shouldn't I be able to live here? There is plenty of everything here – plenty – and I will stay here, I will."

The stove is still on, the grease smoking. She's laughing now, unbending her body, momentarily hovering. "The boys are hungry," my husband says as he enters the room. They spin around me like tops, and I clear her dishes, clear the paper from the table, the bits of leaf, the ketchup, the butter. I clear the counter. I pull out bread, turn the stove off, move the burnt pan. Olga shifts finally, waves past, and saunters out of the kitchen. She is wearing my husband's sweater with the sleeves rolled up. My sons sit there, giggling, tracing the alphabet mazes on their place mats. I move more plates and wipe the table; there are two eggs left and I cook them quickly, my hands careening between the stove and the grimy counter. Olga at least is out of the room, although the smell of perfume and grease sticks in the air. The boys eat quickly, seriously.

I run upstairs to change out of my business clothes. She's in my bedroom, drying her hair with my hair dryer, surveying herself, smiling, in the mirror. The bed is unmade, and her shirt is on the sheet, behind her. I grab clothes from my closet, run into the bathroom, peel off tights, put on jeans, a loose shirt. The smell, undiluted, sickens me, and I see black lace panties on the chrome rack. The counter is jammed with foreign makeup, bits of Kleenex, small bottles of perfume. I lift the panties and open the door to her room, walk through her nest of plastic bags and shoes to throw them on top of her unmade bed. I turn to see my own bedroom door shut; I enter the boys' room, grab clothes from their drawers – underwear, socks, sweatshirts, pants. The room is a mess, the beds unmade, covers pulled off, toys strewn around, their crayons and books in the middle of the room. Suddenly, she's in the doorway. "Kris, I was wondering where to put my dirty laundry, when you will be – how do you say it – washing clothes?"

"Look," I say, "you can use the washing machine."

"Oh no," she says, "I don't know how to use one. We don't have such luxuries in the Ukraine."

"I'll show you," I say, clutching a pile of clothes, searching for a matched pair of little socks.

"Oh no, really, Kris, I couldn't, I would be afraid of breaking it," she smiles idly.

"Look, Olga, it's easy, and I have enough to do."

"But I am going out now: Mark is driving me to meet my friend. I'll just get my laundry and put it on the floor here." She strides into her room, shuts the door. I am shaking with rage and hunger; I clutch the boys' clothes and fly back down the stairs, back into the kitchen.

The boys have eaten mostly everything, and I get them down to the bathroom as my husband shouts "'Bye, Kris, see you at five or so," as she shouts, "Bye, Kris." It's a long process of shirts and overalls, socks, of shoes and jackets; Michael is chattering, and Nicholas is increasingly quiet. They demand a last minute fruit roll-up and then, finally, we're out the door.

IT'S A QUICK RIDE. There's another long clutching moment, then we're out of the car, watching for traffic, two small boys with their hands tight in mine, into the building and up the concrete steps. My whole body grieves the terrible loneliness on Nicholas's face as he enters the kindergarten room; his body caves in with fear and sadness and worry. I hug him hard, hold his lovely head close against me, tell him I'll be back at three-thirty, take Michael's hand and leave the room. We stop at the water fountain for a drink and head down the stairs and into the car. I lean in to fasten his seat belt, slide into my seat. He's still chatting and chatting, joyful to be alone with me. I start the car and drive, my head full of Nicholas's fearful face, his terrible need to be perfect, Michael's incessant chat, his immense pleasure in my exhausted, furious company. I feel the surge of power beneath my hands, cradle the car around the corner, lean back. I drive down Aubrey and on up to Portage, turn left and head west. I want only to continue this movement beneath my body, allow Michael's rhythmic chant to become almost a croon. I want only to drive out to the prairie, find some place to stop. I want only the earth, the sky.

At a gas station stop along the way I park close to the store, lock the doors, run in, and buy sandwiches, juice, coffee. We drive then, my son and I, down Portage and out into the country. I pull off the highway and we get out of the car, find a space of earth, eat and laugh and drink, savouring our impromptu feast. I want only this earth and this body with me, picking grass and singing, drinking apple juice. I want only to feel this black earth through my fingers, the earth that quickened beneath my grandparents' hands, too, as they planted and weeded, the earth they fought with and cried over. They lived in it and on it and with it, their stone house picked from the fields and their dirt floors swept clean with the labours of living. I want to remember them and come home to this ancestry, this true thing that happened, that made me now live in a city with a job and a washing machine and a house and money enough for strawberries and shoes for my children. The girl is from another country, but this earth beneath my fingers is the earth I love. This is my country. I want to lie within it, touch my face to it. I need it on my skin. All the harshness of my own ancestry falls like broken glass between the syllables on the foreign girl's tongue. I press my face close to the earth, lay my hair in it. Michael comes and jumps on me, giggling, kissing me, finally giving me a rare, full-body hug, his body swept still as stone, there in the middle of the prairie.

TRANSLATORS' NOTE

TRANSLATION IS NOT EVEN AN INEXACT SCIENCE: the craft has no principles, no corpus of rules, and only a few practices around which a consensus has emerged. We offer the following remarks to explain how we approach the craft and to elucidate at least some of the references in this book that may puzzle readers.

Both the Canadian and the Ukrainian stories often use Ukrainian terms simply to mark them as Ukrainian, but some Ukrainian elements are also woven into the narrative. These terms can be considered in three groups: personal names, place names, and references to customs, social institutions, and everyday life.

Ukrainian personal names in the Canadian stories posed a challenge when they differed from the forms accepted in present-day Ukraine. We retained only the few deviations that occur when immigrants, who often speak non-standard variants of their native language, adapt to a new country and a new language. Thus most of the Ukrainian personal names in the Canadian stories appear in their standard form. In the Ukrainian stories names function in a more complex way. The de-ukrainization of names of characters in Bohdan Zholdak's "Karma-Yoga" is tied to their grappling with their identity. The references in Oles Ulianenko's "Orders" to Iosif Stalin and Lavrentii Beria, his chief of the NKVD, combine with the protagonist's fond memories of blue riding-breeches to reveal that he once worked for the secret police. The name Marcus in Taras Prokhasko's "Necropolis," which in transliteration would be Markus, is such a patent allusion to things bookish that we spelled it the Latin way.

Sometimes personal names are chosen for their meaning. The question then is whether or not to translate. We decided each case on its own merits. Among references to Satan, Dr. Kovalyk in Yurii Vynnychuk's "Day of the Angel" could have been called Dr. Smith, and Hrushkevych, the protagonist, could have been renamed Pearson, a not accidental choice when we recall that pears are related to apples and that temptation is an important theme in the story. So, too, the name Mlynarsky in "Necropolis," with its allusion to grinding or milling, could have been rendered as Miller. We resisted, so that readers wouldn't wonder what characters with English names are doing in stories set in Ukraine. But the names of the secretaries in Roksana Kharchuk's "Always a Leader," Vira, Nadiia, and Liubov, are so catholic in their meaning that they demanded translation. (Auntie Mania in the same story is, however, an innocent product of transliteration.)

We have given the names of places in Ukraine in their standard Ukrainian forms. Readers will thus find "Kyiv" instead of "Kiev" and "Dnipro" instead of "Dnieper." The use of "Ukraine" without the article is also consistent with current usage. Place names can, of course, be used connotatively: in "Karma-Yoga" Zholdak invokes Khreshchatyk, the main street in Kyiv, for how public and open to view it is, and Lypky as an instance of an exclusive residential district.

In the realm of customs, "Green Sundays" is Patricia Abram's free translation of *Zeleni sviata*, or "green holidays," and whereas the English equivalent is Whitsuntide, the Ukrainian phrase invokes the traditional commemoration of the dead by visits to their gravesites, which is closely tied to the theme of the story. As for social institutions, Ray Serwylo refers in "The Lost Winters of Emerald and Silver" to SUMK, Plast,

UNO, and KUK. The first two are youth groups; the latter are community organizations, and it is significant that Serwylo uses their Ukrainian acronyms, as they would come to the ukrainophone mind, even though both have English acronyms as well – UNF (Ukrainian National Federation) and UCC (Ukrainian Canadian Committee).

Borrowings are a linguistic fact of life. The Camel cigarettes in Yevhenia Kononenko's "Elegy about Old Age" indicate the appeal of Western goods in Ukraine, as do the Western makes of musical instruments in "Karma-Yoga." (The realism of the latter is emphasized by the reference to the Canadian trading company Kobza.) Other languages figure in the stories as well. The Polish word *jazda,* which as an interjection means "come" or "let's go," hints at the western Ukrainian setting of Yurii Izdryk's "Father." The multilingual hues of Martha Blum's "Two Triangles" reflect the linguistic realities of her native Bukovyna, which was under Austrian rule between 1774 and 1918 and had sizeable Jewish, Romanian, and German minorities.

Cookery provides some of the most clichéd, and therefore efficient, markers of ethnicity. But even, or perhaps especially, for such familiar foods as *pyrohy* and *borshch,* spelling can be a problem. The dumplings stuffed with meat, potatoes, cabbage, cheese, or fruit that most Ukrainians know as *varenyky* were brought to Canada by immigrants from Galicia and Bukovyna who called them *pyrohy,* "pies." In Canada, Polish and Russian phonetics interfered, so that dictionaries of Canadian English now list several variants, the most common being *perogies.* So, too, with the word *borshch,* which first meant cow parsnip (and thus is cognate with the English words "burr" and "bristle") and then was transferred first to the soup cooked with cow parsnip as a base and finally to the soup made from beets. Borrowed by other Slavic languages and Yiddish, the word has made its way into English in half a dozen spellings. On the other hand, studenets, jellied pigs' feet, a dish that has not been welcomed by the non-Slavic palate, has failed to establish itself in Canadian dictionaries and cuisine, and when Serwylo uses the term in "The Lost Winters of Emerald and Silver" he provides a description.

A few other facts of daily life in the Ukrainian stories may not be clear to Canadian readers. Slavs drink their vodka neat and help it go down by chewing a piece of bread or, if they don't have one, by sniffing the palm of their hand. Thus when the protagonist in "Always a Leader" sniffs his sleeve, he is revealing both his proletarian origins and his parvenu effort to transcend them. The Ukrainian currency is the *hryvnia* (a word derived from the proto-Slavic word for neck because of the custom of fashioning coins into necklaces), and it is made up of *kopiikas* (an old borrowing from Russian, which took it from the word for a spearhead because small coins showed a mounted prince holding a spear), but the mentions of greenbacks in "An Elegy about Old Age" reveal the reliance of the post-Soviet economy on United States currency. Soviet reality arises in the reference to the "lounge" in "Karma-Yoga," which is actually a "red corner," the place in a residence where students were indoctrinated in communist ideology, and in the mentions of Soviet army ranks in "Orders," which speaks of senior lieutenants and lieutenants rather than the first and second lieutenants we are used to. (The rank of junior lieutenant was never formally abolished, but in practice was replaced by the rank of ensign.) That the Soviet era has passed, however, is made clear by Oksana Zabuzhko in "I, Milena," where the prerevolutionary (and now post-independence) blue-and-yellow Ukrainian flag supplants the red-and-blue flag of Soviet Ukraine.

Translating these stories has been challenging, and sometimes frustrating, but it has also been rewarding. In "Necropolis," the word "plot" was our only possible choice to denote a piece of land in a cemetery, but the fortuitous resonance of its literary meaning in the context of the story consoles us for some of the sacrifices that we have had to make. For his generous help in solving the enigmas that exceeded our abilities, we express our thanks to Evhen Slupsky.

– Marco Carynnyk and Marta Horban,
Toronto, Canada, 1998

BIOGRAPHIES

EDITORS

JANICE KULYK KEEFER has been widely anthologized and praised for her novels, short story collections, poetry, and non-fiction. Her novel *The Green Library,* which is partly set in Kyiv, was nominated for the Governor General's Award for Fiction; her book *Under Eastern Eyes* was nominated for the Governor General's Award for Non-Fiction. She is also a two-time winner of the CBC RADIO Literary Award and the National Magazine Award for her short stories. Two other books have appeared this fall – one a memoir dealing with her own Ukrainian heritage, *Honey and Ashes: The Story of Family,* published by HarperCollins; the other a collection of poetry, *Marrying the Sea*, published by Brick Books. Janice teaches Canadian and English Literature at the University of Guelph. She lives in Eden Mills.

SOLOMEA PAVLYCHKO is a Ukrainian literary scholar, translator, and editor, with a PH.D. in comparative literature from Kyiv State University. Since 1985, she has been working as a research associate of the Institute of Literature, Ukrainian Academy of Sciences. She is the author of three monographs in the field of American and English literature, as well as *Letters from Kiev* (1992), published by the Canadian Institute of Ukrainian Studies Press, and *The Discourse of Modernism in Ukrainian Literature* (1997). Pavlychko translated D.H. Lawrence's *Lady Chatterley's Lover* and William Golding's

Lord of the Flies into Ukrainian; she edited Ukrainian editions of the poetry of T.S. Eliot and Emily Dickinson. She is also the author of numerous articles on Ukrainian and Western literatures, and on feminism and the women's movement. She has taught Ukrainian literature at Harvard, and is currently Editor-in-Chief of Osnovy Publishers. She lives in Kyiv.

AUTHORS – UKRAINE

Yurii Izdryk was born in 1961 and is a graduate of the Lviv Polytechnical Institute. An artist, musician, and writer, Izdryk was a founder and editor of the avant-garde journal *Chetver (Thursday)*, published in Ivano-Frankivsk from 1990 to 1994. His short stories have appeared in literary journals and his novel Votsek was published in 1997. He is a columnist for the popular Ukrainian newspaper *Den* and lives in Kalush.

Svitlana Kasianova was born in 1967 in Kyiv and graduated from the Department of Ukrainian Language of Kyiv University. *My Ant-Like Truth*, a collection of short fiction, appeared in 1998. Kasianova works as a radio journalist in Kyiv.

Roksana Kharchuk was born in Kyiv in 1964. A graduate of Kyiv University's Slavic Department, she is a translator of Polish and English writing. She also holds the degree of Candidate of Sciences in Comparative Literature (1992). Kharchuk teaches Polish literature and language at the University of Kyiv-Mohyla Academy, and also works as a critic and publisher. She lives in Kyiv.

Yevhenia Kononenko was born in Kyiv in 1959. She studied mathematics at Kyiv University, graduating in 1981. In 1994, she graduated from the Kyiv Institute of Foreign Languages with a specialization in French; she has received the French embassy's Zerov Prize for her translations of contemporary French poetry. Kononenko has published a poetry collection, *The Waltz of the First Snow* (1997) and a short story collection, *A Hot Subject* (1998). She lives in Kyiv, where she works as a researcher at the Institute of Cultural Politics.

Vasyl Portiak was born in the Ivano-Frankivsk region in 1952. He graduated from the Department of Journalism of Kyiv University and the Higher Literary Courses in Moscow. His collection of short stories, *Hatbrims*, was published in 1983, and he has numerous publications in literary periodicals. Portiak, who now lives in Kyiv, is also well known as a screenwriter.

Taras Prokhasko was born in 1968 in Ivano-Frankivsk, where he still lives. He is a graduate of the Department of Biology, Lviv University. His collection of short fiction, *Anna's Other Days*, appeared in 1998.

Oles Ulianenko was born in 1962 in Khorol, Poltava oblast, and now makes his home in Kyiv. A veteran of the war in Afghanistan, Ulianenko is a graduate of a merchant-marine school and was also trained as a medical assistant. He has three novels, *Stalinka* (1994), *Winter Tale* (1995), and *Fiery Eye* (1997), as well as many publications in literary periodicals. He received the State Shevchenko Prize in Literature in 1997.

Yurii Vynnychuk was born in Ivano-Frankivsk in 1952 and graduated in 1973 from Ivano-Frankivsk Teachers' College where he was involved in student publications and the *samizdat* underground. His writing was forbidden for publication in official Soviet periodicals and publishing houses for many years; because of fears for his safety, Vynnychuk went underground in Lviv. In post-perestroika times, he has written and edited for the popular Lviv newspaper *Post-Postup*. Besides numerous stories in anthologies and Ukrainian literary periodicals, he has three books of fiction: a short-story collection, *Flash* (1990), a novel, *Ladies of the Night*(1992), and a short novel, *The Harem Life* (1996).

Oksana Zabuzhko was born in Lutsk in 1960. She graduated from the Department of Philosophy at Kyiv Shevchenko University in 1982 and received her doctorate in aesthetics in 1987. She works as an associate of the National Academy of Arts and Sciences in Kyiv. She has taught Ukrainian culture and literature at Pennsylvania State University and was a 1994 Fulbright Scholar at Harvard University. Zabuzhko has three poetry collections: *May Hoarfrost* (1985), *The Conductor of the Last Candle* (1990), and *Hitchhiking* (1994). She has published two novels, *Extraterrestrial Woman* and *Field Studies in Ukrainian Sex* (1996), as well as a scholarly work, *Two Cultures: The Philosophy of the Ukrainian Idea and Its European Context.* As a translator, Zabuzhko has also produced an edition of the poetry of Sylvia Plath in Ukrainian. Her own first book in English translation, *A Kingdom of Fallen Statues,* appeared in 1996.

Bohdan Zholdak was born in 1948 and studied at the Shevchenko State University in Kyiv. Early in his career, he taught Ukrainian language and literature and later directed a children's film studio—until 1978, when he began to concentrate on writing fiction and drama. His plays are widely produced in Ukraine and include *Who'll Betray Brutus?* and *How the Cossack Mamai Achieved Immortality.* His short fiction has been widely published in periodicals; two collections, *Temptations* and *Macabresques,* appeared in 1991. Since that time he has written screenplays, created children's cartoons, and hosted a television program, *Artistic Casino.*

AUTHORS – CANADA

Patricia Abram was born and raised in Toronto, Ontario. She earned a degree in Occupational Therapy from the University of Toronto (1981) and worked as a paediatric occupational therapist for eight years. She has concentrated on creative writing since moving to St. Catharines, Ontario, in 1989. Her poetry has been published in many periodicals and in anthologies, including *Close to the Heart* and *Vintage '96.* She was a finalist in the Second Annual (1994) Writers' Union Short Prose Competition. Her paternal grandfather came to Canada from Ukraine in 1921, her paternal grandmother in 1923. Much of her poetry and fiction is based on their lives and their experiences adjusting to life in a new country. Abram made her first visit to Ukraine in June, 1998.

Martha Blum was born in 1913 in Czernowitz, Austria (now Chernivtsi, Ukraine). With the defeat of Germany and Austria in 1918, the city became part of Romania and remained so while Blum was growing up. Her studies included pharmaceutical chemistry, languages, and music at the Universities of

Bucharest, Prague, Strasbourg, and Paris. World War II found her family at the crossroads of warring and occupying forces, persecuted in turn by Soviet Russia and Germany. She emigrated to Canada in 1951 by way of Israel, and has lived in Saskatoon, Saskatchewan, since 1954. She is married to Dr. Richard Blum, professor emeritus at the University of Saskatchewan. Her first novel, from which the story in this collection is taken, will be published by Coteau Books in the fall of 1999. She is at work on a second novel and has completed a collection of short fiction.

Marusya Bociurkiw is a Vancouver, British Columbia writer and media artist. Her short stories, essays, and reviews have been published in periodicals such as *Fuse*, *Fireweed*, and *Queer Looks*, as well as *The Journey Prize Anthology.* She has published a collection of stories called *The Woman Who Loved Airports*. She teaches women's media studies and is at work on a novel and a new film.

Mary Borsky's father left Bukovyna in 1928 to avoid being drafted into the occupying Romanian army. Borsky's mother and her family left Volhynia in the same year, seeking land and, in her grandfather's case, adventure. They settled at the Ukrainian community of Sunset House in the Peace River Country of northern Alberta, where her father was a trapper and her mother's family homesteaders. After their marriage, her parents moved to High Prairie, forty miles away, where her father ran a poolroom. Borsky was born at High Prairie in 1946. She has written a collection stories set in that time and place, *Influence of the Moon* (Porcupine's Quill, 1995), and is working on a second collection.

Chrystia Chomiak was born in 1948 in a displaced persons' camp in Germany; that same year, her family came to Canada, settling in Edmonton, Alberta. She grew up as part of the Ukrainian émigré community amid the radical movements of the late 1960s. In the 1970s, she pursued her interest in art history and Slavic studies in Toronto, Ontario. An activist and feminist, she has been involved in many community and social causes. She has worked as an art curator, researcher, and editor; currently she and her husband run their own business in Edmonton.

Concerned with exploring the intricacies of intimacy and betrayal, privacy and privilege and hope, **Kathie Kolybaba** wants her fiction to address a trueness of being, a trueness of living as a human on this earth. Originally from Regina, Saskatchewan, she is the daughter of Rose Popadynec and Metro Kolybaba, a third-generation Ukrainian. Currently working on her second collection of short stories, and attempting to place her first, *Private Conversations*, she lives in Winnipeg, Manitoba.

Born and raised in Edmonton, Alberta **Myrna Kostash** is a full-time non-fiction writer and author of the classic *All of Baba's Children* and most recently of the critically acclaimed *Bloodlines: A Journey into Eastern Europe.* Forthcoming is the creative non-fiction book, *The Doomed Bridegroom; True Tales of Obsession.* A chapter from this work has been published in *Why Are You Telling Me This? Eleven Acts of Intimate Journalism* (1997). Besides writing for diverse magazines (from *Border Crossings* to *Chatelaine)* , Kostash has written for theatre cabaret, radio drama, and television documentary. As one of Canada's best-known exponents of creative non-fiction,

Kostash has been writer-in-residence in Minneapolis, Minnesota, the Regina Public Library, and the Whyte Museum, Banff. She has been Max Bell Professor of Journalism at the University of Regina and Ashley Fellow at Trent University. In 1993-94, she served as Chair of The Writer's Union of Canada. She is Alberta representative to the Board of the Canadian Conference of the Arts.

Barbara Scott's grandmother was born in the Ukrainian village of Stove Creek, Saskatchewan, in 1911, the year after her family arrived in Canada. Her grandfather came to Canada from Ukraine in 1924, to escape conscription into the Polish army. Scott has been published in various Canadian periodicals, including *Dandelion* and *Open Letter,* in *Prairie Fire's* "Echoes from Ukrainian Canada" issue, and in the anthologies *Alberta Re/Bound* and *Due West.*

Ray Serwylo teaches high school for the Fisher River First Nation in Koostatak, Manitoba. Some of his writing has appeared in *Prairie Fire* and in the anthologies *Worlds Apart* and *Yarmarok.* He has also published a short novel, *Accordion Lessons,* and a translation of *The Call of the Land (Holoc-Zemli),* by the Ukrainian-Canadian writer Honore Ewach.

Lida Somchynsky was born in 1951. After graduating from the University of Toronto, Ontario with a BA in English and Slavic Studies, she lived in Toronto before moving to Edmonton, Alberta, in 1981. Over the last fifteen years, Somchynsky has worked in the field of multiculturalism. She has co-produced and directed documentaries on Ukrainian-

Canadian identity and youth, along with an overview of multiculturalism and co-operative housing in Western Canada. Somchynsky has also explored writing in other media: scripts and a play (co-written), and is venturing into the realm of short story writing. She lives in a Ukrainian-Canadian housing co-op (the only one in North America) in the historic district of Strathcona Edmonton, with an easy-going cat.

TRANSLATORS

As a writer **Marco Carynnyk** has published, in both English and Ukrainian, poetry, articles, and essays on literature, film, and twentieth-century history and politics. Many of his historical studies are concerned with the Ukrainian famine of 1933, Soviet and Nazi repressions in the 1930s and 1940s, and Jewish-Ukrainian relations. As an editor and translator he has published numerous translations from Ukrainian, Polish, and Russian and has edited several books. As a documentary filmmaker Carynnyk has written scripts and served as a consultant. He has recently been working on a documentary series and a book about Soviet and Nazi mass killings in Ukraine and their political, legal, and ethical consequences.

Marta Horban has an AB in French from Bryn Mawr College and an MA in comparative literature from the University of Toronto, and is working on a PhD thesis on poetry in Quebéc and Ukraine. She has taught French and European literature at the University of Toronto, The University of Western Ontario, and Trent University, and has given papers and lectures and published scholarly articles on Ukrainian and Quebéc literature. Most recently she has been a contributor to the *Oxford*

Companion to Canadian Literature. Marta Horban has been translating for over twenty years, in collaboration with Marco Carynnyk. Their joint translation from the Russian of Victor Nekipelov's dissident memoir, *Institute of Fools*, was published in 1980. A course in French translation that she taught at Trent University culminated in the 1995 publication of a booklet of her students' translations of works by Irish poet Moya Cannon. She is currently doing editorial work on the Hrushevsky Translation Project of the Canadian Institute of Ukrainian Studies at the University of Alberta. She lives in Toronto.

COVER ARTIST

Khrystyna Haidamaka works with distilled, stylized motifs from nature and folk art which, although truly enigmatic, nevertheless border on the decorative. A painter and graphic artist, she has had solo exhibitions of her work in Kyiv and the former Yugoslavia, and her work is included in private collections in Ukraine, USA and other countries.

A Graduate of the Kyiv Applied and Industrial College, Khrystyna was born in Kyiv in 1969, and continues to make her home there.